C000151126

P. Edwards was born in Pontypool in South Wales, and now lives in Newport with her family and two rescue cats. She has a wide range of interests that include listening to music, travel, reading and ancient history, and she loves nothing more than to be traipsing through an ancient forest, or surrounded by some old ancient ruins somewhere. When she's not doing any of this, she simply likes to spend some quality time with old friends or close family.

I dedicate this book to my daughter, Samantha, and my son, Geraint for having faith in me to get this book published.

P. Edwards

THE SERPENT WARRIOR

AUSTIN MACAULEY PUBLISHERS™

LONDON • CAMBRIDGE • NEW YORK • SHARJAH

Copyright © P. Edwards (2021)

The right of P. Edwards to be identified as author of this work has been asserted by the author in accordance with section 77 and 78 of the Copyright, Designs and Patents Act 1988.

All rights reserved. No part of this publication may be reproduced, stored in a retrieval system, or transmitted in any form or by any means, electronic, mechanical, photocopying, recording, or otherwise, without the prior permission of the publishers.

Any person who commits any unauthorised act in relation to this publication may be liable to criminal prosecution and civil claims for damages.

A CIP catalogue record for this title is available from the British Library.

This is a work of fiction. Names, characters, businesses, places, events, locales, and incidents are either the products of the author's imagination or used in a fictitious manner. Any resemblance to actual persons, living or dead, or actual events is purely coincidental.

ISBN 9781528938235 (Paperback)
ISBN 9781528980913 (ePub e-book)

www.austinmacauley.com

First Published (2021)
Austin Macauley Publishers Ltd
25 Canada Square
Canary Wharf
London
E14 5LQ

Table of Contents

Synopsis

A magical, mystical tale of a turbulent and, at times, violent and tragic past-life memory of a life once lived in a land called Scythia around 2400 B.C., of a half Scythian, half Mongolian Hun Warrior called 'Manu Kai', who was the second son of a Scythian tribal Chieftain, and who also belonged to a secretive and mysterious brotherhood otherwise known as 'The Agari'.

Our hero's story begins with a chance encounter with a charismatic market trader, who gives him an ancient Scythian relic, which has the effect of triggering a past life memory of his early childhood in Scythia, and his struggle growing up against a backdrop of the constant threat of war, and of the racist bullying which he experienced as a result of being the first half Mongolian, half Scythian child born into his settlement, and of his very first encounter with the head of the Agari, who would later become his mentor and teacher.

The story continues to unfurl into a mystical world of self-discovery, and as he grows into adulthood, it goes on to tell of his personal inner struggle with trying to combine his duty as a Warrior, and a future leader of his people, with his role as an Agari priest. And also of his endearing friendships, his lovers, personal trials, and initiations, into the Magical Brotherhood of the Agari, and his brutal and continuing conflict with the early Roman/Italian army, which persisted throughout his extraordinary life.

Rich with historical fact – this book will take you on a rollercoaster journey into a long-ago forgotten land, where brave warrior fought against brave warrior, but dragons were never slain, as they were seen as wise and all powerful, and anyway…they only existed in another dimension.

1

Waking the Sleeping Serpent

How quickly the seasons seem to pass, it was already late autumn and a heap of russet and golden-brown leaves lay scattered across the narrow flagstone path of the old Victorian cottage that my girlfriend, Seren, and I had rented together for the past three years. But after discovering that the empty house next door had just been occupied by a small but particularly rowdy group of squatters, whose favourite pastime appeared to be conducting strange satanic type rituals in the back garden of the house, and at all times of ungodly hours of the night was causing us to wonder if it was a good time to move. It had been less than six weeks since their untimely arrival, but already there had been at least a dozen or more occasions that we had both been kept awake for most of the night, having being involuntarily forced to listen to the sound of them all desirously howling and wailing away to some malevolent denizen of the shadow lands, of which I would have thought that if nothing else, would have been enough to have at least raised its interest, and then if only to find out who had been behind the awful din that had given it a headache.

Seren suggested that we should go out for the day, as it might help to take our minds off things for a little while.

"I know…let's go to the market," said Seren enthusiastically.

Even though as a rule I tended to shy away from the hustle and bustle of busy places, I thought a leisurely stroll around our local market might be just what was needed in order to clear our heads for a little while, and if nothing else, it would be a welcome break away from our rowdy new neighbours.

"That sounds like an excellent idea to me," I replied, grabbing my wallet from my bedside table. The market was only about a twenty-minute drive away, and with very little traffic out on the road to hinder our journey, it didn't take us very long before we had arrived at our destination. But unfortunately even at this early time of the morning, the car park was already crammed to bursting point, but after finally finding a parking space, we proceeded to make our way over the time worn but rather uneven coble stone pavement…which in turn led to the recently renovated archway entrance of the old medieval market hall, which although had been miraculously transformed into something quite extraordinary in appearance, was still incorporating most, if not all, of its original features.

As we approached the market, the smell of sausage, eggs, and bacon from the market café drifted out through the open archway and onto the street, issuing an enticing invitation to anyone passing by.

"Mmmm…smell that! Shall we go and get some breakfast first?" I suggested, already beginning to head towards the general direction of the source of the mouth-wateringly irresistible aroma.

"Kai…just what are you like?" said Seren, in a slightly reprimanding tone of voice, while at the same time reaching out and firmly grabbing my arm.

It may have been early, but it was already surprisingly busy, and it would have been very easy to lose sight of each other in amongst the hustle and bustle of the crowd.

"TODAY'S SPECIAL – FRESH STRAWBERRIES – ONLY A POUND A PUNNET," an anonymous voice exclaimed loudly: "POTATOES – FRESH FRUIT AND VEG – GET ALL YOUR FIVE-A-DAY'S HERE."

"Let's get some strawberries," said Seren, tugging at my arm.

"You can buy the whole damn stall later if you like," I said, tugging back. "But let's get some breakfast first."

The café was already quite busy, and although the tables and chairs had certainly seen better days, everything was kept spotlessly clean, and the cooked breakfast that we were eventually served turned out to be satisfyingly well worth the wait. So after a good hearty breakfast inside me, I figured that I was now ready for anything…well almost!

Placing her knife and fork neatly on her plate, Seren leaned back and sighed, she hadn't eaten a cooked breakfast quite like that since the time we had both stayed the weekend with her mother. "Right then – do you want to go and get those strawberries now?" I asked her, downing the last few dregs of my coffee.

Puffing out her cheeks like an over-stuffed hamster, Seren nodded and began stacking up our plates.

"Yes, if I can ever manage to get up from this table that is…"

"Come on then, I suppose we'd better go and get your strawberries before they sell out." As we approached the fruit seller, we could see that there was a large queue, and as I really didn't like being in crowded places, I was already beginning to lose patience.

"Hmm…why don't you go and wait for me over by that curiosity stall over there," said Seren, pointing over to the far side of the market.

She knew that I didn't like crowds, and this made far more sense than getting all hot and bothered just for the sake of a couple of cut-price punnets of strawberries. So I left Seren to go and fight her way through the crowd, while I made my way over to the curiosity stall.

I'd always had a fascination for the old and unusual, and it would be fair to say that over the years I had managed to accumulate quite a collection of artefacts from near and far. Unfortunately, Seren didn't seem to appreciate them quite as much as I did, and as a result, she was always moaning at me for having so many, as to her – they were all just dust-collecting clutter. But, of course, to me they were all fine *objet d'art*. So why she had willingly directed me to just the sort of place that I could possibly find something else to add to the clutter I shall never know. As I approached the stall, my eyes were immediately met by those of the stall's owner. "Hello there," he said, raising his hand to push back the hood of his dark grey hooded jacket, which until now had been partially obscuring his face, as well as hiding his long fair hair, which he wore pulled back into a ponytail.

"Oh…hello!" I replied awkwardly.

I couldn't quite place him, but I had the distinct impression that I was supposed to recognise him from somewhere.

"Have we met before?" I asked him, carefully studying his features.

I didn't want to appear rude, but I just couldn't remember where I'd seen him before, which was a little frustrating as he really did seem familiar.

He began to casually rearrange a few random items on the table in front of me.

"Well," he said, raising one eyebrow, "that is a possibility."

Trying not to appear any more ignorant than I must have made myself look already, I quickly changed the subject, and thinking that perhaps this might help to refresh my jaded memory, I began to strike up a casual conversation instead. But nothing that we spoke of did anything in the way of allaying my amnesia, and just as I was about to admit defeat and just ask him outright where it was that we had obviously met before, he asked me if I would be interested in a very rare Scythian artefact that he had brought along with him. Although I didn't know a great deal about Scythian history, my general love of rare antiquities, coupled with my natural curiosity, were presently acting on me like a moth hopelessly drawn to the light of the flame, and I was fascinated to see what it was.

There was still no sign of Seren, so she was either still fighting her way to the front of the queue, or else she'd been side-tracked; most probably enticed away by the prospect of procuring some irresistible bargain somewhere. So I figured that I still had enough time to take a peek at the very least!

"I guess there's no harm in having a look," I said, trying not to sound overly interested.

"Indeed!" said the stallholder disappearing under the table.

He suddenly re-emerged again clutching a rather old-looking wooden box which had obviously seen better days.

"Here…see what you think of this," he said, opening the box and placing it on the table in front of me.

At first, all that I could see was a rather small and unimpressive-looking hessian drawstring bag.

The stallholder stood silent for a few moments, before giving the box and its contents a further push in my direction.

I picked up the little bag and began tugging away at a knot in the cord, which was tied so securely I almost gave up. A passing glance at the stallholder's face revealed that he was quite visibly amused by my apparent lack of knot untying skills. But obviously not wanting to come across in an interfering manner, he politely said nothing, and just patiently continued to wait for the eventual outcome instead.

With one more determined tug, the knot finally conceded, so after opening the little bag, I gently shook its contents into the palm of my hand. At first sight, I thought that the small golden object might be part of an ornamental broach of some kind, but as I began to examine it more carefully, I realised that although it had unfortunately sustained minor damage, it was still quite possible to make out that the shape was actually that of a dragon, or a serpent of some kind.

It was odd, but I actually felt as though I recognised it from somewhere, although for the life of me I just couldn't think from where.

"This is a really interesting piece…what is it?"

"Part of a Scythian warrior's horse harness, or at least it used to be…somewhere around 500 B.C."

"Hmm – it's quite old then," I said, continuing to mentally absorb its every detail.

I was just about to ask the price, when just at that moment, a ray of sunlight shone through the large glass window opposite, and reflected off the little golden object in my hand creating a dazzling blaze of colour. I became aware of the fact that I could feel a strange tingling sensation in the palm of my hand, and I knew exactly what this meant to me, as in the past I had quite often practiced the art of 'psychometry', which is a form of extra-sensory perception, but I'd never felt anything quite like this before, and the sensation grew so strong at one point that I began to feel a little lightheaded. Everything around me suddenly became oddly translucent; so much so, in fact, that I had to momentarily steady myself by holding onto the edge of the table. I knew that whatever was going on had to have something to do with the object in my hand, so quickly regaining my composure, I handed it back to the slightly concerned looking stallholder.

"Are you okay?" he asked, removing the object from my hand and popping it back into its little bag.

"Yes, I'm fine thanks," I answered, casually dismissing his concerns as I thought that trying to make any attempt at an explanation would most probably only result in making myself look a complete idiot.

"So – how much are you actually asking for it?"

"Well…that all depends on you…how do you fancy a bit of a venture?"

I'd never been one for gambling, but I must admit to feeling a little intrigued by what my new friend had in mind.

"What kind of a venture?" I asked him curiously.

"I hope it won't cause any offence by my asking you this – but are you by any chance a little on the psychic side?"

His question took me a bit by surprise, and the expression on my face must have been a dead giveaway, as he quickly apologised for his assumption.

"You don't need to apologise," I said, even more intrigued at how he could possibly have known this about me. "You're right…but how do you know?"

"Uhm…well, I guess you could say that I'm a little on the psychic side myself," he said with a warm but slightly cheeky smile.

"Fair enough," I said, returning his smile. "So tell me – what is this…uh…little venture of yours?"

There was something about him that intrigued me, and I found it impossible not to feel drawn in by him as he felt so curiously familiar to me.

"Actually…it's really more of a challenge than a venture; as if you can accurately psychometrise an object that I have here in my pocket, which I obviously already know all about – I'm going to give you the Scythian artefact as a gift."

"What if I fail?" I asked, feeling ever so slightly apprehensive of what my side of the venture may turn out to be.

He placed the little bag containing the golden artefact on the table and gave it a slight nudge in my direction.

"All that happens if you fail is that you don't get to own 'this' free of charge."

It was written all over his face that he knew only too damn well that he had me dangling hook line and sinker. There was no way that I could pass by a chance to own that little Scythian treasure completely free of charge, as there was no doubt in my mind that its monetary value must have been way above what I could safely justify spending to Seren, which at best, would only be regarded as just another dust collecting, space cluttering waste of money.

"So then…what do you think? Are you feeling up to the challenge…or not?"

I could see no valid reason to refuse, as it appeared that on the face of it, I had nothing to lose by accepting his rather unusual challenge. Although, I did wonder why he was so interested to test me on my gift of psychometry, but as I could sense no hidden agenda, I agreed to take him up on his challenge.

"Do you want to come around this side of the table? I don't know about you, but I prefer to sit down when I do this kind of thing."

"Yes, I think that's probably a good idea," I said, already beginning to edge my way through the narrow gap.

"Here you go," he said, handing me a small and very unimpressive looking stone.

I sat down on an old wooden chair, which looked as though it must have been here since the market was built, and I began to study the stone. There was certainly no hint of its origin to be found by physical sight alone, so I'd just have to wait and see what, if anything, my inner sight could uncover. So closing my eyes, I took a few deep breaths and forced myself to relax, and it wasn't long before I was able to give a fairly detailed description of the surrounding landscape where the stone had been found, and of some of the sights and sounds that it had managed to record along the way. Of course, at first, I had no way of knowing if any of my information had been correct.

"Well done – you're very good! Well…I guess this belongs to you now then," he said, taking back his little stone, and replacing it with the Scythian artefact.

I was just about to stand up and thank my new friend for his generosity, when out of the corner of my eye I saw Seren, who although hadn't seen me yet, was nevertheless heading straight towards us. She was obviously struggling with the weight of several large carrier bags, so my guess that she'd got side-tracked appeared to have been somewhat correct. Talk about perfect timing though!

I immediately stood up and waved. Seren instantly noticed me, and after allowing her bags to gently fall to the ground, she began frantically waving at me to come and help her.

It didn't seem right to just rush off like this, but the stallholder had already moved the craggy old chair, and with a knowing look he moved to the side allowing me to squeeze past.

"Go gallant knight," he said with a farewell gesture of his hand. "Go and rescue your damsel in distress. Or perhaps it is she who has rescued you. Anyway – don't worry; you can thank me another time – I'm sure we'll meet again soon."

"Yes, I hope so," I said, hurrying past him.

"Oh…my name is Kai by the way – what did you say your name was again?" I asked, reaching out to shake his hand from the other side of the table.

"I'll leave you to try and guess what my name is. You can consider it as your next challenge." And with that he quickly shook my hand, before waving me swiftly on my way.

Carefully placing the bag containing my newly acquired treasure safely in my inside pocket, I hurried over to where Seren was presently standing with her three overstuffed carrier bags, which were still lying there on the ground where she'd practically dropped them.

"Sorry," said Seren apologetically. "I grabbed a few bargains on the way back."

"I can see that! Come on then," I said, lifting the bags from the stone clad flooring. "We'd better get this lot to the car. I've got something to show you when we get back."

The truth is I just couldn't wait to get home so I could psychometrise my newly acquired Scythian treasure. If what I'd experienced in the market was anything to go by, it should turn out be quite interesting.

Arriving back home, I parked the car in the driveway and lugged the heavy bags of shopping from the boot to our front door where Seren was frantically digging around in her bag searching for her door key. Meanwhile, I noticed that one of our lovely new neighbours was sitting on the porch bench next door. He was naked from the waist up, which showed off a rather impressive variety of demonic-looking tattoos, and it would have been extremely difficult to miss the overly large inverted crucifix, which he was wearing on a chain around his neck; no doubt as a proud and loud testimony to his rather inverted faith.

"Hello," I said cheerfully, making a special effort to try and be friendly. After all…everyone has the right to choose their own path – do they not? However, my cordial gesture was returned with a cold blank stare.

"Such a nice and peaceful neighbourhood…don't you think?" I exclaimed loudly.

Giving me a sharp nudge, Seren scowled at me and shook her head disapprovingly. "Ah – here it is," she said, finding her key at last. She gave it a sharp twist in the lock and pushed open the door, before quickly disappearing inside.

"Well…" I said, rolling my eyes as I followed on after her.

Once the shopping was inside, I couldn't wait to show Seren the latest edition to my collection.

"Look what I found at the market," I said, holding it out for her to see. "I'm going to try a bit of psychometry on it soon, so would you mind taking down a few notes for me?"

"What on earth have you gone and bought this time?"

"Ah…well, that's the amazing part, it didn't cost me a penny – I actually won it in a wager."

"Oh, well done," said Seren, suddenly looking a lot less displeased with me. "Well…let's have a look at it then."

As I proudly held out my little prize for Seren to see, I could tell by the look on her face that she wasn't exactly feeling blown away, but then I guess it wasn't all that impressive to look at.

"What is it?" she asked, flipping it over in my hand.

After explaining what I'd been told about it, and how I'd come to be its new owner, I placed it on the small coffee table next to my favourite armchair.

"Right…you know as much about it as I do now, so are you ready to take down some notes for me?"

"Well…I suppose so. You're not going to be happy until you've done your 'thing' on it, are you?" she said, grabbing a pen and a notepad from the sideboard draw.

And after slightly re-positioned another armchair so that she could sit facing me – Seren sat down and placed the notepad on her lap. "Okay…I'm ready…whenever you are."

Seeing Seren sat there intently holding her pen above the paper, I couldn't help smiling to myself. I picked up the little golden serpent, and holding it in my right hand, I proceeded to make myself comfortable.

"Right then," I said, closing my eyes, and after taking a few deep breaths, I allowed myself to drift into a semi trance-like state.

I had only been sat there for a few moments, when I became aware of a rather hazy and distant image, which appeared to be struggling to formulate itself within my mind's eye. It was very frustrating, as I couldn't quite make out what it was.

"I can see something…but it's really misty…I just can't seem to penetrate this damn fogginess," I said with a disheartened sigh.

"Perhaps you just need to focus a bit harder," said Seren in such a simple matter of fact way that it actually had the effect of lifting me. She had such a natural way of making even the most difficult situation sound so easy.

"Yes, maybe," I said, nodding in agreement.

And with renewed and steely determination, I took a long deep breath and began to focus with all my inner strength on the shadowy scene before me. When suddenly and without warning, I was struck by a very vivid and unsettling close up of what appeared to be warriors on horseback, who were obviously engaged in a fierce and bloody battle of some sort. It was almost like watching an action movie on a wide screen television; except that this felt decidedly more up close and personal…to say the least!

My reaction must have been quite obvious. "What…what is it?" asked Seren excitedly. "What can you see?"

Although I was fully aware that Seren was speaking to me, I wasn't immediately able to respond to her question, as I had the strangest sensation that what I was witnessing was actually a far distant memory of mine, and I realised that I was actually beginning to remember all of this. The terrible battle which was now playing out in the inner depths of my mind's eye – was one in which I'd once played an active role in – and I was actually watching…myself.

As I began to verbally describe the things that I was inwardly witnessing, Seren became more and more interested and began to question me about the type of clothes that I was wearing, and if I was able to describe my general appearance. I found that I was somehow able to view the whole scene as though I was watching it from above, and I could actually see myself quite clearly. So I proceeded to describe the clothes that I was wearing, and my physical appearance, and I was rather surprised to see that I had what looked to be Mongolian characteristics, and that my hair was worn in one very long braid which hung down the full length of my back, which I found interesting as I had long hair in this life too, although nowhere near as long as in my vision.

"Do you know the breed of the horse that you're riding? – And are you carrying any weapons of any sort?" asked Seren, successfully managing to regain my attention.

"Uhhh...I'm not exactly sure of the breed...although, it does look very similar to a Mongolian horse. But I can definitely see that I'm carrying a bow and arrows, and the bow looks very much like a Mongolian re-curve horse bow. I can also clearly see a beautifully decorated Gorytos, (bow and arrow case) which is hung from the left side of my belt. I also have...what appear to be...two Mongolian scimitar swords which are being worn in a crosspiece leather harness on my back, which comes right down over my shoulders and crosses over my chest. I also have another short sword worn on my right-hand side (which I later discovered was called an Akinakes). There aren't any stirrups, and instead of a saddle, there's a thick highly decorated woollen saddle blanket, which appears to have been secured to the leather horse harness with bright red cord of some kind. Wow...I looked quite impressive back then...even if I do say so myself."

"Well...I think you look quite impressive now dear," said Seren, in a slightly mocking tone of voice.

Tiredness eventually got the better of me, so opening my eyes, I placed the little golden serpent back down on the table in front of me. Realising that I was done, Seren stood up and placed the notepad and pen next to the Scythian artefact.

"That was really interesting," said Seren, making her way to the kitchen. "So do you have any ideas on who these people might have been?"

"Hmm – at a guess I'd say Mongolian, as although the artefact is undoubtedly of Scythian origin, we just can't take it for granted that 'I' had been. To be honest, I'm not really sure what to think at the moment, so I might try doing a little research on the internet – just to see if anything that I'd seen can be validated in any way."

"That sounds like a good idea," said Seren, returning from the kitchen with two large glasses of perfectly chilled dry white wine.

Picking up my laptop, I sat down next to Seren, and it didn't take us very long before we'd managed to find some fascinating information relating to the Mongol Huns, but something was telling me that this wasn't quite right…and so we began to search all over again, and before we knew it, several hours had passed by.

"Do you realise it's already 2.37 in the morning," I said, glancing up at the clock.

"No, I didn't! Oh well – it's already way past my bedtime, and as interesting as all of this is, I really need to get some sleep now," said Seren, standing up and stretching her arms high above her head.

She was right – it was quite enough for one night. We had been researching Huns and Scythians for hours now, and although it was all fascinating stuff, I would have been quite happy to have left it right there, but as I was about to find out – whatever it was that I'd begun to uncover wasn't going to allow me to forget all about it quite that easily.

I just couldn't get to sleep that night, and this time it had nothing at all to do with the noisy antics of our charming neighbours next door. Every time I tried to relax and close my eyes, I was plagued by vivid images of what were most probably past life memories of mine. It really wouldn't have bothered me as much as it did, except that some of these images were more than a little disturbing to say the least. So I just lay there staring up at the ceiling for a while – not daring to close my eyes, and wondering if I had managed to unearth something that perhaps I shouldn't have. Relentlessly the mental images continued to pursue me to every dark corner of my mind, and the more effort that I made to try and shut them out, the more I realised that my attempts at controlling these images were obviously quite futile; so I reasoned with myself that perhaps the best course of action would be to stop fighting this thing and let it take its course.

The sound of Seren breathing softly next to me was oddly reassuring, and I had to resist the urge to wake her and ask her what she thought I should do. I knew that she wouldn't have known how to help me anyway, and I was just going to have to deal with this alone. I figured that if I wanted to get any sleep at all tonight, I may as well allow these unpleasant memories to form, and hopefully that would prove to be the end of it. So, with a sigh, I closed my eyes and took a few deep breaths before mentally preparing myself for whatever dark images I was about see. I had barely begun to prepare myself when there was a sudden blinding flash of light, and there before me, wrapped in a halo of dazzling white light, was a shimmering silvery blue Serpent. It seemed to come out of nowhere, and it had the speed and hypnotic power of a bolt of lightning, and before I'd even had so much as a split second to react – it proceeded to envelop me. Almost immediately, I began to feel a powerful physical sensation, which I instinctively tried to fight against. But whatever this thing was, it had already managed to completely overwhelm me, and all attempts on my part to fight against it were pointless, and I could do nothing other than to yield to its far greater will. The sensation was impossible to describe, and it grew so strong at one point that I began to wonder if it was actually going to kill me. Gradually, the sensation began to wane, leaving me lying there stunned and wondering what on earth had just happened to me.

I must have eventually fallen asleep, as in the morning I awoke with Seren still lying there fast asleep beside me. Her long dark hair cascaded over her pillow, and fell in gentle waves over her naked shoulders. I continued to watch her for a few moments, and I thought to myself how peaceful she looked when she was asleep. But all too soon my mind began to wander to the events of yesterday. It all felt a little hazy now – like a strange dream that you can't quite recall. And even though I did feel a little odd…different somehow, I knew that I had far more important things to think about. I couldn't afford to spend too much time dwelling on all of this, and I was just going to have to push the whole experience to the back of my mind. But, of course, things don't always go to plan, and the need to understand more about my experience became impossible to ignore, and as a result, I began to lock myself away for hours on end with just my little Scythian artefact for company. Seren often raised her concerns that this whole thing was slowly taking over my life, as no doubt she felt as though she was slowly losing me to some crazy obsession. I knew that she couldn't possibly understand what I was going through, and I didn't expect her to, and although I loved her, and I really didn't want to lose her, all I could do right now was to ask her to be patient with me. And so I carried on with my personal quest regardless of the consequences. I had always had a fascination with dragons, snakes, and serpents, and now at last I was about to finally find out why.

2

Alliance with the
Hun and Earliest Memories

"I'd appreciate it if you didn't disturb me for a couple of hours, I know you'll understand," I said to Seren, heading off to the privacy of the spare bedroom for the sixth time this week.

The truth was I knew that Seren didn't understand, but even so, I just couldn't wait to continue with my newfound quest of psychometrising the Scythian artefact which lay on a shelf in the spare bedroom where I'd left it the previous night.

"Oh…and there was me hoping that we could get to spend some time together tonight; you know…cuddle up and watch a movie…or something!" said Seren with a sigh.

"I'm really sorry, Seren, but I have to do this, I'm right on the brink of uncovering something really important…I know I am! This is important to me, Seren; so please – just try and be patient with me for a just a little while longer and I'll make it up you I promise."

I could tell by the sullen look on her face that she wasn't very happy with me right now, so in order to avoid any possible drama, I quickly made my exit, leaving her alone to sulk no doubt! As I made my way up, the old wooden Victorian staircase, I couldn't help feeling slightly annoyed with Seren. Why on earth she found it so damn difficult to allow me a little personal space now and again I'll never know, and as I entered the room, I made sure to quietly close the door behind me. Seren may have succeeded in making me feel guilty, but I wasn't going to give in to this kind of unreasonable pressure from her. It was a shame that she failed to grasp how important this whole thing was to me, but I couldn't allow her lack of understanding to upset, or to hinder me in any way, so after quietly gathering my thoughts for a few minutes, I picked up the little golden artefact, closed my eyes, and with an effort of my will, I stilled the internal dialogue within, and began to focus on the little piece of Scythian history which was now gently resting in the palm of my hand.

At first, the images were hazy and confused; just as they had been for the last six days, but then a remarkable thing happened…I suddenly felt as though I was being transported back through time and space, and I could clearly see myself as a child back in Scythia. I was around four years old, and I was sitting outside a yurt-like structure, which I later found out was called a kol. I was deeply engrossed in scratching the Scythian symbol of the sun into the slightly damp earth with the aid of a sharp stick, which I'd been allowed to sharpen with a knife just a few minutes earlier…under my father's watchful eye of course. The memories of my childhood in Scythia began to flood through to me in waves of ever-increasing clarity, until everything became so perfectly lucid and crystal clear that I actually found it hard to believe I could have ever forgotten all of this.

I remembered how I loved nothing better than to sit outside my father's kol on a warm summer evening and feel the gentle embrace of the cool breeze as it softly caressed the contours of my face. As a child, I had been deeply fascinated by the Sun and all its radiant splendour, and I'd watch transfixed, as it gradually descended in continuously changing hues of colour which marked the exchange of day into night, until it finally disappeared in a shimmering haze of luminosity below the distant horizon. And as darkness gradually descended upon the earth, I'd feel entranced, as the green of the grass gradually faded to the hue of smoky slate – and my brightly coloured clothes slowly dissolved into ashen shades of grey. I was mesmerised, as if by some magical enchantment, the sun appeared to be sucked downwards towards the earth, and along with all the colours of the day, it slowly drained away into the jaws of the Great Dragon. And there it would have to remain until the great Sun God 'Targitai', who reigned over the sky, would have to come and rescue it from the dragon's jaws, and set it free to pour its life sustaining light down upon the earth once again. The whole process repeating itself over and over again in an endless cycle of renewal, which always drew towards the same immutable conclusion; day would always follow night, and night would always follow day.

I knew that soon I'd have to go inside, as twilight was thought to be the time in which the veil between the two worlds was at its thinnest, and during this time bad spirits could slip through the crack between day and night – light and darkness, and would sometimes attack the very young, the unwary, or the week or feeble of mind, and so Scythians believed that it wasn't safe for young children to be outside alone at this time.

Just then my mother appeared from out of the relative safety of our kol, and called out to me that it was time for me to come inside for a drink of warmed 'ippaka', (mare's milk) mixed with honey. This was always a favourite with Scythian children, and was practically guaranteed to get them to come inside.

My mother was of Mongolian Hun birth and was the sister of the 'Khan', who was given this title as he ruled over three small tribes of Mongol Huns, who had now settled together as one large tribe. My mother had married my father who was the 'Sha Pada', (Chief leader) of our people, as a gesture of political alliance between the two tribes. It was not always an easy alliance to keep, as the times were very unstable, and alliances could be broken with just one wrong word. Complications would often arise due to disputes between tribal leaders, and on a larger scale, concerning alliances that had been made between warring nations which would often demand a choice of standpoint. My father was a hard man, and although at times he could be very difficult to deal with, he had a wise and level approach to dealing with matters of a political nature, and he was always open to the possibility of living a peaceful existence. His people had experienced hundreds of years of fighting and bloodshed, and he was no stranger to all of this. And although he was very politically minded, he tried very hard to sustain a status quo within what had become our settlement. Preferring peace to war – but always ready to fight to the death if necessary.

This was my father's second marriage, as his first wife had died in childbirth bringing my older brother into the world. My brother's name was Buemod, but I called him Bu for short, I also had a younger sister called Trishanna. Both my sister and I were given Scythian names, as my father thought it was more appropriate; although, my mother was quite insistent that we should learn her native language and customs as we were also half Hunnic, and as such were children of 'Great Tengri', the Hunnic God of the sky.

My father had no problem with any of this; quite the opposite, in fact, and I was actively encouraged to learn the Hunnic language and customs. Our people actually had a lot in common, as we were both nomadic races of people who, for one reason or another, had been made outcasts from their original homelands. And although our customs and religious practices may have been very different, there were enough similarities between our people to bridge the gap between understanding and intolerance, and my father was always very mindful of the need to have powerful allies, and his attempts to secure an alliance with the Huns, would eventually lead to the marriage between himself and my mother.

A couple of years before he had entered into an alliance with the Huns and had married my mother, he had sought the wise council of a very well-respected Agari priest. Scythians often relied on shamans and seers, and my father was no exception to this, and it would be fair to say that he relied very heavily at times on the guidance and insights of one particular seer, who happened to be at the head of this brotherhood of priests known as 'The Agari', and he often consulted this 'Derkesthai', (Dragon master – or one who sees clearly), before making any political decisions, or for deeper insight into how best to deal with a problem or a difficult situation.

Before an alliance with the Huns had been made, my father had crossed paths with them on several occasions, and a few skirmishes had inevitably taken place – so it was clear to my father that these people were very proficient warriors, who should be considered as dangerous and formidable opponents, and as such – were generally given a wide berth and avoided if at all possible. But this was not always practical as paths would inevitably cross from time to time.

It was on one very auspicious day that my father decided to seek the wise council of this Agari seer on the matter of the Huns. The Agari seer had told my father that an alliance would be formed between the Scythians and the Huns, and that one day they would unite together as one people, and for a time at least – they would become one of the most powerful nations that the world had ever known. So naturally my father was very intrigued by this. Unfortunately, the Agari priest had failed to mention to my father that this great rise to power was not very likely to happen for hundreds of years to come. But even if he had – it probably wouldn't have made any difference, as my father believed that there was no time like the present. And so he called a meeting with his closest and most trusted warriors, and explaining what he'd been told by the Agari priest, he put forward a proposal, which was: that rather than fighting with these people, a concerted effort should be made to form an alliance with them instead. There were a few initial doubts pertaining to the wisdom of this as you can imagine, but as always, my father eventually managed to talk everyone around to his way of thinking. And so after much discussion it was finally decided that he, and four of his most experienced warriors would embark upon a well-planned mission to approach, and offer the Huns a token of their friendship.

And so laden with fine gifts of gold and finely woven linen cloth, the very first attempt to make peace with the Huns was instigated. They all knew that if this plan didn't quite work out the way that they were hoping, this could possibly turn out be a one-way trip. But my father remained stubbornly optimistic that by what the Agari priest had said, it was well worth taking the risk. My father and his small band of carefully chosen warriors had a fairly good idea of the approximation of the Hun encampment. It wasn't all that far – just a couple of days' ride away, in fact, and all the necessary provisions for the journey, and the impressive gifts that were intended for the Huns, had been chosen and carefully packed away. And after all the prayers and ritual offerings had been made, and all of the signs and omens were seen to be in their favour, they all set off for their appointment with destiny.

Their journey went ahead unhindered, and after two nights and three days of travelling, they finally began to approach Hun territory. They knew that they must be getting very close to the Hun settlement, as there were very clear signals to strangers, or to any would be attackers to think twice before proceeding any further, as just a little way ahead of them there were at least thirty or so wooden spikes which had been hammered firmly into the ground, and each one was crowned with the impaled skull of some unfortunate victim, which had long ago been picked clean by hungry buzzards and crows. They'd clearly been placed there as a warning, and you didn't have to share the same language to understand the meaning behind this.

Scythians also had a long and colourful history of head hunting themselves, but neither my father nor his little band of warriors were in any particular hurry to experience a similar fate. The sight of all these weather-beaten anonymous skulls, now bleached white after long exposure to the elements, seemed to stand as a grim reminder of their own mortality, and it made even the most seasoned warriors amongst them feel more than a little uncomfortable. And as my father stared into the deep empty eye sockets of one of the skulls, which had once upon a time been endowed with eyes and a living brain, he couldn't help wondering who the original owners of these skulls may have been; their only purpose now left to them was to act as a disturbing reminder to others of the very real possibility of joining them.

My father had lost a few good men to the Hun a few years earlier, and they in turn had lost a few good men to my father's tribe, and he felt a cold chill run down the full length of his spine…and all it took was one quick glance at his men for my father to know that they too were feeling a little uneasy right now. It was at this point that he seriously began to wonder if this was going to turn out to be the worst political decision that he'd ever made, and if they'd soon be the next in line to join this impressive collection of disembodied severed heads. But being the fearless warriors that they all were, and after reminding themselves of this fact, they soon regained their composure – steeled themselves – and continued onwards with their peaceful mission. Their fate was now resting in the lap of the Gods, or at very least – upon the mercy of the Hun!

"There…up ahead," shouted out one of the warriors. Several little streams of grey smoke could clearly be seen steadily rising in the distance, and they all knew that their final approach to the Hun encampment lay just moments away.

It was customary with Scythian warriors when approaching other tribal warriors for the very first time, to show their friendly intentions by dismounting and making their final approach on foot; they only hoped that the Huns also upheld, or at least understood this simple rule of good conduct. My father gave the signal for them all to dismount, and making sure that their weapons were clearly seen to be not easily at hand, they continued the last part of their journey on foot…until at last, they had finally reached the Hun encampment. Of course, the Huns were already well aware of their dismounted visitors, and had actually been keeping a careful watch on them for some time. They must have thought that my father and his men had completely lost their minds to just walk straight into the hands of their enemy, as they wouldn't have stood a chance if they had decided to slay them. However, they hadn't been allowed to get very far inside the Hun encampment before being met head on by the leader of the Huns whose name was 'Gui Sen', and a small but formidable-looking army of Hun warriors who, although were currently keeping a respectful distance, were cautiously watching every tiny movement that my father and his men were making. And armed with deadly re-curve horse bows, which were currently being aimed straight towards them, the Huns were ready to respond with a deadly hail of arrows, should my father or any one of his men happen to make a single wrong move, and they were all acutely aware of their great need to tread very carefully at this rather delicate moment in time, as should this brave, but extremely risky plan of my father's happen to take a turn for the worst, they would have absolutely no chance of escape, as there must have been at least fifty or more arrows currently pointing in their direction. But it was far too late to turn back now, and so with the utmost caution, they diligently continued on with their quest.

Gui Sen Khan, although very wary, was also very curious to know what my father and his little troop of warriors were intending to do next, as they were obviously seriously outnumbered, and had completely put themselves at their mercy. But as it happened, it was Hun tradition to make welcome 'any' stranger who had wandered into their camp with friendly intentions, and the Hun were an honourable people and very true to their traditions, so they were unlikely to attack unless they were first provoked into doing so.

With a purposeful glance and a nod of his head, my father signalled to one of his men to bring the gifts. A small ornate ceremonial rug was laid out onto the ground, and the gifts that they had brought with them were very slowly and carefully unpacked, and then judiciously laid out before Gui Sen Khan and some of his finest warriors.

The obvious problem was always going to be the language barrier, but intention towards friendship was by now clearly understood and was soon reciprocated by the Hun leader who in turn gestured to my father and his men to follow him. Clearly relieved that they had at least managed to have survived the first hurdle, my father and his men all proceeded to follow Gui Sen Khan into his brightly decorated yurt. This was obviously the first time that any of them had ever set foot inside a Hun yurt, and as one by one they entered through the doorway, they couldn't resist curiously looking all around – quite fascinated by the strange and unfamiliar décor inside. Although the basic design of the Hun yurt itself was surprisingly similar to the Scythian kol, the furnishings, and the way in which it was laid out inside was very different indeed.

Gui Sen Khan gestured to them all to go and sit around a large low-lying wooden table, which was situated on the right-hand side of the yurt. Relieved that things appeared to be going so well, my father and his men were more than happy to co-operate and immediately went and sat themselves down on some beautifully embroidered cushions, which had been neatly arranged around the table. After which, they respectfully waited to see what was going to happen next.

However, they didn't have to wait very long before food and refreshments were being brought over to the table and laid out before them. They were obviously unfamiliar with Hun tradition, and so patiently waited for further prompting from the Hun leader as to how they should proceed. Gui Sen Khan boldly sat himself down, right next to my father, as it wouldn't have taken much insight to work out who the man in charge was here, and no sooner had he done so then four other Hun warriors immediately joined them by randomly seating themselves in amongst my father and his men.

Gui Sen Khan studied his Scythian guests very carefully; watching their eyes and their facial expressions as they spoke to one another. He wasn't at all sure if he could trust them yet, but he thought they must be very brave men indeed to have just boldly walked into their encampment. Either that...or they must be very stupid as they could have easily killed them all if they had wanted to. But they didn't give the impression of being stupid men, so Gui Sen Khan was feeling rather intrigued by his beguiling guests, and was eager to learn a little more about them and of the reason behind why they had put their lives at risk by walking straight into his encampment with lavish offerings of friendship. And although the fine gifts had been very well received by the Hun leader, it was not these which had managed to impress him, as he secretly doubted whether he would have been quite so brave himself.

Picking up a large grey pitcher that had been placed on the table in front of him, the Hun leader proceeded to pour some of its contents into one of the ornately carved wooden bowls which had been randomly spread out on the table, and after he had taken a small sip of its contents, he passed it to my father, who also took a small sip before looking to Gui Sen Khan for some sort of clue as to what he was supposed to do next. Gui Sen Khan responded by making a facial gesture to my father, which although subtle, clearly expressed his wish for my father to continue to pass it on, and after each man had taken a sip, the bowl was then placed back upon the table. The Hun leader then made a bold gestured for them all to help themselves to the food and drink that had been previously laid out before them.

The contents of the pitcher turned out to be fairly strong in alcohol content, but as my father and his men were mindful to avoid offending their Hunnic hosts, and with a little stout encouragement from the Huns, they soon began to feel the effects of the alcohol. And as they became increasingly more intoxicated as the evening progressed, the Huns felt more and more relaxed in their company, and took great delight in proving that they could out-drink their unexpected guests well into the night. And before very long, there was much drunken revelry with playful slapping on the back, and even though they couldn't understand a single word of one another's language, some attempts were made to converse with one another. The wry drunken humorous antics of the Scythians, and the over enthusiastic attempts of the Huns to impress, seemed to act as a mutual satirical comedy of errors to both parties concerned, and oddly enough, the alcohol seemed to have the effect of transcending the need for a common language, and they found that they were able to understand each other on some entirely different level altogether. In their drunken state everything just seemed to make perfect sense…whatever it was!

The only problem was that there were so many do's and don'ts with the Huns, that between them, my father and his little band of merry men, had successfully managed to break just about every traditional rule of etiquette that they had, and all in the space of time that it took them to get drunk. But luckily for them, the Huns had found themselves demonstrating a surprisingly high level of tolerance towards the shortcomings of their rather amusing Scythian guests, and of their lack of understanding of their culture and traditions…which was just as well really!

The Huns had proved themselves to be excellent hosts, and after putting my father and his some-what inebriated men up for the night – they left them to peacefully sleep off the effects of the alcohol.

The first attempts to bridge the gap had been a success, and many other such meetings would follow. And before three moons had passed, a purposeful exchange of learning one another's language had begun, until at last, a basic verbal communication between the two races could be established, along with a fundamental understanding of one another's cultural traditions and religion – if not always fully appreciated.

My father was still a very young man in his early twenties, and since losing his wife three and a half years previously, he had remained unmarried. It wasn't very long after Gui Sen Khan had stumbled upon this fact that he put forward a proposal of marriage between my father and his seventeen-year-old sister, who although very young, had been widowed just the previous year. Gui Sen Khan thought that there could be no better way of strengthening their alliance than with a bond of marriage between my father and his sister, thus creating a family unity, and a far greater reason to maintain their alliance. This marriage proposal was then submitted to my mother who, although understandably very apprehensive, had eventually agreed to marry my father for the greater good of all concerned, or at least this was what she was most probably forcibly coerced into agreeing to.

The marriage went ahead just a few weeks later in true fine Hunnic tradition, and my father's new Hunnic bride, along with all of her personal possession and a dowry of fine horses and furs, was promptly shipped off to go and live with my father. Obviously, this must have been a very difficult time for my mother, and it didn't help matters that no one but the very few could speak a single word of her language, and she, of course, was unable to speak any Scythian. My father knew that if this marriage of political convenience was ever going to have any chance of working, my mother was just going to have to learn to speak the Scythian language, and so he wholeheartedly threw himself into the task of becoming her personal teacher. He could be a very patient man when necessary, and he indulged my mother in her many emotional outbursts, and complied with her wishes as much as was within an acceptable boundary. And although it took a little time, and a whole heap of patience – my mother gradually settled in, and in time, she even found herself warming to my father's wily charms, and to her great relief, he continued to treat her well, and actively encouraged her to keep in touch with her own people by regularly organising a small group of warriors to accompany her on visits to her Hun family – bringing her back again after a few days. And when he was able, he'd accompany her there himself – genuinely enjoying the visit. And this would become the way in which regular contact between the two tribes was effectively maintained. So it turned out that my uncle's hindsight in using marriage as political glue was actually very well founded.

After I'd been born, and as soon as I was old enough, my father encouraged my mother to take me along with her. He believed that it was probably in the best interest of all concerned if I was given the chance to form a family bond with my Hun relatives and learn all there was to know about that side of my blood heritage. I would then become the perfect mediator between the two races. Not really belonging to either, but instead belonging to both. I was born the result of a political alliance, and an unsuspecting pawn in the games of men, and although I was still far too young to understand any of this yet – it was to become both a curse and a blessing.

So…here I was, still deeply engrossed in the carving of the symbol of the Scythian Sun into the damp earth just outside my parents' family kol. I'd put it there as a reminder to the Sun God Targitai to rescue the sun again first thing in the morning…just in case!

"Kai," shouted my mother for the second time.

I was about to stand up when I felt a hard slap across the back of my head. I didn't have to turn around to know who'd given it to me. It was my brother, Bu, who was nearly five years older than I was.

"Get in horse shit – your mother's calling you," he said, giving me a sharp kick.

Unfortunately, I was used to it as my brother never missed a single opportunity to hit or kick me. He had always been very jealous of me, and this would become more and more apparent as time went on.

3

The Cruelty of the Innocent and
the Great Surprise

It was the eve of the Scythian festival of the Sun God Targitai, and it just so happened that today was also my birthday. Scythians usually kept track of how old they were by counting each winter that they had managed to survive; so going by Scythian terms, I would have been four winters old. Birthdays were rarely celebrated in Scythia, as most people had no idea when they were born, as unless your parents had marked that day in some special way and had retained a record of it for you to keep, it was impossible to know the exact day of your birth. Added to that, many children grew up as orphans, as you could count yourself extremely lucky if both your parents survived to see old age. Children often found themselves dependant on the kindness of relatives, or occasionally at the mercy of anyone who may have been willing to take them in and care for them as one of their own. Or if they were extremely unlucky, they may have ended up being used or even sold as a slave. The result being that even if a record had been kept, it was often forgotten or lost through the passage of time.

The festival of Targitai was always a time of joyful celebration, as it marked the transition from winter into summer as the harsh bitter cold, and the long dark nights of winter were finally drawing to an end. It was also the time that the Para-lati (the common folk or crop growers) could prepare the land ready for sowing.

There was a very important holy man living in our village who bore the title of 'Artim Derkesthai' (celestial dragon master). It was said that he could read the messages that were hidden in the stars, and many people came from near and far to seek his wise council on a wide range of issues both great and small; including the royal Scythians, who summoned him by way of a messenger who would always recite to him exactly the same verbal message of: "You are hereby summoned on a matter of great urgency, and you are given direct order from the royal court to immediately set aside all things of which you may be currently involved, and make haste to the King's aid without any further delay." He knew that he had very little choice other than to obey the royal command which so eagerly demanded his sagacious presence, but he only did so after first completing whatever it was that he may have been doing at the time. The royal Scythians in turn, had very little choice other than to learn the meaning of patience.

This wise and holy Sage appeared to possess a remarkable ability to gain insight into the characteristics and possible destiny of an individual. He did this by mapping out the positions of the sun, moon, and planets, at the time of the individual's birth. But it was obviously only possible for him to do this if the individual's place and time of birth were known.

The whole village was beginning to feel positively charged with an almost electric sense of excitement. And the preparations for the coming festival of Targitai spring renewal were already well underway, and a celebratory bonfire was in the process of being prepared from a huge stockpile of dry wood which had been collected from the nearby forest some time ago.

The larch tree was considered to be sacred by the Scythians, as to them, it represented the cycle of death and re-birth, as during the time that the light of day began to grow shorter, and the darkness of night grew ever longer, the autumn fall soon followed and heralded the approach of the cold winter months to come. And so in order to conserve valuable energy, the larch tree slowly began to shed its leaves, until its skeletal frame stood bare, and in a death-like state of slumber there it would remain…until at last, the icy grip of winter began to loosen up its hold upon the land, and the first faint rays of sunshine began to pierce the morning mist, and tiny little grey buds would gradually begin to appear upon its outstretched branches until once again, it proudly stood in all its former glory.

A large branch of the larch tree had been cut down to make a pole, which was then firmly erected in the very centre of the village. It was then brightly decorated with painted symbols of the sun and of the elements of air, fire, water and earth, and also of the serpent slain, and the serpent reborn. The shed skins of venomous snakes were randomly draped over two long thin branches which had been crossed over in the middle and then secured to the centre pole. They were carefully positioned so that each extended branch roughly marked the direction of each of the four quarters of the northern, eastern, southern, and western hemispheres. We referred to this as 'the tree of life', and to mark the beginning of the festival, people placed offerings of food which had been lovingly prepared for this special occasion around the base of the tree of life, while others hung small treats from its outstretched branches. This fine feast of seasoned meats, cheese, fruit, bread, and all manner of delectable delights to the palate, would then be blessed by an Agari priest, and ceremoniously offered up to Targitai, before being shared equally between everyone in the village. The festivities would then carry on throughout the rest of the day, and well into the night. People would play musical instruments, dance and sing, and there would be incredible displays of talent and dexterity by the shadow dancers, who would always end their show by jumping straight through the flames of the fire in an amazing show of skill and perfect timing.

A fair degree of fermented mares' milk, mead, and cannabis was also consumed, and if you were that way inclined, something a little stronger could often be provided by your friendly neighbourhood shamans.

It was also a good time for people to sort out any personal differences that they may have had, and to lay old grievances or bad feelings to rest. Personal disputes which had remained stagnant and unresolved throughout the year, could finally be faced and dealt with by the individuals concerned, albeit with the aid of an arbiter if necessary. Life was too short to waste by holding onto grudges or bad feelings, which had often been caused from simple misunderstandings or petty disputes which had arisen in the past. No matter how great the pain of injustice was, it was far better for the individuals concerned to try and resolve their outstanding conflict. Of course, there were always those who would either be too proud, stubborn, or arrogant, or simply for one reason or another, would feel unable or just plain unwilling, to let go of their bitterness or anger, and so gradually over time they often found themselves feeling ever more embittered, and increasingly dragged down by the heavy leaden weight of the chains of a self-justifiable misery entirely of their very own making. I was beginning to feel very excited at the thought of the coming festivities and I asked my mother if I could help, so I was a little disappointed when she said that I could help her by going to play outside and staying right out of her way.

My little sister, who was around two years old in modern day terms, was happily playing with small wooden carvings of animals on the floor of the kol.

She looked up at me, and holding up a carved wooden horse she said: "Ippa," which was the Scythian word for horse.

"But I want to help," I pleaded.

"If you are very good and you go outside and play for a while, I will let you help me later," said Mother firmly.

The look of disappointment on my face must have been obvious, as she stopped what she was doing for a moment, and called me over to her. She bent down and quietly whispered in my ear: "Kai…you must be a good boy today as your father has a surprise for you tomorrow."

"What is it?" I asked excitedly.

"Well…if I told you that…it wouldn't be a surprise now, would it? You'll just have to be on your best behaviour and then you'll find out tomorrow."

I immediately forgot about my disappointment at not being allowed to help and began to wonder what this surprise could be instead. My mother's ploy had worked, as I went outside and sat down on the ground near to our kol leaving her alone to get on with what she needed to do. There were few children playing a game of tag just a short distance away from me, so I sat there watching them for a while; still wondering what this mysterious surprise was going to be, when one of the children ran over to me, and shoving me very hard on the shoulder he shouted out loudly: "Tag!"

"But I wasn't playing," I said, rubbing my shoulder.

One of the older children ran over to me – and shoving me even harder, he said: "Double tag." For some reason, they all seemed to find this really funny.

"Why don't you all just go away and leave me alone," I retorted, quickly rising to my feet.

I was always being picked on, so this was nothing new, but I wasn't going to just sit there and allow them all to push me around. But instead of leaving me alone, they all began to taunt and tease me even more, and like a hungry pack of wolves, they began to encircle me, spurring each other on to join in with the attack. This particular group of children often found great delight in making my life a misery, simply because of the way I looked. I was already well aware that I looked a little different from them, and that I stood out due to my racial characteristics and my long hair which was often braided Hun style. Scythian children usually had their hair kept fairly short, as it was much easier to manage that way. But my mother had taught me that my long hair was a sign of my inner strength and power, and that I should never have it cut short. I didn't feel very strong and powerful right now though, I felt scared and upset by the cruel taunts of these children, and struggling to hold back the tears that were beginning to well up in my eyes, I asked them:

"Why are you always so horrible to me?"

They all just stood there staring at me with blank expressions on their faces. None of them were able to give me an answer to my question, and my fear was quickly replaced by anger.

"You'd better leave me alone or I'll put a curse on all of you, and your eyes will shrivel up and fall out of their sockets," I said, spitting on the ground before them.

That, coupled with the angry look in my eyes, was obviously enough to make them all back off a little, which at least gave me a sporting chance to run to the safety of my parent's kol. Once inside, I just sat there wondering to myself why they all hated me so much, but I made my mind up right then and there, that if they didn't like me, then I didn't like them either.

One day, I decided to tell my mother about the constant teasing, and about some of the spiteful names that the children were calling me.

"Hush now," she said, slipping her arm around me. "They tease you because you stand out – you look different from them, Kai. I know that it's very difficult for you to understand, but they are very young, and they don't know that what they do is wrong. But one day they will look back and remember just how badly they treated you, and they will feel ashamed and truly sorry for what they did to you…you'll see."

I know that my mother meant well, but even if that day ever came, which I very much doubted, it was very little consolation to me now.

"Right then," said mother, kissing me goodnight. "No more talking tonight – it's getting quite late now, and it's time for you to go to sleep. Tomorrow is a great day of celebration, and your father has spent many long hours preparing his surprise for you."

My brother had been pretending to be fast asleep, but he had been sneakily listening to everything that had been said.

"Oh dear…is poor little Kai being picked on again? You're so pathetic – it's no wonder that no one likes you. You're a freak of nature – and you should have been drowned at birth."

I thought for a moment before responding: "At least my mother didn't die of fright the first time she saw me like your mother did."

As soon as I'd said it, I wished that I hadn't, but the words just came right out of my mouth before I had a chance to stop them. It was a cruel thing to say and I knew it, but I was so fed up with my brother's constant bullying.

"I hate you…and I'm going to make you pay for that remark, you little pile of horse shit," he hissed. And I knew that he meant it too.

I really wished that I would hurry up and grow a bit bigger, then no one was going to be able to bully me ever again. Perhaps I could go and live with my Hun family – they always treated me well, and I didn't get picked on by the children there either. I didn't see why I had to live here anyway. I just lay there feeling sorry for myself and wondering what delightful punishment my brother had in store for me. For some reason he really hated me, and never missed an opportunity to make my existence on this planet as unpleasant as he possibly could. Staring blankly into the darkness, my feelings of anger towards him grew and grew, and I found myself wishing that he would just disappear out of my life forever, and I was just about to yell out at him to go and fall into a deep hole and die, when there in the half light of a low burning lamp, a tall luminescent shadowy figure slowly began to materialise right before my eyes. It seemed to look right at me for a moment or two before turning towards my brother and heading straight towards him. I watched in amazement as it then reached down and put its shadowy hands around my brother's throat. He immediately awoke with a scream, and began to wrestle with the phantom hands that were still clasped around his throat. I sat bolt upright and I shouted out: "NO!" The figure turned and looked at me once more, before it slowly began to fade away…until nothing more of it remained but empty space.

"You did that, didn't you? It was you …I know it was …you tried to kill me," yelled my brother, clearly shaken by what had just happened.

"I didn't do anything…I wasn't anywhere near you," I yelled back at him.

"You did it with your evil sorcery," he said, holding his throat.

Understandably, all the commotion awoke my mother and father, who both came running over to see what all the fuss was about. "What's going on?" Father asked us both.

"It was him," yelled out my brother. "He tried to strangle me to death."

"What?" said Father, somewhat taken aback by this. "Is this true, Kai?"

"No! I wasn't anywhere near him," I said, protesting my innocence.

"Hmm…very well," said Father thoughtfully. "I think we need to get to the truth of this matter then, don't you? I want to hear both of your sides of the story – one at a time, starting with you, Buemod."

My mother and father both sat and listened to what my brother had to say, and when it was my turn to speak, I told them what had been said between my brother and I, and I did my best to explain to them how it made me feel, and what I'd seen. Neither my mother nor my father said a single word throughout either my own or my brother's side of the story, and when at last we had both finally finished explaining, Father took a deep breath, and resting his chin in his hand he just sat there staring blankly at me. "Hmm," he said thoughtfully.

Father then turned and looked at my mother, and she looked at him, and I looked at both of them, and then they both looked at me. I then looked at my brother, who looked at my parents, and I said: "I didn't do it!"

"We will talk about this tomorrow. We should all try to get some sleep now, and I don't want to hear another word out of either of you," said Father, standing up again.

My brother immediately began to protest, "But Father…Kai tried to kill me with black magic. He's evil."

"No…I didn't…I'm not evil," I shouted back at him.

"ENOUGH!" said Father firmly. "We will deal with this tomorrow. Not one more word from either of you. Do you both understand?"

We both replied back to him in unison, "Yes, Father."

My parents both went back to their bed, and I could hear them quietly whispering to one another, so I strained my ears in an effort to hear what it was that they were saying. I could just about make out a few words here and there, so I knew that they were talking about me, and I definitely heard Father say something to my mother about taking me somewhere to see someone.

But try as I might, I just couldn't quite make out anything else that they were saying. I continued to listen to the sound of their muffled whispering until there was no more to be heard, and then at last, I finally drifted off to asleep.

The morning began with the usual ritual of organised chaos. We all had chores to complete before breakfast. My chore for this morning was to accompany Father to the horse paddock, and check that the horses were all fine, and that none of them had escaped or been stolen during the night.

Father always made sure that the horses were taken down to the river to drink at least once a day, and there could be up to a hundred or more horses at any one time, as he bred them to trade for the things that his family or his people needed. He had his own special favourite horse which he always rode down to the river with the rest of the horses following on behind.

I was already a competent rider, as I was practically born with the reins in my hand, and I always enjoyed our little equestrian trips down to the river. After the horses had had time to quench their thirst, Father always round them back up again by waving a looped piece of leather in the air and making a loud whooping sound, and if one of them was being a little bit stubborn, or just a bit too slow in re-joining the herd for the trip back again, he'd give it a little extra encouragement with a sharp slap on the backside with the leather hoop.

I still had no idea what this surprise was that Father had in store for me. I just hoped that after what had happened last night, he wasn't feeling angry with me and had changed his mind. Perhaps he'd forgotten all about it – highly unlikely…but as nothing more had been said, I decided not to mention it either.

"Kai, I think it's time that you owned your own horse and learned how to take care of it. So…would you like to choose one now?" asked Father as we approached the paddock gate.

I was absolutely thrilled at the idea, of course, but if this was my surprise – and it was a wonderful surprise – it didn't quite fit in with what Mother had said about Father having spent long hours preparing a surprise for me. But anyhow it didn't matter – I was going to have my very own horse.

Father just stood there looking at me with his arms folded. "Well…" he prompted.

"Uh…Yes, I would…I really would," I replied excitedly.

"Good! You can choose any one you want, except for mine, of course, or your mother's or brother's," he said, pointing towards each horse.

I could easily recognise which ones belonged to members of my family, so I just stood there looking at all the others. How on earth was I going to know which one to choose? Your very own horse was supposed to be special, but I didn't know the characters of any of these horses, and they didn't know me. So how would I know if we were going to like each other and get along? I knew that horses were very much like people, and they all had different characteristics and personalities.

"I don't know how to choose," I said, feeling a little confused.

"Hmm, well, you must choose with your heart, Kai…not your eyes. Just look with your heart and it will tell you which one is the right one for you."

I had no idea what Father was talking about, but I didn't want him to think that I was stupid, so I said, "Yes, Father…I will. Can I go inside the paddock? I think I can choose better if I'm in there with them."

"No, you could get injured. You will have to choose from out here," he said, shaking his head.

"Oh!" I said feeling a little disappointed. "Well…what if the paddock gate is left open a little; I can sit over there on the grass and just wait and see which horse comes to me."

"I've never heard it done that way before," he said, scratching his head. "But you can give it a try if you want to."

Father unclipped the paddock gate, and I walked over and sat a short distance away from the entrance. Although I tried very hard to look at the horses with my heart; it was obvious that it was my eyes that were doing all the looking. So closing my eyes I concentrated on trying to see out of my heart, but all that happened was I couldn't see anything at all now…but it did have the strange effect of making me feel all warm and fuzzy inside. The rays of the sun felt warm on my skin, and I could hear the distant buzzing of a bee as it busily hurried on its way. I felt so relaxed and at peace with the world that I'd almost forgotten about choosing a horse, when suddenly I was startled back to reality by the sensation of something nudging my arm. I immediately opened my eyes, and there standing right next to me was a chestnut mare. The expression on Father's face was so funny that it made me laugh.

"Well…I've seen a lot of things, but I've never seen the likes of that before. You have a gift, my son…truly you do! Shall I take it then that the choice has been made?" And not waiting for an answer he continued. "You can ride her tomorrow as we don't have enough time now; besides; I've got something else that I want to show you, and we only have just enough time before the festivities begin – and you don't want to be late for that, do you?"

"No, Father," I replied obediently.

After returning to our kol, we all sat down to an ample breakfast of eggs with honey bread before stacking up our dishes ready for Mother to clear away.

"Right then, Kai, I think you'd better come with me," said Father, as he disappeared through the doorway.

I followed on after him, and after passing several kols, he finally approached the one with a large metal disk attached to the left-hand side of the entrance. It had a metal rod attached to it with a piece of hemp rope, which Father then proceeded to hit the disk with several times.

It made such a loud clanging noise that if anyone was at home, they couldn't fail to hear it. In fact it was so loud that it could probably be heard throughout the whole village.

"Vasmer, are you in there?" he shouted out as he hit the disk one more time.

And a voice coming from inside the kol shouted back…

"Sha Herian…Come in…come in."

"He's a bit deaf," said Father, pulling back the flap of the entrance to the kol and ushering me inside. I stepped through the entrance of the kol closely followed by Father, who was warmly greeted by his right-hand man and closest friend Vasmer.

Vasmer was one of the original warriors who had accompanied Father on the very first visit to the Hun several years ago. He was initially dead set against the whole idea, believing it to be nothing more than a suicide mission. But even though he didn't think they'd ever survive to tell the tale, he still maintained such a loyalty to my father, that he told him that if he was insistent on going on a mission of death and he was unable to talk him out of it, then as far as he was concerned, he would just have to be going on a mission of death too.

"Hello, Kai," said Vasmer, with a big warm friendly smile.

"Hello," I replied back to him.

"Sit…sit," he said, pointing to an enormous pile of fleeces.

I clambered on top and watched as my father walked over to the far side of the kol and picked up a beautifully crafted bow. He then walked straight over to where I was sitting and held the bow out towards me.

"Here you are, Kai – this is for you…"

Reaching out, I took it from his hand and began to study it closely. It was beautifully painted with intricate designs of strange-looking beasts, which completely covered the bow in an interlacing continuous pattern, and I loved it!

"It's beautiful," I said without taking my eyes off it.

"Your father made the bow, and it was I that painted it," said Vasmer, looking rather pleased with his self.

"Thank you…you're very clever."

"Yes, well now you have to do it justice by learning how to use it," said Father, with a satisfied smile.

"Yes, I will…I really will," I said enthusiastically.

"I'll begin to teach you the day after tomorrow," said Father proudly. And I couldn't wait! Adjusting his ceremonial dagger, Father nodded to Vasmer before making his way over to the doorway of the kol.

"Right then, Kai…I'm expecting some Thracian guests. They should be here soon, and I suppose it's only right that I should be there to greet them."

"Don't forget your bow," said Vasmer, with a knowing look on his face. As if…

4

The Blessings

It was almost time for the celebrations to commence. My mother, brother, and little sister had already made their way down to where all the festivities were being held, but I, along with Father, Vasmer, and several other high-status warriors were still waiting for Father's guests to arrive outside our kol.

"There they are," exclaimed Father, sounding somewhat relieved. And there in the distance our guests could just about be seen making their way over the horizon towards us, and not a moment too soon, as it was almost the time of the highest point of the sun, which was the signal for the blessings to begin.

As Father's honoured guests finally approached us, I could see that they consisted of a party of six Thracians; one of whom was a Thracian emissary who had been a regular visitor to our village for some time, and had been involved in political talks with my father concerning the future of their alliance which had been made several years earlier.

Dismounting from their horses, the party of Thracians boldly walked over to where Father and the rest of us were standing. Their horses were promptly led away to the tying posts by a couple of young Scythian warriors, where they would be given fresh water and grain.

The Scythian/Thracian alliance had always been a very temperamental affair, which was becoming increasingly unstable due to the pressure which was being put upon Scythian tribal leaders to break certain alliances which had been made with other nations. Along with every other Scythian tribal leader in the province, Father had always maintained that they were not willing to do this. So the situation was currently one of a stalemate. The Scythians and the Thracians had a long history of alliances made and broken, and there had been several intermarriages between the ruling classes of the two nations, resulting in many blood links between them. This however did not prevent constant political upheavals, some of which had actually resulted in pitched battles between them.

But today was to be an informal visit by the Thracian emissary and his accompanying entourage, as on their previous visit my father had invited them to join us for one of our most important religious festivals, and this was a very welcome opportunity to set aside their political differences for a while, and to enjoy a far more relaxed atmosphere of celebration, along with some very serious partying of course.

I noticed that the Thracian emissary had brought his young son along with him today. It wasn't the first time that he'd accompanied his father to our settlement, as he'd already been here several times before. The idea being, that he should gain experience of our culture and language, and affectively would eventually be groomed into becoming a future emissary himself. His name was Gaidres, and he was around the same age as my brother.

Grasping one another firmly by the forearms, my father and the Thracia emissary embraced one another like old friends. Their affection for each other appeared to be quite genuine, or at least if it wasn't, no one could tell. After all, the fragile political climate which currently existed was no real fault of either man.

Looking across at Gaidres, I noticed that he was stood at his father's side in very similar manner that I was stood next to mine. Gaidres suddenly raised his eyes in my direction catching me staring at him. He responded by giving me a half smile – I half smiled back, and although I was always very suspicious of people I didn't know very well, I thought that he looked quite friendly, and I found myself feeling 'reasonably' comfortable in his company.

We didn't have enough time left for all the usual welcoming niceties, so without further delay we all quickly made our way down to a small stream that ran near the edge of our village, and over towards a large group of people, who were already gathered in readiness for the priest to mark the beginning of the festivities. We had arrived just in the nick of time, and we all hurriedly made our way to the front of the crowd, so that Father could take his position as the Sha Pada (chief leader) of our tribe.

Politely excusing himself to his guests, Father hurriedly made his way over to the priest, who had been very patiently stood there waiting for him, and as soon as he saw him, the priest raised his eyes upwards towards the sky as a gesture that we had only just made it in time.

The priest was impressively dressed in a long white ceremonial robe, which had been lovingly embroidered with intertwining golden serpents near the hem, and a matching golden sash which was tied around his waist. He also wore a solid gold headpiece which had been intricately crafted in the shape of two intertwining serpents upon his head. His long, dark hair reached all the way down to his waist, which on this occasion he had chosen to wear loose. I thought to myself that I might like to wear my hair like that, but then I reasoned with myself that it would most probably just get all tangled up, so I was probably better off by continuing to wear it in a braid…for the time being at least.

The priest then proceeded to bless all the food, which had been brought as offerings to the life-giving Sun of God by the people in the village. And raising his eyes and hands upwards, he spoke in a strange dialect that I didn't understand, before asking my father to stand directly before him in our native tongue.

"I call upon the sons and daughters of Targitai, and all those who are gathered here today…See now this one who humbly stands before us all – and who has been chosen by the mighty and unquestionable wisdom of the all-knowing and all-seeing God of the Sun, to serve 'you'…his people."

The priest then gently rested his hands upon my father's head, and paused for a few moments before he continued:

"Herian – Blessed son of Magog – vessel of the united voice of your people, may you carry that voice high above all else. May you put aside all thoughts of selfish pursuit, and if a day should ever come to pass, that you are faced with such a thing as this – may you never hesitate in laying down your own life in sacrifice for the safe passage of your people, and may the power of all that is pure and wise guide you, and bless you with clarity of vision, good health, and inner strength. May your heart remain true to your calling, and may the Great Spirit remain ever watchful over you, and all your people. Blessed is the tree of life, and all those who choose to follow in its Sacred Wisdom." The priest bent down and picked up a solid gold ritual bowl that had been resting on the ground beside him and scooped up a small amount of water from the stream. He then made the sign of the four-armed cross over the water, which I later learned represented the four kingdoms of the Celestial forces; before adding a tiny amount of powder of some sort.

The priest then offered the bowl to my father, who after taking a small sip of its contents, handed it back to the priest, who then in turn placed the bowl back on the ground. The priest and my father continued to stand directly facing each other, and looking my father squarely in the eye the priest said:

"Herian – Mighty son of the tribe of Magog – return once more, and take your rightful place amongst your people."

Crossing his hands over his chest, my father then bowed to the priest in a gesture of humility. "Venerable Derkesthai – I am truly humbled by your presence here today – and by the great honour of receiving your blessings."

The priest nodded his head in acknowledgment, and my father then proceeded to take three steps backwards before turning around, and walking back to re-join his Thracian guests who along with all the rest of us, had all been stood in respectful silence throughout the whole performance. The priest appeared to have had a magical effect upon me, as while I was stood there watching him perform the blessing ritual on my father, I could plainly see a bluish light which shone all around him, and at certain times he actually appeared to glow. And when he put his hands on my father's head, I saw a shimmering energy of some sort which completely surrounded him for a moment or two, before it appeared to magically disappear into his body.

"Is there anyone here today who would also like to receive a blessing?" asked the priest out loud.

"Would you like to receive a blessing from the priest, Kai?" Father asked me.

I thought for a moment before replying: "Yes, Father, I think I'd like that."

Father smiled, and taking my hand in his, he marched me right up to the front of the queue, cheating the crowd in the process. Luckily no one seemed to mind, as the priest immediately noticed us standing there at the front, and gestured to me to come and stand before him. And with a little help from father, I suddenly found myself standing there knee-high to the priest, who after dipping his finger into the bowl of water, made the sign of the four-armed cross on my forehead.

"There you go, Kai," he said winking at me, and he gave me such a big beaming smile that I felt all warm inside. I smiled back at him, before quickly running back to my father and the relative safety of his protective shadow.

The blessings were set to continue for some time yet, so Father asked his honoured guests to follow him to where a special guest kol had already been set aside and prepared for them, and where light refreshments and a large pitcher of water had already been neatly laid out on a table, so that they could finally refresh themselves after their long journey, as there just wasn't enough time for them to have done this earlier.

Father proceeded to escort his exhausted guests to their kol which was conveniently situated right next to our own, and which was always kept exclusively for guests and the occasional emergency. And after making sure that his guests were happy, Father told them that he was going to have to leave them for a short while in order to tend to his horses, and that he would return very shortly and re-join them.

"Would you like to help me, Kai?" asked Father, placing his hand on my shoulder. "You can ride your new horse if you like."

I didn't need to be asked twice, as I literally jumped at the chance. Father smiled at my obvious enthusiasm.

"Come on then," he said, quickly walking off in the direction of our kol.

I excitedly followed on after him where he quickly stopped by at our kol to grab a couple of harnesses and two brightly coloured saddle cloths, (which were used in place of leather saddles) and his 'Gorytos' (bow and arrow case) containing his bow and arrows.

"Just in case…You never know," he said slinging them over his left shoulder. "Come on then let's go – we don't have a lot of time today."

After arriving at the paddock, Father immediately jumped down off his horse and unclipped the gate. It didn't take him long before he'd located my horse, and after leading her out of the paddock he harnessed her up ready for me.

"Right then Kai," he said, handing me the reins. "She's all ready for you – jump on."

After giving me a leg up and firmly ordering me to remain exactly where I was, he went back inside the paddock and proceeded to harness his own horse, and then with a tight grip he gave the harness a sharp tug downwards, while at the same time issuing a verbal command to his horse, who immediately responded by lowering itself down into a kneeling position on its front legs, allowing my father to easily jump straight onto his back, after which, the horse quickly stood upright again.

"Right then, Kai…come on then, I'll race you," said Father, galloping off ahead of me. I gave my horse a sharp kick, and immediately began to race after him. Father glanced behind him, just to make sure that I along with all the other horses was safely following on behind. After a short while, he began to slow down a little in order to give me a sporting chance to catch up with him. After that, we continued to travel at a much slower and relaxing pace. It didn't take us very long before we'd reached our destination, and as soon as we had, we immediately dismounted and allowed our horses to join the herd, who were already heading towards the riverbank in order to quench their thirst.

As we stood and waited for all the horses to finish drinking, I decided to tell father all about what I'd seen during his blessing by the priest. He just stood there intently listening to what I had to say, and after I'd finished, I fully expected him to be able to give me some sort of an explanation, but instead he just stood there in complete silence, and just stared at me for what seemed like ages before he finally spoke.

"Hmm…that's really interesting, Kai. Perhaps it would be a good idea if you told the priest about what you saw. I was going to have a little chat with him a little later on anyway. Come on then – we should really be heading back by now…"

After making sure that our horses were safely tethered, and placing all the gear inside our kol, we walked back up to re-join my father's guests, who had already been escorted back to where the festivities were taking place by a couple of ambitious young warriors who had been especially assigned the task of looking after them for the day. Father was pleased to see that they had obviously been getting stuck into the arduous task of sampling the very best of this season's mead in his absence, but by the way they were knocking it back, escorting them back to their guest kol again in one piece may turn out to be a task in itself.

Meanwhile, the priest had finally completed his monumental mission of blessing just about every single person in the whole village, and was now sitting quietly to one side enjoying a very well-deserved rest. He wasn't the only Agari priest who happened to live in our village, and presently several other resident priests were just about to begin the process of sharing out the generous offerings of food which had been so lovingly prepared for this special occasion. A few of the resident priests had left our village a few days ago in order to conduct the ceremonies for the 'Royal Scythians', who were also celebrating this day of renewal.

After all of the food offerings had been equally shared out amongst the village, we were all graced by the presence of some wonderfully talented musicians. A young woman was playing a stringed instrument called a lyre. She was accompanied by an older man playing a lute, while two younger men were playing a variety of different types of percussion. There were dancers, singers, story tellers, and numerous displays of warrior skills which carried on throughout the day.

I sat down amongst an audience of people who were enjoying the musical performance when I noticed that my father and the Agari priest who had conducted the blessing earlier were both standing directly opposite me talking about something. They both glanced across in my direction, and they could see that I was watching them. Although Father looked very serious, the priest just looked at me and smiled. He said something to my father, before making his way over to where I was sitting.

"Hello again, Kai," he said, smiling down at me. "Would you mind if I joined you for a short while."

He had kind gentle eyes and a comforting warm smile, and I actually quite liked the idea of him sitting next to me. But speaking to him was quite a different matter entirely, so I just nodded my head to let him know that it was OK.

"They're very talented – don't you think?" he said, sitting down beside me. I replied with a silent nod of my head.

"Yes, some people seem to have a natural talent for playing musical instruments, while others have a natural talent for other things. I would very much like to talk to you about 'your' natural talent Kai…if that's all right with you of course."

"I…uh…I don't have a talent," I said, finally finding my voice.

"Kai, your father has already told me all about you," he said, gently resting his hand on top of mine. "So what do you think then…can we talk later?"

"Oh!" I said, looking straight down at my feet.

"It's all right, Kai – you're not in any trouble you know – I would just like us to talk for a little while that's all."

Raising my eyes up from the ground I studied his face. He had large pale blue eyes, and the kind of face that was very difficult to put an age to; as sometimes he looked quite young and at other times much older. But whatever his age, his face was so full of warmth and kindness that I felt completely at ease with him, and so I nodded my head in agreement.

"Excellent!" he said, clasping his hands together loudly. "I shall see you a little later on then. I shall go and make arrangements with your father to bring you to me."

And with one single movement he arose to his feet and then briskly walked off – leaving me sat there open mouthed and speechless. I began to look all around for my father, as I was dying to tell him what the priest had just said to me, but I couldn't see him anywhere, so I decided to go for a walk and look for him, and thinking that he may have returned to our kol for some reason, I took a little wander in that direction to see if he was there. But instead of finding my father, I almost walked straight into my brother who had been resting just inside the doorway of our kol. I quickly reacted by stepping back outside again, and I was about to head back to where the festivities were taking place when my brother shouted out:

"Oy…Horse dung…Come here…."

And before I'd had a chance to get away from him, he jumped up and grabbed me by my hair.

"I think I owe you something," he said with a snarl.

And with that, he shoved me so hard that I was knocked clean off my feet and sent tumbling to the ground. He immediately responded by jumping straight on top of me and forcing my face into the cold damp earth.

"Get off me," I struggled to yell at him.

"Get off him," said a voice I didn't recognise.

It was the Thracian boy Gaidres. He had been in the guest kol next door and had obviously heard everything.

"Why don't you mind your own bloody business, Thracian? This has got nothing to do with you," barked my brother in response.

Gaidres immediately ran over and gave my brother a really hard shove, which thankfully had the effect of sending him flying off me. Raising himself from the ground, my brother screwed up his face angrily, and forgetting all about me for a moment, he turned to face Gaidres with two clenched fists.

"Come on then…try and hit me if you dare," said Gaidres, taking a protective stance. "What are you waiting for?"

"Forget it – you're just not worth it, Thracian Scum," hissed my brother, before spitting at the ground and angrily storming off. "Are you okay?" asked Gaidres.

I'd sustained a badly grazed cheek during my brother's vicious attack, but apart from that…I was fine.

"Yes, I think so," I said, still sitting on the ground.

Gaidres held out his hand towards me, and I responded by reaching out and grasping hold of his outstretched hand. He effortlessly pulled me back onto my feet again, and looking at my grazed and muddy face he said:

"You should clean that…I can help you if you like."

"No thanks," I said, not wanting to make a fuss.

"I think it would be better if I help you. Come on," he said with a friendly smile.

I wasn't usually allowed in the guest kol, so Gaidres had to first persuade me that it would be fine for me to come in and sit down just for a few of minutes. It took a little persuasion, but eventually I agreed to go inside just long enough to allow him to wash the dirt from my grazed cheek.

"You speak our language really well," I said.

"Thanks. I've been having regular lessons for quite some time now. Do you want me to walk back down with you?"

I thought for a moment, and fearing the very high possibility that I may bump into my brother again, I agreed to allow Gaidres to accompany me. And so with my new friend and albeit temporary bodyguard, I was safely escorted back down to where the festivities were in full swing.

It wasn't long before I found my father. He was obviously enjoying watching the spectacle of a few young warriors who were determined to out-do one another in trials of strength and endurance, and I had to tug at his sleeve several times in order to get him to notice that I was there. "What happened to your face?"

"I tripped and fell over," I lied.

I could tell by the expression on his face that he didn't believe me.

"Are you sure about that?" he asked, taking a closer look.

"Yes," I replied, while avoiding making any direct eye contact with him.

"Hmm…if you say so," he said with a raised expression on his face.

I remained very close to my father's side for the rest of the day, until at last he told me that it was now time for me to go and have my chat with the priest.

"Come on then," he said, looking up at the position of the sun. "It's not good to keep the Derkesthai waiting."

Father led me away from all the people to a quiet secluded spot where the priest was already sat cross legged on the ground patiently waiting for us. As soon as he saw us, he quickly stood up and gave us a big welcoming smile, and as we approached, he held out his hand and beckoned for me to come and join him.

The priest turned to my father and said: "Don't worry – I shall return him safely back to you when we're done, Herian."

"I'll see you later then Kai," said Father, already beginning to walk away.

"What happened to your face?" asked the priest with a frown.

I told him exactly the same cover up story that I'd told my father earlier.

"Hmm – Shall we try that one once again," he said, repeating the question.

I felt so ashamed at having to admit to him that it had been my own brother who had done this to me, but even more ashamed for having lied to him, so I stared downwards towards the ground, concealing the shame that was reflected in my eyes.

"It was my brother – he pushed me over – and he shoved my face into the ground," I said, feeling very sorry for myself.

"Hmm – Well, that wasn't a very nice thing to do at all…but I'm really glad you've been able to be honest with me, Kai," he said sympathetically. "You really don't have any reason to feel ashamed Kai. Sometimes it can be very difficult to admit to the things we find difficult to deal with. Trust me; I really do understand how you feel, but we cannot continue unless you are willing to be completely honest with me. Now then…it would also be really nice if you looked up at me now and again, instead of staring at that invisible speck on the ground…don't you think?"

As I raised my eyes from the ground, they were instantly met by his kind but penetrating gaze. The gentle knowing expression that was plainly written upon his face, gave me no doubt that he really did understand how I was feeling right now.

I found him very easy to talk to. He had a certain way about him which made me feel as though I could talk to him about anything. And sure enough, before very long I found myself opening up to him and telling him all about the strange things that I'd experienced, and about the phantom shadow that tried to strangle my brother. I told him all about what I'd seen earlier on that day during the blessing on my father, and also about several other things that was currently going on with me; things that I'd never dared mention to anyone before. And once I began to open up to him, I found I couldn't stop. It felt so good to be able to talk to someone about these things. He just sat there quietly listening to me talk and talk, without once interrupting, until finally…I'd completely run out of anything else to say.

The priest paused for a moment before proceeding to tell me that my abilities could be a very good thing if they are used wisely…or a very bad thing if they are used unwisely.

"Kai…Would you like me to teach you how to use your abilities wisely?"

"Yes…I think so!"

"Good, because I'd really like to be your teacher, Kai…if you will have me…that is?"

"Yes…I think I'd like that!"

"Good, well that's agreed then, but we're going to have to wait for a few years yet before you're going to be old enough to undertake any serious study. So for now – just try and stay out of trouble. And if you need to talk to me about anything…just ask your father to bring you to me. And in the meantime, I'll talk to him about all of this, and hopefully he will agree."

"How old do I have to be?" I asked him.

"Twelve winters is about usual."

I thought it sounded like a very long time to wait, but at least it would be something that I'd have to look forward to in the future.

And with that, he escorted me back to my father where I was then able to enjoy the rest of the day's festivities, thankfully without any further confrontations with my brother.

Later that day, the priest and my father had a very long conversation. I knew it was all about me…but this time it really didn't bother me at all!

5

A Visit to the Hun

Within the boundaries of our settlement there was a specially enclosed area, which had been set aside for the teaching of young children in the weaponry skills of the horse Warrior, which were absolutely essential if you were to have any chance of surviving in our harsh and sometimes hostile environment.

Father had personally spent many long hours teaching me the correct way to use my bow. And when he thought that I was sufficiently skilled, he began taking me along with my brother on hunting trips. He did this so that we could practice our aim towards an unpredictable and moving target while on horseback, and he was pleasantly surprised to discover that I appeared to have a natural leaning towards archery. In fact, by the age of around seven I'd already developed a sharply focused and accurate aim, which easily equalled many of the more experienced warriors in our tribe.

I didn't care very much for the trivial games of children my own age, and when I wasn't out improving my aim, I enjoyed spending my time alone in the practice area where I could continue to sharpen my bow skills. Sometimes I'd be joined by other children, who would regularly arrive for practice sessions, and although it was not mandatory that every girl should learn to use the bow, they were always given an equal opportunity, and if they wished, they could also learn to use a sword or any of the other weapons. Some of them became excellent warriors, and even fought in battle alongside their men folk as equals. Although this was generally the exception and not the rule, as women faced the added possibility of being raped if they were ever captured, and also women with a young family risked leaving their children motherless.

Sometimes, I was given the job of helping to teach some of the other children how to use a bow.

I saw this as a great responsibility, and I always took my role as teacher very seriously. Although Father would often make light-hearted comments about my obsession for practising, he also encouraged it, as he knew that I was never happier than when I was either practising or teaching. Father was a very proficient swordsman, and with the aid of two wooden practice swords he spent a great deal of time teaching me the basic skills of swordsmanship. And after I'd learned all the basic moves, he appointed one of the most skilled swordsmen in our tribe to be my personal teacher. With all this tuition, I soon excelled in the finer skills of swordsmanship as well as in archery. And my speed and agility at both was quite noticeable even at an early age.

Meanwhile a visit to the Huns was in the process of being organised as it had been quite a while now since our last visit, and my uncle who had already been given prior notice of our forthcoming arrival, was busy preparing a yurt especially for us to stay in for the duration of our visit. I was really looking forward to seeing my Hun family again. It was like having an extended family that lived in a different world from our own, and our visits were always received with genuine warmth and excitement.

I had another little sister by now, but neither of my sisters, or my brother for that matter would be joining us this time around, and would be left under the watchful care of one of my father's three sisters instead.

Mother was busily preparing everything that we were going to need to take along with us, while Father was having a bit of a problem deciding who he should choose to accompany us this time around. He always tried to select a good balance of few good and trusted warriors who hadn't visited the Hun before, with an equal amount who were already familiar with their religious beliefs and traditions. Father was always very mindful to give the inexperienced warriors a preliminary prep talk; explaining to them a few basic codes of conduct that they needed to follow, e.g., never ever stand in the entrance of a yurt or pass anything to anyone across its threshold. Always walk in a clockwise direction around the inside the yurt, and never directly underneath its central supports. And never ever throw any rubbish into a fire after it had been lit, as this was considered very disrespectful to the fire. And perhaps most importantly of all…never pass anything to anyone who was sat to the left of you, as it was considered very bad luck. And a whole bunch of other things that they needed to be made aware of.

Father couldn't help but recount his own very first visit to the Huns, and how between himself and his little band of warriors, they had managed to break just about every single rule of correct conduct that they had. It made him cringe at the memory of how ill-mannered they must have all appeared to the Huns back then. But even so, somehow they had managed to survive to tell the tale.

The Gods must surely have been smiling on them that day for sure, and the rest was now history. We set off on our journey early the next morning, and after a couple of days of steady travelling, we finally arrived at our destination, where we were immediately met by my uncle who was the 'Khan' (leader) of the Hun tribe, and many others who were obviously genuinely pleased to see us.

No sooner had we dismounted from our horses, than they were immediately led away to be taken good care of. And after the usual ritual of greetings had been made, we were all herded inside my uncle's yurt where Mother immediately got stuck into helping my uncle's two wives, who were in the process of preparing food and refreshments for us on the left-hand side of the yurt. The rest of us all sat down on brightly decorated cushions that were randomly scattered around a low-lying table which was situated on the far-right hand side of the yurt, after which, Father proceeded to introduce my uncle to the Scythian newcomers.

Along with my uncle's two wives, Mother carried over the food and set it down on the table, before sitting down with the other two women to eat separately on the other side of the yurt. It was not customary for Hun women to join their men folk while they were entertaining guests as it was considered bad luck.

After everyone had finished eating, Mother helped my uncle's wives quickly clear everything away, after which, they promptly left the yurt. Their work was done for now, and no doubt they were eager for a chance to catch up on all the gossip.

My mother and my uncle's two wives had barely had a chance to take one step outside the yurt before my father and my uncle had ardently begun discussing all the current political situations that may, or may not have concerned them. I have to admit that I was far more interested in what the women might have had to say than I was in listening to the men folk harp on about politics for the next couple of hours, and if truth be known, I would much preferred to have tagged along with them instead.

My father and uncle politely spoke to each other in Scythian for the benefit of those who didn't speak the Hunnic language. I could already speak both languages, but I found politics equally as boring in either language, so you can imagine my relief when I was asked to go outside for a little while so that they could all speak freely to one another on the matters concerning men; of which my little ears were still far too tender in years to hear. Father smiled and told me that I could join them again a little later on. I really didn't need to be told twice, and before he'd had a chance to tell me to close the door after me, I was already through it.

Apart from two rather bored-looking Hun Warriors who were supposed to be keeping watch, the whole place looked pretty deserted, so wandering over to a large upright wooden structure that was used for the practice of knife throwing; I sat myself down on the ground with my back resting up against the splintered wooden frame. However, it didn't take very long before some Hun children suddenly seemed to appear from nowhere and began gathering all around me. I already knew most of them from my previous visits, in fact, I was actually blood related to two of the boys, and three of the girls. It felt really good to see them again, but the fact that they were obviously excited to see me too made me feel really happy. I was always being singled out and bullied in Scythia, so to be the centre of attention for all the right reasons was a very welcome change.

"Ah ha...I see you've brought your bow and arrows along with you," said Altan. Altan was Gui-Sen-Khans son, which of course made him my cousin.

"Are you any good with that?" he asked me, taking a closer look at my bow.

"I might be...why?"

"Well...let's find out then shall we. Come on," he said enthusiastically.

We were eagerly followed over to the practice area by the other children, along with the two bored looking Hun warriors who had been stood idly listening to us, and who obviously had nothing better to do.

"Go on...you can go first," said Altan, waving me on ahead of him.

I knocked my arrow into place and prepared to take aim. I wasn't used to such an audience, and I found the fact that I had one very off putting as it made me feel very self-conscious. Needless to say, my first shot wasn't all that impressive. And when Altan took his turn, he was able beat my shot with ease. So when it was my turn again, I took a deep breath, closed my eyes, and tried to imagine that I was the only person here. And not before I had completely centred myself did I nock my arrow and draw back my bowstring.

A cheer rang out from everyone including the two Hun warriors who were stood nearby watching us. I'd scored a bull's-eye!

Altan looked at me surprised: "Good shot," he said, before walking over to the standing point and taking aim for his second shot.

Another cheer rang out. Altan had also scored a bull's-eye this time.

"That's far too easy – shall we see if we can make it just a little bit more interesting," said one of the Hun warriors who had been stood there watching us.

He walked over to the target and placed a small stone on the top of it.

"Now let's see which one of you will be the first to hit that."

Altan and I both looked at each other. "Go on," I said. "You go first this time."

Altan took first aim but missed, so taking a deep breath I focussed all my attention on the target. I continued to hold my breath as I pulled back my bowstring…aim…and release. My arrow hit the stone square on, and as the stone flew off the top of the wooden target, a huge cheer rang out.

"That was very good!" said the Hun warrior nodding in approval.

"You win for now," said Altan, giving me a somewhat harder than necessary congratulatory slap on the back.

"Wait, before you go why don't we see what else you can do." said the second Hun warrior. And before long, they were setting up all sorts of targets for me to hit. Some I would miss at first, but after a few attempts I would eventually hit them. The targets slowly became more and more difficult, until eventually the level of my skill had clearly been established. One of the Hun Warriors praised me with another hard slap on the back, which almost knocked me clean off my feet this time.

"You're pretty good, aren't you," said Altan, wiping a speck of mud from his bow.

"I've been practising," I said, trying not to appear too smug.

"Hmm," said the Hun warrior with a cold stare. "But I wonder if your bravery is matched by your accuracy with that bow little warrior?"

His piercing deep set dark brown eyes held me captive like a startled animal before he turned his head very slightly to face the horizon. He closed his eyes for a few moments before slowly opening them again in a very deliberate and controlled manner. His head was still facing towards the horizon, but as he slowly opened his eyes, they were already fixed in a freaky looking sideways stare in my direction. I don't know why but he was obviously trying to scare me, and it was working.

"I'll catch up with you later, little warrior," he said with an ominous grin.

He signalled to his companion with a nod of his head, and they both headed back in the general direction that they had come from.

"You shouldn't take any notice of Yesukai," said Altan, resting his hand on my left shoulder. "It's just his way that's all. He's one of the most respected, skilled and feared warriors amongst us, and he has managed to retain the title of 'champion of the bow' for several years running. I think you must have really impressed him. And believe me when I tell you…that's a very difficult thing to do. He's just testing you out by trying to scare you a little…that's all! He obviously believes you must be worth his…uh…attention. And I know that this might sound a bit strange to you, but he probably really likes you, or he wouldn't have even bothered to try and frighten you."

"He didn't just…try to frighten me. He did frighten me…for real! He actually really frightened me."

Altan must have found the look of utter indignation on my face some-what amusing. I could see that he was obviously struggling to keep a straight face, and I began to see the funny side of it too. We both looked at the forced expressions on one another's faces, and burst into fits of hysterical laughter. The other children all started to laugh too, although I'm not quite sure if they were laughing at the same thing we were, or laughing at the spectacle of Altan and myself; neither of whom could see for the tears of laughter that were streaming down our faces. And every time we looked at each other, we just burst out laughing all over again. It felt so good to be able to laugh at the very same thing that had only just a few moments ago seemed so very frightening to me. But the added bonus was that I could now see that the whole thing was nothing more than a cleverly devised and artfully presented illusion which was designed to trigger irrational feelings of confusion and fear. Very clever!

For truth be said, Yesukai hadn't actually done, or said anything to imply that he had had any intention of harming me in any way. So it would seem that he 'was' just testing me after all. Hmm, well if that's the case, I'd just managed to gain a priceless advantage over him, as I could now clearly see that this was nothing but a game, and whatever this test of bravery was that he may have had in store for me, I would now be well and truly prepared for it!

"Would you like to go and pay a visit to the head Shaman of the village, he's always good for a story or two," said Altan, regaining his composure again.

"Yes, but first I really need to talk to my father about something, so I'm going to go and see if they've finished with their 'men talks' yet. You can go on ahead if you like, and I'll join you a bit later."

Standing outside the entrance to the yurt, I tentatively pulled back the flap just enough so that I could take a little peek inside. They were obviously still all busy with their 'talks'. My father caught sight of me peering in through the entrance to the yurt.

"Not just yet, Kai," he said firmly.

I immediately let go of the flap and made my way over to the large wooden board that was used for knife throwing practice, and once again I sat myself down on the ground with my back resting up against the splintered frame. I did think about going to look for Altan, but it was so peaceful that before very long I'd managed to float off into one of my little day dreams. Suddenly, I was jolted back to reality by the loud shrill voice of Yesukai yelling at me.

"Now you'll know what fear tastes like, boy."

Yesukai was stood approximately six metres away from me. He looked very angry, and his features were contorted with rage, but I just continued to sit there calmly looking straight at him; wondering what it was he was going to do next. I wasn't at all afraid of him anymore, as I knew that whatever he did, it was only an act, and I felt quite confident that he wasn't really going to hurt me. Moving towards me aggressively, Yesukai snarled at me: "You don't honestly believe that you can defy me and get away with it…do you, boy?"

I just sat there calmly watching his performance.

"Let's see if you can defy this," said Yesukai, grinning menacingly as he reached for a small dagger that he had strapped to his leg. "It's time for you to die boy."

I watched him draw back his arm with the knife in his hand, and with a forward motion that was almost too fast for my eyes to follow…he released his grip on the knife. While all the time I just continued to sit calmly staring straight at him. There was a dull 'Thuck' sound, and I felt the force of the knife as it hit the board very close to my left shoulder, but still…I hadn't even so much as flinched. Glancing to my left, I could see that the knife was firmly embedded in the wood just a couple of inches away from my shoulder. So standing up I firmly grasped the handle of the knife, and began working it free from the board.

"I wish that I could throw a knife as good as that!" I said, finally freeing the knife.

I walked over to Yesukai with the knife resting in my hand and held it out towards him. I hadn't noticed before, but my father, uncle, and the other men who had been inside of my uncle's yurt, had all been stood outside watching the whole spectacle. And every one of them was looking at me with a grin on his face.

Reaching out, Yesukai retrieved the knife from my hand and smiled. And grasping me by both shoulders he looked me squarely in the eyes and said:

"Your bravery most definitely surpasses your skill, little warrior, and your skill has already ran way ahead of you. You have earned respect today, and the right to call yourself a true Hun Warrior. And if you wish, I will teach you how to deliver an accurate throw with a knife." And turning the handle of the knife so that it faced me – he offered it back to me. "You should keep this one," he said. "I think you've earned it."

"Thank you," I said, bowing to him respectfully.

"When you've learned to use this one properly, I'll have some more made especially for you."

Although I was feeling very pleased with myself, I couldn't help feeling that I'd cheated just a little, as I knew deep down inside that I hadn't really been brave at all; just very confident that this was all some elaborate test of some kind, and that Yesukai hadn't really intended to do me any harm. I looked across at Father, who proudly nodded his head in a gesture of approval. So with my newly acquired prize of throwing knife in hand, I walked on over to join him.

"You did really well there, son, I'm really proud of you," said Father, resting his hands on my shoulders.

I felt elated…and if ever there was a moment of total happiness – this was it, and I would have given anything to have remained frozen in that moment forever. But alas – it was but a fleeting moment through the endless passage of time. I instinctively knew that I should try and hold on to this feeling for as long as was humanly possible, as very soon it would begin to dissolve, and like the distant echo of a long-ago forgotten promise, it would in time become just another faded memory.

Yesukai called over to me: "When do you want to start then?"

"Now…please!" I replied enthusiastically.

"Okay then," he said with a chuckle. "Let's find out how accurate you are at knife throwing then, shall we?"

And that was how I came to learn the art of knife throwing. Yesukai only had to show me the correct technique a couple of times, and with my obsessional drive to perfect the art, I eventually became as accurate at knife throwing as I was with my bow.

6

The First Lessons

When the time had finally come to begin my training with the Agari priest, I received a message requesting that I should come to see him at his kol the following day at around mid-day. And although I was really excited at the prospect of becoming a pupil of an Agari priest, I was also terrified as I didn't have a clue what I was going to be letting myself in for. But whatever it was, I figured that I should at least make an effort to look my very best, and so I washed my body and hair with a kind of soap that we made out of boiled seaweed which had been specially scented with aromatic oils which was usually kept for special occasions; after which, I dressed in my finest clothes. I even asked my mother if she wouldn't mind braiding and decorating my hair for me, and thankfully she was quite happy to oblige. So after several hours of preparing myself both physically and mentally, I finally felt ready to leave our kol and keep my appointment with destiny.

As I made my way towards the priest's kol, I could feel my heart beating fast, and the closer I got the more nervous I felt, and as I hesitantly approached the entrance to the priest's kol I wasn't sure if I should just stand here and wait for him to come out and get me; or call out to make my presence known to him; or even if I should just walk straight in. And as I stood there still deliberating upon the question of what to do next, the priest suddenly called out to me from inside the kol.

"Kai…please come right in."

Lifting up the flap of the entrance, I tentatively crossed over the threshold of the priest's private sanctuary, and I was immediately met with a warm and welcoming smile.

"Please, Kai…come and sit down," he said, standing up to greet me.

The air inside the priest's kol was full of a heady a mixture of incense, and the various herbs that were often used in the preparation of certain medicinal compounds and tinctures. And just on the right-hand side of the doorway was a large pile of well-seasoned wood that was used for burning. A little further along was a wooden shelf unit that was full to bursting with a multitude of different containers and earthenware jars, and placed right next to them was several weaved baskets which had been covered with tightly fitting lids.

Hanging from the inner wooden structure of the kol were many different types of herbs, which had been firmly tied together into neat little bundles before being hung up and left to dry. A low wooden table was presently playing host to a fascinating selection of various fungi which had been carefully laid out and was now left uncovered to dry.

To the left of the priest's kol was his bed, which also doubled up as a seating area, and was presently completely covered over by a huge and lavish sheepskin blanket. A little further over towards the far side of the kol were two very large baskets; one of which the priest used to store his clothes, while the other was used to safely store away the various ritual items that were occasionally used by the Agari. Resting on the ground, and right next to the central fire pit, was a fairly large cauldron with two smaller cooking pots standing like informal sentries nearby, and laying right next to them were a variety of implements; some of which were used for cooking, and others that were only used in the preparation of elixirs, potions, and a whole variety of medicinal concoctions which were regularly used in the treatment of all types of ailments and afflictions – both of the body and of the mind.

Most of the floor of the kol was covered with tough hemp matting, and all across the surrounding wall of the sleeping/sitting area, soft sheepskins had been firmly secured into place, thus creating a very warm and cosy atmosphere.

Another low wooden table had been conveniently situated right next to the sleeping/sitting area, and on it was placed a variety of different items which included amongst other things; several candles which had already been lit, a small golden bowl, and a highly decorated silver incense burner.

The priest had lived here alone for many years, and it was common knowledge that he'd never married; preferring to live a life of celibacy. This was entirely of his own personal choosing, as there were no rules concerning celibacy – or sexuality amongst the Agari.

Sitting himself back down again, the priest beckoned for me to come and sit down next to him.

"Would you like some water, Kai?" he asked me.

"No, thank you!" I said, shaking my head.

"Hmm," he said, leaning in towards me. "If you are not quite feeling up to our meeting today, Kai, we can always do this at some other time you know."

He could obviously sense that I was feeling more than a little nervous right now. However, I was determined not to allow my nervousness to get the better of me.

"No, I'm fine," I replied, shaking my head.

"So then, Kai, do you still want to learn how to use your abilities wisely?" he asked, with a warm smile.

"Yes, of course I do," I replied, eagerly.

The priest then proceeded to explain to me that it wasn't going to be easy, and that it would require many long years of serious study on my part, and only then if I was truly dedicated, would it eventually lead to a deeper understanding of the very nature of all things both seen and unseen. He also explained to me that there may be times when I may be called upon to face, and to overcome, great personal trials along the way.

"So tell me – are you still absolutely sure that you're ready to begin?"

"Yes, I'm really sure," I replied, enthusiastically.

"Good!" he said, leaning forward and resting his hand on my shoulder for a moment. "Then there is no time better than right now. So shall we begin?"

The priest began to re-arrange a few of the items that he'd previously placed on the table in front of us before reciting a short prayer for protection. He said that it was really important to always ask for protection before undertaking any spiritual study or work of any kind.

"Right then, Kai," he said, clasping his hands together. "I think that today we shall begin our studies by first concentrating on a little basic groundwork. Simple though it may be – it will then allow us a firm base on which to lay the very foundations that are so necessary, before we can even think about beginning with the process of building a mighty temple."

I'd never heard anyone speak this way before, so not surprisingly I just sat there with a blank expression on my face, as I didn't really understand all this talk of foundations and temples.

"Don't look so worried; I shall explain," said the priest, with a knowing look on his face.

However, he spent the next half an hour or so just explaining to me the basic meaning behind this one simple sentence. He was certainly going to have his work cut out for him with me as his student that was for sure.

The priest then proceeded to explain to me how important it was that I should first gain a deeper understanding into the hidden and inner workings of nature, and of the apparent duality contained within the elemental kingdom, and how all of this directly relates to the deeper levels of our own selves. He said that all things are connected, and we in turn are connected to all things, and it was possible to gain a deeper understanding of our own self, by first uncovering how the very elements of earth, air, fire, and water, relate to us on a personal level. As each of the elements reflect certain aspects of our own inner selves and of our personality, and when this is truly understood, it can offer us great insight into our individual potential in this life, and of our personal strengths and weaknesses, and armed with this knowledge – we can learn to control, and to bring into balance those very elements within our own being, which may on occasion become a little stormy or out of control, and ultimately over many lifetimes, and with a fair degree of faith, courage, and the inner conviction to succeed, we can slowly bring together our inner polarities, until they eventually merge together as one, and the Alchemical marriage of the ultimate unity of the self with the self will have then been achieved. He said that as the time of my birth was known, he was able to consult the Artim Derkesthai (Celestial Dragon Master) who in turn was able to gain valuable insight into my core nature, and how each of the four elements related to me personally. But before he could explain what this meant to me, I was going to have to understand the positive and negative attributes of each of the four elements, and how by measuring the strength, or weakness, of the presence of each element in a special chart which showed the position of the planets, stars, sun, and moon, in relation to the earth at my time of birth, had given us all some very valuable information. He proceeded to explain the positive and negative aspects of each element, pointing out that all were equally essential to sustain life, but by the law of duality – equally capable of destroying it too. "So then, Kai, we now come to your own personal relationship with the elements and what they have revealed about you," he said with a very serious expression on his face. "Well, firstly, it shows us that your ruling element is undoubtedly air; in fact, nearly two thirds of your chart is ruled by air, while the rest is mostly shared between fire and water, with just enough earth to keep you from falling off the planet altogether. I must say that when we first saw this, it gave rise to some concern, as the lack of the earth element in your chart is going make it very difficult for you to control such an overwhelmingly powerful presence of the element of air. It also shows us that you possess a sharp intellect, and an ability to mentally calculate and respond to situations with incredible speed and agility, and is also responsible for your accuracy and aptitude with weaponry. But most importantly – your chart clearly shows us that you already have several developed Occult faculties, some of which we are already aware, and some of which we are not. Unfortunately, the negative side to all of this is that the great height of the positive side of your nature is currently shadowed by an equal capacity for its negative counterpart. And if the negative side of the emotional aspects of water; or the hot temperament and driving force of fire are not brought under control, it could potentially become inwardly or outwardly destructive, and possibly even dangerous, as there is very little of the earth element to cause a grounding effect. If the negative side of your nature was ever to become problematic, it would then be left up to the discretionary intervention of certain others to try and gain control over the situation."

I found it all very confusing and I began to feel a little bit frightened at the seriousness of it all.

"Kai...I know it must have been very difficult for you to hear all of this," said the priest, with obvious concern in his eyes. "But it's for the best that you know the truth right from the very beginning. I can't change any of this, but I 'can' help you. There are certain things that can be done in order to help you to develop a closer link to the earth element, and that will go a long way in helping you to ground the other elements. So please don't worry too much. You're not put together this way by accident – there is always a reason for everything. One thing is for sure – although you may be a bit of an unknown quantity at the moment, you also have great potential. And a really positive thing about all of this is – that there are some very negative human sentiments that you will never have to deal with, as you are completely incapable of feeling them...Jealousy, greed, competitiveness, hunger for Power or for wealth. All of these feelings will remain strangers to you. But you 'will' have to watch your tendency for impulsive behaviour, and keep a firm grip on your fiery temper and your emotions, and you must remain ever mindful of keeping a very tight lid on that shadow side of yourself, of which we really don't ever want to see. I'd like you to come and see me at the same time every day until I tell you otherwise, after

67

which, we will reduce that to every other day, until eventually once every seven days will suffice. Now before we end our lesson for today, I would just like to stress to you the importance of never repeating, or revealing anything that is ever said between us, or that you may experience during your study time here with me to anyone. Do you understand?"

I nodded my head and answered that I did.

"Are you willing to swear a blood oath to that?"

I'd seen people do this sort of thing before, but I could never understand why anyone would want to do such a thing as to cut their own hand. But I trusted the priest, so I thought to myself that if he thought it was necessary for me to prove my loyalty in this way, then I would just have to do it.

But I really didn't want to!

Hmm – a blood oath. "Okay…so what do I have to do?" I asked, nervously.

"You don't have to look so worried," he said, resting his hand on my arm. "It's really quite simple. All you have to do is make a tiny little cut on the side of your left hand, and repeat a few words after me. All new pupils of the Agari are asked do this as a way of showing their commitment. And also if anyone should ever try and push you for information concerning what you may have learned, you can tell them that you have sworn a blood oath of secrecy, and that you dare not tell, and they will most probably leave you alone after that."

The priest then began to unravel a small bundle of clean white linen; revealing a very sharp looking ritual knife which up until this moment, had been discreetly resting upon the table, and as soon as I saw it – I immediately began to feel a little nervous again. I must have cut myself dozens of times before, but never actually on purpose, and I really wasn't sure if I could do it.

"Don't worry – the knife has already been purified," he said, sensing my concerns.

After smoothing out the white linen upon the table, he gently rested the knife on top of it. He then proceeded to pour some liquid from a small silver bottle onto another piece of clean linen, and told me to clean my hands with it. I had already washed my hands before I'd arrived so I didn't see the point of having to do it again, but all the same I obediently followed his instructions, giving both of my hands a thorough wipe over with the soggy piece of linen, after which I promptly handed it back to him. Discarding the cloth, he picked up the knife and placing it flat in the palm of his hand he held it out towards me. At first, I was a little hesitant, but I didn't want him to think I was a coward, so reaching out – I grasped the knife by its delicately ornate handle and took it from his hand.

"You're doing very well," said the priest, proceeding to place a small solid gold dish which had been lined with a piece of clean wool directly in front of me.

"I am now going to say a few words, and I want you to repeat them after me," he said, looking me straight in the eyes. "After which, I want you to make a small cut on the edge of your right hand with the knife, and then allow a few drops of your blood to fall onto that piece of wool in the bowl in front of you. When you've done that, I want you to pick up the piece of wool and hold it over the flame of the candle until it starts to burn, and then quickly return it to the dish before the fire begins to burn your hand."

Still maintaining eye contact, he then asked me to repeat after him: "With my life blood, I swear a Sacred Oath of Silence that I shall never under any circumstance repeat anything that I may see, anything I may hear, or anything that I may experience to anyone outside of the Agari brotherhood during the whole of my time here on earth, spent either as a pupil of the Agari or otherwise." After I had repeated the words exactly as he had spoken them, the priest then gave me a little nod of his head as if to say 'go ahead!' And after a brief moment of hesitation, I picked up the knife and held the sharp edge of the blade against the outside of my right hand, and not wanting to give myself a chance to think about it, I quickly made a small cut, after which I held my hand over the piece of wool lying in the dish, and then watched as a few drops of my blood dripped onto the wool.

"Now hold the wool over the flame," instructed the priest.

So picking up the little piece of blood-stained wool, I held it there for a second or two until it began to burn, and then I quickly returned it to the dish.

"That's it – well done," said the priest, smiling at me. "Now let me see your hand."

I held my hand out towards him. "Yes, that's fine. It will be healed in a day or two," he said, proceeding to tie a small strip of linen cloth around my hand to stem any further bleeding.

"Right then – I think that's enough for today," he said with a satisfied smile. "We will continue again tomorrow at the same time. I have another pupil arriving soon. He also has special abilities – and is another one who has given us reason for concern in the past. So you see, Kai – you're not the only one."

Standing up to leave, I respectfully bowed to my new teacher before making my way to the doorway of the kol. I was surprised to be met head on by a fair-haired boy who looked to be around fourteen or fifteen winters of age, and as we passed each other I couldn't resist turning around to get a better look at him, and he was also doing exactly the same thing to me. We both gave each other a little smile of mutual respect, before he disappeared into the priest's kol. I'd later learn that his name was Sai, and that he lived on the far easterly side of our village.

As I approached my father's kol, I could see by all the fuss that was going on outside that he was obviously entertaining visitors. It was a party of Thracians; including the regular emissary and his son Gaidres who must have been around sixteen or seventeen winters by now. They had unexpectedly arrived requesting an urgent meeting with my father. This wasn't anything particularly unusual in itself as there was always something going on somewhere with someone.

Gaidres was presently sitting on a large wooden tree trunk outside the guest kol, and seeing that he was sat there alone, I briskly walked up to him and asked him how he was doing.

"I'm fine," he replied. "What about you? What have you been up to since the last time I was here?"

"Well, actually…I've just began training to be an Agari Priest," I said, unsure of how he was going to react to what was probably going to come as surprising news.

"Really…I didn't know that the son of a Chief was allowed to join the Agari," said Gaidres, raising his eyebrows.

"Yes, it is allowed – but only under certain conditions."

The look of utter surprise on his face said it all. I thought I'd better quickly change the subject before he fell off the tree trunk. "Anyway…Never mind about all of that – how do you fancy some weapon practice."

"You're still allowed to use weapons then…now that you're training to become an Agari priest and all that?" he asked me, looking even more confused than ever.

"Come on," I said, quickly grabbing my bow and throwing knives which were lying just inside my father's kol.

There was always plenty of wooden practice swords left lying around in the practice area so we didn't need to take any.

During our practice sessions together, we often spoke about many things. Gaidres told me that in Thracia they had special warrior schools, where men and boys would regularly go and learn to master many different types of weapons. He told me that back home in Thracia, he was receiving private lessons from the finest swordsman that ever lived. Although I didn't see how he could possibly make such an enormous claim as to being taught by 'the finest swordsman that ever lived', I did think that a warrior school sounded like a really good idea though, and I asked him if he wouldn't mind demonstrating some of the sword techniques that he'd been taught by this master swordsman. Gaidres seemed more than happy for the chance to show off his new sword skills, and I in turn was eager for the opportunity to show off mine. And so we continued to spar until the light began to fade, and as neither of us wanted to be the first to admit to the other that we were thoroughly worn out after a gruelling few hours of solid kick ass sparring, when we eventually returned to my father's kol, we were both totally exhausted.

I wondered what the urgency of the talks was all about this time. And I hoped and prayed that my father and our warriors were not going to have to leave for battle again. We lost several good men during the last battle that was fought against the Celts. And my father would have died for sure had it not been for the immediate attention that he'd received from one of the Agari priests who had accompanied them. It was quite common for a few Agari priest to accompany our warriors into battle, so that they would be on hand and ready to administer to any of the wounded, and many lives had been saved this way. As it was; he'd returned home with serious and life-threatening injuries. But thanks to the continued attention of the very same Agari priest who had been there to save his life on the battlefield – my father eventually recovered.

There was an increasing threat coming from the west from these Celts, as they had been periodically attacking us for some time. And although we had always been successful in blocking their attacks, they must have known that they were having the overall effect of making our position here increasingly unstable.

Early the next morning just as the sun was beginning to rise; the Thracian's were already preparing to leave. And before the dust of their horses' hooves had had time to settle, my father called a meeting with all of his best and most trusted men. After which, he dutifully informed my mother along with the all rest of us, that he was going to have to call a meeting with the royal Scythians, and as many tribal leaders as they could possibly manage to get hold of at such short notice. This obviously meant that they were going to have to leave immediately, and would most probably not return again for several moons (months).

Although this was usually not a very good sign, it didn't necessarily mean that there was going to be another battle. So I would just have to try and remain positive.

The next day I decided to leave early for my appointment with my Derkesthai (Dragon Master) as I wanted to make a good impression, so on reaching my destination, I hung around outside for a few moments in order to compose myself, and to brush away all the dust from my trousers that I'd managed to collect along the way. But I'd barely had a chance to gather my thoughts before I heard the priest call out for me to enter. I wasn't feeling quite so nervous today, so taking a deep breath, I boldly pulled aside the heavy leather doorway and stepped inside.

"How are you feeling today, Kai?" asked the priest, standing up to greet me.

"I'm feeling a lot less nervous today than I did yesterday," I answered, still brushing the dust from my trousers.

"Good! – That's very good! Please come and sit yourself down," he said warmly. "I would like us to cover three very important issues today. The first is concerning the lack of the presence of the earth element in your chart, and how we may be able to develop it by creating a slightly stronger link to the earth. The second thing is the issue of blood, and why it has such an important role in the rituals and practices of both the Agari, and the Scythian people as a whole. Although there are very few people living in this village that understand why. And the third and final issue concerns the use of snake venom.

"So firstly, and concerning the first issue – I'm going to give you a new name. Don't worry – it won't replace your given name – but will simply add onto it. This name isn't just any old name, as it carries with it a strong vibrational link, which has been built up by association and repetition over many ages of time. The name that I'm referring to is Manu, and as you know, it's also the word that Scythians use when referring to the presiding spirit of the earth. So from now on – you shall be known as Manu Kai."

I had always been told that the name Kai was a very ancient name, and that it meant warrior, so a rough translation of my name was now 'Earth Warrior'.

My Agari teacher then went on to say, that it would probably benefit me a great deal if I became a little more acquainted with the earth itself, as it would help in the process of building up a more solid connection with the earth element.

"How am I going to do that?" I asked him puzzled.

"Well, I'm so glad that you asked me that," he said with a slight but detectable twinkle in his eye.

And as he began to explain what he had in store for me, my jaw began to drop in total astonishment.

"I'm going to make arrangements for you to stay with the 'Pa-ra-lati', who you will have already come to know as the common folk, or the 'crop growers' for two moons, so that you can gain some hands on experience with the principle of the earth element, and this you will do by learning how to till the soil and grow crops. That should certainly ground you a little," he said with a satisfied look on his face.

I really didn't much like the sound of this one little bit, but if my Derkesthai thought that this was necessary for me, then I didn't really have a lot of choice in the matter…did I?

Studying my reaction very carefully, he raised his eyebrows a little, and with a concerted effort not to show 'too' much amusement at the shocked expression on my face – he quickly changed the subject.

"Right then – Now that we've got that out of the way. The second thing I want to talk to you about today is the blood issue.

"Blood contains within itself far more than what we can see with our mortal eyes Kai. It contains within itself a vital conscious link to the quality of the character of the individual who it belongs to, and as a result of this, it's very important that the ancient Scythian tradition of young warriors having to drink the blood of a defeated enemy, should be tempered with an understanding of the dangers of indulging in this practice; as unless the character of the owner of the blood is known to be of a high and morally pure disposition, it can have an albeit temporary, but very undesirable effect on those who may be particularly sensitive, especially if they are also actively involved in higher pursuits of an Occult nature."

He continued to explain that blood was sometimes used in the rituals of the Agari in order to form a stronger vibrational link between them, and that this was particularly beneficial when undertaking certain ventures that were dependent upon joint co-operation.

I found all of this deeply interesting, as I'd never really given much thought to blood being anything more than what we all had inside us in order to keep us alive. The priest then paused for a few moments to give me time to think about what he'd just said before continuing.

"The last thing that we are going to speak of today is about the use of snake venom by the Agari, and although I'll save the deeper explanation of the relevance of the 'Serpent' for tomorrow. I will concentrate today on the physical use of Venom and its inherent benefits."

He continued to explain the Agari practice of building up an immunity to snake venom by gradually, and over a long period of time, slowly introducing tiny amounts of venom into the blood stream. And that drinking a potent mixture of certain herbs mixed with snake venom, was actually beneficial in promoting a healthy immune system, as well as in the prevention of many illnesses and diseases. He said that snake venom had many medicinal uses, and it could even be used to stop bleeding and to heal wounds. He said that many Scythian warriors took the precaution of building up their own immunity to snake venom under the supervision of an Agari priest, as they were very partial to using snake venom to poison the tips of their arrows and other weapons; so if they should ever have the misfortune to come into direct contact with the sharp edge of their own weapons, they themselves would not fall foul of the undesirable effects of the venom, as they would have already acquired an immunity. I was aware of the use of snake venom as a poison, but not so familiar with its medicinal uses, I was absolutely amazed to learn that it could be used for so many things. The priest suddenly stood up and walked over to the two baskets with the secure lids.

"I want to show you something, Kai," he said, removing one of the lids and putting his hand into the basket.

I couldn't believe my eyes when he pulled out a very much alive and highly poisonous Steppe Viper. I immediately recoiled at the shock of seeing him do this.

"Don't worry – I'm not going to let it bite you," he said, placing the lid back on the basket. "I'm just going to show you how the venom is extracted from the snake."

Reaching towards a nearby shelf, he took a small jar that had a smooth piece of linen cloth tightly secured around the top. He then proceeded to entice the snake to bite him, but instead of biting him, it bit into the cloth instead. He then extracted the venom by pushing its head firmly down against the tightly stretched linen, after which, he returned the unharmed snake back to the basket, and making sure that the lid was firmly secured again, he showed me the venom that had just been extracted.

"This is done on a regular basis to all my captive snakes," said the priest, while replacing the jar back on the shelf.

"How many snakes have you got?" I asked him curiously.

"I keep six. But some of our Agari brothers like to keep more than this. You can begin the process of building your own immunity to the venom today…if you wish that is," he said in a rather nonchalant easy-going tone of voice.

Perhaps he was just trying to sound as though this was no big deal. Perhaps it wasn't. Or maybe he was just trying to sound as though it wasn't, when in fact it really 'was' a big deal. I thought for a moment or two before reaching the conclusion that if I was going to do it at all, then now was as good a time as any…regardless of whether it was a big deal or not. So rather reluctantly I agreed to begin the process today.

"It will probably take several years before you will become totally immune to the venom, and it will have to be regularly maintained after that. So it is in fact a lifelong commitment; as is the practice of ingesting the venom," he said, sitting back down again. "These practices actually serve a dual purpose, as it is not just for its purely physical benefits that the Agari engage in these practices, but they also have a very spiritual significance, and we shall discuss that tomorrow. You will most probably feel a little unwell after the first few times of having the venom introduced into your system, but don't worry, as this is all perfectly normal and expected, and is no reason for concern as it will soon pass. There are several different ways of introducing the venom into the system, but the easiest way for you today would be to use the small cut that you made yesterday." I looked at the little cut on my hand, it had already begun to heal.

"You can re-open it just a little which will allow the venom to enter into your bloodstream," he said, handing me a clean piece of linen which had previously been allowed to soak in the cleaning solution from the silver container on the table.

As I carefully cleaned my hands with the solution, the priest proceeded to explain that introducing snake venom directly into your bloodstream was potentially 'very' dangerous, and was only ever to be done under the highly trained supervision of an Agari priest. He then told me to reopen the wound a little, and after I'd done this, he dipped a thin white stick into the jar containing the freshly extracted venom, and after removing it again, he carefully wiped off any excess venom before rubbing the stick lightly over the cut on my hand. He then wrapped my hand in a clean linen bandage once again.

"Right – that's it! – all done for now," he said, lightly tapping my arm. "Please don't remove the bandage for a good while. And now I suggest that you go straight home and rest, as you may begin to feel a little unwell – as I explained earlier."

After first thanking my Agari teacher, I immediately left, and hurriedly making my way back home, I headed straight over to my bed and sat down. And as nausea began to wash over me, I began to wonder what I'd actually let myself in for. Well…it was too damn late to change my mind now, so I decided that the best thing, and indeed the only thing for me to do, was to lie down and ride it out.

My mother hadn't been home when I'd got back, but on her return she noticed that I was in bed and asked me what was wrong, but remembering my oath of silence, I felt that I couldn't tell her the real reason why I wasn't feeling my usual self, so I just told her that I was feeling a little bit tired.

And after asking her if she wouldn't mind fetching me some water, I curled up and continued to ride out the initial effects of the venom. The feeling of nausea lasted for a good couple of hours, but slowly I began to feel a little better, and by the next day I had completely recovered.

I returned to the priest's kol the same time the next day, and once again I repeated the same process of waiting outside the entrance until he called me in. I don't know how he knew, but no matter how quite I was – somehow he always seemed to know exactly when I arrived.

"Come straight in, Kai," he called out.

"How are you feeling today?" he asked me.

"I feel much better now thank you!" I politely replied.

"Good!" he said with a smile. "It can make you feel a little poorly the first few times, but these effects will lessen with time."

After giving me a few minutes to settle down, the priest then continued where he left off the day before, explaining that the snake was not just important for its venom, but that it was also very symbolic to the Agari, as for one thing, it was representative of the Sacred Serpent and its Holy and dualistic principles, and to seek to understand it was to seek to understand the Holy mysteries themselves. He said that our Goddess Tabiti was an outward expression of the feminine creative aspect of this principle, and that under certain conditions she could actually appear to take on the tangible physical appearance of a Serpent or a Woman, or sometimes even a mixture of 'both'. He then went on to say that visions of this nature are only a way in which the human mind could relate more easily to something that in truth is pure energy, and has no solid form in actuality. But this energy has often been described as a Serpent by those who had bravely stood their ground and watched as it appeared to take on this form.

I was held spellbound by his words, I knew that what he was saying was the truth, and I asked him if I would ever get to see this for myself.

"I hope so, Manu Kai, I truly hope so," was his honest reply to me.

He continued to explain that the duality of the Serpent energy was like the positive and negative aspects of our own selves, and that I should remember that we are connected to all things, and this Serpent energy was no exception. He said that it contains within itself the primordial creative and destructive active intelligent life force energy, that resounds throughout the height and depth of the whole universe, and it cannot ever be truly understood by the limitations of the human mind. But in reaching out to try to gain a deeper understanding of its mysteries, we can expand the limits of our own consciousness.

And he went on to tell me that the active, masculine, forceful principles of the Serpent was represented by the colour red, and the responsive feminine nurturing side of the Serpent, was represented by a silvery pale blue. And both were just different aspects of the spectrum that could be found within the colour white, which of course was not any colour, but the presence of all colour in its purest form. He said that colour contained within itself a vibrational energy, and that is the reason why the colour red was often worn in battle, as it represented amongst other things – the active forceful male energy that was often attributed to blood and war. And pale blue was often recognised as a peaceful colour. I asked him if black was the opposite of white, and he said that it was. I then asked him that if white contained all colour, did that mean that black contained no colour.

"Very good, Manu Kai, Yes, you are correct – black is not actually a colour at all – it is simply the absence of colour."

"What about silver and gold?"

He explained that Gold is the symbol of perfection, and the highest esoteric principles of the Sun, and it also symbolises man's quest for spiritual purity and enlightenment. He said that there are certain types of people called 'Alchemists', who are dedicated to trying to unravel the mysteries of just this one principle alone, so it cannot be easily explained. But it's a subject that we will be entering into during the course of my studies. He then explained that Silver was attuned to, and represented the Moon, and the feminine psychic and intuitive watery aspects of our inner nature.

"I know that the last three days have been a lot for you to take in, Manu Kai," he said with a sigh. "So I think I will give you a couple of days off so that you can have some time to take all of this in before we continue any further, and it will also give me time to make arrangements with the Pa-ra-lati for you to go and stay with them, so that you can begin to develop your connectedness to the earth. Oh, and don't forget to return here three days from now."

And he gave me such a heartfelt smile that I felt as though everything in the whole universe was just doing just fine.

And so it was that he continued to teach me many more things over the next few weeks, and during that time, my father and his men had returned home once again. I was thankful that he'd returned home safely this time, as I hated it when he was away on these so called 'meetings', as there was always the possibility that he wouldn't return one day. My father had also been to see my Derkesthai, and after having been informed of his plan to send me to stay with the Pa-ra-lati for a little while; he was now resting in our kol. And as soon as I walked in, he called me over to him.

"I hear you have a new name, and that we are to call you Manu Kai from now on, and also that you're going to be spending some time with the Pa-ra-lati learning how to grow crops."

With one raised eyebrow, he smiled at me, and unable to disguise his obvious amusement at my impending predicament, he stood up and began to walk away.

"This I'd really love to see," he said, still walking away chuckling to himself.

7

First Contact with the Pa-Ra-Lati

The very next time I met up with my Derkesthai, he informed me that all the arrangements had been made for me to go and stay with the Pa-ra-lati, and that I was to immediately go home and gather together all the things that I was going to need for the two moon duration of my stay. He said that I was to leave early the following morning, and that my father was going to personally escort me there himself. I had never been to this part of Scythia before, and I had absolutely no idea what to expect; or for that matter…what was going to be expected of me. This was also going to be the very first time that I'd ever been away from home by myself, and I don't mind admitting that the thought of having to stay alone with total strangers, and in unfamiliar surroundings, gave me a feeling of having giant butterflies in my stomach, and I was filled with a sickening feeling of dread. My Derkesthai was obviously well aware that I would most probably feel this, and so he said to me:

"Manu Kai…I understand that you're finding the task that I've set before you very daunting right now, and that you're probably feeling a little nervous at the prospect of being left alone in a place that is completely unfamiliar to you, but I would never have arranged all of this, if I didn't have complete and total confidence in your ability to handle this. And Manu Kai…you are 'more' than capable of handling this; you just don't know it yet. Now go home and prepare for tomorrow, and try not to worry too much. I shall come and visit you regularly during your stay with the Pa-ra-lati to check up on you, and to make sure that you're doing okay, and also to retain the practice of administering the snake venom into your system."

Obediently I did exactly what he told me to do, and immediately went straight home and informed my mother that it had all been arranged for me to leave tomorrow for my stay with the Para-lati. "I already know," said Mother, softly resting a comforting hand on my shoulder. "Your father has already told me all about it earlier. I've already begun packing your clothes ready to take with you. Try not to worry so much Kai – I'm sure everything will work out just fine."

Sensing that I was feeling a little apprehensive about tomorrow, Mother began to tell me all about the time that she'd married my father, and had felt terrified at the prospect of moving to a strange place amongst strange people, as although she'd already met my father on several occasions, she didn't really know him, and she certainly didn't know how he would treat her after they were married. But as it happened, he turned out to be a wonderful husband and father, and she couldn't have hoped for better.

"Manu Kai...it's often the fear of the unknown that gives rise to so much unnecessary anguish," she said with a sigh. "I'm sure that your Derkesthai knows what he's doing, and I know for sure that your father would never have agreed to you going to stay with these people, if there was 'any' genuine reason to worry."

Just about then, my father who had been busy tending to the horses arrived back at the kol; he had obviously overheard at least part of the conversation between Mother and me, as he walked straight over, and with a knowing expression on his face he gently rested his hand on my shoulder.

"So then Manu Kai – are you all ready for tomorrow?"

"Yes, I think so," I answered, with a deep sigh. "Can I take my bow and throwing knives with me?"

"Yes, of course you can," he said, ruffling my hair.

Breathing a sigh of relief I relaxed just a little...at least I could still keep up with my practice sessions.

Father suddenly turned to face me, and grabbing me firmly by both shoulders he looked me squarely in the eyes and said:

"Are you sure you want to go ahead with this Kai. You know you don't have to – if you really don't want to...that is."

Seeing the slightly concerned expression on his face, I asked him if he knew of any reason why I shouldn't go.

"Kai – let's talk for a while," he said, sitting down beside me.

Father was normally a man of very few words, so when he actually asked me to sit with him and talk, I knew that he must have had something very important to say.

"Manu Kai...there are many trials that you are going to have to face during this life, and maybe this is going to be one of them, but we should never feel forced to do anything against our better judgement, or just because someone else thinks that we should…Do you understand?"

"Yes, Father," I replied, wondering where he was actually heading with this.

I felt his eyes boring into mine…searching for some small clue as to how I was really feeling about all of this.

"Hmm…Then answer me this: Are you doing this simply because you've been told to, or because this is something you feel is important for you to do…for yourself?"

"Yes, Father," I said, trying to sound confident. "I think I really 'do' need to do this. And it's not just because my Derkesthai has told me that it's important for me, but because I trust him enough to know that if he believes that there's a good reason why I should do this, then I know that there has to be one."

"Good! That's all I needed to hear. We ride out at daybreak, so make all of your preparations tonight, as although it's not very far – I'd like us to leave as early as possible."

That night, I found it very difficult to get any sleep, my mind kept turning over the same questions over and over again. What were the people like? Would they like me? Would I like them? Would I do well? Or would I make a total mess of everything? I must have eventually dropped off to sleep, as the next thing I can remember is my father shaking me by the shoulder. I struggled to gather my thoughts together, and after wondering why he'd woken me up in the middle of the night, I realised that it was already morning.

"Shhh – Don't wake your sisters – I'll see you outside," he said, before leaving me alone to get ready.

Just as my father left the kol, my brother half fell in through the doorway. He was obviously worse the wear for alcohol after an all-night session somewhere, and rubbing his bloodshot eyes he stumbled towards the general direction of his bed…knocking into me in the process.

"Oh yeah…that's right! You're being dumped off with the Pa-ra-lati today. I've heard they eat people, and that they're particularly fond of little half breeds like you. So I guess we won't be seeing you again," he said, cackling with amusement at his own dim-witted remark.

I glared at him for a moment, before deciding that it was probably best to ignore his stupid comment. It wouldn't be very long now before he moved out of our kol for good. He was to be married off very soon, to the daughter of another neighbouring Scythian Chieftain, and she would be coming to live with him here in our village as was the custom. So at least I might finally get some peace at last. But all the same, I really did pity this poor girl who ever she may turn out to be.

"Fetch me some water," he demanded.

"Shhh…or you'll wake the girls. And I'm not your slave, so go and fetch your own water." "I told you to fetch me some water," he scowled malevolently, "so if you know what's good for you, you had better go and fetch me some water."

Stumbling heavily onto his bed, he lay there sprawled out amongst the mud and grass which now covered half his bed from the earth sodden boots that he was far too drunk to remove. Seeing him lying there I couldn't help wondering to myself why I couldn't have had a slightly more agreeable brother instead of him.

"You can either get it yourself or die of thirst for all I care," was my somewhat indifferent reply.

I could see that he really wanted to punch me at this point in time, but fortunately for me he was far too drunk to catch me even if he wanted to, so instead he just glared at me angrily and said:

"You just don't get it do you? One day I'm going to be Sha Pada of this village, and then you'll be sorry, as one of the first things I'm going to do is rid this village of all the disgusting little vermin like you."

"May the Gods take pity on us all should such a terrible day ever come to pass," I said, turning my back on him.

I really couldn't understand why he hated me so much, I figured that maybe it was a past life thing, or perhaps I should just ask him outright why he despised me so much, but somehow I doubt very much if he knew the answer to that question himself.

I quickly got dressed, and after fastening my belt and dagger around my waist, and securing my leg straps which were specially designed to hold my throwing knives, I slung my 'Gorytos' containing my bow and arrows over my shoulder and grabbed my little bundle of clothes. I was about to hurry outside when my mother who was already awake and quite used to my brothers' abusive outbursts, quietly called me over to her.

"May Hoh Tenger (God of the blue skies) watch over you and keep you safe Manu Kai." Kneeling down beside her, I could plainly see the sadness in her eyes, although I knew that she was doing her very best to try and hide it from me. I gave her a little smile, and I hoped that it was enough to conceal my own feelings of melancholy, and as I left her side, and turned to walk towards the entrance to our kol, I fought the urge to take one last look behind me, as this was thought to be very unlucky before setting off on a journey. So instead, I just closed my eyes for a moment, and took a long deep breath before lifting up the flap of the doorway, and doing my very best to act as cool and as laid back as I possibly could, I casually ambled out through the door. I was instantly met by the some-what eerie sight of a very low-lying mist. It was almost as though it was purposely trying to cling on to the dampness of the earth below; albeit in a very noble but completely pointless attempt at prolonging its comfortable existence here. Perhaps it was somehow aware that it wouldn't be very long now before the Sun would be sending forth its life giving rays to bless the earth once more, and the cold grey icy fingers of the mist would be forced to release its grip upon the earth, and to yield to the Sun's mighty will once again; only to be whisked away and carried off to some strange and unfamiliar place. I felt as though the mist and I were connected somehow, and that it knew exactly how I was feeling. One thing was for certain…the mist wasn't the only thing around here that was presently finding it a little difficult to bravely take a leap of faith straight into the vastness of the unknown, for as far as I was concerned, it might as well have been another planet that I was being sent to. The cold chill of the morning air suddenly caused me to shudder involuntarily, and I noticed how still everything felt this morning. It was as if the very air itself was holding its breath in anticipation of the coming day ahead.

Father had already made ready our horses, and was now patiently waiting for me just outside our kol, along with the five other warriors who were to be our travelling companions for the day. I walked over to my father and I asked him if it was true that the Pa-ra-lati ate people. He laughed and asked me how I'd managed to come by that little gem of information:

"Bu just told me," I said, shivering with a mixture of cold and anxiety.

"That figures! No, they don't eat people. You're quite safe. If anything, it was us lot that managed to earn that reputation, but as far as I know it doesn't go on any more, or at least if it does, no one has ever bothered to offer me any," he said, laughing to himself.

"Don't look so worried…I was only joking!" he said, seeing the utter look of horror and disgust that was written all over my face.

One of our travelling companions gave me a leg up and secured my neatly wrapped bundle of clothes to my horse. I fastened my Gorytos to the left side of the horse harness, and when everyone was ready – we headed off to planet unknown.

The journey went well, and we arrived at our destination a lot sooner than I'd expected, and as we made our way into the heart of the village I was amazed at how big it was. There were so many people, and their kol's were not quite the same as ours. They also had other types of dwellings that were entirely different to anything that I'd ever seen before. I tried to take in the scene that was set before me but there was far too much going on, and I found the strangeness of it all completely overwhelming. Everywhere I looked, there were people staring at us, and I could feel their eyes boring into me. I was suddenly struck by a feeling of total panic, and I was seised by an overwhelming urge to turn my horse around and gallop off as fast as my horse could carry me out of this place and straight back home again. Just at that very moment my father began to ride very close along side of me.

"Whoa there," he said, reaching out and grabbing my horses head harness. "You weren't actually thinking of changing your mind already, were you, Kai?"

Father had obviously been watching me very carefully, and he could tell that I was feeling more than just a little bit nervous right now.

"Kai…look at me, son," he said, bringing my horse to a halt. "Do you remember that time with the Hun, when you earned the right to call yourself a true Hun warrior by proving how brave you were?"

I thought back to that time for a moment, and how I had managed to fool them all into thinking that I was being brave, when really I hadn't been brave at all.

"Father, please don't try to convince me what a brave little warrior I am – as I really don't think I could stand to listen to that right now. The truth is father – I wasn't really being brave at all. I knew all along that it was all just some silly little game, and that Yesukai wasn't really going to hurt me. So you see father…bravery had nothing to do with it. So now that you know the real truth about your 'brave' son…I expect you feel ashamed of me now…don't you?"

Father was obviously quite taken aback by my sharp and indignant attitude towards him. I knew that I shouldn't have spoken to him the way that I had, and I instantly regretted it. The words just seemed to pour out of my mouth before I'd had a chance to stop them. I was expecting him to be absolutely furious with me, and I was quite prepared for his wrath that I felt quite certain was about to come my way. But he just calmly carried on looking straight at me, and taking a deep breath, he slowly exhaled and gave a little sigh. He let go of my horse's harness, and shifting his seating position, he leant in a little closer towards me – and speaking to me calmly and quietly in a very clear and concise tone of voice, he said:

"Hmm…so if that's the case then, Manu Kai, you actually did a lot better than I, or anyone else for that matter, has ever given you true credit for. You used your intelligence to work out what was really going on, and you were able to see straight through the 'silly little game' as you call it. Many brave warriors lay slain, simply because they weren't able to see through an enemy's artful trickery. I don't think any less of you my son for the knowing of this. And another thing; there has never been a true warrior born of a woman, who hasn't at one time or another experienced the bitter taste of fear – and it would serve you best to remain mindful of that fact in the future."

I couldn't believe that I'd actually got away with speaking to him like that, and I was just about to breathe a sigh of relief when…

"Oh – and by the way – if you ever dare speak to me like that again – I'll have you horse whipped," he said, giving me a rather unsettlingly malevolent smile, which coupled with the dark brooding look in his eyes was certainly chilling enough to turn the mightiest of rivers into a solid block of ice. I'd never seen this side of him before, and it came as quite a shock, and I knew that even though I may have got away with it this time, it was highly unlikely that I would get off quite so lightly the next time. I thought I knew my father well, but there was obviously a side to him that I was as yet totally unaware of.

"Right then," said father, breaking the intensity of the moment. "Now that you've had a chance to vent out your emotions, are you feeling a little better now?"

The five accompanying warriors who had silently stood by, and had witnessed the whole dramatic episode began to laugh. I felt as though they were all mocking me, and I felt embarrassed by my emotional outburst. I could feel my face beginning to glow with embarrassment, and I hung my head in shame.

"Yes, Father – I feel much better now – and I'm sorry for the way I spoke to you!"

"Good! – Now let's just get on with this then shall we?" he said, raising his right hand upwards in a signal for us all to move on.

Two of the warriors who were accompanying us had been far too busy flirting with a group of young women, who were obviously encouraging them, to have noticed their leaders hand signal. My father just rolled his eyes upwards and let out a long drawn out sigh, and folding his arms he just sat there allowing the pair of them to blatantly continue with their outrageously flirtatious display, quite oblivious to the fact that we were all watching them. Until at last my father just couldn't stand it any longer, and in a loud commanding tone of voice he said:

"Could we all try to put our personal interests on hold for just a little while longer please, and finish what we are here to do first?"

The two guilty warriors immediately froze, and realising that my father was referring directly to them; they both cringed, and glanced at one another guiltily, before responding in perfect unison:

"Whoops...sorry Chief."

The other three warriors had obviously found their reactions to being caught out quite funny, and were unable to control their obvious amusement at all of this, and it took them several minutes before they were finally able to regain their composure again. My father just continued to sit there pan faced with his arms folded, and how he had managed to retain such a serious expression throughout all of this tomfoolery I shall never know.

"Right!" said Father, looking at each one of us in turn. "If everyone has completely finished performing for now – shall we continue?"

As we rode deeper into the village, I noticed that not a single person had approached us, and appeared to be purposely keeping their distance from us instead. I questioned my father about this, and his reply to me was:

"That's because we belong to a very high-status warrior caste – and these people are 'Pa-ra-lati' – (common people) and they're strictly forbidden to approach us unless they have a valid reason, or unless they have been requested by one of us to do so. They're technically subservient to us, and their job is to provide us with livestock and grain, both for our own consumption and for trade, and in return we protect them, and leave them in peace to live as free men and women. They're allowed to keep a percentage of what they produce for their own consumption, and if the yield is high, they are amply rewarded for this, and that's just the way it is."

"Ah! I think we have arrived! You're going to be staying with a really nice couple, Kai. They're getting on a little in years, and have never been blessed with any children of their own. So they're absolutely thrilled to have been given this opportunity to take care of 'you' for a little while that's for sure. It's also a great honour for them – and they won't go unrewarded."

We all dismounted, and father asked the warriors who had accompanied us to find somewhere suitable to secure our horses, and then to immediately return and wait for him here.

"Right then, Kai," said father, firmly resting his hand on my shoulder. "Let's go and meet your temporary guardians then shall we?"

I was still feeling a few little twinges of nerves, but nothing like I felt earlier. So we walked up to the entrance to a little 'Ger' (dwelling place) that was similar in shape to our own kol, but unlike ours, it had a roof that was made of wood and straw. The doorway was left open, and I could see two people who were sat inside, and as soon as they saw us they both immediately stood up and rushed over to greet us. They were both smiling and appeared to be really happy to see us.

"Please come in and make yourselves comfortable – we are truly honoured by your visit sir," said the man to my father, who was still maintaining a subtle, but reasonably firm contact with my left shoulder…just in case I decided to do a runner no doubt!

The woman just stood there staring at me with a big smile on her face. She was a homely looking woman, and little on the portly side, but she had a kind and friendly warmth about her, and I found myself liking her immediately.

"So this is Manu Kai…He's absolutely gorgeous," she said with such exuberance that I was quite taken aback. I'd never been called gorgeous before, and I began to blush with embarrassment.

"Now stop that already Nessa. Can't you see that you're embarrassing the boy," said the man. I looked up at my father, and the look on his face was absolutely priceless. I could see that he was obviously finding all of this very entertaining, and he was genuinely struggling to keep a straight face.

"Don't mind the wife," said the man winking at me. "She's always had a weakness for a handsome face as you can see."

The man gave me a big toothless grin, and he looked so funny that I started to laugh. I wasn't really sure what to make of them at first, but they were both so natural and unpretentious, that I was already beginning to relax a little in their company, seeing this; Father finally relaxed his grip on my shoulder a little.

"Oh – but where are our manners," said the woman. "Please make yourselves at home…can we offer you some refreshments?"

"Yes…That would be nice…thank you," said Father, sitting himself down and resting his chin in his hand, which I noticed, also had the added benefit of hiding half his face. He'd been carefully watching my reactions to these people the whole time, and I think that he would have been quite prepared 'despite it all' to bring me straight back home again, if I really didn't like either one of them.

The woman who I'd already gathered by now was called 'Nessa', handed my father a drink of some sort, after which she fetched one over for me.

"Thank you," I said politely.

The man pointed to my bow, which I was presently tightly gripping onto.

"That's a very nice bow you have there, Manu Kai. But can you use it…that's the thing?"

"Yes, I can," was my rather short – but definite response to his question.

"Excellent! And what about those," he said, pointing to the knives strapped around my legs.

"Yes, I can use those too," I replied, in very much the same manner.

My father happened to be very proud of my weaponry skills, and he could never resist a single opportunity to get me to show them off.

"If you ask him, maybe he'll give you a demonstration some time – he's actually very talented," said Father, standing up and passing his empty cup to Nessa. "Please excuse us for a moment," he said, gesturing for me to follow him outside.

Father's men were all sat outside waiting for him as they had been requested to do, and as soon as we emerged they all immediately stood up. He made a simple hand gesture for them all to sit back down again.

"So what do you think of them, Kai?" he asked me.

"They seem nice," I replied.

"I think your Derkesthai did well to choose these people for you to stay with, and I feel pretty confident that it will be safe enough to let you stay with them," he said, running his fingers through his beard.

"Haven't you met them before?" I asked him, feeling a little confused.

"No…that was the first time – and that's why I wanted to personally escort you here, so that I could meet them myself."

"How did you know which dwelling they live in?" I asked him, puzzled.

"I just followed Garenhir's…I mean your Derkesthai's instructions – that's all."

So – Garenhir was his name. I'd never thought to ask him what his name was. It was an unusual name for this part of the world, and it started to get me wondering where he was from, as I'd heard it mentioned before that he wasn't originally from Scythia.

"I want two volunteers to stay here for the first six days to watch over Kai for me, after which you'll be replaced by two others," said Father loudly.

One of the two warriors, who had been flirting with the group of women earlier, immediately raised his hand, and said:

"I will, chief."

His partner in crime responded to this by quickly raising his hand saying that he'd stay too. "Well, isn't that a surprise," said Father, looking at the two of them through narrowed eyes. "But what worries me is who's going to be keeping an eye on you pair? Kai...I'm afraid that's going to have to be your job. You must let me know if they get up to any mischief."

"You didn't really think I was going to leave you here alone without any supervision did you?" he said, raising one eyebrow.

Father ordered the other three warriors who were standing nearby to go and make ready the horses. They all immediately responded with a nod of their heads, before continuing on with their rather heated debate about how best to capture a wild horse. Father just stood watching the three of them for a moment or two before shaking his head with an air of indifference. Turning his attention back to his two amorous volunteers, he gestured to them to follow us back into the elderly couple's little home where they had been sat patiently awaiting his verdict.

"I would like you to meet two of my finest warriors," he said, pointing to the one with fair hair. "This is Merren," and then pointing to the one with dark hair he said: "And this is Aptien...and they're both going to be staying behind to make sure my son behaves himself. So if you have any problems at all – talk to one of these two men about it. And if they can't sort it out themselves, they can get word out to me, and I'll come and deal with it personally."

Father then asked the old man if it was possible for him to find somewhere for his men to sleep, and that he'd make fair compensation to anyone who was inconvenienced by this in any way.

"That won't be a problem at all, sir," said the old man with a smile. "Anyone here would be more than honoured to give them a place to stay."

"Good," said Father, smiling back at him. "Then I'll leave them both in your capable hands. The rest of us will be heading back now, so make sure you take good care of my son. But mind you don't pamper him either, he might grow too accustomed to it – and 'I' have to live with him when he returns back home again."

He then gave Merren, Aptien, and me a little gesture for the three of us to follow him outside again. He wished the old couple safe keeping, and heading out through the doorway, he told them he would see them both again very soon.

"Right then you two," said Father. "I don't want to hear any bad reports about either of you, so you'd both better be on your best behaviour. And if you do become a little 'side tracked' at any time, and the temptation to misbehave gets a little too much for either of you to bear…then please be discreet about it…do we understand each other?"

Merren and Aptien both said that they did, and I couldn't help thinking to myself: "Yes, I bet you do!"

"Right then, Manu Kai," said Father, turning his full attention to me. "I have to leave you now in what I trust are safe hands, so you'd better make sure that you behave yourself too…do you hear me? I will see you very soon."

Meanwhile, the other three warriors had returned with the horses, and were already mounted and ready to go. Father took a running jump, and grabbing the horse harness with his left hand, he hoisted himself straight onto the back of his horse. He gave us a fair-well wave, and without looking back, he and his men immediately rode away. I watched them till they'd completely disappeared out of sight, and I began to feel a little anxious about how I was going to cope. I was suddenly surrounded by strangers in an even stranger land, and although it may have been just a few miles away, it might as well have been mars.

"Come on then, Manu Kai – let's get you settled in then shall we?" said Nessa, wrapping her arm around my shoulder.

Merren and Aptien were currently just standing there looking a lot like two spare thumbs. It was somehow reassuring to me that they both appeared to be feeling as lost as I was.

"Why don't you both come and wait inside?" instructed Nessa. "And while Kess is sorting out somewhere for you to stay – I shall make us all something nice to drink."

They both gave Nessa a big smile, and all three of us followed her back inside the little hut, or kol…or whatever it was.

"Please sit," said Nessa pointing to some wooden chairs. "Well…I must say; this is all very exciting. What a sight for sore eyes the three of you make sat there together. You all look very handsome."

I almost said: "Don't tell them that…they're bad enough already." But I just rolled my eyes upwards instead. Nessa turned her back to us for a few moments in order to prepare whatever drink she was going to make, and Aptien leant across to Merren and whispered to him:

"I think we're in here mate." At which they both fell about laughing.

I couldn't help but laugh either, although I did feel a little guilty, as Nessa was such a nice lady. Nessa turned around and glowered at each of us in turn. We immediately froze…it must have been obvious that each of us was struggling not to laugh.

"Hmm," said Nessa, thoughtfully. "Handsome you most certainly are, but I bet you pair are as slippery as an eel covered in goose fat. A poor lass couldn't keep a fare grip on either one of you for longer than it would take you to put your boots back on…and isn't that the truth!"

The three of us just sat there looking at each other in stunned silence, until Merren finally broke the silence by loudly slapping his thigh.

"Woman, I have to hand it to you. I know that we've just been firmly put in our place, but if truth be said…I'm also just a little impressed."

"I feel as though I should respond to that in some way, but I really can't think of anything suitable to say right now, said Aptien, shaking his head."

"Well, mate…All I can say is: if Nessa here is any example to go by – we may as well go help Manu Kai dig some holes," said Merren, looking somewhat chastised. "Yes, and one that's big enough for the both of us to throw ourselves into I reckon mate," replied Aptien, who was looking refreshingly more humble right now.

I was laughing so much at this point that my sides were beginning to hurt. Nessa just smiled, and handed each of us a cup of her special herbal brew. I was unable to hold onto mine as I was still laughing too much, so Nessa had to put it down on the floor for me.

"Now, now, Manu Kai – best behaviour and all that," said Merren, taking a tiny sip of his drink. "Yes, shame on you, Manu Kai. And don't embarrass us by slurping either," added Aptien, also taking a tiny little sip of his drink.

"Please don't say anything else – as I really don't think I can stand anymore," I said, quickly walking outside in an effort to try and regain a little composure.

And after I was able to catch my breath again, I decided that perhaps my stay here wasn't going to be so bad after all.

8

Tihanna

Kess had returned with the good news that he'd found somewhere suitable for Merren and Aptien to stay, and he said that if they would both like to follow him he would take them there right away, and just before disappearing through the doorway, Aptien turned his head towards me, and giving me a slightly wicked looking grin he said:

"Don't you forget now, Manu Kai…best behaviour!"

He was swiftly followed by Merren, who purposely brushing past me on his way out said:

"See you soon, handsome."

"I'd better show you where you'll be sleeping," said Nessa giving me a knowing smile and pointing to the far side of the cottage. "That's your own little place over there in the corner. You can take your belongings and put them over there for now," she said, pointing to a very cosy looking little bed that had already been prepared for me.

Picking up my little bundle of clothes and my Gorytos containing my bow and arrows, I walked over to the far corner of the hut where my sleeping quarters had been placed and slung them on my bed. I could feel Nessa watching me, and when I turned around to face her again she said: "You wear your hair very long Manu Kai, do you always wear it in a single braid like that?"

"No…Not always!"

Nessa thought for a moment before continuing:

"You have quite a dark complexion and pale blue eyes…such an unusual combination – quite striking."

I could tell by her mannerisms that she really wanted to ask me something but was hesitant to just ask me straight out.

"I don't mind if you want to ask me something – so if you just ask me – I'll most probably tell you."

"Oh dear…am I really being that obvious? I know that it's none of my business – and you can remind me of that fact if you want to. And please forgive me if I step out of place here, but you don't look much like any Scythian I've ever seen before Manu Kai."

"That's okay," I said, giving her a little smile. "I really don't mind. I can't blame you for noticing. I'm actually half Scythian and half Mongolian."

"Is that the truth of it? Well – I suppose that's what makes you so special then my handsome isn't it?" she said, smiling back at me.

Her curiosity satiated for the time being, Nessa left off with the questions for a while, and began to attend to the fire that was burning low and steady in the centre of the hut. I wasn't doing anything, so I asked her if she needed any help.

"No my handsome," she said hanging a large pot over the fire. "Tomorrow is going to be a busy day for you, so you'd better make the most of this little rest while you can."

"How old are you, Manu Kai?" she asked, continuing to chop up large pieces of mutton so that they were small enough to fit into the pot.

"I was born at the festival of renewal…and on the next one I will have seen thirteen winters…why?"

"I was just wondering that's all. That will be on the next full moon," she said, stopping for a moment and looking up from what she was doing.

I had forgotten it was so soon, I was going to miss the festivities back home this year, and I wondered if the Pa-ra-lati celebrated it the same way that we did.

"Do you have a celebration here?" I asked her.

"Yes, we do! We build a huge fire, and after all the offerings have been made we have a big party that goes on all through the night and well into the next day."

It didn't sound very different to our own celebrations, and I was quite looking forward to it. "When Kess comes back, he'll take you on a little tour of the village as you will need to know where the toilets and the fresh water wells are situated. While you're here you can help me collect water for the cooking and washing."

Scythians never washed themselves or their clothes directly in the river, as this was thought to pollute the water. So water was always collected for washing and then disposed of by tipping it onto the ground.

It wasn't very long before Kess returned, and as he entered the hut he gave me a big toothless grin and said to me:

"Right then, Manu Kai – that's your friends sorted out. I've invited them both to come back here to eat with us later, and after we've all eaten they can show you where they're both staying so that you'll know where to find them if and when you need to. And talking of which – I think it's about time I showed you around a few places so that you'll know where everything is."

Kess proceeded to show me around the village, proudly introducing me to anyone and everyone that we met along the way. It was clear to me that my presence was causing more than a little interest amongst the people living here. Everyone seemed very curious about why this strange-looking visitor of high warrior caste was staying at their village.

As Kess proceeded to show me around the village, I couldn't help noticing a small group of five young girls who were all roughly around the same age as I was, as although they were keeping their distance, they were obviously following us, and as soon as they saw that I'd noticed them, they all began to giggle amongst themselves.

"I think you've already got yourself a few admirers there Manu Kai," said Kess, giving me a gentle nudge. "It looks like I might have to keep a careful watch on you, if this is anything to go by."

Turning my head to face them for a moment, my eyes were instantly drawn to one girl in particular who was standing in amongst them. Her hair was the colour of sunshine and she just seemed to stand out from the rest by a mile. Just for a very brief moment we made eye contact, she gave me a little smile before shyly lowering her eyes and covering her face with her hand. I was instantly captivated by her. I thought how pretty she was, and I really couldn't help staring at her. And the more I watched her, the more I began to feel a very odd sensation inside. I guess you could say that I was smitten.

"Yes, indeed," said Kess, nudging me again…only slightly harder this time. "Come on then young man, I think it's about time we headed back now…don't you?"

As we turned to make our way back, I couldn't resist glancing behind me, and I saw that the girl with the golden hair was also looking at me. So I gave her a little smile, and all of the other girls instantly gathered all around her and began to chatter furiously amongst themselves. I'd never wanted to know what a bunch of girls were saying to each other so much in my life. And just at that very moment, Merren and Aptien seemed to suddenly spring out of nowhere. Aptien grabbed me by my arm, and sharply pulling me backwards, he allowed Kess to walk on a little way ahead of us, before he quietly said to me: "We saw that, Manu Kai…"

"Saw what?" I asked him, feeling a little taken aback by his rude intrusion into my private moment.

"Manu Kai – we were both stood there watching you the whole time. We don't know if we should be impressed, or just a little bit concerned…that's the problem."

I could see by his face that he did have a look of genuine concern about him, and as I turned to look at Merren who was walking very close to me on my other side, he raised one eyebrow and shook his head and tutted. And placing his arm very gently around my shoulder he said:

"Well…should we be concerned, Manu Kai?"

With an air of righteous indignation I shrugged myself free of Merren's arm. "Don't you dare judge me by your own lowly standards," I retorted back at the pair of them. "I'm not the same as either of you two so back off."

Raising both hands upwards in a gesture of submission, Merren immediately took a step back.

"Whoa – steady on. And keep your voice down. We're just doing our job Manu Kai…that's all."

Both Merren and Aptien just continued to stand there looking very remissive for a moment or two, until Aptien gave a long drawn out sigh and said:

"Okay chief, maybe we were a bit quick off the mark there. So…are we forgiven?"

"Yes, you're both forgiven. Now let's just all go and eat shall we?" I said sharply.

They both gave each other a very vacant look; I knew it was meant to conceal a deeper meaning between the two of them. I may have been young – but I wasn't stupid!

"OK, you're the boss," said Merren.

Rolling my eyes upwards to the sky in a manner of vexation, I briskly marched off. I think they must have both thought I was out of earshot, but with a little effort I could just about hear what was said between them.

"I think we may have got our work cut out for us here mate," said Merren.

Maybe I should have warned them that I had exceptionally good hearing…or on second thought…maybe not!

It suddenly began to thunder, and a few seconds later there was a bolt of lightning and a loud crack of thunder which sounded as though the sky above us had been ripped in two. A few heavy drops of rain began to hit the dry ground around us causing little puffs of dust to rise, and we all ran as fast as we could in a mad determined effort to win the race against the rain. We got back just in time, as the storm was one of the heaviest that I've ever witnessed.

We all ate our mutton stew to the sound of the raging storm outside, and every now and again there would be a particularly bright flash, which had the effect of making us all freeze in mid motion, and await for the loud crack of thunder that almost instantly followed, and which appeared at times to be a little too close for comfort.

After we had all eaten, and the storm had finally subsided, Merren and Aptien showed me where they were presently staying, and it seemed to me that everywhere I went, there was either a group of children, young girls, or a mixture of both trailing along behind me. I looked around to see if the pretty girl with the golden hair that I'd seen earlier was amongst any of them, but alas – she was nowhere to be seen. And later that evening, I just couldn't stop thinking about her, and I told myself that the very next time that I did see her I would bravely walk right up to her and ask her what her name was.

The morning light came all too soon, and Nessa was already up and busy preparing a breakfast of fried fish coated with a spicy seasoning of some sort, and a drink of warmed sweetened goat's milk to wash it all down with. Even though I had a curtain to protect my modesty it was a cold morning so I quickly got dressed under the large woollen blanket that completely covered my bed, after which I went through my normal ritual of attaching my dagger and throwing knives to my belt and leg straps. I noticed that Kess was watching me; he was obviously fascinated by the amount of weapons that I'd finally managed to attach to myself.

"Do you always go everywhere armed up to the teeth?" he eventually asked me.

"Yes, I do – I never go anywhere without my bow, dagger, and throwing knives. My father told me that the day that I did would most probably be the day that I'd regret it."

After I'd finished my breakfast Kess told me that I was going to learn how to plough a field today, and that he was going to take me up to one of the fields where someone would be waiting for me. He then informed me that he would be leaving me with this person for a while, as they were the one who would be showing me what to do.

"Right…Are you ready?"

"As ready as I'm ever going to be I guess," I replied.

"Good lad – come on then – let's get going shall we?"

We made our way right up to the top field, and as we approached I could see two men leaning on some wooden fence posts, they were obviously waiting for me to arrive. And there, in a very muddy looking field stood the largest beast that I'd ever set eyes upon. It had massive horns protruding from its head, I had never seen anything quite like it before, and I felt sure it was going to trample us and kill us all.

"What in the name of mercy is that?" I asked Kess, pointing to the beast.

"That fine-looking fellow is an ox my dear boy, but we call him old slow-tooth, and it's his job to pull the wooden plough that is presently fixed to the harness or 'yolk' around his neck." Kess proceeded to tell me that I was going to learn how to get the beast to do my bidding, and how to get it to walk in a nice straight line. He went on to say that the plough which it was attached to would make a deep furrow in the soil ready for the planting of the grain. I looked at the size of this beast compared to the size of me, and I had visions of it being me that would end up getting planted in the ground along with the grain.

"Please somebody tell me that this is just a joke. You are just kidding me aren't you?"

"No! I'm afraid not!" replied Kess, shaking his head.

Kess tried to divert my attention away from the beast by introducing me to the two men who were still leaning up against the fence posts.

"Well, my lad," said Kess. "I'm going to be leaving you now so that you can get on with it. Good luck…and I'll see you later!"

And with that he walked off leaving me standing there completely mortified. I wondered if Merren and Aptien would bother to turn up. I seriously hoped that they wouldn't as this was going to be bad enough without the added humiliation of those pair stood watching me make a complete idiot of myself.

One of the two men whose name was Urak then walked up to me and said:

"So you're the famous Manu Kai? Well, it's an honour to meet you. We've been told that this has got something to do with your training to become a member of the Agari…is that true?"

"Uhm…Yes, it's true," I said, as I watched Kess slowly walk further and further away into the distance…until he finally disappeared out of sight all together.

Instinctively scanning the surrounding area, I began to look for the easiest escape route – just in case I should happen feel the need to make a rapid exit at any point.

"OK…well…I suppose I'd better run through a few things with you first, and then you can give it a go if you like," said Urak, trying his best to gain my attention.

Oh boy! …I was most definitely 'not' liking the sound of this one little bit.

"Uh…yeah…that's uh…" I couldn't even speak any more. I couldn't take my eyes off that enormous beast. I was going to end up getting trampled to death for sure. Urak could obviously see that I was absolutely terrified of this beast.

"Oh…you don't have to worry about old slow-tooth over there…he's as gentle as a lamb, and once you get to know him a bit better, you'll look back and laugh when you remember how scared you were of him in the beginning."

Urak explained to me that old slow-tooth was trained to respond to a mixture of certain words that when spoken in a clear and commanding tone of voice, and accompanied by a sharp tap from a stick would respond accordingly.

"I'll give you a demonstration and I'll show you exactly what I mean, and after that – you can have a go at it yourself if you like."

Picking up the stick that lay on the ground by his feet, Urak jumped onto the wooden plough and tapped the beast on the back with it, while at the same time shouting the command of 'walk on' Old slow-tooth, 'as he was affectionately known' – slowly began to walk forward, and Urak maintained his balance by distributing his body weight accordingly with every little bump. He made it all look so easy that I thought to myself that if that was all there was to it, I should be able to do it standing on my head.

"Do you want to have a go now?" asked Urak, jumping down from the plough. I was feeling slightly more confident now after seeing how easy it was.

"Yes, okay then!"

The other man who had remained silent up until now finally spoke.

"You might want to remove all your weapons first little warrior, I don't know if you've noticed but it's a bit muddy over there, and it'll save you a great deal of time and effort cleaning all the mud off them later – 'should' you happen to slip and fall. That's a fine looking Akinakes (dagger) you've got there for one so young as yourself. It's probably best you don't get it all covered in mud if you really don't have to. You can safely leave all your weapons over here with me, I'll watch over them and keep them safe for you."

I thought about it for a minute, and I realised that he was probably right. So I removed all of my weapons and handed them all over to him.

"Do you mind if I ask you where you got this?" he asked, examining my dagger with interest. "My father gave it to me," I replied. "It was given to him by his father, who had it given to him by the King."

"Hmm – I thought it looked very grand. Your father must think very highly of you to have given this to you so young," he said, still studying it.

I thought back to the day that my father had given it to me; it was actually quite recent – just a few moons ago in fact. I'd managed to disarm him during a practice session, and he looked at me very seriously before he told me that this was going to be the very last time that I would ever disarm him. For a moment I thought that I'd done something wrong, and that I had upset him, but then he gave me a big beaming smile and said:

"Manu Kai, your skill has already surpassed my own. The pupil has now become the teacher, and I really don't think that there's anything else that I can teach you."

He presented me with the Akinakes later on that day, and as he handed it to me he told me that my brother had been after it for years, but he didn't feel as though he'd ever earned the right to own it. And so he was giving it to me, partly as a lesson to my brother, but more importantly because he felt I'd genuinely earned it, and he was sure that my grandfather would have done exactly the same thing. And although I knew that my father's gift would undoubtedly only fuel my brother's hatred towards me, I dared not refuse his gift, as at the end of the day, it was up to him who he chose to give it to.

I'd never really given it much thought, but it was probably very valuable too, as the scabbard was made of solid gold, and it was set with many different types of gemstones. I'd never dared trust it to a stranger before, but I somehow knew in my heart that I could trust this man.

Finally, I was ready to give it a go, and picking up the long stick, I climbed onto the wooden plough and carefully balanced my weight as evenly as I could, and remembering exactly what Urak had showed me, I tapped old slow tooth on the back and yelled out:

"WALK!"…Nothing! – The beast didn't move an inch. So I tried again, but this time I made sure to hit him a lot harder, and I yelled at him much louder too!

"WALK!" Old slow tooth responded with a sudden jerk forward; causing me to completely lose my balance. I tried to recover my dignity by attempting to land on my feet, but I slipped and fell straight into the mud instead. This was met by loud cheers and the sound of hysterical laughter. I recognised those merry tones, and sure enough, Merren and Aptien were in absolute stitches at my expense. I just couldn't believe it, of all the times for them to turn up. I hadn't physically hurt myself as the soft mud had cushioned my fall, but my pride...or what was left of it was more than a little bit dented. I stood up and the wet mud was just dripping off me from head to toe. I thought about my Derkesthai, and how pleased he would be if only he knew just how well I was doing at making a connection with the earth right now. Well...at very least the earth had managed to make a very good connection with me...all over me in fact.

Struggling to assemble what little dignity I had left, I demurely walked over to where Merren and Aptien were standing and just stood there...dripping!

"Manu Kai...you're a star," said Aptien, managing to compose himself for a few moments.

"And it's so nice to see how willing you are to just 'throw' yourself right into the task ahead with such enthusiasm."

And with that they both fell about in hysterics again.

"Don't worry, Manu Kai," said Urak, doing his best to conceal his obvious amusement at my present predicament. "You can try again tomorrow."

"Excellent! I can hardly wait," piped in Merren.

"Sorry Manu Kai," said Merren apologetically. "But if you could only see yourself right now you'd understand." And with that he burst out laughing once again. The other man, whose name I just couldn't remember said:

"Look on the bright side – at least your weapons were saved from the mud."

And just when I thought things just couldn't get any worse...they did! A group of children had obviously found out where I was and were heading straight this way...and guess who was with them?...Yep! Why me?

Oh well – So much for my plan of confidently walking over to her and asking her what her name was. I could feel my stomach turning over as I walked over to Aptien.

"You know that hole you were on about digging yesterday; the one that's big enough for the both of you to throw yourselves into. Well...can you dig it really fast – and do you think you could make it big enough for three?"

Both Aptien and Merren simultaneously turned to look who was heading this way, and on seeing it was my heart's desire they both cringed.

"Ouch," said Merren, screwing up his face. "This is going to hurt. It's really not your day, is it, Manu Kai?"

"Will you do me a favour?" I asked the both of them. "Would you at least carry my weapons back for me, so that they don't end up as sodden as my pride right now?"

"No problem at all, Chief," said Aptien. "I think that in the circumstances that's the very least we can do."

The group of kids – including the object of my affections, were now all stood around silently staring at the sorry spectacle of me covered in mud from head to foot.

"Hello…so how are you all today?" I said, giving them all a little wave of my muddy hand. They all responded enthusiastically, and as I looked at the pretty golden-haired girl standing there before me, my heart rate began to rise, and desperately trying to act as cool as possibly…despite the mud! I walked up to her and asked her what her name was.

"Tihanna," she said, giving me a little smile. "You've got a little bit of mud…just there," she said, pointing to my face.

We both started to chuckle, and that broke the ice perfectly. I was about to tell her my name when she said:

"I already know your name – it's Manu Kai."

Glancing across at Merren and Aptien, I was slightly compensated by the fact that they were both stood there staring at me with a look of complete amazement on their faces, so I gloated at them for a brief moment before quickly turning my attention back to Tihanna.

"I'm going to walk back now and wash this…Uhm…this little bit of mud off my face," I said, pointing to my chin. "Would you like to walk with me?"

"Okay," she said shyly.

Merren and Aptien were both still rendered quite speechless, and without saying a single word, they both just quietly walked over to where my weapons were laying on the ground, and began gathering them all up. And as we began to walk back, Tihanna pointed to my bow which Aptien was currently still carrying in his hand.

"People say that you're really good with the bow."

"I'm not too bad I suppose," I said, trying to sound humble.

"Can you use a bow at all?"

"No – I'm afraid not," she replied.

"I'll teach you if you like," I said enthusiastically.

Tihanna told me that she'd like that very much, so with my head held high, I proudly walked back into the village completely covered from head to foot in mud with Tihanna at my side – and a refreshingly speechless Merren and Aptien trailing along behind us. I suddenly realised that I really didn't give a damn how dishevelled I looked right now. Oddly enough, it felt strangely liberating. I may have looked a total mess on the outside – but inside I felt like a king.

9

Secrets

I told Tihanna that I'd have to catch up with her sometime later that afternoon, as begrudgingly I really needed to go and get cleaned up. Merren and Aptien accompanied me to the little home of Kess and Nessa as they were carrying all my weapons, and as I really didn't want to walk straight into the old couples neatly kept little home all covered in mud, I peered in through the doorway and called out to let them know that I was back…and just a little on the muddy side.

After placing my weapons just inside the doorway, Merren gave me a much-needed hand to remove my muddy boots.

"When you're ready, Kai, would you mind paying us a visit, I really think we need to have a little chat," said Merren, tossing my boots over in the corner.

Kess and Nessa both stood there gawking at the state of me for a few moments before they just couldn't contain themselves any longer and began to laugh. I must have looked a right mess after my baptism in mud, and after they had finally managed to compose themselves again, Kess raised his eyebrows and said:

"We guessed that this might happen, so we've already warmed some water ready for you to wash. Come on, lad – I'll show you where you can get cleaned up."

Taking me by the arm, Kess led me around to the back of their hut and showed me a small extension which he'd made especially so that I would have somewhere private to wash myself. Nessa followed on behind us, and after handing me some clean clothes and a bucket of warm water, she gave me a small wooden bowl containing a powder of some sort.

"Here you are," she said. "Just add a little water to this and then rub it all over yourself, and then wash it all off again, and you'll soon be gleaming like a little ray of sunshine."

There was a slight chill in the air this afternoon, so after getting cleaned up again, I quickly pulled on my clean clothes, and hurried back to the warmth of the hut. The fire was glowing brightly, and would shortly provide the necessary heat needed to prepare enough food for five. It was a welcoming sight, and I took full advantage of the heat from the fire to dry my hair. I noticed that Nessa was watching me as I repeatedly run my fingers through my hair in an effort to keep it tangle free.

"Do you want me to comb your hair through for you?" she asked me.

I stopped what I was doing for a moment, and I looked up at her and smiled. My mother always combed and styled my hair for me back home, so it would be nice to have someone to do it for me here too.

"Yes, if you want to…I'd like that. But I have to go and see Merren and Aptien first," I replied with a smile.

I could guess what Aptien and Merren probably wanted to 'have a little chat' with me about, but all the same, I thought it was best to get it over and done with, so I decided to head over to their kol where I knew they'd both be waiting for me to turn up.

When I arrived at the kol that they were staying in, I didn't bother to announce my arrival by calling out from outside as they were already expecting me, so I walked straight in and caught them right in the middle of discussing my 'behaviour'. They immediately ceased their conversation, and I could see that they were both obviously a little embarrassed by the fact that I'd caught them talking about me. There was one of those 'awkward' silences, so I just stood there with my arms folded, and waited for either one of them to be the first to say something. However, they both very quickly regained their decorum, and proceeded to call me over to come and sit down with them, so I confidently sauntered over and sat myself down, and waited to hear whatever it was that they had to say to me.

Merren leant forward towards me, and began to stroke his beard.

"We really don't think that it's a good idea for you to encourage this girl Manu Kai. You must know that no good can ever come of it," he said very seriously.

"What do you mean?"

Aptien scratched his head and rubbed his nose, and then looking me squarely in the eyes he said: "Well…It's like this little warrior. – If your father was ever to find out that you're seeing a 'Pa-ra-lati' girl…I think we would be correct in assuming that he wouldn't exactly be very happy for you and he would never permit it to continue, and then it would be our necks on the block for allowing it to happen in the first place. So you see…all things taken into consideration, we both think that any thoughts you might be having right now about getting to know this girl a bit better…(at which point he gave me a knowing wink) …should end right now before it goes any further." I honestly hadn't given any thought about the caste problem, and it did seem a little unfair that we weren't supposed to like each other, just because we were from different backgrounds.

"I don't care if my father doesn't approve – I like her…and I'll see her if I want to!" I retorted back at him defiantly.

Aptien shook his head and narrowed his eyes, and taking a slightly more dominant approach he leant forward and sharply pointed his finger towards me.

"That's all very well Manu Kai, but you have to understand that this puts us in a very difficult position as we're due to be replaced in a few days, and if this carries on and it gets reported back to your father, guess who's going to get the blame for failing to deal with this situation by nipping it in the bud right from the start."

In all fairness I could see their point. But I still wasn't willing to bow down to something that I felt was deeply unfair and fundamentally wrong, so I told them exactly how I felt, and where they both stood in all of this.

Merren sighed: "Well, if that's going to be the case," he said, "then the only thing that we can do is to stay here with you for the whole damn duration of your stay, and somehow try and prevent your father from ever finding out about this, or its going to be us who'll be getting the horse whipping."

I did feel sorry for them, but I still wasn't prepared to back down. They both turned and stared at one-another for a few moments…after which, Aptien raised his arms over his head and arched his back, and then raising his eyebrows, he leant back and gestured to Merren to help him remove his boots.

"OK then, Manu Kai – so how do you feel about having to put up with our company for the rest of your stay then?"

Aptien began waving his foot in the air. Merren tutted, and narrowing his eyebrows he grabbed at Aptien's foot – pulled off his boot – and promptly threw it at him. Aptien managed to dodge out the way, and then smugly held up his other foot for Merren to pull that boot off for him too. As I watched their antics, I realised that I actually quite liked the idea of having Merren and Aptien around.

The truth of it was – I had already developed a warm spot for them both, and as long as they were willing – then so was I.

This time, Merren grabbed a firm hold of Aptien's leg with both hands and proceeded to drag him right off his bed and onto the floor, before sharply tugging off his boot and hurling it towards him with the velocity of a launched missile. Aptien quickly responded by raising his hands in an attempt to deflect the incoming boot, but somehow managing to catch it instead, he promptly hurled it back at Merren, who narrowly escaped the incoming projectile by quickly ducking out of its way. Unfortunately…the boot may have missed him, but it made direct contact with a rather ill-fated earthenware pitcher instead; knocking it clean off a low-lying wooden table, and sending it smashing to the ground in the process. I couldn't think why anyone wouldn't want this pair of clowns for company – except perhaps for the owner of the pitcher.

The very next morning, Merren rode back to our village to inform my father of their decision to remain with me for the whole duration of my stay, saying that it was by my own request that they should do so. The plan being; that as long as my father gave it the go ahead, Merren would then gather enough clean clothes for them both, and ride back again the very same day.

Merren returned again that evening, and informed both Aptien and myself, that my father had given them all his blessings to go ahead with their plan. And so it was, that Merren and Aptien were to be my somewhat bemused, and totally unprepared guardians for the whole two moon duration of my stay. You had to feel a little bit sorry for them.

I continued to see Tihanna on a daily basis after that. And after eight days, I finally got the hang of the plough thing. I think Nessa must have felt just a little relieved when I finally stopped falling in the mud, as even though she never complained, it couldn't have been much fun washing all the mud out of my clothes every day.

On the ninth day of my stay, my Derkesthai turned up to see how I was getting on, and to attend to the matter of administering the snake venom into my system, as he said that it was very important at such an early stage that it should continue to be done on a regular basis. We did this in the privacy of Merren and Aptien's lodgings, and it also gave us an excellent opportunity to talk in private. My Derkesthai asked me how I was getting along. I told him that I thought I was doing okay, and I wondered if I should mention anything to him about Tihanna. I wanted to…and I almost did, but I began to hesitate while I thought about it for a few moments. He immediately picked up on this, and began studying my face very carefully before leaning across and resting his right hand on my arm.

"If there's something you need to tell me, Manu Kai...then now's your chance."

I knew that I needed to be honest with him about this, but for some reason I was finding it very difficult, so we just sat in silence for a few moments while my Derkesthai continued to watch me carefully until he finally broke the silence.

"Manu Kai – before you say anything else, I can see that you're quite prepared to tell me, but before you do – first answer me this: Is this going to be something that you would prefer that your father didn't know about?"

"Yes, it is," I answered, honestly.

"Then I think in this case it's probably better if you don't tell me, as I also have a loyalty to your father both as a personal friend of mine, and as our leader. I have sworn a moral oath to never knowingly conceal anything from him that he should probably know about; or to deceive, or to lie to him, and if anything you are about to tell me will compromise that oath in any way, then I really don't wish to be put in the almost impossible position of being forced to choose between my loyalty to you, and my loyalty to him."

I hadn't thought of that, and lowering my eyes a little, I just nodded my head in agreement. As the Derkesthai of our village he was at the head of the Agari, and as such, he wielded a great deal of power within our village. It was a requisite formality that on the day that he obtained the title of 'Derkesthai', he also had to take a moral oath of obedience and loyalty to my father, and as a man of the highest moral standing, this was an oath that he took very seriously indeed. There was plenty of other stuff for us to talk about, so I told him all about the many other things that had happened to me since I'd been here, completely managing to avoid the subject of Tihanna, of course. He appeared to be very pleased to hear that I seemed to be getting on so well. My time with him seemed to pass so quickly, and I couldn't help feeling a little sad when he told me that he was going to have to leave and be on his way. However I did feel a little better when he told me that he would return again in eight days' time. So after Garenhir and I had said our fond farewells, I immediately set off to go and find Tihanna.

It was very clear that I was beginning to weave a very complex web of secrets. A web which was being spun from the sticky threads of deceit, and one which would inevitably cause others to become tangled up within its glutinous strands along with me, but I was still very young, and far too head strong to even begin to envisage the possible consequences of all of this, and of course, I could have absolutely no idea as to where it was all eventually going to lead.

Time went on, and very soon it was the day before the festival of the Sun God Targitai, and throughout the day people were busying themselves with the preparations. A huge bonfire was being built, and wooden tree trunks had been placed all around it, so that people could sit around the fire later on in the evening. I'd been given a couple of days off from ploughing the field, so I took the opportunity to begin teaching Tihanna how to use a bow. It wasn't long before we managed to draw quite a crowd, and I was eventually persuaded to give everyone a demonstration of my skills. This inevitably led to me giving lessons to interested beginners, along with those who just wanted the chance to improve on their skills. I didn't mind at all, in fact I quite enjoyed taking the role of teacher as it reminded me of home.

Merren and Aptien had been standing around watching…as usual, but it hadn't taken very long before they had also got roped into giving a few lessons themselves. It was quite amusing watching them both struggling to cope with all the female attention that they were getting; in the guise of wanting to be taught how to use a bow – but at least it gave us all a chance to relax and just let our hair down a little…so to speak!

At last the day of the festival had arrived, and as there was no Agari priest present to conduct the ceremony, it was more like a huge social gathering than a religious observance. And later as the evening approached and the sun began its leisurely decent. I couldn't help thinking that it looked as though it was slowly melting, like warmed honey running down the side of a pot. This time of the day still fascinated me, and I continued to watch the sun go down until at last it had completely disappeared behind the horizon in a shimmering haze of colour. And as the light of day gradually faded into a dusky twilight – the fire was set ablaze to the raucous sounds of whoops and cheers. People soon began to gather around; drawn to the irresistible warm hypnotic glow of the flames which flickered and danced; beguiling and enticing all with its bewitchingly seductive charms. Tihanna and I walked up to one of the tree trunks that had been placed around the fire and sat down next to one another.

Kess and Nessa, who were all too well aware by now, of the growing relationship between Tihanna and me had walked over to ask us if we were enjoying the festival. We both replied that we were. Kess pointed over to a couple of men who were sharing a pitcher of mead.

"Mind you, don't drink too much of that brew which is going around now, won't you. I've been told it's got a fair old kick to it."

"Don't worry – we won't," I said to him, genuinely believing the words that had just come out of my mouth.

Right on cue as usual, Merren and Aptien suddenly materialised out of thin air. They were like a pair of silent, but some-what intimidating spectres. And their sudden appearance made me jump.

"I really wish you wouldn't keep doing that," I said, giving Merren a shove.

I guess I should have been more used to them by now, but they still managed to startle me every time they did it. Merren smiled at Kess and Nessa, and giving them a wink of his eye he said:

"You don't have to worry – we'll keep an eye on things here."

Merren turned to look at me, and as he did he gave me a wide grin that exaggerated his missing front tooth, (lost in a fist fight no doubt) before uninvitedly sitting himself down right next to Tihanna. He was swiftly followed by Aptien, who sat himself down right next to me. Kess and Nessa both smiled, and seeming to be quite happy to leave us in the watchful presence of Merren and Aptien, they both wandered off again. I could tell that both Merren and Aptien had already been sampling the so called 'brew', and I was about to make a comment to the fact, when Aptien nudged me and said:

"Well…aren't you going to introduce us then?"

I couldn't really see the point in introducing them, as Tihanna already knew who they were, and they certainly knew who she was – but I politely went through the motions just for peace sake. Merren and Aptien's behaviour was unusually well mannered and polite, and I couldn't help thinking that they were up to something.

"We'll be back again in a short while," said Merren, giving Aptien a little nudge.

They both stood up and promptly walked off, leaving Tihanna and myself sitting on the bench alone together.

"Do you want to try some of the brew?" asked Tihanna, obviously meaning to take full advantage of the fact that we were left alone and unsupervised.

"Yes, okay – why not!" I really couldn't see any harm in just trying it.

Smiling excitedly, Tihanna rose to her feet, and quickly disappeared in the direction of where the brew was being served; leaving me sitting on the bench all by myself. I began looking around at all the people that were gathered here.

The party was definitely in full swing, and the atmosphere was positively alive with the raucous sound of people casting all their cares and worries to the wind and enjoying themselves for a little while. It actually felt really good to be amongst them, and I quietly smiled to myself.

I watched the flames of the fire as they flickered and danced, the gentle crackling sound of the burning logs reminded me of home, and I wondered what my Derkesthai was doing right now. I'd always found staring into fire fascinating, it seemed to have a very hypnotic effect on me, and very soon, albeit quite unintentionally, I'd managed to slip into a semi hypnotic trance. I suddenly became aware of a rather peculiar looking warrior who was obviously staring at me. He was sat on the same tree trunk as I was, and as I turned my head to get a better to look at him, he very rudely carried on staring straight back at me. I hadn't even noticed him walk over, and I certainly hadn't seen him around here before, so I politely introduced myself, and waited for him to respond. But after continuing to stare blankly at me for a few seconds, he suddenly stood up and walked over to the fire instead. I thought his actions were very rude, as he had just completely ignored me, and now he was stood facing the fire with his back to me. He remained like this for a moment or two before he turned around again, and then very slowly he began to walk back over towards me until he finally stood directly facing me. He then pointed over towards a couple of trees in the distance, and I looked over to where he was pointing, but apart from the silhouette of the trees in the distance, it was really difficult to see anything at all in this light, so I asked him what he was pointing at. But once again he didn't reply. I thought that perhaps he was unable to speak for some reason. He continued to stand directly in front of me, and then raising his right hand, he held up three fingers. I was feeling very confused by now, and I didn't have a single clue as to what he meant by all of this. "What exactly are you trying to tell me?" I asked him. But he just pointed over towards the trees again, and then began walking off in the same direction that he had just been pointing towards, until finally – he completely disappeared out of sight.

There were few people sat nearby, and after I had managed to get their attention, I asked them if they knew who the strange warrior was that I had just been talking to.

"What warrior?" asked one of the men looking all around?

"The one who was standing right there," I said, pointing to where he had stood just a few moments ago.

"No – can't say I noticed anyone," said the man, shaking his head.

They all began looking at me a bit strangely, so I gave them a brief description of what he looked like and what he was wearing. One of the men stood up and slowly walked over to me, and keeping in mind my high-ranking status, he respectfully asked me if I minded him sitting down right next to me for a few minutes. I gestured to him to sit down, after which he very quietly and very politely assured me that I had been on my own the whole time, and there was no warrior of that description anywhere around here, and also what I had just described was more in keeping with a Scythian warrior of times now long since passed.

It slowly dawned on me that I had been the only one who had seen him. But this wasn't the first time that this type of thing had happened to me, so I didn't feel particularly spooked by it, just very interested to know who he was, and what it was that he was obviously trying to tell me.

Tihanna finally returned with two large beakers of the alcoholic brew, and sitting herself down right next to me, she handed me one of the beakers. There was still no sign of Aptien or Merren, but you never really knew with that pair if they were watching or not. So quickly scanning the area, and feeling satisfied that no one seemed to be taking any notice of us, I cautiously took a small sip of the brew. It had a pleasant warming effect as it went down, and several mouthfuls later, I realised that it was also having a pleasurably relaxing effect on me. Tihanna and I were sat closer together than was probably correct, and I could feel the warmth of her body as she nestled close against me. At first I felt a little uncomfortable, and I began to look around for disapproving glances, but as nobody seemed to care…or even notice, I began to relax a little, and encouraged by her bodily signals, I coyly wrapped my arm protectively around her. We continued to sit cuddled up together making small talk for a while, and very soon I found myself confiding in her, and telling her many things about myself, including all about my Hun family, and the real reason behind why I was here in the first place. Tihanna appeared genuinely fascinated by it all, and she told me that her life was so different to mine, as she'd been orphaned shortly after being born, and had been raised by an aunt, and that she'd never once set foot outside the confines of this village. I guess my life must have sounded pretty fascinating compared to hers.

It turned out that Tihanna was a tiny bit older than I was, in fact just a little more than one winter. So to put it in plain and modern terms, she was around fourteen and a half years old. But I didn't mind, I figured that what I lacked in age, I more than made up for in experience.

I'd soon managed to finish off the contents of the beaker, and forgetting my words of earlier, I asked Tihanna if she could get me some more.

"I'll try," she said, taking the beaker from my hand.

I watched her walk away from me until she had completely disappeared into the crowd once more. I found it impossible to take my eyes off her. I felt so completely captivated by her, that if only she knew right now...she could have made me her slave.

While Tihanna was away, Merren and Aptien had decided to show up again. But this time they were accompanied by two young women who I hadn't seen before. "Where's Tihanna?" Merren asked, looking all around.

"She's gone to try and get some brew." I couldn't see the point of lying to him, as he was going to find out the truth as soon as Tihanna returns with two full beakers of the stuff.

"Ah! Well, you'd better make sure that you don't drink too much of this stuff," he said, taking a large swig from a pitcher that he was carrying. He passed it to Aptien before introducing me to the two women. I just politely said hello to the both of them, as I figured it was really none of my business anyway. And with that – they all sat down and joined me around the fire.

Without giving them a chance to settle, I beckoned to them to come closer to me. They both immediately stood up and walked over to where I was sitting, and obviously intrigued to find out what it was that I was about to tell them, they both crouched down in front of me. I proceeded to tell them all about the phantom warrior that I'd just seen. I was normally more reticent than this whenever I'd experienced anything 'strange', but due to the effects of the alcohol, I was currently feeling a little less guarded than usual, and uncharacteristically complaisant.

They both listened to what I had to say with great interest. Merren gave me a look of such intensity that he actually made me feel a little uncomfortable.

"I've heard people say that you can see and do some pretty weird stuff – so I guess it's all true then is it?" asked Aptien curiously.

"Yes, it's true," I said, feeling strangely obligated to be honest with the pair of them right now. Merren just continued staring at me, he was obviously a little unsure of how he was supposed to react.

"Well I suppose that would make a lot of sense. I guess that's why he's training for the Agari," said Aptien.

Merren nodded in agreement, and finally finding his voice he made sure that he was looking me squarely in the eyes before he asked me…"What other stuff can you do then, Manu Kai?"

"Just…things," I replied, breaking away from his eye contact. I was already beginning to regret saying anything.

Aptien passed me the pitcher; I drank a few mouthfuls before passing it back to him.

"Come on then tell us…what things?" pressed Aptien.

I shook my head, I was suddenly uncomfortable with saying any more, as I didn't want them to regard me any differently, as even though it was perfectly fine for me to talk to my Derkesthai about these things, he had warned me never tell anyone outside of the Agari about my gifts, as if people knew about some of the things that I could do, they may become afraid of me, and that could only lead to bad things.

"I really don't want to say right now – maybe I'll tell you some other time," I said, looking around for any sign of Tihanna.

Aptien gave me a rather prolonged look: "Hmm…just things eh?"

Sighing to himself, Aptien stood up and walked over to the fire and began poking at one of the hot stones with a sturdy looking stick which had been lying on the ground nearby, and after separating it from the fire, he carefully rolled it a little closer to where we were all sitting, and after untying a little pouch which had been fastened to his belt, he opened it and sprinkled some of its contents onto the stone, and just as it started to smoke, he immediately inhaled it through a long hollow tube which he had also brought along with him. He then handed the tube and the pouch to Merren, who did exactly the same thing as he did. Merren who was obviously aware of my curiosity, and of the fact that I was watching his every move, held out the hollow tube towards me and said:

"Do you want some of this?"

I'd never tried it before, and I was very curious to know what it was like, so without saying a word, I stood up and took the tube off Merren, who responded by giving me a little nod of approval. He sprinkled a little more of the contents of the pouch onto the hot stone, and I waited a moment for it to smoke and then inhaled it through the tube, exactly as I'd seen it done so many times before. It instantly made me cough, and for some reason everyone thought that this was highly amusing and they all began to laugh. Merren sprinkled a little more of the bag's contents onto the stone.

"Don't worry – I almost coughed up my liver the first time I did it. You'll soon get used to it. Go on – have another go."

I tried it again, and it didn't make me cough quite so badly the second time around. I was beginning to feel very light headed though, so I decided to go and sit back down again. Aptien took the tube from my hand and just grinned at me.

"Nice one chief; good stuff…don't you think?"

I just nodded in agreement, and allowed them to carry on without me. I'd had enough cannabis for the time being. It would be fair to say that I certainly knew what the term 'being stoned' actually felt like now. Aptien offered the tube to their female companions, who needed very little encouragement in order for them to join them in their quest to be the first human beings to step foot on another planet.

Tihanna had finally returned with the brew. The two women who were with Aptien and Merren both watched Tihanna as she sat down next to me. Tihanna just gave them a little smile, and they both smiled back at her. They obviously all recognised one another, which was hardly surprising as they did all live in the same village after all. Tihanna handed me the beaker containing the brew. I noticed that she seemed to be upset about something, so after taking a few good swigs of the brew, I asked her what was wrong.

"It's nothing," was her slightly convoluted reply.

Her answer didn't make any sense to me at all, as if it was really nothing, why was she obviously so upset? So I questioned her further on just this very point, and she sharply turned to me and said:

"Well, if you really must know, someone has just told me that I'd be far better off staying well away from you, as your father is never going to permit us to be together, and that you already know this, and that you'll just use me, and then you'll leave here forever and forget all about me. Is this true, Manu Kai? Please – you have to tell me the truth."

Merren was sat right next to me, and he was obviously close enough to have overheard all of this, and he very quietly whispered in my ear:

"I think that it's about time you were honest with the girl…don't you, Manu Kai?"

Placing the beaker down on the ground, I rudely turned my back on Merren and turned to face Tihanna, and taking both her hands in mine, I looked deeply into her beautiful sky-blue eyes. I didn't want to admit it, but Merren was right, and I knew that I was just going to have to come clean and tell her the truth about our current situation.

"I'm afraid that it's true about my father not being happy if he knew about us right now, but I don't care…I want to marry you Tihanna, and my father is just going to have to accept it."

"You know damn well it's never going to happen," said Merren, quietly whispering in my ear.

I didn't care what anyone said…it was up to me who I married and that was all there was to it, and fuelled with a heady mixture of cannabis and alcohol – and in full view of everyone present, I kissed Tihanna for the very first time. I was briefly aware of the sound of Merren tutting away in the background, but soon I was completely lost in the moment, and oblivious to everything else that may have been going on around me.

The birds were beginning to mark the start of a new day with their dawn chorus, and after Aptien had failed several times to get my attention, he finally resorted to gently tapping me on the shoulder.

"I think that it's about time we all got some sleep now don't you? Come on, Kai…we'll see that you both get back safely."

Tihanna and I finally re-surfaced for air, and I heard Merren ask their female companions to wait for them in their kol, saying that they wouldn't be very long. I finished off what was left in the beaker before tutting disapprovingly. Merren just looked at me and laughed as he ran his fingers through his dark curly hair.

"Yes, well, guess what? We won't tell if you don't!"

We walked…or perhaps it would be more accurate to say – drunkenly staggered Tihanna safely back to her kol. I really didn't want to leave her, and Aptien and Merren had to practically drag me away. And in all fairness to the both of them, they made absolutely sure that I also got back safely and all in one piece; as if I'm honest – I could barely walk by now. And after they had quietly helped me inside Kess and Nessa's hut, well, as quietly as was humanly possible for them to do so considering the given circumstances…they removed my boots and weapons, and then they even helped me to get undressed; after which they left me alone to sleep off the effects of the cannabis and alcohol.

The very next thing that I can remember is being woken up by someone gently shaking me. For a moment I didn't remember where I was, and I didn't have a clue what time of the day it was either. Coming to my senses I sat bolt upright.

"Hmm, good night last night then was it?" said Garenhir. I had completely forgotten that it was his day to visit.

"Uhm…Yes, I think so," I replied, trying my best to sound convincingly coherent. Garenhir just smiled knowingly.

"What if I go and wait in Merren and Aptien's kol for you. That way it will give you a chance to gather your thoughts together. Just make your way over when you're ready."

"Have you seen them yet?"

"Yes, they're both up and about. Apparently they popped around to see you earlier, but you were still fast asleep."

Garenhir left me alone to give me some time to sort myself out, and although I was feeling a little hung-over, I quickly pulled on my clothes and made my way over to Merren and Aptien's kol, where they were both sat with Garenhir who was patiently waiting for me to turn up. As soon as I arrived, Merren and Aptien both stood up and politely acknowledged me before quickly disappearing outside. Garenhir asked me how I was feeling this morning, and I wondered if Merren and Aptien had already told him about how inebriated I'd managed to get. But if he doesn't ask me outright, then I didn't see any point in telling him, so I just told him that I felt fine.

"Good I'm very glad to hear it. And in case you were wondering Manu Kai – your two fine friends have not betrayed any of your secrets," he said, raising his eyebrows a little.

I felt very transparent all of a sudden. I should have known that there was no way that I was going to be able to keep anything hidden from Garenhir for very long, and I felt drawn to look into his eyes for a moment, and as I did, I just knew without any doubt that he was already aware about my relationship with Tihanna, and feeling very guilty for purposely trying to keep so many things from him, I threw myself at his feet…and at his mercy.

"Manu Kai, will you please get up off the floor, and keeping in mind what I've already said to you before, I have a feeling that there may be at least a couple things that you may want to tell me about."

Raising myself up from the ground, I rather sheepishly sat down directly opposite Garenhir and slowly began to recall the events of the night before, and of the phantom warrior who had come to me with a message of some sort, and after I had delivered my tale as accurately as I could recall it, I asked Garenhir if he had any idea what it could all mean. He paused for a few moments before speaking...

"The problem with this sort of thing Manu Kai is that sometimes these type of messages are so vague and unclear, that more often than not, it's practically impossible to decipher the meaning behind them. There's obviously a message there somewhere. But exactly what it could be, right now I honestly couldn't say."

"Have you any idea who he could have been?"

"Again – it's impossible to say. There was a great battle here once, and many warriors were slain. It's possible that what you saw could be a phantom of some sort. But that's highly unlikely after all this time. He may even be something entirely different, a non-human entity of some sort perhaps, who has just taken on the appearance of a warrior of the past, but again going on what you've said, it's very difficult to know."

As we continued to discuss how I was getting along, and some of the things which I'd experienced since I'd been here, Garenhir carried on with the business of administering the snake venom into my system via a small nick to the inside of my arm; while all the time I skilfully managed to completely avoid the subject of Tihanna. I even owned up to getting so intoxicated the night before that Merren and Aptien had to put me to bed. But instead of the scolding that I was expecting, Garenhir just shook his head and tutted. When the time came for him to leave, he bade me farewell and said that he would return after eight days had passed.

In the peaceful solitude of the empty kol, I soon became so lost in an ocean of my own thoughts that I hadn't noticed Merren and Aptien had quietly let themselves in and were both stood by the doorway staring at me.

"Is everything alright?" asked Aptien, walking over sitting down beside me.

It took me a moment or two before I could gather my thoughts enough to be able to answer him.

"Yes, everything's fine," I finally answered with a sigh. Merren who had remained standing said:

"You know that you can always talk to us about things if you need to, Kai, and it'll never go any further...you know that don't you?"

118

I could tell by the look in his eyes that his words were coming straight from the heart, and all things said and done, I knew that when it came down to it, I could trust them both implicitly.

"Yes, I know – but I'm okay, but it's good to know anyway!"

"We just wanted to make sure that you knew…that's all," said Aptien, still looking a little concerned.

There was no more that really needed to be said, so for now at least we were all just happy to leave it at that.

10

First Kill

As my relationship with Tihanna continued to blossom, I secretly began to wonder how we were ever going to continue seeing each other once I had returned home again. I had promised Tihanna that somehow I would find a way, and even though I really meant it; just how I was ever going to turn this into a reality I really didn't know.

One morning after lying awake half the night thinking about it, I decided that I had nothing to lose by talking it over with Merren and Aptien. I'd come to trust them during our stay here, and they were the only ones that I could actually talk to about this, and as they had said that I could talk to them at any time, right now seemed as good a time as any. So being very careful not to wake Kess and Nessa, I quietly got dressed and made my way over to their kol.

As I quietly let myself in through the doorway of Merren and Aptien's Kol, I was struck by how dark it was inside. The shutters hadn't been opened yet to allow any daylight to shine through so I couldn't see a thing; so after standing there for a few moments to allow my eyes time to adjust to the darkness, I could just about make out Aptien who was still sleeping soundly on the left hand side of the kol, so walking over to him I plonked myself down on the edge of his bed. He immediately sat bolt upright and made a grab for his sword which was down on the floor next to his bed.

"Sorry to wake you," I said apologetically.

"Kai…it's you…what the hell! What are you doing here at this time of the morning?" he said, rubbing his eyes. "Merren…wake up – Manu Kai is here."

Merren began to stir from the other side of the kol. My eyes were beginning to acclimatise to the darkness, and I noticed that he wasn't alone. It was the woman that he'd been with on the evening of the festival. Merren got out of bed, and after quickly pulling on his trousers he came over and sat next to me on Aptien's bed. His female companion modestly got dressed beneath the cover of the sheepskin blankets, and then without saying a single word, she quickly left the kol. I didn't really know what to say either, so I just sat there and waited for someone else to be the first to say anything about the situation.

"Look, Manu Kai…before you say anything," said Merren, raising his hands to his head. "I know what you're thinking. But don't you be so quick to judge me. I know you probably won't believe me – but I actually have genuine feelings for that woman. I don't know how it happened – but I do."

To be honest I didn't really care if he had a woman in bed with him or not, but he seemed to think that I did, so I decided to play along with it for a while.

"If you really have feelings for her, then how come you've kept it hidden from me?"

"Because she asked me to Kai," he said, pausing to take a deep breath. "Plain and simple, but it doesn't matter anymore because you know now, and do you know what? I'm actually glad that you do. Do you have any idea how hard it's been trying to keep this from you?"

I thought about my own situation for a moment: "Yes, I think I probably do."

"I think Kai may have a pretty good idea of how hard it is to keep this sort of thing a secret from someone close to you…eh Manu Kai?" said Aptien.

I nodded in agreement, and then I began to see the funny side of all of this. Merren had actually fallen for a woman, and a Pa-ra-lati woman at that. This was pure gold, and I just couldn't help but laugh.

"What's so damn funny?" asked Merren, scowling at me.

"You…this…everything," I replied.

I could see that Aptien was trying his best not to laugh at this very moment too, but in the end he just couldn't help himself either.

"He's right you know, mate, it is pretty funny if you think about it," said Aptien, with a stupid grin on his face.

"Yeah, hilarious I'm sure," said Merren, staring down at his bare feet.

Merren let out a long sigh, and raising his gaze slightly from the ground, he could see that both Aptien and myself were staring at him with silly smirks on our faces, until at last, Merren also began to see the funny side of all of this.

I'd almost managed to completely forget that I'd come to see them for a reason. It's just as well that Aptien reminded me, or I may well have just gone on my way without saying anything.

"So…what's going on then, Manu Kai? You must have come here for a reason."

"Oh…I just wanted to talk to you both about something that's all."

"Well…you certainly know how to get our full attention, I'll give you that much," said Merren, shaking his head.

Something suddenly dawned on me. Merren was going to be in the same position as I was…well almost.

"How are you going to manage to see each other after we go back?" I asked him.

"I don't know yet, I'm going to have to try and come up with some reasonable excuse why I have to regularly disappear, but I just can't think of anything at the moment," he replied, rubbing his chin thoughtfully.

"I can…"

Silently I thanked the Great Spirit for giving me this opportunity. Merren and Aptien both listened intently as I explained my plan. I told them that if Merren was willing, I could tell my father that I'd really like to come back here on a regular basis to visit Kess and Nessa. And I'd ask him if Merren could be the one who accompanies me and no one will suspect a thing. And that way I can carry on seeing Tihanna, and Merren can carry on seeing his latest flame.

"I would like to keep in touch with Kess and Nessa anyway, and I 'will' pop in and see them while I'm here, so I won't actually be lying," I said with a smug grin. They both stared at me open mouthed.

"Well, I've got to hand it to you Manu Kai; you're one scheming son of a bitch. I'm beginning to see a slightly wider picture of you," said Aptien, shaking his head. "It takes one to know one," I said, glaring at him.

"Well, that's all very well," said Merren with a sigh. "But I don't know if you realise it Manu Kai, but if I were to agree to this, and it ever got back to your father; he could have me executed."

"Yes, I know – but I've already thought about that, and if he was to ever find out about Tihanna and me, I'll simply tell him that you didn't know anything about it, and that I'd managed to deceive you too."

"You're something else, Manu Kai – you really are. But I need some time to think about all of this."

"So what was it you actually wanted to talk to us about?" asked Aptien.

"Uhm…it doesn't really matter now," I replied, rising to my feet.

And leaving them both sitting there looking quite stunned, I headed back to Kess and Nessa's hut where Nessa was already busy preparing breakfast. I was feeling particularly pleased with myself this morning, and it must have been quite obvious that I was up to something, as Nessa asked me what I'd been up to.

"I needed to see Merren and Aptien about something that's all," I said with a little sigh.

"No problems I hope," she said, narrowing her eyebrows.

"No…I think it's all been sorted now…thanks!"

The rest of the day passed by without incident, and with all my chores completed for the day, I stepped outside for some fresh air just in time to see the last rays of the light of day slowly replaced by a rather eerie twilight mist. I felt a cold chill run down the full length of my spine, and for some reason I began to feel uneasy. There was definitely something in the air tonight, but I just couldn't put my finger on it, so with a shudder, I walked back inside the kol and began to clean my weapons, along with the added entertainment of watching Kess and Nessa's desperate attempts to capture a family of mice which were running riot all around the hut.

We were suddenly disturbed by the sound of frantic screaming which was coming from outside. I quickly grabbed my bow and arrows, and Kess told Nessa and me to stay in the hut. He was about to unhook a long-handled Scythe which was hanging on the wall, when two men burst in through the entrance. Nessa screamed, and Kess quickly pushed her down to the ground, and as I'd done so many times before, I drew back my bow – took aim – and loosed my arrow. The only difference being…that this was the first time that I'd ever actually aimed at a real person. My arrow hit one of them straight in the head, and he instantly fell to the ground. The other man roared with anger, and with hate blazing in his eyes he drew back his bow, and aimed it straight at me. I'd already knocked another arrow, took aim and loosed. Unfortunately for me he had done exactly the same thing, and as I dived to the ground I thought to myself: "That's it…I'm dead!"

I felt a sharp searing pain tear through my left shoulder, and as I fell to the ground I knew that his arrow had hit me, but I also knew that my arrow must have hit him too, as he staggered and fell to the ground just as the first man had done before him. My arrow had actually hit him in the throat, and I watched frozen with sheer terror as he reached out towards me – his eyes ablaze with such fury and hatred that I felt my blood run cold. His cold steely eyes were still fixed in an unnerving stare towards me as he rasped his last laboured breath and then lay still. Both men were now lying on the ground right in front of me. Kess was just about to run over to help me, when another man burst in through the entrance. I couldn't use my bow this time, as I was unable to lift my left arm. So I instinctively reacted by reaching for one of my throwing knives instead, and with my one good arm I had delivered it with such speed that there was little time to know if my aim had been true before it was very quickly followed by another. However, both knives had managed to hit their intended target. One had hit him squarely in the chest, while the other had hit him just below the left eye. The expression on his face was a mixture of shock and anger, and with a final effort of defiance, he staggered a few more steps towards me before finally collapsing on top of one of his companions; thus joining him in a deathly embrace.

Nessa, who'd been huddled in the corner, looked over at me and screamed: "Manu Kai…oh no…you've been hit!"

I didn't need to be told…It bloody hurt! I looked at the arrow which was still sticking out of my shoulder, and I could see that it had gone in pretty deep. I looked down towards the three men that I'd just slain lying on the ground in a large pool of their own blood, and I suddenly felt my knees give way from under me. Kess ran over, and managed to catch me before I hit the ground. He was still in the process of helping me over to my bed, when Aptien burst in through the doorway, almost falling over the pile of dead bodies that lay at his feet. He just stood there staring at them for a few moments, before realising that I'd been hit.

"Can't leave you for a minute can we…Just look at this mess! I see you've managed to get yourself a bit of a splinter there, mate. Don't worry…you'll be okay," he said, trying his best not to sound too concerned.

Aptien helped Kess to make me as comfortable as possible, and after taking a closer look at the wound, he told Kess to go and see to Nessa who was understandably very shook up. "If it hadn't have been for Manu Kai, we'd be dead now for sure," said Nessa, with tears streaming down the side of her face.

Merren burst in next, and just as Aptien had done before him, he almost went flying over the three dead raiders.

"Watch you don't fall over the bodies mate…and as you can see…Kai's been wounded," said Aptien.

"Today is turning out to be one shit of a day," said Merren, stepping over the bodies and making his way over to where I was still being propped up by Aptien.

Removing his knife from its sheath, Merren began cutting away at my tunic, and on seeing how deep the arrow had gone in, he turned to Aptien and sighed:

"We're going to need some help here mate."

Merren removed the rest of my tunic, tore it into strips, and tied it around my shoulder to stem the bleeding.

"It's not bleeding too badly Kai," said Merren, carefully wrapping a blanket around me so as to avoid the protruding arrow. "You've been very lucky that the arrow has missed the artery, so it's just going to be a matter of getting the damn thing out of you now."

"Who are they?" I asked staring at the three body's still lying there on the ground.

"They belong to a nomadic tribe of pillaging cut throat scum. They like to prey on easy targets, and raid villages like these. They rape and kill women and children, and steal whatever they can, including children to sell to the slave trade. But I don't think they'll bother to come back here again in a hurry," answered Aptien.

"One of us is going to have to ride back and fetch Garenhir; if you like I'll do it while you stay here with Kai. Sorry to leave you to clear up the mess," said Merren to Aptien.

That's OK, mate, just be careful in case there's any more of them lurking around.

"Your first kill, aren't they?" asked Aptien, staring down at the three dead men lying in a heap on the ground.

"Yes," I replied.

"You know that as a Scythian Warrior, it's customary to drink the blood of your first kill...don't you?" asked Aptien, very quietly.

I remembered what my Derkesthai had said about drinking blood.

"Yes, but I don't want to."

"It's tradition...and you only have to do it once."

"I don't care what it is, I'm half Hun...and I'm...I'm also in training for the Agari – so I'm excused anyway."

"OK," he said, shrugging his shoulders.

Aptien walked over to the bodies, and after dipping his fingers into a pool of blood, he walked back over to me, and with one swift movement, he smeared it across my forehead, and all the way down my left cheek.

"There – well I guess that will just have to do then," he said with an air of satisfaction. "You did really well there Manu Kai, and regardless of what you said to your father about you not being brave and all that, well this is the proof…if any was needed, that you really are a true warrior. So hang on in there little Chief, and you'll be okay."

Kess gave Aptien a hand to drag the bodies outside, where Aptien retrieved my two throwing knives, after which they both returned inside again.

"You were a little bit sloppy there, Chief," said Aptien, wiping the blood from my knives. "One of them was not quite dead yet, so I finished him off for you."

I didn't bother to ask him which one, as I was feeling rather nauseous as it was, and along with being in a great deal of pain I was also trembling and noticeably in shock. Aptien's mask of indifference was beginning to slip, and he was beginning to look a little more worried. He asked Kess if he knew if there was any alcohol around anywhere.

Kess ran outside, and about five minutes later he returned with a full jug of the strongest that was available. After having a fair old swig of it himself, Aptien poured some of it into a drinking bowl and sat down right next to me.

"Here – just take a few sips of this Kai – it'll help with the pain."

I was trembling so much that he had to hold it to my mouth so that I could drink it, after which, he pulled another sheepskin blanket over me in an effort to try and keep me warm. I really wanted to lie down, but Aptien wouldn't allow me to – insisting instead that I remain sat in an upright position.

By now word had got around that I was injured, and it wasn't long before Tihanna come bursting in through the doorway and ran straight over to me, and seeing the awful state that I was in she began to cry, I really didn't want her to be upset, so did my best to try and put on a brave face just for her sake.

"Don't worry – I'm going to be just fine," I said, as convincingly as I could manage in the present circumstances.

But obviously I was not convincing enough, as Tihanna was getting in such a state that I began to wonder if I may have been far worse off than I actually was.

Aptien could see that Tihanna wasn't really helping matters right now, so he told her that he'd make sure that I was okay, and it would be much better if she left me alone for a little while so that I could conserve my strength. Aptien then went on to tell her that I was going to need all my strength when the arrow was finally removed. Tihanna reluctantly agreed to leave, but before she did, I asked her if she knew how many people had either been injured or killed?

"No one was killed thankfully…only the raiders. There's a few people injured, but they're all being taken care…." Tihanna had barely had a chance to finish her sentence before Aptien had ushered her outside.

"How many of them did you get, Aptien?" I asked him.

"Five…I think!"

"We got fourteen of them altogether between the three of us. The villagers managed to get a few more, the rest all managed to escape," he said, taking another swig from the pitcher.

"Here – have a couple more sips of this," said Aptien, pouring a little more into the beaker.

"That should do you for now."

All we could do now was to sit tight and wait for help to arrive.

"What will you do with all the bodies?" I asked Kess, who was still comforting a badly traumatised Nessa.

"They'll all be taken outside the village and either burned, or buried in a joint grave," answered Kess.

Suddenly, my father burst in through the doorway, he was quickly followed by Merren, my Derkesthai, and another of his pupils who I'd previously bumped into a couple of times before called Sai. They were also accompanied by several other warriors from our village. My father immediately rushed to my side and knelt down in front of me, and looking deeply concerned he asked me how I was doing.

Although it was pretty obvious to everyone by now, all I could think of to say to him was…"I've got an arrow in my shoulder."

"Yes, I know," he said gravely, "Don't worry though, we'll have that out for you very soon." My father then stood up and moved aside so that Garenhir could remove the makeshift bandage and take a good look at the wound.

"Hmm – It's not that far from having gone all the way through by the looks of things," he said to my father. "There's no bone blocking it, and luckily it's missed the artery, so by the look of things it's going to be a lot easier, and a lot less traumatic to just knock it straight through – I'm going to need some help to steady him though."

Garenhir then asked for someone to fetch a wooden stool that was stood next to the fire place, and after asking my father to give him a hand to sit me on it, he asked him to hold me steady by standing directly behind me and placing both his hands on the top half of my back. He then asked Merren and Aptien to get one on either side of me, and to link one of their arms through mine and hold me very still. Then without giving me any warning, Garenhir quickly snipped off the fletching part of the arrow, and immediately poured an alcohol solution all over my shoulder and what was now left of the remaining protruding shaft. He then put on a specially designed leather fingerless glove, which had a layer of extra thick leather attached to the palm, and kneeling down in front of me he looked me straight in the eyes.

"I promise that this will all be over very soon, Manu Kai," he said in a very calm and reassuring tone of voice.

He then gave me a piece of thick leather to bite down on, and although he appeared very confident, his eyes betrayed his secret concern, but I was also aware of a deep sense of compassion which seemed to radiate from him towards me, and I trusted him implicitly. I knew full well that I really couldn't be in better hands right now than his. I think he must have picked up on my thoughts as he gave me a knowing smile, and he gently rested both his hands on my head for a few moments, and almost instantly I began to feel a deep sense of calm wash over me.

"Ready?" asked Garenhir, standing up again.

And everyone, including myself answered: "Yes!"

I felt both Aptien and Merren tighten their grip on me, and as swift as the arrow that had first pierced my flesh, Garenhir then struck the shaft of the protruding arrow with a single sharp blow using the palm of his hand, and in doing so, had succeeded in pushing the arrow head right through to the other side of my shoulder, which he then very quickly pulled out. It hurt like mad, and the intensity of the pain made me feel sick. Garenhir poured even more alcohol over my shoulder, and if I thought it hurt before – this time it was excruciating. I bit down hard on the piece of leather, and then I spat it out angrily onto the ground. Garenhir then covered both sides of the arrow wound with a herbal poultice of some kind that he had brought with him, before binding my shoulder with a clean linen bandage, and then strapping my arm across my chest. He said that he wasn't going to stitch it, as it was best left as it was for now so that any dirt would have a chance to work its way out through the open wounds.

"The worry now is infection, so it's going to need very careful attention for a little while," said Garenhir, wiping the blood from my still trembling body.

I was aware of my father asking me how I was feeling, but his voice sounded very distant, and I just couldn't find it within me to answer him. I was beginning to drift into unconsciousness, but I can remember hearing Garenhir say that I needed to sleep now, and that I shouldn't move around too much for a few days. At which point he lifted me up from the stool and carried me over to my bed, and after propping me up with a couple of rolled up sheepskins, he asked someone to fetch some fresh drinking water. Kess handed him a beaker of water which Garenhir then held to my mouth.

"Manu Kai…Drink some of this water," he said firmly.

I managed to take a few sips before he covered me over with a soft woollen blanket. I was so thankful that the arrow was finally gone, now at last I could finally lie down and go to sleep. The sound of people's voices faded in and out, until completely exhausted – I sank into a very deep sleep.

I must have slept throughout the night, as the next thing that I can remember is opening my eyes and seeing my father's face looking down at me. He smiled, and asked me how I was feeling. I tried to sit up, but my shoulder was just too painful.

"Can I have some water?" I asked him.

My father helped me to sit upright, while Garenhir, who was also at my bedside, went to fetch me some water. I looked all around, and I could see that everyone who had been here last night were still here this morning. And all eyes were presently focussed on me.

"I'm feeling a lot better now," I said, seeing the concerned look on everyone's faces. Garenhir sat down next to me and handed me the water.

"Kai, I'm very happy to hear you say that you're feeling a lot better this morning, as unfortunately I'm going to have to leave you for a little while as I've been summoned by the King. He says it's an emergency – so I have to go. But don't worry as I'm going to be leaving you in the very capable hands of Sai here. He has a remarkable gift for healing, and I have complete faith in him to be able to take care of you in my absence. Sai and I have already administered to all who were wounded here, so hopefully everyone will make a full recovery."

I looked across at Sai who was quietly sitting on a wooden bench nearby. He just nodded to me and gave me a little smile. Garenhir then said that he would return as soon as it was possible for him to do so. And after giving everyone his blessings – he hastily left.

Nessa was feeling a lot better now too, and was busy preparing a large pot of stew, while Merren, Aptien, and Kess, along with the three other accompanying warriors were busy with the task of removing every minute trace of blood from Kess and Nessa's little home.

My father, who was looking relieved to know that I was feeling so much better, sat down beside me and he said:

"Kai, I'm also going to have to leave you for a while as I'm going back to organise a hunting party. I've decided to track down the rest of that worthless scum and exterminate them like the vermin they are. They dare to call themselves 'Skudat'. They insult us by calling themselves by the same name. I won't rest until every last one of them is slain." And I knew that he meant every word of it too!

As my father prepared to leave, I began to recall a dream that I'd had during the deep sleep that I'd fallen into after having the arrow removed from my shoulder. In this dream – the Phantom warrior appeared to me once again. He stood in front of me; just as he'd done when I was sitting by the fire, and he held up three fingers. But when I looked closely at his fingers, they each resembled one of the three men that I'd slain. The phantom warrior then pointed towards some trees, and as I looked at these trees, they slowly began to multiply until they had become a huge forest. That was it…they were hiding in the forest!

"I know where they're hiding," I said excitedly.

"What – How do you know?" my father asked me puzzled.

"I've…I've had a message from a…from a dead warrior. He showed me the three men that I'd slain. I know now that he was trying to show me where the rest of them are hiding, they're in the forest!" I replied, emotionally.

Along with everyone else – Merren and Aptien had been listening in with great interest to our conversation.

"That's right," said Merren. "I can remember you telling us about your phantom warrior friend." My father looked at Merren for a moment, and then back to me again.

"I'm going to trust you on this son, but is there anything else that you can remember which might help us to narrow down which part of the forest they may be hiding in – that's a very large forest."

I thought about the phantom warrior's actions on the night of the festival, and the direction that he was facing when he'd turned his back on me and faced the fire – he was actually facing south.

"They're heading for the southern region," I said confidently.

"Are you quite sure of this, Kai?" asked my father.

"Yes, I'm sure," I replied.

"Excellent! Then I'll organise a little surprise party for them as soon as I get back," he said with a rather malevolent looking glint in his eye.

By now Nessa's huge pot of stew was ready, she had made sure that there was more than enough to go around, so after everyone had eaten a good hearty meal of ample proportion, my father and his little band of warriors politely thanked their hosts for their kind hospitality, before they all set off and headed back home again in order to organise the attack.

Nessa soon turned her attention towards Sai, who had barely spoken two words since arriving the previous day.

"So…you're going to be looking after Manu Kai then are you?"

Sai, who had obviously been deep in thought, suddenly realised that Nessa was actually talking to him.

"Sorry, Yes…I'm going to be looking after him."

"Are you a healer or something? You're very young," asked Kess, who was in the process of fixing the wooden door, which had been made unstable when one the raiders had kicked it open.

"He's in training for the Agari, the same as Manu Kai," replied Aptien, who was presently having a well-earned rest.

"Goodness," said Kess, looking back at Sai. "You can't be much older than Manu Kai."

"I'm around sixteen winters," said Sai rather shyly.

Nessa had made a little bed up for him right next to mine. And after helping Nessa clear away all the dishes from our meal, Sai sat down on his bed, and began to take some things out of a bag that Garenhir had brought with them. I watched him intently as he began to lay it all out on his bed before him.

"I'm going to have to change your dressing now," he said, leaning over to help me sit on the edge of my bed, which would allow him to remove my soiled dressings more easily.

After carefully cleaning my wounds, Sai then covered them in some kind of herbal paste before re-applying the clean dressings, and then finally, he finished off by strapping my arm across my chest again.

"I think it's best to keep your arm immobilised for a couple more days," he said, as he began to tidy everything away.

It was easy to see why our Derkesthai had such confidence in him; he really did appear to possess a natural ability as a healer, and although very young, he displayed total competence in everything he did. It would be fair to say that he had a certain way about him which made me feel totally at ease in his company, and perhaps more importantly – completely secure about being left in his hands.

Aptien and Merren both looked totally exhausted, and Merren said that they were going to make their way back to their sleeping quarters and get their heads down for a little while. They both wished us all a good night…and then they left. Shortly after that Tihanna popped around to check on how I was doing, so we just sat and talked for a little while until the light began to fade. After she had left, Sai asked me if she was my girlfriend. I hesitated for a moment or two before replying.

"Yes, she is, but please don't tell anyone, as my father wouldn't approve if he knew that I was seeing a Pa-ra-lati girl. I will tell him, but in my own time, so I'd appreciate it if you just kept it to yourself for now."

"No problem – your secret is safe with me," he said, raising his finger to his mouth.

"Thanks…It's just that I really don't think I'm quite up to him finding out at the moment." I knew that Sai was as good as his word, and I was happy to tell him all about Tihanna and myself…in Kess and Nessa's absence, of course. It wasn't that I didn't trust them, as I knew that they were all already well aware of our relationship. But I just didn't feel comfortable talking about these things in front of them.

It felt really good to be able to talk freely to someone about my feelings for Tihanna, and I found myself being able to speak to Sai about all sorts of things that I simply couldn't say to anyone else – not even Garenhir. I knew that Sai and I were going to become good friends as well as future Agari brothers. I asked him if he had a girlfriend, but he just shook his head and said that he didn't. A few days later my father returned again with a small party of warriors. I was able to get up and about a little better now, and he looked really happy when he saw that I was making such good progress. He told me that they'd found the raiders exactly where I'd said they'd be, and that they'd managed to totally catch them off guard, and as a result, they were able to slay most of them with relative ease. He said that a couple of his warriors had sustained minor injuries in the process, but that was only to be expected, but no one had been either badly wounded or killed, and all of our warriors were expected to make a full recovery.

"Your time here is almost over son," said father, with a certain amount of relief in his voice. "So as soon as you're well enough to ride, Merren and Aptien can escort you home. I have to go straight back, as I've very important business to take care of, but before I go, I need to have a little chat with Kess."

My father then asked Kess to step outside with him for a few moments, and when they returned it was obvious that he'd given Kess something of value, as he immediately hid it under his bed. "Please do me a huge favour and avoid getting into any more scrapes. I have to go now, but I'll see you soon," said Father, walking backwards towards the door.

And with that, he turned and quickly disappeared through the doorway.

Garenhir turned up the following day and was obviously delighted to learn that I was making such a good recovery.

"How is your shoulder feeling now?" he asked me.

"It's still painful...but I'm feeling much better now."

He smiled at me and said, "Good! Let's have a look at it then."

Garenhir carefully removed the dressings, and seeing how well the wounds were healing he nodded in approval.

"Hmm – it's healing very well indeed. I told you Sai was an excellent healer didn't I?"

After applying fresh dressings, Garenhir said that he thought I was probably well enough to ride back, but it would be best to wait for at least another week – just to be on the safe side.

"If this hasn't grounded you a little – I don't know what will," he said, raising his eyebrows.

I had very mixed feelings about going back, but I knew that I'd have to go home at some point. But I was determined to keep my word to Tihanna and return again soon, and nothing was going to stop me.

11

The Horse Whipping

After I was well enough to return home, my thoughts inevitably returned to the problem of how on earth I was ever going to arrange regular visits for myself to the Pa-ra-lati village in order to see Tihanna without my father finding out about our relationship. So after much deliberation, I eventually plucked up the courage to ask him if it would be possible for me to visit Kess and Nessa now and again. I told him that I had grown very fond of them both during my stay with the Pa-ra-lati, and if Merren and Aptien didn't mind, I would prefer it if they were my escorts, as during the time that they had stayed there, they had both got on really well with the locals, and as they already knew their way around the place, it would be a lot easier for all concerned if they were the ones to accompany me. I was so relieved when my father said that he couldn't see a problem with this, just as long as Merren and Aptien were willing. He told me that he'd have a word with them, and he'd let me know what they said later that afternoon.

I wasn't present when he asked either one of them, but I can imagine what must have been going through their heads when he approached them on the matter. But whatever their thoughts had been – they'd both agreed. And so it was that I was able to pay regular visits to the Pa-ra-lati village and continue seeing Tihanna in secret. And of course this also made it much easier for Merren to continue seeing his girlfriend there too. And all the while I kept promising myself that there was going be a right time to tell my father about Tihanna, while still upholding my solemn promise to Merren and Aptien, to make sure that they'd be seen as blameless in all of this should my father ever find out. But as time went on, there never did seem to be a 'right' time to tell my father, and before I knew it, weeks had turned into months, and eventually two whole years had managed to pass and I still hadn't found the courage to tell my father.

Although my brother was married now, and had long moved into his own kol, he still delighted in getting at me any way that he could. It would seem that time alone had not succeeded in offering me any respite from his constant and senseless harassment. That is until one fateful day when I was around fifteen winters of age, and I was finally just about big enough to be able to stand up to him. I was about to leave for my appointment with Garenhir, and I'd only just managed to have taken one step outside of our kol, when my brother who had apparently been looking for my father purposely barged right into me. I did my best to ignore him, and I would have just carried on my way had he not suddenly reached out and grabbed me by my braided hair, and to my horror he drew his knife from its sheath and held it to my throat.

"I really think that it's about time you had a haircut," he said, sneering at me like something possessed.

It was probably a culmination of a lifetime of bullying from him, and the fact that I was no longer a small and vulnerable child – and not too far off from becoming a man myself, but whatever it was, my natural instincts had kicked in before he, or even I for that matter had had a chance to even blink, with lightning speed I reached up and knocked the knife from his hand, and spinning around I lunged at his face with a clawed hand, and in doing so, I'd managed to poke my fingers into both of his eyes. He was completely taken off guard and yelling out in pain he stumbled backwards with his hands held up to his eyes, and as he did, I followed the momentum by leaping at him and grabbing him around the throat, which culminated in him toppling over backwards and falling to the ground with me landing right on top of him, and then with both hands still firmly attached to his throat, I proceeded to attempt to squeeze the very life out of him.

Stunned and unable to see out of his eyes, he blindly grabbed at my hands, but to no avail, and on the one attempt that he made to use his superior strength in an effort to push me off him, I responded by sharply bringing my knee into direct contact with his groin. The next thing that I can recall is someone grabbing me firmly by my shoulders.

"Kai, let him go…Kai, let him go or you're going to kill him."

It was my father, and seeing the horrified look on his face seemed to snap me back to my normal senses again, and I immediately released my death grip on my brother's throat and swiftly jumped to my feet. My brother immediately began coughing and gasping for air, and staggering to his feet, he wiped away the tears that were still streaming down his embittered face. I just stood there glaring at him, almost daring him to retaliate until I was satisfied that it was truly over. I had finally managed to successfully stand up to his senseless and unrelenting bullying, and feeling morally victorious in my defeat over him – I calmly walked away. I could still hear him whining away to my father about how I'd attacked him for no reason, but I just ignored him and carried on walking. As unless I was asked to do so, I couldn't even be bothered to stick around long enough to give my side of the story, after all, I wasn't exactly very big for my age, and my brother was much heavier and a lot taller than I was.

"Well – that was well overdue," said one of my father's men as I walked past him. "Maybe he'll leave you alone now…if he's got any sense he will anyway."

My brother never did physically touch me again after that…but even so – I was still a long way from being entirely free of him.

My studies with Garenhir began to intensify. And as time went on, I threw myself wholeheartedly into whatever task he set for me, and the practical application of the truths which he taught me. But the fact that I was deceiving my father continued to gnaw away at me. And even though Merren's relationship hadn't worked out as his girlfriend had suddenly ended their relationship after she had finally realised that Merren was never going to marry her, as to do so would effectually make him an outcast, as he'd never be able to set foot in our village again. But even so – both he and Aptien still continued to accompany me on my visits to see Tihanna. Tihanna's aunt had been very poorly for some time, and on one occasion when I'd returned to the Pa-ra-lati village, Tihanna told me that her Aunt had passed away during my absence, and as a result of this, she had inherited her Aunt's kol and was now living there by herself. This was very sad news of course, but it did allow us a lot more opportunity to be alone together. And after that, it was only going to be a matter of time…but on my very next visit, Tihanna swiftly informed me that she was pregnant with my child.

Well…that was it. I really didn't have much choice now other than to face my father and tell him the truth. I told Tihanna that I intended to be true to my word and marry her, and I don't know if I was trying to convince her or myself, but I assured her that everything was going to be just fine.

If only it could have been that simple…

As I headed back home again with Merren and Aptien by my side, I thought that it was probably best if I pre-warn them of my plan to tell my father about Tihanna and me, and to reassure them that neither of them would be implicated in any way. So bringing my horse to a complete standstill, I waited for Merren and Aptien to realise that I'd stopped and head back to me. And there in the middle of nowhere in particular, I informed them of my predicament. Aptien put his hands to his head in a gesture of despair and said:

"You know your father's going to go crazy don't you? He's never going to allow you to marry a Pa-ra-lati girl."

"He's going to kill us all for sure," said Merren, with a sigh.

"Just tell him you didn't know anything about it…don't worry…I'll back you up."

"Maybe, but I've still got a really bad feeling about all of this," said Merren, shaking his head.

"Yeah…me too, mate," said Aptien in agreement. "But I'm more worried about what's going to happen to the Chief here than I am about us. Oh well…May the Great Spirit have mercy on us all…that's all I can say!"

There was nothing more to be said, I'd obviously made up my mind, and they both knew only too well by now that there was no chance in a month of Sundays that I was ever going to change it. Back home I wasted no time at all in seeking out my father's whereabouts. I was told that he was attending to the horses, so this would be an ideal time to catch him on his own. So making my way down to the paddock, I was relieved to find that he was still there. I felt fairly confident as I strode over to him and boldly told him that I had something very important to tell him, but before I did, he must first promise to let me finish telling him the whole story before he reacted. He could see by the serious expression on my face, that whatever it was that I was about to tell him must have been very important to me, so he agreed to hear my whole story before reacting.

As I proceeded to explain about Tihanna and myself, and about her being pregnant, and of my intention to marry her, a look of utter consternation began to spread across his face. I could see the fury clearly building in his eyes, but true to his word – he held his tongue. I blatantly lied about Merren and Aptien being totally unaware of my relationship with Tihanna, and that I'd only decided to tell them on the way back home, and as such, they couldn't and shouldn't, be implicated in any way. And after I'd finally finished confessing all, I was really hopeful that my father would see reason, but instead he looked so angry by now, that I really thought he might explode at any moment, and I felt my confidence melt away as fast as a snow flake in a furnace.

"Have you completely lost your mind? You stupid boy – it's completely out of the question. I forbid you ever to see her again. Whatever were you thinking?

I can never permit you to marry a Pa-ra-lati girl. How do you think it would look if I was to allow my own son to marry a Pa-ra-lati?

"Don't you realise the consequences of such a marriage? If I were to allow this…it would open the door for others to follow suit, and that is just totally unacceptable. We depend upon the strict rules, and the definite order of a caste system for the continuation and stability of our whole society, and without it, our very way of life would just crumble to dust. And I'm sorry to say this son, but I can't allow 'any one' to jeopardise that balance. NO ONE! …And that means you too! So you can just forget all about it right now! I don't want to hear another word spoken on the matter…ever! Do you hear me?"

There was no doubt in my mind that he meant every word, but I wasn't going to give in that easily.

"But she's carrying my child – your grandchild. Don't you care about that at all?" I pleaded.

"No! …I don't," he replied sharply. "There are far more important things at stake here, and there's no room for foolish sentiment. You're forbidden from ever going there again, and you're never to mention anything about this matter to me, or to anyone else ever again, and that's my final word on the matter. This conversation is over."

And with that he angrily walked off leaving me standing there alone. If that's the way he wanted it – then so be it. I could be just as stubborn as he could…if not more so. I was just going to have to show him that I meant business too – and that he couldn't just order me to do something that I knew was inherently wrong, and just expect me to meekly obey him without question. And regardless of what he said, I was still determined to marry Tihanna. So I went back to our kol, took a harness and a saddle blanket, walked back to the paddock, harnessed up my horse and defiantly disobeyed him by riding off alone to be with Tihanna.

I don't know exactly how long it took my father before he'd worked out what I'd done, but it couldn't have been very long, as within a couple of hours of me arriving at the Pa-ra-lati village, a party of six of my father's finest warriors had arrived to track me down and bring me back home again…forcibly if necessary. I knew that sooner or later they'd come looking for me, so I just sat with Tihanna waiting for them to turn up. And as I had made no real attempt to hide, they were soon able to catch up with me.

"Manu Kai…I'm really sorry, but we're here to take you back by the direct order of your father – with force if necessary," said one of them, after they had barged straight into Tihanna's kol. I knew that there was very little point in trying to argue with them, so without making a fuss, I allowed them to quietly escort me to my horse. I also knew that my father was going to be absolutely furious with me for disobeying him – but at least I had made my point. So now I was just going to have to face up to the consequences of my actions when I got back, and no sooner had we done so, than I was immediately frog marched straight to my father's kol where he was sat there awaiting my return.

Merren and Aptien had obviously guessed what I'd done, and were now purposely hanging around in an attempt to find out what was happening. I had to pass them on my way to see my father, they were both just helplessly stood there like two orphaned lambs, and I could see by the look on their faces that they were obviously both very concerned.

My father had obviously made sure that my mother and sisters were somewhere else right now so that we could talk in private, and as soon as his men had delivered me to him, he immediately signalled for them to leave us.

"Sit down, Kai – we need to talk," he said coldly pointing to a wooden stool.

I sat down and stared down at the floor preparing myself for his wrath. I was expecting him to be really angry with me, but instead he just calmly proceeded to explain to me how unacceptable my actions were, and that my defiance would not be tolerated. And although he understood my feelings, I was also going to have to understand that we are all governed by certain rules and a strict code of conduct, and I was just going to have to learn to accept this fact, and my behaviour was not only unacceptable, but a complete waste of everybody's time, as nothing I did was ever going to change a single thing. And one way or another I would just have to yield and give up this infantile display of defiance, or unfortunately he would be forced to punish me until I did yield. He asked me if I understood, and my reply to that was that I did.

"Good!" he said, and to my utter relief, he allowed me to leave.

Although I fully understood everything he'd just said to me, it made absolutely no difference whatsoever, as I immediately jumped straight back on my horse, and I rode all the way back to Tihanna's village.

I wasn't there for very long, when the same party of six very annoyed looking warriors turned up to fetch me back once again. They had completely surrounded me, and they just stood there with their arms folded across their chests silently staring at me with totally blank expressions on their faces. And as I stood looking around at them all, I couldn't help thinking what a fine sight they made, and how between them all they had even managed to slightly intimidate me. I just nodded, and meekly allowed them to escort me to my horse. They had my father's full permission to forcibly bring me back if necessary, so I knew better than to try and resist.

Arriving back, I was once again immediately escorted to face my father's wrath. To say he looked furious would be an understatement, and glowering at me menacingly; he pointed to the same wooden stool and loudly commanded me to sit! I immediately sat down, and 'he' immediately stood up and began to pace up and down the kol.

"What's it going to take before it finally sinks in, Kai? Do you want to force me to horse whip some sense into you?" he said, angrily banging his fist down hard on a table. "Well…do you?"

"No, Father – I just want to marry Tihanna – that's all I want," was my unrelenting reply.

"I've been very patient with you, Kai, but my patience is fast running out, and right now you are very close to a horse whipping. This is your last and final warning. If you do this again, you'll leave me with no other alternative but to punish you severely. DO YOU UNDERSTAND?"

"Yes, Father," was all that I could really say. And so once again – I was allowed to walk away scot free.

I walked out through the doorway of my father's kol, and straight into Merren and Aptien, who'd been quietly eves-dropping along with the six warriors who had been sent to fetch me back again. Merren and Aptien immediately sandwiched me in between the pair of them, and linking their arms through mine, they practically lifted me off my feet.

"A word in your ear young warrior," said Merren.

"How would you like to come and hang out with us for a while?" asked Aptien. "And what if I don't want to?" I asked, looking at them both in turn.

"You would…well that's excellent! So let's all go then shall we?" said Aptien, grinning at me. And with that, they quite forcibly frog marched me all the way to their kol – and straight in through the doorway.

"Sit down, Kai," ordered Merren.

Merren and Aptien shared this kol with two other warriors as it made far more sense for them all to live together, as none of them had any family, and they could all share the chores and the cooking between the four of them. The kol was empty at the moment, so it was quite private, and perfect for their so called…word in my ear!

"Just sit down, Manu Kai…you're not going anywhere," said Aptien, standing in front of the doorway blocking my escape.

"You can't keep me a prisoner here," I protested.

Merren sighed, and slammed his hand so hard against the inner structure of the kol that he actually managed to crack the wood.

"Look, Manu Kai, we can't just stand by and let you do this – you're really pushing your luck now. Your father doesn't want to punish you – that's obvious, but if you do this again, he's not going to have any choice, and we really don't want to see you get a horse whipping. So please, by the very breath of our ancestors – just yield damn you!"

"I can't, you don't understand…if I back down now…I've lost! I'm not going to give up, so you might as well let me go now, as you have to let me go eventually. I really don't care if I get a whipping, that won't stop me either," I said defiantly.

"Manu Kai – as much as we respect your sheer determination to win this impossible battle of wits, you just don't know your father like we do. You are your father's son for sure – but you have no idea what you're up against," said Aptien, shaking his head.

"How long do you intend on keeping me here?"

"For as long as it takes to get you to see some sense," replied Aptien.

"OK," I said, humbly looking down at the ground. "What you've said has made a lot of sense to me, I know that I'm stubborn, and I'm causing everyone loads of problems, and I'm really sorry. Now will you let me go?"

"Nice try, Manu Kai, but you're going to have to be a little bit more convincing than that," said Merren.

Well…that didn't work, but I figured that I probably had a reasonably good chance of making a run for it, but first I had to make sure that both of them were far enough away from me, so I asked if I could have a drink of water. Merren nodded, and he walked over to a table on the far side of the kol to fetch the water. Aptien had moved away from the doorway, and was presently approximately a metre away from me. So seising my chance, I leapt to my feet and made a bolt for the doorway. Aptien tried to grab me, but I was just a little too quick for him, and I was out through the doorway before either of them could stop me. I ran as fast as I could with both of them giving chase behind me. I spotted a horse just a short distance ahead, which luckily for me was already harnessed and ready to go. It had obviously been left un-tethered outside someone's kol, so seising the opportunity – I leapt straight onto its back, gave it a sharp kick, and I galloped off as fast as I possibly could. I figured that the owner of the horse would get it back eventually, but for now, I was just going to have to borrow it for a little while.

I knew that Merren and Aptien had my best interests at heart, but at the end of the day, it was out of their hands what I chose to do. But even so, I really did appreciate their noble efforts to try and protect me from myself. They were just a little out of their depth on this occasion. So once again, I rode all the way back to the Pa-ra-lati village. And just as before, it wasn't very long after I had arrived before my usual escort home had turned up looking for me. I made no attempt to hide, and they knew the most likely place to find me. So they all just casually stood in front of the kol doorway staring at me. One of them then walked over to me, and placing his hand firmly on my arm he said: "We all feel really bad about having to fetch you back this time Manu Kai, but I'm afraid we don't have any choice. You know you're in for a horse whipping this time don't you?"

"Yes, I know," I answered with a deep sigh.

The harsh reality of a horse whipping was beginning to sink in, and I really wasn't relishing the idea, so I began to think about making a bolt for it. I was pretty fast, and I'd certainly give them a fair old run for their troubles. What did I have to lose? Nothing!!!And so, I waited for just the right moment and I made my escape. They all immediately gave chase, and although I really did give it my best shot, they eventually had me cornered. I made a last ditch attempt to get past them, but as I did, two of them grabbed me, and after that – they kept a much tighter grip on me. They certainly weren't going to risk me getting away again that was for sure! "OK…I yield," I said, frowning at one of them.

"Sorry, Manu Kai," he said shrugging his shoulders. "But we've been ordered to tie your hands if you tried to escape…Hold out your hands."

I held out my hands, and he proceeded to tie my wrists together, and then he tied an extra piece of rope between my bound hands for holding onto.

Oh well…I certainly wasn't going anywhere now. They led me over to the horse that I'd 'borrowed', and I was promptly lifted onto its back. It was then securely tied to one of their own horses to ensure that there was going to be absolutely no chance of me making any further attempts to escape.

As soon as we arrived back home again, I was immediately escorted to my father with my hands still bound together. Merren and Aptien were stood close by our kol, and could only stand by and watch helplessly as I was marched straight past them, and in through the entrance of my father's kol. They both looked so utterly miserable, that I actually felt a little sorry for them. My father was sat inside quietly waiting for me once again. He didn't even bother to look at me this time, but just kept staring blankly into space. I knew what was coming to me, and so did everyone else. My father finally stood up, and still not bothering to look at me he said:

"I have tried to give you every chance, Manu Kai, but you were determined to defy me. So with great regret you have given me no other alternative…it's a horse whipping for you this time I'm afraid."

After ordering me to kneel down, my father told one of his men to tie the rope that was still dangling from my tethered hands tightly to the inner structure of the bottom part of the kol. After this had been done, he ordered all his men to leave. I watched as he removed a leather horse whip from a hook on the wall, and as he turned to walk towards me, I immediately looked down at the floor, purposely avoiding making any eye contact with him, and steeling myself, I tensed every muscle in my body and waited for what I knew was coming.

"You wouldn't learn the easy way Manu Kai, so perhaps 'this' will help you to understand." As the first lash of the whip left its mark across my back, I was shocked at the sheer intensity of the pain as it shot through my whole body. I tried very hard not to flinch, as to do so was to show weakness, but it was impossible. And as my father struck me with that whip, over and over again, every lash increasingly more painful than the last, the whole of my back felt as though it was on fire, but even so, I swore a silent oath to myself that I would rather die than allow my father to break my spirit.

After my father had dealt me five lashes of the whip, he stopped and asked me:

"Are you ready to yield now?"

I raised my eyes from the ground for the first time since I'd been forcibly brought to him, and defiantly staring him in the eyes I replied:

"No…never!"

"Have it your way," he said, and he proceeded to give me five more lashes, after which he asked me the same question again. But even though the pain was excruciating, I still refused to yield, and so he gave me another five lashes, and then once more – he asked me the very same question.

"NO NEVER!" I yelled at him.

"You will yield damn you. YIELD," he shouted back at me angrily, striking me again and again. The pain was so great by now, that I really thought he was probably going to kill me; when suddenly I found myself standing on the other side of the kol, and although I could clearly see myself lying limp upon the ground, and my father who was still standing over me with the whip. I felt strangely detached and removed from the whole situation. And best of all – I couldn't feel any pain any more.

Just then Garenhir suddenly burst in through the entrance to the kol, and in a very commanding tone of voice he shouted:

"HERIAN…ENOUGH! Can't you see that he's had enough, you must stop this now or you are going to kill him…that is if you haven't done so already."

Allowing the whip to fall from his hand, my father just stood there motionless as Garenhir hurried over to where I lay unconscious upon the ground; the whip which had been used to render me so, now lay coiled upon the ground next to me like a venomous snake.

"He refused to yield Garenhir," said my father, grimly. "What was I supposed to do?" "He was never going to yield Herian – you're just going to end up killing him," replied Garenhir, sharply.

Garenhir knelt down in front of me, and using a small blade which he always carried, he quickly freed my hands.

"Manu Kai," he said, lifting my head very slightly.

But after failing to get any response, he quickly fetched a pitcher of water, and after splashing my face a couple of times, he began repeating my name over and over again.

On seeing that Garenhir was still unable to get any response, my father stared blankly at the horse whip that now lay discarded upon the ground for a few moments before taking a few steps backwards, and slumping heavily onto a wooden stool.

"What have I done, Garenhir? …What have I done?" he lamented.

Garenhir checked my pulse:

"Don't worry…you haven't killed him. But I dread to think…if I hadn't intervened when I did, Herian."

I was still stood outside my body; watching and listening to everything that was going on, but I felt so peaceful and so liberated from all the pain and suffering of this earthly plane of existence, that I was certainly in no hurry to return to my physical body. I continued to watch as Garenhir made a sign of some sort on my forehead before placing both of his hands on my head. He then began to speak in a strange dialect, and although I couldn't understand the words, they had a strange effect on me, and I immediately felt a pulling sensation, and then very suddenly I felt myself hovering just above my physical body. I could hear a strange crackling sound which was very much like the sound of static electricity – only much louder, and I felt myself being drawn back into my body again. And in a flash of silvery blue crackling light...I was back.

I was immediately struck by an overwhelming intensity of pain which made me I cry out. I was aware of Garenhir telling me to take some deep breaths. But as I looked at my father sitting there watching me, I felt such anger towards him for having done this to me, that really I wanted him to suffer just as I was suffering now, and so with vengeance in my heart I yelled at him:

"FEEL PAIN," and with that, my father immediately folded up in agony and collapsed to the ground.

"Manu Kai...NO! STOP!" commanded Garenhir.

But to no avail. So in order to break my focus, he slapped me across the face, and holding me by the shoulders, he forced me to look into his eyes.

"Manu Kai...You must stop!"

This time Garenhir had managed to break my focus, and I cried out in frustration, anger, and pain. Garenhir concerns turned to my father, who was by now speechless with shock, and still obviously in a great deal of pain.

"Herian I'm going to have to get him out of here...now! So I'll come back and see to you just as soon as I possibly can."

Garenhir ran outside, and seeing that Merren and Aptien were both still hanging around outside, he called them over to give him a hand to get me to his kol. They both immediately ran over, and on entering the kol they must have wondered what on earth had happened, as both my father and I were still on the ground, and obviously both in need of medical assistance.

"What's going on?" asked Merren confused.

"Never mind about that now...just get Manu Kai out of here," replied Garenhir.

And on seeing the state that I was in, both Merren and Aptien quickly linked their arms through mine, and lifted me up from the ground. Garenhir told them to take me straight to his kol. He then asked my father if he would be all right if he left him for a short time, as he was obviously still in a lot of pain. Unable to speak, my father nodded his head in response. Garenhir told him to remain exactly where he was, and that he'd send someone to go and fetch his trusted friend Vasmer to come and stay with him until he could return.

After we had reached Garenhir's kol, Merren and Aptien helped me inside and gently sat me down on a pile of soft sheepskin blankets. Garenhir then told Merren and Aptien to quickly go and fetch all the Agari that they could find. He then removed my boots, and proceeded to paint symbols on the soles of my feet and the palms of my hands, and then on my forehead and throat. He removed my tunic and proceeded to paint symbols all down the front of my body, while all the while mumbling incantations of some sort to himself. He then cast a full circle all around me, and told me not to step outside of it. He then began to mix together some sort of potion, adding many different ingredients that he kept in clay jars. And after he had given it a good stir, he handed it to me, and told me to drink it straight down.

"What is it?" I asked him.

"It will help you…just drink it," he ordered.

I drank it down in one go. "It tastes disgusting," I said, pulling a face.

"Yes, I know – it is pretty bad. But it's going to help you, and that's the important thing."

Merren and Aptien arrived back with five Agari priests…and Sai. They all just stood there staring at me dumbfounded, as none of them had a clue what was going on. So Garenhir proceeded to explain everything that had happened, and that he had already taken every precaution as was fitting for this situation, and that he'd also given me a powerful sedative and pain killer. I looked at Merren and Aptien, who were both listening intently, and when Garenhir explained the part about me having inflicted pain on my father with a force of my will – they both just stared at me open mouthed in astonishment. I suppose their reaction was only to be expected. I would have preferred they hadn't got to know about it though. Not because I didn't trust them, but because I was afraid that they might think differently of me now.

"Whoa," said Aptien looking at Merren, who raised his eyebrows and said: "Well I'll be damned."

"You two shouldn't really have heard that," said Garenhir, realising his mistake. "So please promise me that it'll never go any further, I must have your word that it will stay between just the two of you."

Both Merren and Aptien swore to Garenhir that anything they heard or saw would never go any further than between the two of them.

"Good!" said Garenhir, before informing everyone that he was going to have to go and look in on my father, now that all immediate concerns had been addressed.

"I'm going to have to leave it to you to tend to Kai's back," said Garenhir to Sai.

"That looks a bit sore," said Merren, wincing. "How many lashes was that?" he asked, taking a closer look at the deep welts on my back.

"I don't know…I think I must have passed out after about thirty," I answered very groggily.

"That's just crazy," said Aptien, shaking his head in a gesture of despair.

He was about to say something else, but he just pursed his lips and raised his eyes to the roof and sighed instead.

The sedative was beginning to kick in by now, and I was finding it very hard to focus on anything. And even remaining in an upright position was becoming increasingly difficult. Seeing this – Sai walked over to me and said:

"Kai, if you lie down on your front, I can clean your back for you…if that's okay with you of course."

I could tell by the look on his face, that he knew exactly what Garenhir had given me, and most likely – how it would affect me too. He was our Derkesthai's prodigy after all…"Yes, okay – you're the boss," I said submissively.

However my compliant behaviour didn't go entirely unnoticed by Merren and Aptien, who just couldn't resist having a little dig at me. I suppose under the circumstances you couldn't really blame them.

"Well…that's the very first time I've ever heard you say that to anyone before. All I can say is it's a pity you couldn't have been quite so agreeable when we tried to prevent all this from happening in the first place," said Merren, scowling at me.

I actually found Merren's vexation strangely reassuring, as it proved that even after learning what I'd been able to do to my father, he didn't appear to be all that affected by it, and I hoped the same was going to be true of Aptien.

Sai said nothing, and just continued to help me lie face down so that he could tend to my back.

"This all feels strangely familiar," I said, looking up at Sai.

"Yes, it does a bit," he said with a little smile. "It looks like you're just going to have to put up with me again."

As Sai began to gently clean my back, I couldn't help yelping as it was very sore.

"Sorry!" he said apologetically.

"You will be if you do that again," I said sarcastically.

Sai stopped what he was doing for a moment, and after seeing the slightly twisted smirk on my face, and realising that I was only teasing, he tutted loudly, and narrowing his eyes a little he quietly whispered in my ear:

"Just remember…I have you at my mercy right now."

"Just get on with it," I said with a sigh.

Aptien and Merren walked over to sit with the Agari priests, while Sai tended to my back. They were all just quietly talking amongst themselves, and for some reason it made me think of the strange friendship which had somehow managed to form between Merren, Aptien, and myself. They kind of reminded me of two faithful hounds, as they were never too far away, and they always followed me around everywhere I went. But for the life of me, I really couldn't think why as all I ever seemed to do was to cause them trouble.

Garenhir returned after a short while, and kneeling down beside me he said:

"Kai – your father is fully recovered now, and he's genuinely very sorry for losing control and causing you so much harm. He really wants to talk to you, and he's going be coming over to see you shortly."

"I don't want to see him," I said sharply. "I need some time to think about what I'm going to do, as when I'm well enough, I'm planning on leaving here for good, and I don't want him trying to influence me. So please tell him to leave me alone."

"Leaving…But where will you go?" asked Garenhir, looking rather shocked by my sudden announcement.

"I plan to go and see Tihanna first, and then if she's willing, we'll both go and live with the Hun. They don't have a caste system, and I know that we'll 'both' be welcome there."

Garenhir told the other Agari priests that they may as well all go home for now, as it was very late, and if he needed them for any reason he would send word to them. And so they all wished us a very good night before going on their way.

Merren and Aptien also looked a little surprised to hear of my plan, as did Sai. I could see Merren and Aptien quietly whispering to one another with their backs turned to the rest of us, and then suddenly they both turned around.

"If you're leaving…then we're both coming with you, Kai," said Merren.

"We'll talk about it some other time," I said, not really caring a great deal about anything right now.

After realising that I was pretty much out of it right now, Merren and Aptien also left to get some sleep. Merren told Garenhir that they'd come and check in on me tomorrow, and just seconds after they had left – my father arrived. I really didn't want him anywhere near me right now, so Garenhir had to ask him to step outside so that they could talk. I could hear Garenhir explaining to my father that he'd given me a strong sedative, and that I wasn't really up to seeing him just yet, and also that he felt it was his duty to inform him, that I intended to go and live with the Huns as soon as I was fit enough. I then heard my father asking him what he thought he should do.

"You have to let him go Herian – I don't see what else you can do," replied Garenhir.

To which my father replied, "I've gone and lost my son…haven't I?"

"All we can do I'm afraid is to hope that one day he'll return of his own free will."

My father had obviously decided to head back to his kol, as Garenhir came back inside again and told Sai that he should also head back to his kol now and get some sleep, and then after making me as comfortable as he possibly could, he finally settled down for the night himself. I had a feeling that it was going to be a long one…

It seemed to take forever, but I'd obviously managed to drop off eventually, as the next thing I can remember is Garenhir waking me with some breakfast. I didn't really feel like eating, but as he'd gone to the trouble of making it for me, I thought I'd better try and eat some of it at very least. A little while later Sai turned up, and sitting himself down right next to me he asked me how I was feeling. I answered that apart from my back, and the fact that my whole life was in a total mess right now…I was never better!

Sai already knew of my relationship with Tihanna, and he was fully aware of the situation that had led up to all of this. However; he had remained true to

149

his word and had kept his promise to keep my secret safe, and for that reason I knew that he was a friend in the truest sense, and I would surely miss him when I left here. I would also miss my mother and sisters, and although I was still very angry with him, I knew that I would probably miss my father too. But most of all I was going to Miss Garenhir, and although it saddened me, I felt that I had no choice other than to leave after what has happened.

Sai stood up to make room for Garenhir, who had made it quite plain to him that he wanted to sit down next to me.

"Manu Kai, I just want you to know that we are always going to be here for you, and if ever you need to talk about something, or you are in need of any help or advice of any kind, just remember…I am still your Derkesthai. There can be no turning your back on the path that you have chosen – so please remember that also. So whenever you're ready…I'll be here waiting for you."

One week later, and my back had already healed well, and now at last I felt well enough to travel. So after saying my goodbyes to everyone, I began to gather any personal belongings that I wanted to take with me from my father's kol. And even though my father kept a respectful distance the whole time, I would have much preferred him not to have been there at all. And although we only made eye contact once, I could plainly see the sadness in his eyes, so I made sure that I was careful to avoid making any further eye contact with him after that. Neither of us had won this battle of wits. We were both stuck somewhere in between hard choices, and nowhere. And so without a single word being exchanged between us, I carefully placed the Akinakes that he'd given me on his bed. And without glancing back – I quickly walked out and joined Merren and Aptien who were patiently waiting for me outside. They had already received my father's blessings to go with me when they had explained to him of their plan to do so the previous day.

And so it was that I left the home that I'd known for the first fifteen winters of my life, and with Merren and Aptien at my side, I rode out to go and get Tihanna.

12

Winds of Change

We arrived at the Pa-ra-lati village just as we had done so many times before, but this time it was very different, as we wouldn't be staying for a few days before returning home again to my father's village; we'd be heading straight to the Huns instead.

Tihanna looked horrified as I proceeded to explain to her exactly what had happened since the last time I'd seen her. And after she insisted on taking a look at the damage to my back, I told her of my plans for the both of us, and that if she didn't want to come with me and live with the Huns, I would understand, and although I would obviously be a little upset, I would accept her decision, as this was obviously going to be a massive step for her to take. But I also explained to her that this was the only way that we were ever going to be together, and although I loved her very much and I wanted her to come with me, she needed to take some time to think about what was going to be the best thing for her and our child. And only if she was absolutely sure that it was what she truly wanted should she make the decision to come with me. I told her that we were going to stay here for a couple of days which would give her some time to think things over, and it would also give her enough time to gather up her belongings, and to take care of anything that she needed to, 'if' she decided to come with us.

Tihanna had no hesitation in telling me that she didn't care where we went, just as long as we could get married and be together. I was obviously overjoyed to hear her say that, but even so, I still insisted in her having a little time to think it over first.

I wanted to cause as little fuss as possible, so we all bunked down together in Tihanna's kol for a few nights, while she took care of the few things that she needed to before leaving. I told her not to give her kol away for the time being, and just to entrust it to someone for safe keeping instead…just in case she ever changed her mind and wanted to return for any reason. I truly wanted her to be happy, and I would never have tried to stop her if she ever wanted to leave me and return home. Tihanna remained adamant that all she ever needed to make her happy was to be with me. But even at my young age, I was wise enough to know how quickly one's apparent needs can alter with a sudden change of circumstances. It's very hard to imagine that your feelings for someone; or for the things that you feel so passionate about, could one day become swept up by the winds of change, and just like the autumn leaves on a tree they can crumble and turn to dust.

After a couple more days, we all finally set out from the Pa-ra-lati village for our three-day journey to the Hun encampment. I'm glad to say that our journey went unhindered. And when we finally arrived we were given an enthusiastic welcome, and although my uncle, and my cousin Altan, were both genuinely pleased to see me, they was also equally concerned as they obviously knew that there had to be something very wrong for me to have just turned up out of the blue like this with Merren, Aptien, and a pregnant woman.

Altan ordered two Hun warriors to take good care of our horses, and they were promptly led away. Altan had grown into a fine young warrior, and had managed to earn himself a lot of respect in the process, and he now proudly stood as the second in command to his father – and the next in line for the position of Khan.

My uncle ordered that refreshments should be brought for us immediately. He couldn't fail to notice that Tihanna was pregnant, and so he made sure that she was made as comfortable as possible before requesting that I, along with Merren and Aptien, should come and sit with Altan and himself for talks. We were immediately joined by a couple of my uncle's right-hand men, who just so happened to have been close by as we'd arrived. My uncle was understandably very eager for me to explain to him the circumstances which had led to our very unexpected and impromptu visit.

One of the warriors present was Yesukai; the very same warrior who I'd once managed to impress with my bow skills as a young child. He just nodded to me respectfully, and I respectfully nodded back, and sitting down around the very same table that my father and his extremely brave little band of warriors had been seated all those years previously, I proceeded to explain the reason that we were here.

Merren and Aptien had both managed to pick up a little of the Hun language during their previous visits here, but not quite enough as yet for them to be able to follow a full conversation. So after I had given my uncle the full explanation as to why I was presently homeless, and expressed to him my wish for the four of us to join with the Huns as permanent residents in his native tongue, I asked him if he'd mind if we spoke in Scythian for a little while, so that Aptien and Merren could understand what was being said.

"If they want to live here permanently, they had better learn to speak our language, and so should your woman over there," replied my uncle.

I just nodded in agreement, not really wanting to push the subject. However; I was pleased when he showed respect for my wishes, and began speaking in Scythian while Merren and Aptien were present.

I knew that my uncle had always hoped that one day I would choose to come and live with the Huns, and so although he appeared outwardly very sad that things had worked out the way that they had for me, I knew that deep down he was secretly pleased that I had been pushed into making this decision. And as I proceeded to explain to him that as Tihanna was pregnant with my child, it was very important to me that we should be married, he looked absolutely delighted, and nodding his head in agreement, he said that he would make all the necessary arrangements as soon as possible. He then asked one of his men to go and immediately organise the building of two yurts, and to include all basic comforts and amenities so that all of our immediate needs were taken care of. My uncle then turned to Merren and Aptien, and speaking to them in broken Scythian he said:

"You two go…with Altan…help erect yurts…you go help now."

All three of them obediently stood up, and Merren and Aptien both looked across at me for my approval before leaving. I nodded to them, and they both proceeded to follow Altan outside. Glancing across at Tihanna, I could see that she was engrossed in the study of the typical Hun décor of my uncle's yurt, when suddenly she noticed that I was looking at her. She looked so lost and vulnerable right now, that I really wanted to leave my uncles side and sit beside her and sooth her fears with gentle words of comfort, but I gave her a reassuring smile instead. I knew that all of this must have been very overwhelming for her, as the nearest she had ever come to having any contact with the Huns was me, and if anything, I was culturally a lot more Scythian than I was Hunnic.

My uncle had obviously picked up on my concern for Tihanna.

"Don't worry, Kai…she'll be well taken care of."

"Thank you, Uncle – I deeply appreciate all of this, and I shall forever be in your debt."

"Kai…you are like a long-lost son to me; a son who has finally returned home after a long journey, I'm simply welcoming you back home again. Why don't you go and sit with your woman for a while…what's her name again?"
"It's Tihanna."

"Ahhh…yes, that's it, she looks very nervous, and that's not good for the baby. I'll go and see how they're getting on with erecting these yurts, you go and join her for a while," he said, signalling to Yesukai and the other remaining Hun warriors to follow him outside.

I immediately walked over and sat down next to Tihanna, and as I gently took her hand in mine, I noticed that she was trembling like a frightened calf about to be sacrificed.

"There's no reason at all for you to be afraid," I said, giving her a reassuring hug. "That Hun warrior that I was just talking to…well, he's actually my uncle, and it just so happens that he's also the Chief here…the word is 'Khan' in Hunnic, and he will personally to go out of his way to make sure that you are well taken care of. You'll probably find things a bit strange here at first, but you'll soon get used to the ways of the Huns, and eventually you'll even learn to speak the language, and remember…you always have the option of returning to your people if ever want to."

"You didn't tell me your uncle was the chief of the Huns," she said, looking very surprised.

"Well…I guess there are a few things about me that I haven't quite got around to telling you yet Tihanna," I said, shrugging my shoulders. "But maybe it's about time that I did. You probably have a right to know, I'm just not sure where to start that's all. But for now at least please trust me when I tell you that no harm will ever come to you here."

Three days later, Tihanna and I were married. The only Scythians present were Merren and Aptien, and although I was happy that at last we could get married, my happiness was marred by thoughts of my father and mother, and for my Derkesthai, and all my dear friends that I'd left behind in Scythia. But I did my very best to hide my sadness for Tihanna's sake.

We all got on with the job of trying to settle down to a new life with the Huns, especially Tihanna, who had surprised us all by passionately embracing her new role as the wife of an Imperial Hun warrior, and she took to learning the

154

language, traditions, and the religious beliefs of the Huns with such enthusiasm, that I really couldn't have hoped for more. Tihanna proved herself to be a very bright and astute pupil, and within a few short months, she had managed to learn enough of the Hun language to be able to hold a simple conversation.

Merren and Aptien had also managed to surprise me, as I secretly didn't really expect them to have stayed as long as they had. But they were both like extra sticky glue, and had faithfully managed to remain firmly stuck to me throughout the thick and the thin of it.

One evening Merren, Aptien, and I, had joined Yesukai and my cousin Altan, along with a dozen or so young Hun warriors around a camp fire. This was a favourite tradition of the Hun, as it was an excellent way in which the younger warriors could get together and have a few drinks. I'd had one or two myself, so I decided now was as good a time as any to ask Merren and Aptien why they'd both decided to follow me here...I asked Merren first. "Oh...I don't know," he said, "someone's got to look after you."

"What about you, Aptien?"

"What...and miss all this. Anyway – I just followed him," he said, pointing at Merren.

"You're both quite mad – you know that don't you?" I said, shaking my head.

Raising his hands upwards in a nonchalant manner, Aptien just shrugged his shoulders and then carried on drinking.

"Maybe...But hey! What's with all the questions all of a sudden? We're here because we chose to be – Isn't that enough?" said Merren.

"I was just wondering what I was going to have to do to get rid of the pair of you...that's all," I said, screwing up my face.

Aptien tutted loudly, and he gave me a hard dig in the arm with his elbow.

"Is that so – well, enough of all your wonderings for now, and pass me that instead."

Aptien pointed to a large pitcher of fermented mare's milk which was presently resting on a flat stone down by my feet.

"Get it yourself," I said, rubbing my arm.

And I shoved him so hard in avengement for my bruised arm that he collided into Merren.

"Oy...Watch it!" said Merren, giving Aptien a really hard shove in return.

Aptien glared icily at Merren before returning his hard shove with an even harder one, which resulted in Merren completely losing his balance, and

155

somehow managing to strike Yesukai squarely in the side of the head as he flailed his arms about in order to steady himself. Yesukai stared coldly at Merren, giving him one of his finest, 'I'm going to kill you any second now' stares.

Merren looked absolutely mortified. He didn't know Yesukai quite as well as the rest of us did. Altan had been sat opposite quietly watching our antics. He was obviously finding it all very amusing, and as soon as our eyes met we both burst out laughing. It felt just like old times, and I couldn't help but remember my very first encounter with Yesukai, and how he was able to freeze me to the very spot with one of his infamous stares. I guess the look on Merren's face was just too much even for Yesukai, as he began to laugh too. Merren quickly realised the joke was all on him, and he gave a genuine sigh of relief before pretending to wipe the sweat from his brow.

"Phew...you really had me going there for a moment," he said to Yesukai, in the best Hunnic that I'd ever heard him speak so far.

"I know..." said Yesukai, with a satisfied grin on his face. "You should have seen the look on your face."

Yesukai then surprised Merren by giving him a really hard shove, which ended up with him crashing straight into Aptien, who in his valiant attempt to try and move out of the way, had somehow managed to send me sprawling to the ground in the process. Everyone was in fits of laughter by now.

"Cheers, mate!" I said, glowering at Aptien.

"Whoops...Sorry, Chief!" said Aptien, rolling his eyes. "But while you're down there – do you think you could pass that jug up to me?"

I responded by making a very rude gesture at him, before relenting and picking up the jug and passing it up to him. Aptien just shook his head and tutted as he took the jug from my outstretched hand. He drank some of its contents before passing it to Merren, who then did the same before passing it to Yesukai, who responded by giving him a friendly slap on the back. Yesukai took a long drink from the jug, and after wiping his mouth with the back of his hand he turned back to Merren, and obviously worse for wear due to all the alcohol that he'd already managed to consume, he put his arm around Merren's shoulder, and told him that he was determined to make Huns out of the both of them...even if it killed them. *I can hardly wait*, I thought to myself, as I picked myself up from the ground brushing away some of the dust from my trousers.

Just then Tihanna, who had been resting in our yurt, came walking over to me and quietly whispered in my ear:

"Kai...I think the baby's coming."

"Go straight back to our yurt and I'd go and fetch someone," I said, suddenly feeling a lot more sober. "Yes...I will," she said, turning to make her way back again.

There was no shortage of people here who could be called upon to help deliver a baby, including five shamans. But it didn't stop me panicking, and in my confusion I couldn't think straight.

"Hay...just stay calm," said Aptien, grabbing me by the arm. "Why don't you go and sit with her for a while; Merren and I will go and find someone."

"Good idea," I said, hurrying off to catch up Tihanna, who by the look of her was obviously in a lot of pain.

As we walked in through the yurt entrance, I asked her how long she'd been getting the pains, and she told me that she had been getting pains since yesterday, but she didn't want to say anything, until she knew that she was closer to the time of actually giving birth.

A few minutes later, Merren and Aptien arrived with two female shamans, and taking one look at Tihanna, they both promptly ordered us all to leave, telling us that we were not allowed to return again until we had received word that it was alright for us to do so.

"He'll be in our yurt with us," said Merren, wrapping his arm around my shoulders and firmly guiding me outside.

The three of us walked the short distance to Merren and Aptien's yurt, after which we waited for what seemed to me like an eternity. Until finally...I heard one of the two female shamans calling to me, so racing outside I could barely contain myself as one of the shamans began to speak, at which point I was joined by an equally impatient Merren and Aptien.

"Relax...everything's fine," said the shaman. "You have a baby daughter."

I found it difficult to take it all in...I was a father!!!I just stood there staring at her open mouthed.

"You can go in...if you want to," prompted the shaman.

"Yes, of course I do...are you kidding?" I said, suddenly finding my voice again.

The female shaman wished us all well then bowed respectfully before taking her leave. Merren and Aptien both looked as relieved and as happy as I was. And they both began to whoop and cheer loudly.

"Wait here for a minute," said Merren, before promptly disappearing back into the yurt. However, he wasn't gone long before he soon reappeared again, this time with the jug of fermented mare's milk that he'd had the hindsight to take back to the yurt with him.

"Here!" he said, thrusting it towards me.

I took a couple of good swigs, before handing it to Aptien who did the same, before passing it back to Merren who after gulping down a fair few mouthfuls himself, proceeded to tip the remainder of what was left in the jug all over the three of us.

"Let's go then shall we," said Aptien, grabbing me by my soggy arm, and with the three of us smelling as though we'd spent the night floating in a vat of fermented mare's milk, we made our way over to the yurt that I shared with Tihanna. But just as we reached the doorway, Merren suddenly came to a halt.

"I think it's probably best if me and Aptien wait outside…just for now," he said, grabbing Aptien, who was about to lift up the flap of the yurt.

"Yes, okay," I said, as I caught a glimpse into the yurt as the wind caught the flap and blew it slightly open.

As I stepped inside the yurt, the other female shaman who was still sat with Tihanna stood up to greet me and smiled. She told me that she'd pop in again tomorrow – just to make sure that everything was okay, and then she gave blessings to the three of us and left. Tihanna was obviously very tired after just giving birth, but she looked happy to see me.

"Look, Kai," she said proudly. "We have a little daughter."

And there lying by the side of her, wrapped in a soft felt blanket, was this tiny little person.

"She's beautiful – just like you," I said, sitting down beside her and giving her a gentle hug. I wanted so much for Merren and Aptien to share this moment, as they'd been there right by my side for so long now that they had almost become a part of me, so I asked Tihanna if she'd mind if Merren and Aptien came in for a moment to see the baby. Tihanna smiled and said that she didn't mind. So I walked over to the doorway and popping my head outside, I asked them if they wanted to come in for a minute, and without saying a word they both quietly stepped inside. It was obvious that neither of them really knew what to say, as they both just stood there looking as awkward as two eunuchs in a brothel, until Aptien finally broke the silence by asking:

"What are you going to call her?"

"We've decided to call her Nymadawa," replied Tihanna.

"That's a Hun name, isn't it?" asked Merren.

"You are quite correct – It most certainly is," I replied proudly.

"I think we'd better go and leave them alone now, it's getting quite late," said Merren, giving Aptien a little nudge.

Aptien nodded in agreement, and wished us a restful night's sleep before letting themselves out.

"It's starting to rain," said Aptien, closing the yurt doorway from the outside.

Suddenly there was to be heard the loud rumbling of thunder, which was quickly followed by the loud clattering of thousands of heavy droplets of water, which were now mercilessly laying siege to the outside of our yurt.

"Run," I heard Merren shout, as an almighty bolt of lightning lit up the whole yurt, which was quickly followed by a very loud crack of thunder.

Most of the Huns didn't like thunder storms at all, as they believed that it was a sign that the great God of the sky was angry – but 'I' loved it, and even more than that – I actually felt empowered by it. The intensity of such a sheer and blatant display of the mighty power of the electrical forces of nature seemed to have some kind of magnetic pull on my senses and I felt an irresistible urge to run outside. I gazed down at Tihanna peacefully lying there with our daughter in her arms and I gave her a little smile. She must have thought that I'd finally lost my mind, as I suddenly pulled off my tunic and my boots, and ran half naked out into the storm. And raising my face upwards towards the sky, I closed my eyes and stretched out my arms as I allowed the cool rain to splash all over my face and body. The feeling was almost intoxicating, as each lightning bolt that split the silence of the night sent a thrill to my already heightened senses. I felt so connected to the elemental forces of nature that I was unable to hold onto the sheer intensity of the sensation any longer…and I opened my eyes.

At first, I was unable to take in the sight that beset my eyes, as everything was shimmering with what I can only describe as a conscious active energy of some sort. Garenhir had often spoken of a life force energy which he called 'Prana', he said that all living things were imbued with it – and nothing could exist without it. I was so overwhelmed by the phosphorescent beauty of it all that I was beginning to feel a little giddy; so sitting down cross legged upon the rain soaked ground, I began to study the energy field around my fingers, as both my hands and everything around me began to glow in a blaze of bright vivid shades of living colour. I felt as though I was beginning to dissolve into the very substance of nature itself, and at last I finally understood exactly what my Derkesthai had tried to explain to me about the connectedness of all things, and I knew that everything he had said to me was true.

After I'd had a chance to gather my thoughts together, I stood up and slowly walked back into our yurt. I was completely drenched, and I could see that Tihanna was fast asleep with our baby daughter sleeping soundly next to her. So not wanting to disturb them, I quietly took off my saturated trousers, and after drying myself off as best as I possibly could, I made myself a makeshift bed next to Tihanna and baby Nymadawa. And crawling into my soft bed of furs, I extinguished the flame from the oil lamp which I'd placed next to me, and I made myself comfortable for the night. All that was left now was the low distant murmuring of thunder, and the drip – drip – dripping sound of the water, which was now leaking in through a little hole in the roof of the yurt. As I lay awake reflecting upon the events of the day, my thoughts soon began to wander to my mother and father, and how badly things had turned out between my father and me. I really wished that things could have been different, and that both of my parents could have been here today to share my joy in becoming a father for the first time. I would never had admitted it, but I missed them a lot more at this moment in time than I even wanted to admit to myself. I also missed my Derkesthai, and I longed to be able to tell him all about my experience in the storm. I really hadn't realised until this very moment just how badly I did miss him. I'd neglected my spiritual life since I'd been here, and this very night had managed to find me out.

Dawn wasn't far away, and it was just beginning to get a little lighter, and as I looked across at Tihanna and this new little person who was blissfully sleeping by her side, I thought how perfect they both looked, and I knew that I should have been blissfully happy right now, but there was a deep hole inside of me that even they hadn't managed to fill.

The morning had come all too soon, and it wasn't long before visitors began to arrive with gifts for the new arrival. My uncle was one of the first to arrive, and he brought many fine gifts for the three of us; including some fine new Hunnic clothes and boots for both Tihanna and myself, which he'd had especially made for us, and were all expertly crafted from the finest materials, and to the highest standard possible.

After my uncle had left, I changed into my new clothes and felt every inch a true Imperial Hun warrior. I began to wonder if I was ever really Scythian at all, and as time passed I became more and more Hunnic, and less and less Scythian. I rode with the Hun, I fought alongside the Hun...and unfortunately, I could also drink as hard as any Hun, and oh boy...could they drink!

The blood that coursed through my veins was the blood of a true Hun warrior, and I did my best to bury my Scythian past as deeply within myself as I possibly could. I also did my best to fill the ever deepening hole which was slowly growing inside of me, by constantly anesthetising myself with copious amounts of alcohol, often to the point of passing out. My behaviour was even beginning to concern Merren and Aptien who would often voice their growing concerns, but all to no avail, and it soon became a regular occurrence for them to have to carry me back to my yurt. It must have been very tough on Tihanna too, as although I loved both her and our sweet baby daughter deeply, I was slowly beginning to distance myself further and further away from them. Tihanna often tried to get me to talk to her about whatever it was that was going on with me, but unfortunately this just had the opposite effect, and I'd just close down even more. I knew that my behaviour was making her unhappy, and I sometimes wondered if she'd be much better off if she were to return to her own people; as time and time again it would end up with Tihanna in tears, and me walking out of our yurt and riding off to find somewhere quieter. Only to eventually return and have to repeat the whole process all over again.

One morning Altan came to my yurt to see me, I was still in bed recovering from the night before, and I was in no mood for such an early morning call.

"Come on, Kai – wake up," he insisted ...much to my growing annoyance.

Altan grabbed my blanket, and after failing to grab it back again, I sat upright, folded my arms, and glowered at him. He just stood there with my blanket in his hands, and proceeded to explain to me that he and a few young warriors had planned to head out to the forest today, and go in search of bird of prey eggs. (These would be hatched out and hand reared, and then trained for the use in sport and for hunting.) And he asked me if I fancied coming along with them; in fact he literally wouldn't take no for an answer, and so after much irritation, I eventually gave up and very reluctantly agreed to go. So moaning and complaining the whole time I got dressed and fastened my weapons, and after packing a few provisions I quickly informed Tihanna of the plan before leaving our yurt and harnessing up my horse. Altan and six other young Hun warriors had all been patiently waiting for me at the westerly point of entrance to the encampment. But just as we were all about to leave, for some reason I began to feel a strong sense of uneasiness. But when I tried to explain this to Altan he just casually brushed off my concerns saying…

"You know you need to stop drinking so much, it's already beginning to rot your brain. Come on, cousin – it's time we headed off. We can talk later."

Altan gave his horse a little kick and sped off ahead of us. I just sighed deeply, and along with the other six warriors in the group – I proceeded to follow on after him.

Perhaps he was right – maybe all the alcohol really was starting to screw with my head. I knew that I was definitely very close to alcoholism. I began to think about what Altan had just said to me, and although he hadn't really said anything which hadn't already been said to me by several others before…including Merren and Aptien. For some reason, something just seemed to click into place with me this time, and I made myself a promise that as soon we got back, I would get myself sorted out – even if I had to ask others for help in order to do it.

13
Goodbye Old Friend

We continued to ride at a steady pace until we eventually reached the half way point of a shallow river, and as it was beginning to get quite dark by now, we decided that it would be best to make camp and to rest here for the night, and to cross the river first thing in the morning. There was quite a large thicket of trees and bushes growing nearby which would offer us some protection from the elements at least, as there was a very cold chill to be felt in the air here tonight.

The moon was almost full, and the sky was perfectly clear, so there was enough natural light to allow us all to go and search for enough fallen twigs and branches to build a good fire. We all headed off towards the thicket of trees taking different directions as we went. It wasn't long before I'd managed to collect as many fallen twigs as I could possibly carry. So returning back to camp, I dropped off my bundle of twigs and immediately left to go and collect more. But instead of heading back in the same direction, I decided to take the widest route around the back of the trees; just to see if there were any larger pieces of wood in that area. I could see by the lack of footprints that no one else had been this way. There were plenty of dead branches lying undisturbed on the ground, so I quietly began collecting up a few of the larger fallen branches, when I suddenly became aware of what sounded like two people whispering to one another. The voices seemed to be coming from in amongst the trees, and I was naturally curious to know who it could be. I suppose if I'm to be honest…I was being a bit nosey. Cautiously I made my silent approach to try and see who it was, and if I was able to hear what it was that they were so covertly whispering about. I clearly recognised Altan's voice, and I know this may sound a little bit paranoid, but I wondered if he was actually talking about me, as with all of my problems of late it wouldn't have surprised me at all. I listened very intently to what was being said, and very soon I recognised a second voice, it was the voice of a young warrior called Guyuk, but I couldn't quite make out what he was saying, as he was whispering very quietly, but then I heard Altan say:

"I know…but what are we supposed to do?"

I was really curious to know what they were talking about, and I tried very hard to focus in on what they were saying, but even with my exceptional hearing, I could hear nothing but the occasional rustling of a small rodent crawling around in the fallen leaves. My curiosity began to get the better of me, so I decided to move in a little closer to try and see what was going on. So with the silent stealth of a cat hunting its prey, I moved in closer…and closer…until I could finally see them. At first I couldn't believe the information my eyes were receiving. Put it this way…there could be no doubt about it – Altan and Guyuk were definitely lovers. I don't know what I was expecting to see – but it certainly wasn't this. I was so shocked that I totally forgot myself and stepped out from my hiding place behind the trees, and I just stood there aghast in stunned silence – just openly staring at the pair of them. Guyuk saw me first, and he quickly alerted Altan. They both looked totally mortified to see me standing there, as they both knew that I'd obviously been watching them. I didn't know how to react to this situation, so I just quickly turned around and began to walk away.

Altan called out to me: "Kai…wait."

I took a deep breath, and I waited for him to catch me up. I couldn't look him in the eyes right now, so I just fixed my gaze firmly to the ground. It wasn't that I was uncomfortable with homosexual relationships, as I'd spent the first fifteen years of my life in Scythia where it was just accepted as a natural part of everyday life, and people could be relaxed and open about their sexuality as they chose without any fear of retribution. Unfortunately, it was just the complete opposite with the Huns, and homosexuality was seen as unnatural and completely unacceptable, and was not tolerated at all. In fact the punishment for offenders was very harsh indeed, a public flogging for first offenders, and repeat offenders could actually be executed. I think that it was a mixture of knowing this fact, and the shock of finding out about Altan's sexuality in the way that I had, which had caused me to react in the way that I did. Altan was like the brother I would have liked to have had, and also one of my dearest friends. So I certainly wasn't going to feel any differently towards him just because of his sexuality. And after I'd had a chance to recover from the initial shock, I actually felt okay about it. Altan reached out to me, and he was just about to put his hand on my arm, but he obviously thought better of it, and he held his head in his hands instead. I could see that he was desperately struggling to find something to say to me, and he was obviously deeply distraught.

"Kai…I really wish you hadn't seen that," he finally managed to blurt out. "But you did! So now you know! Please…Please Kai…Don't hate me."

Raising my eyes from the ground, I forced myself to look him in straight in the eyes this time. I could see that he was desperately searching for a clue to how I felt about him right now.

"Of course I don't hate you," I said, shaking my head. "I don't give a damn about your sexuality. You should have been more honest with me though, and then I wouldn't have had to find out like this. You're very lucky that it was me that saw you together and not anyone else. You need to be a lot more careful, Altan. You must promise me that you'll be more careful. Can you imagine if your father ever found out? In the name of our ancestors…you're the next in line for the position of Khan. For pity's sake…listen to me Altan – I messed up big time, and I'm still suffering for it. Why do you think I drink so much all the time eh? But 'you' can't afford to mess up…and especially not like this."

Altan was so relieved by my reaction that he dropped to the ground on his knees before me.

"Oh for pity's sake…get up," I said, dragging him back up to his feet again.

"I was so afraid you'd hate me now that you know…"

There was nothing else left to say, so avoiding drawing this out any longer that was necessary I beckoned to Guyuk, who had been quietly keeping his distance to come and join us. He must have been feeling equally as distraught as Altan.

Struggling to regain some sort of normality I just nodded to him and said: "I think we should all just grab some wood now and head back to the camp – before any one begins to wonder where we are."

"Thank you, Kai," said Guyuk, nodding his head in agreement.

I must admit that I was relieved to discover that the fire had already been lit, and that the other five warriors had returned before us and were now all sat around the fire. What remained of our food rations for the day had also been equally shared out between everyone, so all Altan, Guyuk, and I had to do, was to add our bundles of wood to the pile, and join our comrades for supper before settling down and making ourselves as comfortable as possible for the night. So shielding myself from the direct rays of the moonlight, I pulled my blanket up over my head, and did my best to get some sleep…but it was no use, I was far

165

too restless. For some reason I was plagued by an overbearing sense of uneasiness. It was very much like the sensation that I'd felt just before we'd set out on this journey, and I could feel myself becoming increasingly agitated. I hadn't had any alcohol all day, so thinking that it might be just what I needed to help me get some sleep, I quietly crept over to my horse and unfastened the leather water bottle that I'd brought with me, and twisting off the wooden stop, I took a large swig of its contents. It was just about then that I became aware of someone hiding in the shadows, so quickly pulling out one of my throwing knives from its sheath I turned and faced the intruder.

"Who goes there?" I demanded to know.

Altan stepped out from the cover of darkness, and raising his hands upwards he said:

"Whoa – it's me! You seem a little jittery tonight."

"Yes, well…You should know better than to creep up behind me like that. I could have killed you," I said, tucking my knife back into its sheath.

I took another swig from the bottle, and I was about to put it away when Altan held out his hand and said:

"Before you put that away…"

Altan walked over to me and I handed him the bottle.

"How did you know?" I asked him.

Altan took the bottle from my hand, and after taking a large swig, he wiped his mouth with the back of his hand.

"I guess I know you better than you think I do."

"I just needed something to help me sleep…that's all," I said with a sigh.

Taking another couple of swigs, Altan nodded in agreement before handing me back the bottle.

"Yes, I know what you mean. You don't need to explain. But seriously Kai…if you need my help…or just someone to talk to – just remember…I'm always here for you cousin."

I took one last swig from the bottle before sealing and fastening it back onto the back of my horse.

I didn't really know how to respond to Altan's offer of help, so I just looked at him and nodded. "I guess we both have our problems Kai," he said, nodding back. "But at least your problem can be sorted. You can stop drinking but I can't change who I am…can I?"

"No, I don't suppose you can, and even if I was to become as wise as a God, I'll still not have wisdom enough to judge another for who they fall in love with."

Altan paused for a moment: "Hmm…And how wise are you dear cousin to be able to speak of such things?"

"Wise enough to know of my own stupidity…unfortunately," I said, resting my hand on his shoulder. "But you have my word that I'll sort myself out when we get back."

Altan smiled, and walking back over to the camp arm in arm, we both settled back down in an effort to get some much-needed sleep before sunrise.

In the morning, we all ate a light breakfast of dried smoked mutton and corn bread, before breaking camp and setting off again. We crossed the river at the shallowest point that we could find, and with the crisp chill of the morning mist still clinging to the ground, we headed off in a westerly direction straight towards the great forest.

It took us two more days before we finally reached the edge of the forest. We were able to ride a little way into the wild woods before being forced to dismount and lead our horses on foot into the deeper part of the forest.

The bird of prey eggs that we were searching for were that of a large falcon, which later became known as the 'Saka falcon'. Finding a nest wasn't actually all that difficult, as all you needed was a keen eye, a sharp ear, and loads of patience. But once located, it was not such an easy task actually collecting the eggs of these birds, as they always nested very high up in the tallest trees, and usually in an old nest which had been previously made by another bird of prey, or sometimes even another large bird such as a raven. Locating a nest was the first stage, and climbing up the tree and getting to it was the second. And if that wasn't hard enough, getting back down again safely with the egg in one piece was probably the most difficult part of all, and that's why we had an expert climber amongst us called Chinna.

As soon as we'd located a nest, he began to climb up the tree with such ease and confidence, that the rest of us could only look on in admiration. We watched him as he climbed higher and higher, until he finally reached the nest. I held my breath as he reached out and removed one of the eggs from the nest, and steadying himself, he carefully wrapped it in a cloth and then placed it in a bag which he had strapped to his back. As a mark of respect for the parent birds, he only ever took one egg from each nest that we found, and also it was thought to bring bad luck, if you took more than one egg from the same nest.

Chinna had already begun his descent, when I suddenly became aware of the sound of voices in the distance.

"Hurry up, Chinna…I can hear voices," I said, waving him down.

Everyone suddenly froze in silence. You could clearly hear the sound of heavy footsteps and twigs cracking under foot which grew steadily louder.

"Hurry, Chinna," added Altan, also frantically waving him down.

Just as Chinna's feet touched the ground – and before we'd had a chance to hide, they were already upon us. We all just stood staring at them, and they in turn just froze in their tracks and stared back at us. They were obviously just as surprised to see us as we were to see them. The odd-looking strangers were somewhat similar in appearance to the Greek soldiers of whom I was already quite familiar with, but there were some obvious differences; especially in the weapons that they were carrying. I don't know how many of them there were in total, but there did appear to be quite a lot of them, at least forty – maybe even fifty, and every part of my being was telling me to run.

"RUN!" I shouted, but before we'd had a chance to move, a couple of them began throwing spears at us. One of the spears hit Chinna in the chest and he immediately fell to ground. Another spear hit Altan in the shoulder, and the rest of us returned their aggression with a hail of arrows. We managed to bring down at least five of them before the rest of them took cover. I could see that Chinna was obviously dead, and there was nothing more that could be done for him right now. So the rest of us grabbed Altan and hauled him onto a horse. I could see that he was losing a lot of blood, so I jumped on the same horse behind him, and I held onto him tightly while we made our escape as fast as we were able through the denseness of the forest.

As soon as we thought that we were out of the forest and a safe enough distance away, we stopped so that we could tend to Altan. We got him down from the horse and made him as comfortable as possible. He had already lost a lot of blood, and using what skills I'd already learned during my time with the Agari, I managed to stem the bleeding by applying hard and constant pressure to the wound, while a couple of others made a small fire. I placed the blade end of one of my small throwing knives in the fire, and allowed it to heat up until it glowed, and then after allowing it to cool down just a little, I asked Guyuk and another of the warriors to hold Altan steady, and after giving Altan something to bite down on, I quickly cauterised his wound.

Altan was feeling too week to continue the journey home, so we had no other choice but to make camp, and try and keep him as comfortable and as warm as we possibly could. Altan knew all too well that his condition was very serious, and shivering with the cold, he looked up at me and said:

"Kai…I don't think I'm going to make it back. So please tell my father that I'm sorry that I let him down."

Altan beckoned Guyuk to come closer to him, and after quietly whispering something to him, he took his hand in his, and after one last look in my direction he closed his eyes. And there on the open planes – somewhere between Hun and Scythian territory, Altan took his last and final breath. A tear rolled down Guyuk's cheek, and as he began to weep, I cried out in sorrow, and in my embittered pain and anger at the loss of my dear friend, I cursed the strangers, and swore an oath to avenge both his, and Chinna's death …even if it took me until the very end of time.

As we secured Altan's body to one of the horses, my heart felt so heavy that I thought it might drag me down into the cold earth below me, and as we were now one horse short, Guyuk and I both shared a horse, and thoroughly demoralised – we set out on our three day journey back to the Hun encampment.

Hardly a word was spoken amongst us the whole of the journey back, and with our heads bowed low we solemnly rode into the village. Word had already reached my uncle of our arrival, and as soon as he saw us, he hurried over and began to untie the ropes that we'd used to secure Altan to the horse. We all dismounted and helped him carry Altan's body inside his yurt.

"How did this happen …Who did this, Kai?" asked my uncle, looking me squarely in the eyes. I proceeded to explain to him exactly what had happened. I was able to give him a fairly accurate description of what the men responsible looked like; after which I told him what Altan had asked me to tell him with his dying breath.

"We will bury my son immediately, and then ride out with a war party to see if we can find the scum that did this. I don't expect you, or the others involved to come with us," he said, resting his hand on my shoulder.

"Oh – I'm coming," I said with the insatiable need for revenge still burning deep within my heart. And without hesitation, every man present said that they would also be joining the war party. My uncle just nodded to us all, and he ordered that preparations for Altan's funeral be made immediately, and that a large band of warriors should be gathered together in readiness to ride out and hunt down the ones responsible for his death.

"We will have time to mourn Altan and Chinna when we return, 'after' we have avenged them both," said my uncle, solemnly.

Merren and Aptien were also soon on the scene, and after hearing about what had happened, they immediately said that they would also be joining our war party. I had a brief chance to explain to Tihanna what had happened, and of our plan to ride out in search of these men and take our revenge, before I had to leave her all alone once again.

As was tradition, Altan was immediately buried in an unmarked grave, and after quickly preparing ourselves, and fuelled with the solemn intention on avenging the deaths of both Altan and Chinna, we rode out in search of our enemy for to slay.

We travelled lightly and with great haste. We stopped only to relieve ourselves, and to rest and water our horses. And after we had reached the forest, it didn't take us very long before we were able to track them down. They had made a make shift camp in another part of the forest, and the battle that ensued was short and bloody, and I don't wish to go into too much detail as this book is not meant to be a horror story, but I took great pleasure in personally killing as many of them as I possibly could. I lost count…but not satisfied with that; I along with several others, hacked them into pieces, and left their mutilated corpses as offerings to the carnivores of the forest. After which, we impaled their severed heads on stakes as a warning – lest any more of their kind should happen by. A small number of them had managed to escape, but what they didn't know was that we had purposely allowed them to; just so that they could live to tell their story, and hopefully tell a tale so terrifying, that no more of them would ever dare to venture this way ever again.

We never did find Chinna's body…

14

A Light in the Darkness

We rode back into the Hun encampment victorious, but there were no celebrations; just a dark and sombre atmosphere of satiated revengeful blood lust. I was not the only one, but I was completely covered in the blood of our enemies, and when I walked back into our yurt, Tihanna just stood there with a look of sheer horror on her face. I'd completely forgotten that I was covered in blood, and I looked down at my hands, and at my clothes, and all I could think of to say was…

"It's okay…it's not mine…I'll take them off now."

"I'll get some water," she said, grabbing a water pail and quickly carrying it outside.

I removed my boots, and stripped off all of my blood-soaked clothes and threw them in a heap on the floor. And just as I began to un-braid my hair, Tihanna walked back into our yurt with the pale full of water.

"I'll help you to get cleaned up," she said, carefully avoiding making any eye contact with me. Tihanna picked up all my soiled clothes and threw them in a bucket.

"I'll put these to soak later," she said, walking back over to me.

As she began to wipe the dried blood from my face, I could plainly see that she was purposely avoiding making eye contact. I couldn't really blame her, and as I looked down at our sweet daughter who was peacefully sleeping in her crib, I thought that it was a blessing at least, that she was so mercifully unaware of the cold-blooded killer that was standing so close to her right now. "You don't have to do this," I said, grabbing the cloth from Tihanna's hand.

"Kai…I know I don't have to," she said, grabbing it back again. "It's fine…I want to do it, I love you and I just wish you'd stop shutting me out all the time."

"No you don't Tihanna," I said, grabbing her wrist. "You might be in love with who I used to be, but not who I am now. You wouldn't love me if you knew

171

what was in my heart right now. Let me tell you something – I actually enjoyed killing those men. I'm not who you think I am Tihanna. I don't even know who I am any more…I really don't deserve you."

I grabbed a pair of trousers from a neat pile of clean laundry that Tihanna had placed on our bed earlier, and quickly pulled them on before walking out of our yurt bare foot.

"Please, Kai – don't do this," Tihanna shouted after me.

"I'm sorry, Tihanna – you really don't deserve this," I said, walking away.

I made my way down to the nearby river and half stumbling down the riverbank, I waded straight out into the very middle of the river and knelt down. The river was quite shallow at this point, and although it barely covered my ankles, it was quite fast flowing, and I could feel the power and the energy of this mighty river as it gushed forcefully against my knees.

I tried to wash away the blood from my hands and face, but it was so deeply ground into my skin and nails that I just couldn't remove it. There were some plants growing nearby that we called soap plants, because if you rubbed the leaves between your hands they would produce an alkaline lather that was very good for removing blood and dirt. So after wading back onto the dry land to pick some, I removed my wet trousers and slung them over a bush to dry out before returning to the river, and after vigorously rubbing the plants between my hands until they had produced a soapy lather, I used them to scrub away all the dried blood from my skin and hair. I guess I must have conveniently chosen to forget all about the Scythian tradition of not bathing in the river.

Casting aside the mushy soap plants, I waded into the deepest part of the river, and completely submerging myself for a few moments, I allowed the natural flow of the water to thoroughly cleanse my body and ease my troubled soul. I remained in that river until I finally began to feel somewhere near clean again; after which I stood up and walked back on to the dry land where I'd left my trousers, and after pulling them back on again, I sat down on the embankment and began to stare downwards into the water where I soon become lost in the quagmire of my own mind. Nothing made any sense, and I really didn't know who I was any more.

"Who are you?" I asked myself, staring blankly at my reflection in the river.

And closing my eyes I began to pray…for something…anything…to make some sense to me. I could hear the sound of the river as it continued on its endless journey, and I wondered if it secretly carried within itself all the answers to my many questions. Did the river know who I was?

And if it did – would it tell me? Did it even give a damn?

I was beginning to shiver from the cold, so I decided that it was time to return to my yurt where I knew that Tihanna would be waiting for me.

I was in no mood to talk to her right now, but I could see that she'd been crying. None of this was her fault, and I felt bad that I was causing her to be unhappy.

"Tihanna…I'm sorry…you really don't deserve this, and I promise you that we'll talk later, but right now I must mourn my slain brothers."

Tihanna didn't respond, so grabbing my weapons which were still lying in a heap where I'd left them, I walked back outside again.

It was Scythian tradition to announce the loss of a loved one with a public display of drawing one's own blood. So standing in the very centre of the Hun encampment, I took one of my own knives and slowly began to draw the sharp edge of the blade across the back of my arm. I watched with some satisfaction as my life blood began to drip onto the cold earth, after which, I repeated the same process several more times before finally falling to my knees. The next thing I can remember is hearing Aptien's voice.

"Come on, chief – I think that's enough for now."

I just continued to stare down at the ground; so in typical time tested fashion, both he and Merren, 'who was also stood close by', each linked one of their arms through mine, and after physically lifting me up off the ground and back onto my feet again – they quietly escorted me to their yurt.

"Right," said Merren, fetching a clean linen bandage from a large brightly decorated wooden chest. "Let's get that arm sorted."

As Merren began bandaging my arm, I just sat there blankly staring into space. I could hear him asking me if I was okay, but his voice sounded muffled and distant, and it was more than I could do to answer him.

"Here drink this," he said, handing me a cup. I still didn't respond, so kneeling directly in front of me he held out the cup.

"KAI…DRINK THIS," he said rather loudly.

His voice had managed to jolt me back into a state of responsiveness, and without asking what was in the cup, I took it from his hand and drank its contents straight down in one go. Merren stood up and taking the cup from my hand, he refilled it before handing it back to me. I drank that straight down too, and I could see by the look which was etched on the faces of both Merren and Aptian that I must have given them both cause for concern. "I'm lost," I finally said.

"Nahh…you can't be lost chief…or we wouldn't have been able to find you," said Aptien, picking up the empty cup that I'd allowed to fall to the floor. "We're going to help you get through this…you'll be fine."

They were the most unlikely Guardian Angels that anyone could ever have, but it was true, they were never too far away, and always ready to pick me up off the ground and put me back on my feet again…literally at times. I began to realise the fundamental truth in this, and I began to laugh.

"What's so funny?" asked Aptien confused.

"Oh…It's nothing."

"Go on…tell us what's so funny," said Merren, pulling up a stool and sitting himself down opposite me.

"If you get me another drink I might tell you."

"Well…given the current circumstances," he said. Merren stood up, and went to pour me another drink.

"You know – I've always questioned why you guys stick around, and then it suddenly struck me, maybe the Gods have decreed that you should be my Guardians."

"I don't know about that, but by the sound of things I think you've probably had enough to drink for now, said Merren, raising his eyebrows."

Aptien stood there thinking about what I'd just said for a few moments.

"Well, I'd say it was more likely to be a past life debt of some kind…if anything."

"Who knows, but I just want you both to know how much I appreciate all your help."

"Hey…don't you dare start getting all slushy on us, I can handle most things – but not that," said Aptien, removing the empty cup from my hands and placing it loudly on a table behind him.

"I shall have to keep that in mind," I said with a slightly malevolent smile on my face. "Actually in retrospect – I think I prefer the slush," he said, giving me back the empty cup and then walking off.

Life went on, and in time I'd managed to come to terms with the sad loss of Altan and Guyuk. And with Merren and Aptien's help and supervision, I'd succeeded in gaining some control over my problem with alcohol abuse. I still had a few drinks now and again, but this time it was in moderation.

During my recovery, I made several visits to a shaman called Shi Dochin. He was renowned for his remarkable understanding of magic and herbalism, and I was soon to learn that his knowledge was based more on dark Sorcery than anything else. This was something that Garenhir had always warned me to steer well clear of, as it would be detrimental to my physical and spiritual wellbeing, and to the safety and wellbeing of everyone else around me. But unfortunately my natural curiosity had managed to get the better of me once more, and it just so happened that Shi Dochin was looking for a suitable apprentice, and he obviously saw in me a prospective pupil. At first I was some-what hesitant, as Garenhir's words kept echoing in my mind, but gradually Shi Dochin convinced me that all knowledge was good knowledge, and he cleverly articulated his point across to me in such a skilful way, that the pull on the darker side of my nature became too strong for me to resist, and I eventually agreed to become Shi Dochin's Apprentice.

Unfortunately for me – I appeared to have a natural aptitude towards the black arts. In fact things came to me so easily that in a very short time, I had begun to realise that it was my teacher who was actually learning from me, and he was using me to gain access to certain dark forces that he had obviously failed to do himself. This could have potentially had the effect of creating a monster out of both of us, as the energies that were becoming available to me were so intoxicating, and so powerfully magnetic, that I was being drawn deeper and deeper into the Abyss, and I was in serious danger of 'truly' losing my way altogether this time. But something deep within the very core of my inner being, or higher self, or whatever else you want to call it, had reached out to my conscious mind to take a reality check, and although deep down inside I knew that ultimately this wasn't who I really was, I found the depths that I had so easily managed to descend into, were not quite so easy to climb back out of again.

During this time I became ever more secretive, and more withdrawn into myself than ever before. Merren and Aptien had some idea of what I was getting myself into, but there wasn't anything that they could have done; except perhaps to keep an ever watchful but safe distance. Both Merren and Aptien were already well aware of some of the things that I was capable of, but now with the forces of darkness as my companion, and only my higher conscience to hold back the reins, I was a potential danger to all who came into contact with me, and I was still only eighteen winters of age.

But thankfully, I decided that I was no longer willing to be Shi Dochin's 'so called' pupil, and I told him so in no uncertain terms. But he in turn made it quite plain that he was not willing to relinquish his hold on me that easily, and in an effort to frighten me into yielding to his will, he sent an evil elementary which he had under his control to attack me. Unfortunately for him he underestimated my understanding of how these things work, and I returned what he'd sent to me with such a force that it killed him outright, and Shi Dochin was found dead the following morning. I really didn't intend to cause him any serious harm, and although he'd left me with very little choice other than to do what I did, I was as shocked by his sudden death as everyone else was, but I kept the truth of what really happened to myself.

One day not long after this, I received a summons from my uncle saying that I was to come to his yurt immediately as he needed to talk to me about something very important. I knew better than to keep my uncle waiting, so laying aside what I was doing, I made my way over to my uncle's yurt and respectfully called out from outside and waited for him to reply before entering as usual. Once inside, my uncle gestured for me to sit down directly opposite him, and he wasted no time at all before getting straight to the point.

"Kai…you know that you've always been like a son to me, and since the death of Altan I have no one to take my place when the time comes. I know that you're a competent and skilled warrior, and I'm sure you have what it takes to make a good Khan. What would you say if I asked you to stand as my second in command, and that would also put you in the position of next in line to the title of Khan?"

His direct and no-nonsense approach took me completely by surprise, and for a moment I just sat there staring blankly at him. "Well…what is your answer?"

"I…uh…Can I think about it for a couple of days and I'll…uh…and then I'll give you my answer?" I stuttered.

"I shall give you two days to make up your mind, after which you will come back to see me with your answer," he replied, standing up and resting his hand on my shoulder for a moment, before sitting back down again.

And without another word said between us, I promptly stood up and left his yurt.

I knew that I needed to give my uncle's proposition some very serious thought indeed, so I grabbed a few provisions before riding off alone down to the river in order to give myself some time to think clearly for a while. I ended up staying there for nearly two days, but by the end of it – I'd finally managed to reach a decision. I was going to accept my uncle's proposal and stand as his second in command and become the next in line for the position of Khan. It was a huge step to take, but I believed that a position of authority would be good move forward for me, as it would give me more responsibility and hopefully keep me on the straight and narrow, as I'd need to keep a clear head at all times.

After informing my uncle of my decision, the very next two people that I sought to tell were Merren and Aptien. It wasn't long before I found the two of them down by the river spearing fish. There were of course far easier ways to catch fish, but they weren't half as much fun as trying to spear them, so after pulling off my boots and placing them on the bank, I grabbed one of the spears that was left lying on the embankment and joined them. It was also a perfect opportunity to inform them both of my new position here with the Hun. They both just stopped dead in their tracks and stared at me open mouthed.

"Well don't just stand there looking so surprised," I said, spearing a fish. "Say something at least."

"I can't help wondering what your father is going to make of all this when he gets word," said Merren, scratching his head.

I hadn't really given much thought at all to my father, or what he was going to think about me becoming next in line to my uncle. But even better still…my brother!

Who was as far as I knew – still next in line for the position of Sha Pada (chief leader) of the Saka tribe…this was pure gold!

"I hadn't thought about that until you just mentioned it – but now that you have, I don't think I'll wait for word to travel, I think I might just deliver the message in person."

"Oh boy – Why did you have to go and open your big mouth," said Aptien, scowling at Merren.

I hadn't seen my father; or any of my Scythian family for that matter, since that fateful day over two years ago. When I'd left my home in Scythia to go and live with the Hun, I was still just a boy, but I would soon return to Scythia as a Hun warrior, and as a leader of men. I let my uncle know of my intentions, and he agreed that news of my new position would probably be better delivered coming directly from me. And so dressed in my finest Hun regalia, and with over thirty Hun warriors at my side…including Merren and Aptien – who just wouldn't take no for an answer! – I set out and headed straight for Scythia.

We rode straight into my father's village unchallenged. Word had already reached my father that a band of Huns were fast approaching the village. And as we approached my father's kol, I could see him standing there waiting for us with my brother stood proudly by his side, and I felt a sudden and unexpected wave of anxiety, which reminded of the panic attack that I'd experienced all those years ago when I'd first ridden into the Pa-ra-lati village as a boy, but I wasn't going to let my highly strung nature get the better of me, so taking a few deep breaths, I continued to approach my father with my band of Hun warriors following closely behind me.

Stopping directly opposite my father, I waited to see if he would actually recognise me. I really don't think he did at first, then suddenly it dawned on him, and he just stared at me open mouthed for a few moments before speaking…

"Kai…Is that you?"

"Hello, Father," I said somewhat ominously in Hunnic.

Merren and Aptien rode up beside me and respectfully acknowledged my father, who reciprocated by nodding back to them. Just then my mother appeared from inside the kol, she instantly recognised me, and was about to run over to greet me, but my father quickly grabbed her by the arm and prevented her from doing so.

"It's okay," I said in Scythian, and my father responded by letting go of her arm. My mother immediately came running over to me.

"I've missed you, son. You've got another sister now," she said, reaching up to me tearfully.

I really didn't want to let my guard down at this present time, and I couldn't allow my mother to jeopardise my icy demeanour, so even though I really wanted to get down off my horse and give her a hug, I just gave her a little smile and very quietly told her that I'd missed her too.

"It's good to see you, son…come inside and talk for a while," said my father, cautiously walking over and standing next to my mother.

"Why don't you come inside, son…we should talk," he said, gently stroking my horse's neck. "Maybe later," I said coldly. "But first I should tell you that I'm now first in line for the position of Khan."

At which point I turned my attention to my brother, and with a vengeful sneer I continued: "And if the day should ever come that 'you' become Sha Pada here,

178

dear brother – I shall declare war on all of you and I shall raze this village to the ground."

Merren and Aptien both looked at me completely mortified, and turning to my father they both shook their heads and raised their hands palms upwards as a show to my father that they were completely unaware of any of this, and it was as much as a shock to them as it was to him. I know they weren't expecting me to come out with that little gem. My father was unable to hide the look of sheer horror on his face, and I can only imagine what must have been going through his mind, as his worst nightmare was beginning to take form right before his eyes, and everything that he'd worked so hard to gain by forming an alliance with the Huns, was now in very real danger of crumbling to dust, but worse than that, it would be his very own son who was going be the one responsible for eventually leading the Hun into battle against him.

"Please, Kai…dismount and come inside so that we can talk," said my father, almost pleading with me.

"Like I said…maybe later, but you'd better make sure that 'he's' no-where in sight," I said coldly pointing to my brother. "I'm sorry, Father, but it wasn't you that I really came to see. Where's Garenhir?"

"He's in his kol – as far as I know," answered my father uneasily.

"Please take good care of my men," I said, as I gave the order for them to dismount before riding off to find Garenhir.

Word had travelled fast, and Garenhir had already been informed of my arrival into the village, and by the time I'd reached his kol, he was already standing outside waiting for me. Sai had obviously heard too, and was also standing there next to Garenhir.

As soon as I saw them, I dismounted, and although I was secretly feeling a little nervous, I walked over to greet them both as though I owned the whole world.

"Hello, Manu Kai – welcome back," said Garenhir, with a big beaming smile on his face. "Wow…look at you…you've grown, and you look so…Whoa…be still," said Sai, holding his hand to his heart. Garenhir raised his eyebrows a little, and turning to Sai, he quietly said to him:

"Steady on there…eh!"

"Hello, Sai," I said with a wry smile on my face, as I actually found his reaction to me quite amusing.

"I've come to talk to you Derkesthai," I said, turning my attention to Garenhir.

"Of course – I know that Sai won't mind leaving us alone to talk for a while, will you Sai?" he said with a wink of his eye.

"No – I don't mind at all – I'll see you later," said Sai, as he walked off leaving us alone to talk in private.

Garenhir asked me to follow him inside his kol, and after asking me to sit down, he positioned a chair so that we were sat facing one another. Garenhir patiently waited for me to be the first to say something. I thought about all the times that I'd wished I could talk to him, but now that I was here – I really didn't know where to start. I also realised at this point, that I found it impossible to make eye contact with him. He must have known that I was finding all of this very difficult, and thankfully he decided to take the initiative.

"You look very impressive on the outside, Manu Kai, but the question is – how are you doing on the inside?"

Even now I found it impossible to lie to Garenhir.

"Not so good I'm afraid," I said, staring down at the ground. "I can see that…Can you look at me?"

"No, I don't think I can," I replied, still averting my gaze.

"Go on…give it a try," he said with a certain air of command in his voice.

I raised my eyes upwards from the ground, and for a brief moment our eyes met, but as they did I felt so overcome, that I actually found it difficult to breath, and I quickly ran outside and vomited around the back of Garenhir's kol.

I can't do this, I thought to myself, and I was just about to jump straight back on my horse and ride off again, when Sai suddenly appeared from nowhere with five Agari priests. I looked at them all just stood there staring at me, and all the fight just seemed to drain right out of me, and for some reason I found myself allowing them to calmly walk me back into Garenhir's kol.

"There's no point in this…I know that now – it's too late, Garenhir…I walk in shadow now," I protested, while carefully avoiding making any further eye contact with him. As I continued to remonstrate, Garenhir finally ordered me to sit down.

"Manu Kai, please shut up for a moment and listen to what I have to say. We're not giving up on you that easily as it's clear that some part of you is asking for our help, or you wouldn't have come here in the first place."

"It's a mistake that's all," I continued.

"There's no mistake," he said sharply.

"You can't hold me here against my will," I protested.

"No…not officially we can't…but we can ask you to stay here of your own free will for a few days. Just to give us a little more time to talk. And perhaps we can even try and help you to deal with any issues that might have been bothering you lately."

"Please, Manu Kai," said Sai, in a pleading tone of voice. "It's just for a few days – that's all!"

"Fine…you win…but just for a few days," I said with a sigh.

"Do we have your word that you won't just ride off again the very first chance that you get?" asked Sai, not leaving anything to chance.

He knew me well enough to know that no matter how badly I'd been affected, I was still the same person deep down inside. And therefore – if I gave my word, I could still be trusted to keep it.

"Yes, I give you my word," I replied a little reluctantly.

"Good! Now that we've got that little matter settled, I think that it would be a very good idea if your men were made aware of your intentions," said Garenhir.

"Perhaps it would be a good idea if you went and fetched Merren and Aptien," he said, turning to Sai. "So that Manu Kai can let them know what's going on, and they in turn can let the rest of Manu Kai's men know that they'll be staying here for a couple of days. Oh…and you'd better let Herian know too, so that he can make all the necessary arrangements."

"You really don't trust me, do you? I gave you my word," I said to Garenhir.

"I'm afraid it's not you that I don't trust Manu Kai," he replied, raising his eyebrows. Sai immediately left to go and fetch Merren and Aptien, and when they arrived at Garenhir's kol, they were obviously a little surprised to find me surrounded by Agari Priests. It must have been somewhat reminiscent of the time that I'd just received a horse whipping from my father. I just sat there with my chin resting in the palm of my hand as I spoke to them.

"Please inform everyone concerned that we'll be staying here for a couple of days."

They both just stood there with their arms folded, I could see that they were both desperately searching for some small hint of what was really going on.

"Just do it," I said rather sharply.

They both just nodded, and without saying a word, they both hurried back outside again. "Everything is going to be fine Manu Kai – you'll see," said Garenhir, placing his hand on top of mine.

"How can you say that?" I said, standing up. "You have absolutely no idea who I am anymore."

"Be still, Kai. We understand more than you think we do," said Garenhir calmly.

"Then I hope you'll understand this," I said, suddenly raising my arms upwards.

And with an effort of my will, I called upon the dark forces which I'd learned to harness and there was a sound like the howling and the whistling of the wind on a blustery day, which was then accompanied by what sounded like pottery smashing to the ground – but in reality everything remained exactly where it was!

The fire in the centre of the kol suddenly flared upwards for a moment or two, before it went out completely. At which point I was immediately grabbed by two priests and tightly restrained. "Don't you know that everyone here could do that too if they were so inclined to do so Manu Kai," said Garenhir, standing directly in front of me. "But we prefer not to indulge ourselves in such a gratuitous display of misguided egocentric folly. So please don't do it again, as nobody here is even slightly impressed, and if you do it again, you will force us to act upon you in such a way that it will serve to render you a little less aggressive for a while. It's up to you, so what is it going to be?"

I really didn't want to hurt any of them, and I don't know why I did it. I knew that they were only trying to help me, so I agreed to try and behave myself, and to listen to what Garenhir had to say to me. So still flanked by the two priests who had managed to restrain me, I was released from the clutches of Agari hands, and allowed to sit down again, and feeling suitably chastised, I gave in and allowed Garenhir to get on with whatever it was that he intended to do with me.

"Before we begin would you like me to give you something to help you relax a little?" Garenhir asked me with a little sigh.

"Yes…that might be a good idea," I said, wrapping my arms around myself.

Garenhir nodded to Sai to go and prepare me a sedative of some sort, and when he handed it to me, I drank it straight down without even bothering to ask him what was in it. I stared into the empty cup for a moment or two before handing it back to him, and we all just sat in total silence for about fifteen minutes or so, in order to allow the sedative a little time to take effect.

"Right then, Manu Kai," said Garenhir, breaking the silence. "Shall we start again?"

Kneeling down in front of me, he gently rested his hands palm upwards on my knees.

"I want you to take hold of both my hands and look straight at me…if you can," he said calmly. I was still feeling a little nauseous, and as soon as Garenhir touched me I began to tremble, but the sedative had already kicked in, and had successfully prevented me from reacting aggressively. So taking a deep breath I did as Garenhir had instructed, and placing my hands on top of his I forced myself to look straight into his eyes, and as I did, I instantly felt a shock wave reverberate throughout my whole system, which was immediately followed by a blinding flash of light, which felt as though it had penetrated deep into my very being.

"Well done, Manu Kai," said Garenhir taking a deep breath. "I think you'll be OK now." Garenhir stood up and walked over to the other Agari priests, I heard him say that he should be able to cope with me on his own now, and that they could all go about their business, and that he would let them know if he needed them again, and so they all left – all except for Sai that is, who had remained sitting quietly in the background throughout the whole episode.

"Would you like some water to drink," Garenhir asked me.

I nodded that I did, and Sai immediately jumped up to fetch me a beaker of water. Garenhir smiled, and asked me how I was feeling.

"OK…I think!" I said, still trembling a little.

"That's the worst over for now, but it's just the beginning in the way of pointing you back in the right direction again Manu Kai. I want you to rest for now as your body's obviously gone into shock, so we'll talk later. I have to pop out for a short while. Sai will look after you as always," he said with a smile.

Sai walked over and sat himself down directly in front of me, and he continued to sit there staring at me, until I found it impossible to ignore him any longer.

"If you want to say something, Sai…just get it over and done with – just say it."

"Well…Yes, there is something…but perhaps now is not the best time," he said with a sigh. I raised my eyes to briefly meet with his, and on doing so, I instantly picked up on his vibe.

"You've got to be kidding me, Sai…right?"

"No, I'm really not kidding, I've always had feelings for you, Kai. Please don't tell me you didn't know this," he said, averting his gaze and staring down at his feet.

"Well…Yes, I mean no…Oh…I don't know! I suppose I did have some idea, but you're supposed to be my friend. I really don't know how I'm supposed to react to this," I said, feeling more than a little awkward.

Sai stood up and gently touched the side of my face, but I reacted by shaking my head and gently removing his hand.

"That's OK," he said, sitting back down again. "You might change your mind one day." "Oh! – And just for the record, I was impressed if no one else was," he said with a sideways glance in my direction.

After that, we both sat in complete silence and awaited Garenhir's return.

15

The Dweller on the Threshold

When Garenhir returned, he took one look at the pair of us just sitting there in total silence and tutted.

"Did I miss something?" he asked.

"No, nothing importance anyway," I replied.

"Not to you maybe," said Sai rather dejectedly.

"Ah…I see. Well, you can go now if you want to Sai, but please make sure that you come back again tomorrow," said Garenhir, with raised eyebrows.

"OK…I'll see you tomorrow then," said Sai, leaving me alone with Garenhir to talk in private.

To say that we had a fair amount of catching up to do would be an understatement, and Garenhir wasted no time at all in asking me to update him about all the things that I'd experienced since I had been living with the Huns. It felt good to be able to confide in him, and allow myself into his wise counsel once again.

"I'm not going to beat around the bush, I would really like you to consider coming back to live here, and then when you feel that the time is right, perhaps you would like to even continue with your studies," said Garenhir, looking me straight in the eye.

"Is that going to be possible?"

"With a little dedication on your part, I can see no reason why it shouldn't be."

"Have you forgotten about Tihanna and my daughter? I can't, and I won't just abandon them." "Who said you'd have to?"

"And what about my promise to my uncle, I've given him my word now, and I can't just walk away."

"Of course not, but what if there was a way around all of this?" asked Garenhir, sitting himself down directly opposite me.

"Even if that was possible…I know better than to try and hide anything from you. I have a lot of blood on my hands Garenhir. And what about my involvement with negative forces? What if I can't control that part of myself Garenhir – you've seen it for yourself."

"Hmm…Well I'm well aware that there are a few issues that we will need to work on, but hopefully your past involvement with negative forces is something that you will have learnt from, and can now put behind you. I also know that you can be controlled…for now at least. And may the Gods forbid, but if you were ever to experience any problems from that direction again, we will be here to help you, just as we've been able to help you this time, and hopefully as time goes by it will cease to be a problem for you anymore. Listen Manu Kai, although I was aware of the possibility of certain problems arising with you right from the onset, I had no hesitation in accepting the responsibility that taking you on as my pupil would inevitably entail, and as far as I'm concerned…you're still my pupil!"

"I don't know…I've killed so many men, and no matter what I do in the future, I can't change the past."

Garenhir looked thoughtful for a moment.

"How many men have you actually killed, Manu Kai?"

"I honestly don't know."

"You don't know or you just don't want to tell me? You must have some idea, Kai. Ten…twenty…thirty?"

"I really don't know," I said, shaking my head. "I'd say around a hundred…maybe even more than that."

Garenhir's eyes widened, he let out a long sigh, and the expression on his face said it all, and for the first time I realised just how bad what I'd done had been.

"Yes, exactly," I said, staring down at my feet. "And you know what makes it even worse? Quite a few of them were Thracians, and I know it's the least of my problems right now, but that isn't exactly going to fare too well with my father if he ever gets to find out."

"Well I must admit that is quite a lot more than I was expecting, and there can be no doubt that you've certainly played an active role in the terrible evil that's running riot on this planet right now. And although it's true that you can't change what's been done, you can change the path ahead Manu Kai. You have a choice, you can either stop all of the killing now, throw yourself back into your studies and adopt a far more positive role for yourself, or continue on the downward path of destruction and spiral into oblivion. You see it's really very simple Manu Kai – if you are continually focused on all that is negative in this world – then you will inevitably become attuned to it, and if you focus on more positive things you will soon find that you will be able to move away from all the negativity and sorrow in your life, and you will slowly begin to rebuild your life and be happy again. This is the true Law of Cause and Effect. There is no Karma – there is only attunement. We are like mirrors to the universe Manu Kai, and each of us reflect back to ourselves 'that' which we attune to."

"So are you saying that we should all turn our backs on everything negative, and try and forget that it even exists?"

"No absolutely not. In fact it would be very foolish indeed to turn our backs on all the darkness and suffering in this world, but we should only look upon such things if we have the intention to help in some way. It may even become necessary for us to gain first-hand experience into these dark conditions…and that which may abide there, but we should never dwell on it, because to do so would be to attune with it. What I'm actually saying is that we need to be consciously aware that there are very active dark forces at work. But recognising them is one thing – attuning to them is quite another…Do you understand?"

"Yes, but what if it really is too late for me?"

"It's never too late to make positive changes, Manu Kai. You are still very young, and you've still got a lot to learn. There are no coincidences, and I'm sure that you must have learnt much since you've been away. So perhaps now that you have had a chance to gain some personal understanding into dark forces and conditions, you will be able to think of all that's happened to you as simply an unpleasant but necessary part of your studies, and can now move forward to continuing your studies of more positive nature."

"I want to…but I'm not naive enough to believe that I can just start up again where I left off. The boy you once knew and taught is gone forever, and why you would even see fit to offer me this chance of redemption I really don't know. You're bound to know that it's not going to be easy."

"I'm sorry, Derkesthai, but I'm very tired right now and I just can't think straight any more. I have to sleep now," I said wearily.

"I'll make you up a bed. I've already had a word with your father, so he's aware of what's going on, but I'll pop back around and let him know that you'll speak with him tomorrow. I also bumped into Merren and Aptien earlier. They were both understandably very concerned about you, and they asked me what was going on. I told them that you were OK and that as it was Agari business, it was all they really needed to know right now. They're both very loyal to you Manu Kai, and they deserved to know that you were okay at very least. I'll let them know that they'll be able to see and talk with you tomorrow."

"Yes, that fine. They're both good men. And thank you Derkesthai for all your help. And just for the record – I'm sorry for acting up earlier and doing what I did. I can see now just how much I needed your help – I really did need help, didn't I?"

"Yes, you really did Manu Kai – and you still do," he said, busily preparing me a bed for the night.

"There," he said, handing me a soft sheepskin blanket. "Try and get some rest now – and Manu Kai…it's truly wonderful to have you back with us again."

That night I slept like a log – I really couldn't remember the last time that I'd slept that soundly, and I didn't wake up until late the next morning. When I finally did wake up – I opened my eyes, and the first thing that I saw was Sai who was sat by the fire looking at me.

"Where's Garenhir?" I asked him.

"He's had to pop out and take care of some business, but he'll be back shortly," he replied.

"I've already prepared breakfast – would you like some?"

"What do you think? I haven't eaten for over two bloody days."

Sai placed some freshly cooked seasoned fried fish, and a type of bread that was made from finely ground grain and butter milk on a flat wooden platter.

"Here you are then my dark lord," he said, handing me the platter.

"Please…don't call me that."

"Sorry – did I touch a raw nerve," he said with a look of amusement on his face.

"I'm so glad you find all of this so amusing," I responded indignantly. "If you knew what I've been through perhaps you wouldn't be so quick to mock me."

"Fair comment, but I'm willing to learn Manu Kai. And when you're ready to talk – I'll be ready to listen. You should know by now that I'll always be here for you whatever happens," he said, handing me a drink of water.

I hadn't noticed before, but I could see that Sai had done something to his tongue, so I asked him:

"What have you done to your tongue?"

Sai poked out his tongue which was split like a serpents, and then baring his teeth, he showed me that two of his top teeth had been filed to a point.

"Whoa! ...When did you do that?"

"Not long after you left."

Just then Garenhir walked in: "I'm glad to see that the two of you have kissed and made up again," he said, winking at me.

"I wish;" said Sai thoughtfully.

Garenhir had a very wicked sense of humour at times...

"Your father is waiting for you to go and see him whenever you're ready Manu Kai," said Garenhir.

There were many things that I would need to sort out, but the first thing that I really had to do was to go and talk to my father. This wasn't going to be easy for either of us, but it had to be done. So after finishing my breakfast, I took a deep breath and said:

"Right then...wish me luck."

As I made my way to my father's kol, I had to pass a group of Hun warriors, so I took a little time out to let them know that everything was fine, and that I was on my way to have talks with my father.

"Do you know where Merren and Aptien are?" I asked them.

"I think they might be with your father right now," replied one of them.

That figured...my father was probably giving them both a thorough de briefing, but I knew that neither of them would ever betray anything that I had told them in confidence, so as I reached my father's kol I took another deep breath, and straightening my back, I held my head up high and loudly and confidently announced my presence from the outside.

"Come on in Manu Kai," responded my father.

Pulling back the leather flap covering the doorway to the kol, I boldly made my entrance. Merren and Aptien immediately stood up, and after respectfully bowing to my father, took three steps backwards before turning around and heading for the doorway.

"Good luck," said Aptien quietly, as he brushed passed me.

"It's good to see you son," said my father, standing up to greet me.

Seeing him standing there with that welcoming smile on his face brought back warm memories of happy times that I'd spent with him as a child, and I have to admit – it did feel good to see him too.

"It's good to see you too father."

"You've grown son – you're a man now. And from what I've heard, you've been making quite a name for yourself."

"Have I?" I said genuinely unaware of the fact.

My father took a step back and studied me for a moment before nodding to himself approvingly.

"I've missed you son," he said with a sigh. "I'm so sorry for my past mistakes. If I had the power to go back in time I would do things so differently. But I don't – so all I can do is to try and make it up to you now."

"What's done is done! So much water has flowed under the bridge since the day I left, but I really would like another chance at being your son."

My father just stood there silently regarding me for a few moments, before he finally reached out and warmly embraced me.

"Please…sit down, Manu Kai. I am really happy to hear you say that, as I really need to talk to you about matters that have been bothering me for some time. Please come and sit with me for a while,"

"I'm not going to beat about the bush Manu Kai. I may as well come straight to the point and tell you exactly what's on my mind. Firstly, I want you to come back and live here again – and of course, Tihanna will also be made welcome, and I hear that I have a granddaughter now too."

"Yes, you do," I replied.

"Secondly…and you must keep this to yourself for now. I want you to stand as second in command, and to take the position above your brother as next in line for Sha Pada."

"What?" I said, completely taken aback.

"Your brother is a fool Manu Kai, and I know that he doesn't have what it takes to govern our people. When the time comes 'you' are going to have to be the one who will take my place here as leader."

"But I've already promised my uncle that I'll take over from him," I said, raising my hands to my head in a mixture of bewilderment and confusion.

"Yes, I'm already aware of this…but we'll work something out. Garenhir and I have spoken, and he also believes that it's in your best interest to return here and continue with your studies as an Agari priest. I haven't told him of my plan to speak to you about standing next in line yet. I wanted to talk to you about it first."

190

I just sat there staring at him speechless. I really couldn't think of one single appropriate thing to say right now – and that was pretty damn unusual for me.

"So – What do you think?" he prompted.

Talk about being put on the spot. I knew that I needed some time alone to think.

"I'm going to need a little time before I can give you my answer," was the only rational thing that I could think of to say.

So without saying another word, I stood up and briskly walked out of my father's kol…leaving him there wondering what decision I would eventually return with.

Returning back to the relative privacy of Garenhir's kol, I must admit that I was somewhat relieved to find it empty. So sprawling out upon the bed that Garenhir had made up for me the night before, I began to think deeply about the new situation that I'd unwittingly found myself in. It did feel good to be back that was for sure. But how I was ever going to be able to return to Scythia and stand as second in line to my father without letting my uncle down, I had absolutely no idea right now. And if nothing else, I knew that I couldn't disappoint my uncle. But I also knew that my rightful place was here. I was feeling very confused and I really needed some impartial advice right now, but from whom? As even though there were people around me that I knew I could trust, I wasn't sure who would be impartial enough, and at the same time have the necessary wisdom to be able to offer me some real solid advice? I could ask Garenhir I suppose – he was certainly wise enough, and I could certainly trust him that was for sure. But I knew he didn't like keeping secrets between my father and me. And as my father had requested that I tell no one, it would put Garenhir in a very awkward position, and I really didn't want to do that to him. So involving Garenhir was certainly out of the question, and in any case, taking any position of leadership was not going to mix well with my studies as an Agari priest. I could trust Merren and Aptien with any secret, but I knew that even with all their wily ways they wouldn't be able to offer me the kind of wisdom and insight that solving this little problem would require. It seemed to me that whatever decision I made, I was going to have to upset someone. How on earth did I get myself into this one?

It felt as though history was repeating itself. So leaving the shelter of Garenhir's kol, I walked down to the river and sat down upon the edge of the embankment. And after removing my boots, I dangled my feet over the edge into the water, and focussed on the sensation of the water as it rushed between my toes. And as I sat there listening to the sound of the river as it hurried along on its endless journey, I closed my eyes and found myself saying a silent prayer for guidance, and for someone…or something, to show me what I should do.

It was then that I became aware of the presence of something or someone nearby, so opening my eyes…I quickly turned around, and there sitting quietly about twenty metres directly behind me, was Sai. I hadn't heard him approach, which was very unusual for me. I continued to watch him as he stood up and briskly walked over to where I was sitting.

"You look like you might be in need of someone to talk to?" he said, sitting down next to me.

"I doubt if you could help me with this one Sai – but thanks all the same."

"If you want to be left alone – I'll leave," he said, waiting a few moments before beginning to stand up again.

"No! – Please stay for a while," I said, grabbing his arm firmly. "If you want to…that is." We just sat there without speaking for what seemed like an age; the sound of the flowing river conveniently filling in for the lack of conversation between us.

"I know that I can trust you Sai," I said, finally breaking the silence. "But I have to have your word that if I confide in you today, you won't repeat a single word that I say to you to anyone…not even to Garenhir."

"Yes, of course – you have my word," he said, very seriously.

I knew on every level that I could trust him, so I proceeded to explain the whole situation, and that I didn't have a clue what I should do about it. Sai listened intently to what I had to say, and when I'd finished explaining everything to him he said:

"The question is…what do 'you' want to do Manu Kai?"

"I don't know – that's just the thing. I really don't know what to do for the best."

"You're going have to search very deep if you want to find the answer to this one Kai. I think the only thing that you can do here is to try and be true to yourself and allow your heart to guide you." I thought about what Sai had said for a moment. I could remember my father telling me once to see with my heart when I was trying to choose my first horse. It worked then – so why not now. So closing my eyes I allowed whatever was truly in my heart to have its say.

"I want to return and continue my studies as an Agari Priest," I said, opening my eyes again.

"But at the same time I really don't want to let either my uncle or my father down. And of course…if my brother ever took the position of Sha-Pada…well, it just doesn't bare thinking about…and that puts a lot of pressure on me as I know I have the power to prevent it. But I also feel partially responsible for Altan and Chinna's deaths, as I had a very bad feeling before setting out on that ill-fated journey, but I failed to act upon it. I know now that I could have done so much more to have prevented it from happening. If only I hadn't allowed my reliance on alcohol to cloud my vision, both Altan and Chinna would most probably still be alive today. But because I didn't listen to what my higher senses were telling me, the Huns lost two good men, one of them destined to be their Khan, I lost a dear friend, and my uncle is now left without a suitable heir. By the Gods – what am I supposed to do Sai?"

"I know what I'd do if I was in your position."

His filed teeth had the effect of making him look slightly menacing, but I knew him well enough to know the truth behind his illusionary mask. There was a slight pause as he was obviously waiting for me to ask him.

"Well…go on then…are you going to tell me or what?" I responded impatiently.

Sai Pulled his hair back from his face, and tied it in place with a braided headband before responding.

"If I was where you are now, I'd cross over into the spirit realm and I'd seek my answers there." "OK, you've got my attention – go on I'm listening," I said, folding my arms.

"You need to enter into an altered state of consciousness, and journey into the spirit realm in your spirit body, and face the dweller on the threshold," he said with just a hint of a smug smile. "And if you show no fear, it will stand aside and allow you to cross over the threshold and enter into the realm of higher understanding."

I didn't like the sound of this one little bit, but I tried my best to hide my fear by bluffing it out and acting arrogant.

"You know exactly what my next question is going to be Sai, but I'll ask you anyway. So pray tell me wise Magus…and just 'how' am I supposed to do that?"

"Would you like me to show you…oh sarcastic lord of the shadow?" said Sai, smugly. "Hmm…There's really no need to be so bitchy now is there?" I retorted, with an equally smug sense of 'straight back at you.'

Sai responded by sticking his forked tongue out at me, which made me laugh and eased my fears a little. I didn't particularly like the sound of 'thresholds', and 'dwellers', but if it meant finding the answer to my question, then it had to be worth a try.

"I'm willing to try anything…well…almost anything, 'if' it will help me to find answers to all of this. And yes, you know damn well that I'd like you to show me."

"OK! Then meet me here at sundown. Oh…and by the way – don't eat anything for the rest of the day."

And without another word spoken, Sai stood up and headed back in the direction of the village. I waited for about twenty minutes or so, before making my own way back. I wondered what on earth he had in store for me. The uncertainty of what I was going to have to face was beginning to make me feel physically sick, so I couldn't eat anything even if I'd wanted to. So I just rested in my kol until just before sundown, and then hastily made my way back down to the river bank where I found Sai was already waiting for me. I walked on over to where he was sitting and sat down next to him. He nodded at me and smiled, and I thought how his filed teeth gave an edge to his otherwise slightly effeminate demeanour. Neither of us had grown a typical Scythian beard yet, and although he was above average height for a Scythian man, it would be true to say that he was actually quite androgynous in appearance.

"You turned up then," he said.

"Obviously," I replied, sarcastically.

Pulling my knees up to my chest I wrapped my arms tightly around my legs.

"You look a little bit nervous sat there Manu Kai," he said, untying a little leather bag that he had fastened to his belt.

"Me…nervous…well maybe just a little," I said, pulling my knee's up even tighter.

"Hmm…" he said, "I find that quite interesting after some of the stuff that you've obviously been messing about with."

"You don't know what I've been…as you say…messing about with."

"I've got a very good idea though. So tell me, Manu Kai, did your journey into the shadow land actually teach you anything of value?"

194

"Yes, actually it did. I saw a few things that I wish I hadn't. And the reason why I'm feeling very nervous right now is because I've already stood on one threshold…the threshold of the Abyss, and even though I only caught a quick glimpse of what terrible things lurk there, something saw me, and it tried to possess me, and although it failed, it did manage to get some kind of a hold on me for quite a while, and…well…you saw the result. I saw it Sai…the problem is that it saw me too. It's real…and I'm terrified it might be waiting for me at the threshold that you speak of. Just promise me you'll never get tempted to wander down that path. There are terrible things there, and some of them are very clever. They can get a grip on you, and even though they will feed you with unnatural power, they're only using you as a channel to work through, until finally they will destroy you altogether."

There was a moment of silence until Sai said:

"Hmm…I could actually feel it; it was as if it was trying to make a connection with you as you were talking. Maybe you shouldn't talk about it again unless you have a very good reason to." I nodded in agreement. "So, come on then – let's get on with whatever it is that you're going to teach me shall we."

"OK, my impatient friend," he said, clapping his hands together.

Sai proceeded to explain that he was going to give me something to drink which would cause me to experience an altered state of reality. He said that he'd done this many times himself, and that I could trust him implicitly as he'd already attained a high degree of understanding in this field of shamanic practice. He told me that he was going to act as my guide throughout my whole journey into the spirit world and back again, and hopefully I would bring back the answers to my questions. He hesitated for a moment, before telling me that he was going to guide me right up to the threshold, but I, and I alone, would have to successfully overcome whatever it was that was going to be waiting for me there, he said that this was the one part of the journey that I was going to have to face by myself, as he was not going to be able to do anything to help me at this point.

"What exactly is it that I'm going to have to face?" I asked him nervously. But his answer to my question did nothing to help calm my nerves at all.

"Something most terrifying I'm afraid – and many seekers fail at this point. Your heart must be strong, and your faith must be unshakable in the knowledge that if you bravely stand your ground, 'it', or 'they', will stand aside and allow you to pass."

"Great…I can hardly wait. Come on then let's do it," I said, taking a deep breath.

Sai opened the small leather bag which was tied to his belt and pulled out a little clay bottle, and twisting off the top, he held it out to me. I hesitated for a moment, so he gave me a little prompt by giving the contents of the bottle a little swirl before holding it out towards me once again. I was about to ask him how much of it I should drink, but he had already anticipated my question, and before I'd had a chance to speak again he said: "All of it!"

"Oh well…here goes," I said.

And taking the bottle from his hand and raising it to my mouth, I drank its contents straight down in one go.

"How long will it take to kick in?" I asked him.

"It won't be very long before you begin to feel strange, and you'll probably feel a bit sick for a little while. After that, the full hallucinogenic effects will rapidly start to kick in, and then we can begin."

After a short while I began to notice that everything was beginning to look a lot brighter, and I couldn't judge the size or the distance of anything anymore, I also began to feel nauseous.

"I think I need to lie down for a little while," I said, curling up on the ground.

As I continued to lay there for a while waiting for the nausea to pass, I noticed that Sai, who appeared to be doing his level best to ignore me right now, was beginning to look quite peculiar. It was as if I was actually seeing him for the very first time, and I realised that there was so much more to him than I could see with my normal senses. And although he had only seen twenty-one winters, he had the presence of someone much older than his years, and I felt as though we had known each other somewhere before – long ago in another life perhaps. And as I looked around at the surrounding landscape, it began to rapidly change shape all around me, and I was instantly transported back to another place and time. I realised that I no longer felt nauseous anymore, so feeling the need to sit upright, I looked down at the ground in order to steady myself, but unfortunately everything appeared to have taken on a life of its own, and was presently in a weird state of constant change and motion – which was making it very difficult to co-ordinate. But after some effort on my part, I finally managed to sit upright again.

"I think I can remember you from another life," I said, still struggling to make some sense of it all.

Sai's face although translucent, was about the only thing which was still barely recognisable to me. Suddenly I began to feel a little bit panicky, and Sai had obviously picked up on this.

"You're perfectly safe, Manu Kai. Just take a few deep breaths and keep looking at me." I did as he said, and I began to study his face. The tattoo across his forehead, and down the full length of his nose which marked him as an Agari priest, seemed to take on a whole different meaning, and I could now see why he'd had it done. The braids in his hair had all morphed into living snakes, and the light that radiated from all around him gave him the appearance of some sort of unearthly messenger of the Gods. And as I looked deeper and deeper, I began to realise that I was actually able to see beyond his outer physical form, and into his hidden inner self. I was even aware that he knew exactly what I was doing, and that he was presently permitting me to do this. He allowed me to continue until I was able to pierce right through his inner veil, and even gain some access into his deeper spiritual self, 'the man behind the mask so to speak.' I was fascinated to learn about the many complicated and diverse aspects of his inner nature. It was like looking into a mighty inner universe, with all of its many stars and planets, and each one reflecting the outer universe itself, and all of which came together as a whole, and made him the sum total of who he actually was.

I knew that if I tried, I would actually be able to look right into his mind right now. I tried to look into his eyes, but somehow he must have known what I was about to do, as he suddenly looked away. "Sorry, Manu Kai," he said, "But I can't permit even you to look that deeply. You're actually the only one I've ever allowed to go that far, but there are still some things that I'm not quite ready to share with you...yet! But you can already understand the potent possibilities of being where you are right now."

I just couldn't take my eyes off him, and he smiled at me and said:

"Am I really that fascinating?"

I suddenly realised that I really did find him fascinating. In fact, as difficult as it was for me to accept, I realised that I was actually feeling strongly attracted to him right now. His whole countenance was one of altruistic benevolence, and there was no doubt in my mind whatsoever that he had my very best interests at heart, and that he really did have genuine feelings for me.

I began to feel very confused by my feelings for Sai, and I could tell by the way he was looking at me right now that he must have picked up on this. I felt embarrassed, and lowering my gaze I stared down at my hands; except...they didn't really look like my hands anymore; so raising my right hand I began to study it, and I soon realised that I could actually see straight through it. I was fascinated as my hand began to fade in and out of view, until it appeared to completely disappear altogether. I suddenly felt as though my whole body was melting into millions of tiny little individual versions of myself. And if that didn't feel weird enough, I was actually able to look through all of my many eyes…and all at the same time. And each one of the little ME's were all looking at all the other little ME's.

That was it…I was gone. I wasn't even sure which way up the ground was any more, and I hoped that my body wouldn't forget to keep on breathing, as I didn't even feel as though I had a body right now.

That's when I became aware of Sai's voice…

"Manu Kai…just focus on my voice, and allow yourself to be guided by my words. I'm going to guide you step by step until you reach the dweller on the threshold, at which point you must trust that no matter how terrifying it may appear, it can do you no harm if you remain calm and unafraid, and it will soon yield to your will and allow you to pass unharmed."

Sai began to guide me through the process, until I could just about make out the menacing shadowy outline of the 'thing' that I must come face to face with and somehow overcome. I could see something in the distance which was looming ominously straight up ahead of me. So remembering Sai's words, I continued to move closer and closer, until I could clearly see what it looked like. It was indeed more terrifying to behold than I could ever have imagined possible, and as I continued my approach, it began to move in such an unearthly way, that it appeared to be what I can only describe as…multi-dimensional. Every movement that it made was repeated several times over, as if it was stuck in some kind of time warp. Layer upon layer of movement which was constantly overlapping, and which effectively gave it an overall appearance of something quite terrifying. This was bad enough, when suddenly without warning, it reached out as if to attack me, and as it did, it began to split into a multitude of monstrous gaping mouths, which snarled and snapped at me from every direction. And each one oozed foul liquids, and spat decaying flesh from rancid yellow teeth which were as big as my whole body.

I heard Sai's voice echo in the distance: "Remember to hold your ground."

Hearing Sai's words filled me with the knowledge that I had nothing to be afraid of, and fearlessly standing my ground, I waited until at last it finally withdrew…sliding back into the shadows from whence it had come.

The way ahead was now clear for me to step across the threshold, and to enter into the domain of higher understanding and clarity of vision, and as I took that small…but massive step, and crossed over into the domain of understanding, I instantly felt an unmistakable sense of perception and clarity of thought, and I immediately knew the answer to my question. It all seemed so obvious to me now, that I wondered why I couldn't see it before.

I became aware of Sai's voice telling me to turn around, and to step back over the threshold. I immediately did what he said, and in an instant I was back in my body again, and sitting bolt upright, I grabbed hold of Sai by the arm.

"I did it…I know what I've got to do now," I said, excitedly.

"I know – Well done, Manu Kai, I knew that you could do it," he said smiling. I soon realised that although I was still heavily under the influence of a very powerful hallucinogenic, I felt a lot more in control now, so much so, that I even managed to stand on my feet again…albeit a little unsteadily at first. And after staring at the ground for a couple of minutes, I insisted on going for a walk. Sai had very little choice other than to indulge me in this, and luckily for me he was quite happy to walk along side of me, and make sure that I remained safely out of harm's way until the effects of the hallucinogenic eventually wore off. At one point he had to physically drag me out of the river after I'd insisted on sitting in the middle of it, and then apparently – I'd flatly refused to come back out again. It could have been a lot worse; at least I'd chosen a shallow part of the river to decide to become one with nature.

I felt as though a huge weight had been lifted from me, and I knew that I only had Sai to thank for this one. He'd been able to offer me so much more than the simple advice I was initially looking for.

Eventually the effects of the hallucinogenic had worn off enough for Sai to be able to return me to Garenhir's kol, and hopefully to get some sleep. As I lay down and closed my eyes, I began to think about what I had to do, and I could see how all of this could actually work out for the better. The only thing that was really bothering me right now, was the confusing feelings that I'd felt for Sai earlier. There really wasn't any point in trying to kid myself that I hadn't had those feelings, as I knew damn well that I'd actually felt quite strongly attracted to him at one point. The worst thing was that I knew he'd picked up on it. But his high moral standards would have prevented him from acting upon the situation. He was obviously aware that this was the very first time I'd ever experienced a strong hallucinogenic, and I would have been very vulnerable and not in any fit state to be responsible for my feelings, or how I chose to act upon them. I even began to wonder if he'd actually done something to me to make me feel that way, but I quickly dismissed those thoughts, as I knew Sai well enough to know that even if he was capable of purposely affecting me in that way – he would never have allowed himself to stoop so low. It was most probably nothing more than the intoxicating effects of the hallucinogenic, and the best thing to do was to forget all about it and hope that I was mistaken, and that Sai hadn't really picked up on my feelings at all. I don't know who I was trying to kid but it wasn't working very well…Oh boy!

16

The Proposal

Between the residual effects of the hallucinogenic, and the fact that my mind seemed hell bent on churning over the events of the last few days, I didn't actually manage to get a lot of sleep that night, but even so, I must have eventually managed to drift off, as I was awoken by the sound of someone calling my name and shaking me. Blearily I opened my eyes to the sight of Garenhir peering down at me.

"Good morning…I'm sorry to have to wake you Manu Kai, but some of your men are becoming a little restless, and they are demanding to see you. I think they just want to make sure that you're OK, and no amount of assurance from me will suffice."

"Oh, for pity's sake. Tell them I said: *Khümüüs end untaj chadakhgüi baina.* They will know that's from me."

Realising that I was naked, I began looking around for my clothes. I couldn't even remember taking them off. Garenhir had disappeared outside to relay my message, so I had to wait until he came back in again before I could ask him if he knew what had happened to them.

"Ah! Yes, apparently you went for a little dip in the river, so I gave you a hand to get out of them before I hung them up to dry. Here they are," he said, grabbing them from behind a wooden screen and handing them to me.

"Thank you. Yes, I did do that didn't I? I don't remember you helping me undress though," I replied, struggling to recall the events of the previous evening.

"So – how did it go after?"

"It went well," I said, rubbing my eyes. "At least I think it did. Do you know what happened?"

"No, not exactly," said Garenhir, shaking his head. "But Sai did have a little chat with me beforehand, he didn't tell me the reason, but he did say that he thought you might benefit from a guided shamanic journey as it may help you to gain some insight into a difficult decision that you needed to make, and he just wanted to clear it with me first. Sai is a very talented student, and I know him well enough to be able to trust his insight, and I had no doubt that you'd be perfectly safe in his hands, so I had no hesitation in giving him my blessing to go ahead."

"Well…it's thanks to Sai's help and guidance that I know exactly what I need to do. Unfortunately Derkesthai – I can't tell you everything just yet…even though I really want to, but I can tell you that I've made the decision to return and continue with my studies."

"I respect the fact that you must have a very good reason for choosing not to share certain things with me at this present moment in time Manu Kai," he said, resting his hand on my shoulder. "But I'm so glad to hear that you've made the decision to return and persevere with your studies, as it's of great importance that you continue. You've probably realised by now that there really isn't any going back, and whatever it is that you feel unable to tell me about right now, I'm quite sure that you will have gained some equally wise insight into the best way ahead there also."

"I truly hope so Derkesthai…I really do."

"Right then," I said, rubbing my hands together, "I'd better get myself ready to face my men."

As I stepped outside, I found the brightness of the daylight very uncomfortable. I held one hand up to shield my eyes from the harsh glare of a cloudy day, and I was surprised to see at least ten Hun warriors all sat around outside patiently waiting for me to emerge, and as soon as they saw me, they all stood up and walked over to greet me, so I informed them that we would all be travelling back a little later on this day, and that they should make ready the horses, as I would be ready to leave just as soon as I'd had a chance to speak with my father.

Just then Sai showed up and gave me a rather knowing look. I suddenly recalled having felt very attracted to him the night before and I began to feel very awkward.

"Sai – can I have a quiet word with you?" I asked him, reaching out and grabbing him by the arm as he went to walk past me.

I walked him right over to the far side of Garenhir's kol so that we could talk in private, but when we got there I found it very difficult to even look him in the eyes, and whatever it was that I had intended to say to him had suddenly crumbled to dust, along with all my resolve.

"I…Uhm…I just wanted to thank you for your help last night…that's all. I'm going to be leaving soon, so I'll see you when I get back."

As I turned to leave, I briefly allowed my eyes to meet with his, and holding my gaze for as long as he could, he gave me that slightly crooked half smile of his, which was accompanied by a very slight nod of his head, so I quickly nodded back to him before briskly walking off. He hadn't even said a single word. Damn it…He didn't need to! The look on his face had told me everything that I really didn't want to know.

I made my way straight over to my father's kol, and when I arrived my mother was sat outside with my three sisters, the youngest of whom was still a babe in arms. As soon as they saw me they all began calling out to me.

"Kai…Kai…"

My mother threw down the dress that she had been sewing.

"Son…I've missed you. It's been such a long time. Look how much you've grown. Are you going to be coming back for good now?" she managed to blurt out all in one breath.

"I've missed you too. And yes…I'll be coming back soon."

My mother threw herself to the floor and raised her hands in thanks to the Gods and began to cry. I wanted to hug her, but I was about to face my father, and I couldn't risk him seeing any sign of emotional weakness in me, so I quickly changed the subject and asked her where Father was instead.

"He's inside," she said, slowly rising to her feet. "I'll let him know you're here son," she said, disappearing into the kol.

Straining my ears to try and hear what was being said, I hushed my sisters to be quiet.

"Kai is here to speak with you Herian," I heard my mother say.

"He wants you to go right in," she said, suddenly reappearing through the doorway. I walked through the entrance with an air of unwavering confidence, and my father immediately stood up to greet me.

"Will you sit down, Kai," he said with a sweeping gesture of his hand.

We both sat down facing one another, and as usual, he didn't waste any time in getting straight to the point.

"So have you decided what you're going to do yet?"

"Yes, Father, I've made my decision."

"Well…what is it?" he prompted impatiently.

"I have decided to return with Tihanna and our daughter, and I will also accept your proposal to stand second in line for leadership…but only if I can continue with my studies as an Agari. Oh! And there's just one other thing."

I hesitated for a moment and I took a deep breath before continuing, I could see that my father was hanging on my every word, and a part of me was actually enjoying keeping him in suspense.

"As you know I've already promised my uncle that I'll stand second in line to him, and the thing is – I really don't want to let him down…so this is what I'm going to do. I will let my uncle know that I'm going be moving back here to continue my studies as an Agari priest, and that you have also asked me to stand as second in line to you and to take the position of 'Sha Pada' when the time finally comes. I shall tell him that I will no longer be able to stand as his second in command, as it's going to be too impractical, as I'm going to be spending most of my time here. But if anything should happen to him, I'll immediately return and claim the position of Khan. And as long as all the right people are made aware of this, there shouldn't be any problems. And in the meantime, I shall keep regular and frequent visits, so that I'm kept right up to date on current affairs."

"But if you take the position of Khan, what do you plan to do if anything should happen to me, Kai?" he asked, with a very puzzled expression on his face.

Leaning in towards me, my father rested his chin in his hand, and staring very hard in my direction, he awaited my reply with intense interest.

"Well – if that should happen," I continued. "I shall step up and also make claim to the position of Sha Pada. And if anything should happen to you before my uncle, I will claim the position of Sha Pada first. And again, as long as you make sure that all the necessary people are informed of this before-hand, there shouldn't be a problem with any of this. Then if anything should happen to my uncle after I've already taken the position of Sha Pada, I will also lay claim to the position of Khan, and ultimately unite both tribes as one. You've always insisted that I should be aware of my Hun heritage father, but it's a lot more complicated than that now…the result being, is that I'm equally both Scythian and Hun. I've thought deeply about this, and I can see no good reason why both tribes couldn't be united as one."

My father just continued to sit there staring at me with both eyebrows raised.

"Well," he said, rubbing his chin. "I've got to hand it to you son – you've certainly got high ideals. I don't know if what you've said is actually going to be achievable; mostly due to cultural differences. But I'm impressed by your far-sightedness I must say that much."

"Hmm, well 'I've' managed to embrace and to integrate the two cultures haven't I? Of course, I have yet to present all of this to my uncle, so I'll have to wait and see how he responds first."

I ruminated on this for a few moments before continuing…

"I'll be leaving today, but before the moon is full I shall return, and then I'll be able to inform you of my uncle's response. I have to go now as my men are waiting for me, but we'll talk further on this when I return."

As I stood up, my father immediately followed suit, and we embraced each other with genuine affection before I turned to leave.

"I'll make preparations for your return son," said my father, just as I was about to make my exit. I didn't turn around to respond to this, as it would have been considered very bad luck just before a journey. So without glancing back, I hesitated for a moment.

"Thank you, Father," I said, before continuing on my way.

Merren and Aptien had obviously received word that we would be leaving very soon, and it would seem that so had everyone else, as they were all gathered together and waiting for me outside my father's kol, along with my horse who had also been made ready and waiting for me. So without further notice – we immediately headed back to Hun territory.

I hadn't had much chance to talk to Merren and Aptien about any of my plans, and indeed there was much I couldn't share with them at this present moment in time…even if I wanted to. So whatever they needed to know would just have to wait until after we had arrived back at the Hun encampment.

We continued to ride non-stop until it began to get dark, and then we stopped to make our camp for the night, and just as I'd expected, Merren and Aptien soon began to bombard me with questions. They weren't stupid, and they obviously knew that something had happened since we'd returned to Scythia, and it was the not knowing exactly what it was, that was presently killing the pair of them. They were beginning to drive me quite mad, and I knew that they were both doing it on purpose, and it was pretty obvious that they weren't going to let it rest until I'd told them at least something of what was going on.

"OK – let's all go for a little walk then, shall we?" I said, before their constant nagging had succeeded in driving me completely insane.

So leaving the rest of the men sitting around the camp fire, we found ourselves somewhere a little more private. And no sooner had our backsides managed to touch the ground, than Merren immediately began asking what all the fuss was about with the Agari.

"Ah – I'm afraid I can't tell you that, Merren, as I'm sworn by a blood oath never to repeat anything that goes on within the circle of the Agari brotherhood, and as much as I trust you both, I'm held by that oath."

"As you're not actually part of the Agari anymore, we didn't think that oath applied to you anymore," said Merren, thoughtfully.

"Well – guess what? I've decided to return to Scythia and continue my studies with the Agari. But even if I wasn't, I would still have to uphold my sacred oath to the Agari brotherhood." "See…I was right! What did I say? – I knew it!" said Aptien, giving Merren a little shove. Merren just looked at Aptien and nodded.

"This news comes as no surprise Manu Kai. We were half expecting you to tell us this anyway. But what's with all the hush hush?" asked Merren, carefully studying my expression for a moment before continuing: "There's a bit more to this…isn't there Kai?"

Merren began stroking his beard thoughtfully, and along with Aptien, he just sat there silently staring at me. I really don't know which was worst, the two of them bombarding me with questions, or the two of them staring at me in total silence. I was almost relieved when Aptien finally broke the silence.

"So are you going to tell us?"

"I guess you both deserve to know the truth," I said with a sigh.

It just felt wrong somehow to conceal the truth from them, after all the loyalty they had both shown me time and time again…although; I never could quite understand why.

"You must both swear to me that you will never repeat what I'm about to tell you to anyone," I said, in a very serious tone of voice.

"Well obviously," said Merren.

"That should go without saying," added Aptien.

"Maybe – but just humour me. Now both swear."

"Yes, OK – I swear never to repeat what you tell us to anyone," said Merren, placing his hand to his chest.

"Me too…I mean yes, I swear. I'm not going to repeat anything you say to anyone. You should know that by now. But yes…I'll even swear a blood oath to that fact, if it makes you feel any better," said Aptien, drawing his knife from its sheath.

"No, that won't be necessary…a verbal oath will be just fine. Right then…here goes." And so, I proceeded to explain the whole story from start to finish…well almost. I left out the bit about Sai and my hallucinogenic journey into the spirit world. The looks on their faces went from deep interest to amazement, until they were both just sat there staring at me with their mouths open in total astonishment. Merren shook his head in awe, and then raising his hands and eyes upwards towards the sky he said:

"That's the craziest damn thing that I've ever heard for sure. Manu Kai, if ever I had any doubts about you – and yes, I must admit, there have been times…well…I'm sorry! I take it all back. This answers it all I suppose…That's just damn crazy."

Aptien began to laugh…he had obviously found Merren's verbal ramblings quite amusing.

"What's so funny?" Merren asked him pan faced.

And for some reason, that made Aptien laugh even more. His laughter was very infectious, and before long all three of us were in complete hysterics. I hadn't laughed like that since…I can't remember! And it felt so good to be able to laugh again.

After a little while, the three of us re-joined the rest of the men, and after a rather late supper, we finally settled ourselves down for the night.

The sky was really clear tonight, so I just lay there staring up at the stars in the night sky for a while wondering to myself why my life always had to be so damn complicated? Talk about having a dual nature…I must have been duality manifested in the flesh! Garenhir often spoke to me of polarities, and about bringing the two conflicting sides of my inner nature together as one. He explained that we all have what can be described as an inner pendulum, and the further it is capable of swinging in one direction, the further it is capable of swinging in the other. He said if you rested a paint brush on a piece of parchment paper, and then drew downwards at opposite angles from a single point, and then joined those lines together at the bottom, you'd have a triangle. And if you draw a circle around it, it symbolises the total capacity of the expanse of conscious awareness that an individual has developed over many life times. A reversed triangle placed over the top of the upright one symbolises the necessary balance between opposites, and the dualistic nature of all things. He said that the centre point in the middle of the upward and downward pointing triangles, symbolised the eye, or point of true vision, which can only be attained when all the necessary alignments have been made. Only when this has been achieved can the initiate see with the eyes of a Serpent of Wisdom. The initiate then reaches a state of perfect equilibrium, and eventually becomes a very powerful centre point of wisdom and higher consciousness. Garenhir also told me that there were several other meanings for this symbol, but this explanation was the one that the Agari preferred above all the others.

As soon as we arrived at the Hun encampment, I wasted no time at all in seeking out my uncle, and luckily, I was able to speak to him immediately as he was alone resting in his yurt. I explained to him about my father having asked me to stand next in line for the position of Sha Pada, and the reasons why I felt that I had very little choice other than to accept. And without giving him a chance to react, I then quickly presented him with my proposal, telling him that I'd already spoken to my father, and that he's fully prepared to offer me his full support, and as long as he, (my uncle) had no objections, then my father couldn't see any reason why my idea couldn't be achievable. My uncle just sat staring at me for a little while before he finally responded.

"Hmm…" he said thoughtfully. "I think that your proposal to unite our two tribes is a very interesting concept. When you get back, tell your father we need to organise a meeting so that we can discuss this further."

"Of course, Uncle," I said standing up, as I could see that our talks had ended for now; so respectfully I bowed to him, before leaving him alone to reflect upon what I'd just said.

Next stop was to inform Tihanna that we would soon be leaving to go and live at my father's village.

As I approached the entrance to our yurt, I must admit to feeling a little apprehensive about how Tihanna was going to react to this news, after all, my father wasn't exactly thrilled after he'd learned of her existence. But all of my fears just melted away the moment that I walked in through the entrance to our yurt and I saw her happily playing with our daughter Nymadawa. It felt so good to be home again, and I realised just how much I'd missed out on all of this. I loved them both so much, and how I'd ever allowed myself to shut them out the way that I had, and descend into such a contemptible state of destructive behaviour I'll never know.

I just quietly stood there watching the two of them for a few moments, until Tihanna finally noticed me. She smiled and stood up to great me, so walking up to her, I reached out and pulled her close to me, and we immediately fell into a passionate embrace.

"I'm so sorry, Tihanna," I said in a soft voice. "Please forgive me for everything that I've put you through."

"I've never stopped loving you Kai…through it all," she said with tears in her eyes. "How could I ever do anything else but to forgive you?"

"I don't deserve you, Tihanna – and I know that, but I've actually got something very important to tell you, so let's go and sit down…and I'll explain."

And taking her by the hand, I led her to our bed, where I'm quite sure things would have progressed further from there had Nymadawa not been around, but she was, so we just sat down next to one another instead, and I proceeded to tell her all about my plan for us to move to my father's village, and that I was also going to continue with my studies as an Agari priest. Tihanna's mouth dropped open in surprise, and her eyes immediately filled up with tears before she excitedly grabbed me around the neck – kissing me over and over again.

"Oh, Kai, that's excellent news," she said with tears now streaming down both sides of her face.

"I was a bit worried that you might not want to…after what happened and all that," I said, feeling somewhat relieved by her obvious enthusiasm. That night we made sure to make up for lost time…

A meeting was promptly arranged between my father, my uncle, and me, along with everyone else who needed to be made directly aware of this rather ambitious plan of mine. My proposal was unanimously accepted. And so that was that…Sorted!

And very soon all of the necessary preliminary preparations had been made, and within a very short time, I, along with Tihanna, our daughter Nymadawa, and Merren and Aptien, all headed home to Scythia.

17

Painful Memories

We arrived back to a warm welcome, and my father had already made sure that two new kol's had been especially built and furnished ready for our return. There was one for Merren and Aptien, and one for Tihanna, Nymadawa, and me, and although it all felt a little strange to be back at first, especially for Tihanna and Nymadawa; it didn't take very long before we had all settled in. Poor little Nymadawa found it very frustrating that no one seemed to understand a single word that she said, as the only language she could speak was Hunnic. It didn't take her very long though, before she began learning to speak the Scythian language. I guess children that age pick things up pretty quickly.

I whole heartedly threw myself straight back into my studies, and Garenhir promptly reinstated the practice of building up my immunity towards snake venom. I found myself taking my studies even more seriously than I had before, and it wasn't very long before Garenhir informed me that I was to take my first initiation into the outer circle of the Agari, and this would require travelling to the mountain cave that was used by the Agari for their secret meetings and rituals. I had no idea what this would entail, only that I would have to successfully accomplish a series of set tasks in readiness for my inauguration into the Agari proper. These tasks were given to the neophyte in order to prove that he had reached a high enough degree of understanding, concentration, and mental control, which was an essential requirement during some of the secret practices and rituals that were an integral part of being a member of the Agari priesthood. During this time I was also taught the different medicinal properties of certain herbs, tree barks, and fungi. And, of course – snake venom, along with an array of other poisonous and narcotic substances. This was a specialised subject in itself, and some Agari dedicated themselves to the study of this above all else, and although I found it very interesting, it wasn't really my calling so to speak. I also became more accustomed to the use of certain hallucinogens which were used exclusively to attain heightened states of consciousness, and I also had to prove that I could successfully carry out certain tasks while I was under the influence of these hallucinogens.

One day Garenhir and I were discussing the different kinds of relationships that can exist between two people, when I became curious as to why he had chosen to live alone, as in all the time that I'd known him, I'd never once seen him with a woman, or a man for that matter. So I decided to come right out with it and ask him straight.

"Derkesthai – can I ask you a personal question?"

"You can ask, but I can't guarantee that I'll give you an answer," he said, chuckling to himself. "Go on then Manu Kai fire away. Whatever it is that you feel the need to ask me – now's your chance."

"I know it's really nothing to do with me Derkesthai, but I've never known you to have a lover – and I was wondering why you choose to remain alone."

"Hmm…I suppose it's only natural for you to wonder. Come and sit opposite me Manu Kai and I'll try to explain," he said with a sigh.

I did as he asked, and he began to explain to me that there were several reasons why he chose to remain alone. And one of them was that he had dedicated this life to his spiritual study and to teaching, and he felt that having a partner would only be a distraction to this. Plus, he genuinely enjoyed the times of solitude that living alone gave him.

"And in order to save you the trouble of asking me the next question, Manu Kai…Yes, I am celibate, and if this was not the case, then my choice of partner would have most definitely have been female. Does this answer all of your questions?" he asked, with a slight air of satisfaction at having correctly anticipated my next two questions. "Nearly all I guess…But can I ask you just one more?"

"If you must," he replied.

I knew that I was probably over stepping the mark here, but I figured that if he didn't want to answer any of my questions, he'd soon let me know.

"Have you 'ever' had a lover?" I asked, cringing at my own blatant intrusion into his private life.

However, he didn't really seem to mind.

"Yes, Manu Kai…I have. I was actually very much in love once. It was a very long time ago before I came to live here."

"What happened?" I asked, curiously.

"Ahhh…Manu Kai," said Garenhir, with a sad and distant look in his eyes. "It's a very long story, and I really don't want to bore you with all the details. I've never spoken of it since leaving my home land all those years ago, and besides; you probably wouldn't find it all that interesting."

"Actually I 'do' find it interesting – please tell me," I said, both captivated and intrigued by the secret that he'd kept hidden for all of this time.

Garenhir sighed very deeply, and looking very thoughtful he said:

"Very well then, Manu Kai."

I listened with great interest as he began to share his story with me.

"Just where do I start? Well… As I said, it was a long time ago Manu Kai, I was younger than you are now. It was back in my homeland, in a place quite far from here across the water which we called 'Don', (Britain) where I lived amongst a Warrior tribe of people called 'The Shaul' (Siluries – People of the wise, or 'Northern' star)I was in training to become a priest within a religious brotherhood very much like this one, who are called 'Druids', and part of my duties there was to tend to our temple fire which was always kept burning. And every night I'd walk down to the temple alone, and after tending to the fire, I sometimes took the opportunity that the peaceful silence of the night gave me to meditate for a while. One evening I was surprised to find a young woman sat alone in the sacred grove. I instantly recognised her as belonging to the royal family that lived nearby, as she along with other members of her family, would often come and attend the religious ceremonies that were held throughout the year. At first I was unsure if I should say anything to her or not, so I remained silent and just carried on with my duties, but as I walked past her, I could see that she had obviously been crying, and I wondered if she might need someone to talk to. So plucking up the courage, I nervously asked her if she was OK, and if she needed to talk. She looked up at me and started to cry again, and not really knowing what to do or say, I tentatively sat down next to her. No further prompting on my part was needed before she began to explain that she had been promised in marriage to a man that she really didn't want to marry, and that the thought of this was making her feel very unhappy. I didn't really know what to say to her, as I was very young and I didn't have any answers. So I just continued to sit with her for a while, until she graciously thanked me for my time and for listening to her. And after thanking me once more – she stood up to leave. But before she left, I told her that I was here every night about this time, and if she ever needed someone to talk to in the future I would be happy to listen, and that she could trust that anything she said to me would be treated as confidential.

"I didn't realise it then, but her visits were to become a regular thing. And as time went by, I found myself actually looking forward to our secret rendezvous. I never meant for it to happen, but I became increasingly fond of her, until eventually my every waking thought was entirely wrapped up with just being with her once again. I was aware that my feelings were misplaced, and that it was wrong of me to feel this way – but what could I do? I was trapped in a hopeless situation. I knew that I'd fallen in love with her. I hadn't seen it coming – and now it was too late. My feelings for her terrified me, but I was so hopelessly in love, and so caught up in the tide of my emotions, that I began to wonder if I should just tell her how I felt, at least then I'd know if she had similar feelings for me. But what if she did? – What would we do then? I couldn't stand it any longer, so I decided that whatever the outcome, I was just going to have to tell her how I felt. Then at least if she didn't feel the same way, I'd know where I stood, and could then begin the process of trying to move on with my life.

"That night I arrived at the temple early...and I waited...terrified at the thought of what I was about to do. When she finally arrived, she walked over and sat down next to me as usual, but I was so nervous that I began to tremble. She noticed this and asked me what was wrong, so turning to face her, I told her that I had something very important that I needed to tell her, and as terrified as I was...it was going to be now or never, so I just blurted out that I was in love with her, and even though I knew that it was wrong for me to feel this way, I really couldn't help my feelings and that she had a right to know. She just sat there staring at me the whole time, and I hardly dared to wonder at her response, so you can imagine how relieved I felt when she told me that she had feelings for me too, but that she had been too afraid to say anything in case I didn't feel the same way about her. I felt both elated, and terrified at the same time.

"'What are we going to do?' I asked her.

"'I don't know – just hold me,' she replied. And we fell into each other's arms and into the throws of such intoxicating forbidden passion, that neither of us was prepared for what was to happen between us that fateful evening.

"And so it was that we continued to embark upon our passionate and illicit secret love affair, which continued right up until the time had finally arrived for her arranged marriage to take place. She begged me to run away with her, to some place far away where we wouldn't be found. But I was just a novice Druid, and she was a princess. How could I provide for her? And where would we go? I had nothing to offer her but my love. So although it broke my heart in two, I decided that the best thing that I could do for her was to leave this place forever, and in time she would forget all about me and get on with her life, and hopefully, she would be happy someday. So without even saying goodbye, I packed a few personal belongings and set off to wherever my destiny would carry me. I continued to wander from place to place for some time, but I was unable to settle as I was continually haunted by my memories of her. She was always in my waking thoughts no matter how hard I tried to forget her, and she always managed to find me in my dreams at night.

"After many days of wandering, I eventually found myself on board a ship sailing to where? I knew not, and I cared even less.

"Years passed by…but still haunted by her memory I continued to move from place to place. The only comfort that I felt was in knowing that I'd done the right thing. Until one day the unbearable truth had finally managed to catch up with me in the shape of a fellow traveller from my homeland, who had been trying his fortune at prospecting for gold.

"One night while we were sharing a camp fire and casually engaging in small talk, he had told me that the princess from our native homeland had taken her own life, and probably not long after I'd left by the sound of things. He went on to say that it was rumoured that she had been having a secret love affair and that she had become pregnant by this unknown secret lover. And on hearing this, I immediately plummeted into the depths of utter despair, and not caring what happened to me, I set out and just walked and walked. I wouldn't eat, and I only slept when I was too exhausted to continue. Unwashed and emaciated, I finally collapsed, and praying for death to come swiftly, I just lay there awaiting my own demise. I was barely conscious and close to death, when I was discovered by an Agari Priest, who after fetching help to carry me to his kol, took care of me and gradually nurtured me back to health, and was to eventually become my own teacher. It took a while before I was well again, but after I had regained my strength, I swore that I would dedicate the rest of my life to my spiritual studies, and after my teacher left for India, I took his place here as Derkesthai, and I've remained here ever since. So now you know all about my sordid past, Manu Kai, I hope that you will not look upon me any less kindly."

I just sat and stared at him speechless. I was completely blown away by his tale of love and tragedy. He had never so much as even hinted towards any of this during the whole time that I'd known him.

"No! – Of course not. That's an incredible story – I had no idea that you'd been through all of that."

"Sometimes it's necessary for us to experience our darkest moment before we can begin to rise back up towards the light again. It was very difficult for me to speak to you of this, so I truly hope that this has been of some value to you Manu Kai."

It was time for me to leave him alone so that he could carry on with his personal daily meditations. So leaving him in peace, I began to make my way back to my kol, when up ahead I could see that we obviously had visitors. I thought that I had better do the politically correct thing and drop by and see who it was, and as I walked into my father's kol, I immediately recognised my old Thracian friend Gaidres, who was accompanied by several other Thracian's, and some other men who instantly had the effect of transporting me back in time to that fateful day in the forest when I was living with the Hun. The horrified expression on my face didn't go unnoticed by my father, who quickly reacted by grabbing me by the arm, and quietly but firmly accompanying me outside.

"Who are those men?" I demanded to know.

"They're from Italy – they've come to talk…that's all," he replied.

"I don't care what they've come for," I retorted rather angrily. "They're wearing the same type of clothes as the men who killed Altan and Chinna – and I'll have nothing to do with them." My father continued to hold onto my arm firmly.

"Shhh…keep your voice down. Yes, maybe! – But from what I hear, 'you' amongst others, wreaked a suitably bloody revenge. Do you want them to know who you are? Look! – just stay out of it for now – and I'll talk to you later."

I felt all of the painful emotions that up until now, I believed that I'd dealt with suddenly resurface again. And like a tempestuous storm, I rose up in my father's face, and with bared teeth, and white knuckles – I wrenched myself free from his strong grip before angrily marching off. I made my way straight to my kol, and when I got there I felt so angry, and so frustrated, that I didn't know what to do with myself. Part of me wanted to kill them, while another part of me desperately struggled to keep these feelings under control, as I knew that it was wrong for me to feel this way. Thankfully Tihanna was spending some time with a few friends that she'd recently made, so she was not around to see me like this. But I knew one thing for sure – I was never going be able to put what had happened behind me, and the Hun part of me was always going to react in a negative way to these so-called Italians. I had cursed them all once, and the aftertaste of that curse was still lingering heavily on my breath.

Sitting alone in my kol, I was suddenly disturbed by the sound of someone calling my name from outside, so I stood up and walked over to see who it was. It was Gaidres who had obviously enquired where I could be found, and had come looking for me. We both stood looking at each other for a few seconds before he broke into a wide grin.

"You've grown a bit since the last time I saw you – well are you going to ask me in or what?"

"Yes, of course…sorry! – I was just a bit surprised to see you standing there, I wasn't really expecting you. Come in my friend – it's nice to see you."

We talked about nothing of any real importance for a while, until he inevitably brought up the subject of my time spent with the Hun. I was dreading this for obvious reasons. The Hun and the Thracians were not exactly on the best of terms right now, and I had personally been involved in several skirmishes with Thracians during my time spent living with the Hun, but what was worse was that I had personally been responsible for the deaths of at least twenty…perhaps even more of them than that. And I wasn't even sure if Gaidres knew what had actually taken place between the Huns, and whom I now knew were called Italians. We had purposely allowed a few of them to escape, so that they could tell others what had happened. But now I found myself wishing that we'd had enough hindsight back then to have realised that it may turn out to be a huge mistake. Gaidres continued to artfully skirt around the real issues here, and I was beginning to feel a little agitated; so resting my chin in my hand I leant forward towards him and said:

"You've undoubtedly brought this up for a reason Gaidres, you know that I'm half Hun, and you obviously know that I've spent several years living with the Huns, so perhaps it would be better for both of us, if you just cut straight to the point."

"Look…I'm sorry, Kai," said Gaidres, scratching his head. "I wasn't trying to make you feel uncomfortable. I know what happened with your cousin. And I'm not stupid…I know that you were most probably involved in the massacre of the unit of Italians in the forest, but you don't have to worry – that lot over there in your father's kol don't know who you are – and they're not going to find out from me. What does worry me though, is where you stand between your Scythian half which is allied to us, and your Hun half which presently lies in conflict. Where would you stand, Kai, if say…push actually did come to shove?"

I didn't much appreciate being put on the spot like this, but even so, I could understand why Gaidres felt the need to question me on this. He must obviously have wondered just how many Thracians had fallen in battle directly due to me.

Taking a sharp intake of breath, I walked over to the table on the far side of the kol and began to pour us both a beaker of the finest wine that my father had presented me with as a gift on my return to Scythia.

"Gaidres…I need you to understand that as I'm about to be initiated into the Agari priesthood, I'm not supposed to take 'any' aggressive standpoint."

Gaidres just sat there and stared at me for a moment, and then he shook his head and said: "Oh that's good! That's a very clever answer…I'll give you that Kai. But I think you forget something. You're still walking around armed up to the teeth, and I saw how you reacted earlier to the sight of those Italians. So please don't bother trying to fool me into believing that you've managed to put your past behind you, because you've already blown any chance that you may have had of doing that."

"Yes, okay! I'll admit that old habits are proving to be a bit of a challenge. And I'm not going to deny that seeing those men earlier really did catch me off guard. But the rational side of me has the last say, and I stand by my convictions."

"Very well – but one day you may be forced to make that choice, and I can't help but wonder what that choice would be," said Gaidres, thoughtfully.

"I know that you'll probably find this really hard to understand Gaidres, but I'll never make that choice…how can I?" I replied with a sigh.

I was just grateful that he'd seen fit to spare me the question that I was dreading more than anything else which was, if I'd actually killed any Thracians during my time spent living with the Huns. Although, I'm quite sure he must have had a pretty good idea what that answer would have been if he'd only had the guts to come right out with it and had asked me straight.

"So do you still teach weapon skills and all that?" he asked me, completely changing the subject.

"Yes, I still teach…Why?"

"So, I take it that you're still allowed to spar then?" he asked, with a little smile on his face.

"Yes, of course. Why – Do you fancy trying your luck?" "Why not," he said, grinning at me.

And with that he stood up and briskly walked outside.

I took a deep breath, thankful that the subject of my time with the Huns and where my loyalties lay had ended, and I followed on after him.

In days gone by, we'd spent many hours sparring and swapping sword techniques, and as we reached the training ground, it reminded me so much of old times again. We always used blunted weapons which were kept just for training purposes, so walking over to the far side of the enclosure I began removing all of my weapons while Gaidres did the same.

While I was living with the Hun, I'd got into the habit of carrying two Hunnic curved swords which I wore crossed over my back, and this hadn't gone unnoticed by Gaidres, and as I began to remove them, I guess Gaidres couldn't resist making a little comment.

"Nice swords…Hun, aren't they?"

I'd learned the art of fighting with these two swords while I was living with the Hun, and I'd used them on more than one occasion in battle. And I'm sorry to admit that they'd been responsible for many a Thracians bloody demise. So you can imagine how awkward I felt as I glanced across at Gaidres, who was just standing there blatantly smirking at me. I knew that he was doing it on purpose, so I didn't bother to answer his question, but continued to quietly remove every last one of my weapons…including the Hunnic swords, and gently laid them upon the ground.

As I uncovered the practice swords and picked one up, Gaidres gave a shrug of disapproval at my lack of response to his question before he also picked up one of the practice swords. We both walked into the middle of the training enclosure, and immediately turned to face one another. Gaidres instantly lunged in with a heavy swing, which thankfully, I was able to effectively block. He then began raining blow after blow down upon me, while I simply blocked each one. For all I knew, he may have lost someone close to him in one of those 'skirmishes' that I was involved in, and who knows – I may have even been personally responsible for their death. And that thought…or something very much like it, must have been in his head as it was in mine, and I just couldn't bring myself to fight back.

Unfortunately Gaidres became increasingly more aggressive, until finally he pushed me just a little too far, and I retaliated by first disarming him, and then by holding my blunt sword provocatively to his throat.

"Lost none of your old skills then I see," he said sarcastically.

I'd really had quite enough of this, so throwing my practice sword down onto the ground; I marched off and began picking up my real weapons. I knew that I'd probably dented his Thracian pride a little just then, but at the same time, I really wasn't prepared to allow him to vent out his anger towards me so aggressively with a sword…even if it was a blunt one.

"Look Gaidres, I can understand how you must feel, I really can," I said, strapping my throwing knife back around my leg. "But I can't help who I am, and whatever I've done in the past is done, and I can't change any of it…even if I wanted to. We've been friends for many years now, and I hope that we can continue to stay friends, but I can't remove the Hun part of me, and if we are to have any chance of continuing our friendship, you're just going to have to accept that."

Gaidres walked over, and began picking up his own weapons which still lay where he'd left them on the ground.

"I want to, Kai – I really do believe me. We were good friends once it's true, and I know you can't help who you are, but when I look at you…you remind me of another good friend of mine who was slain by the Hun." So I was right it would seem…

"I'm really sorry for your loss Gaidres. We've all lost someone close to us, and I can truly empathise. But even if you knew for sure that it was me who killed your friend, would you be prepared to draw a blade across my throat? For if the answer is no, we must be prepared to put all of this behind us. And if the answer is yes, then it would be best for us both if we stayed well away from each another."

Gaidres placed his sword back in its sheath, but even so – I still wasn't turning my back on him just yet. He began toying with a loose clump of earth with his foot, and after kicking it outside the enclosure, he held out his hand in a gesture of friendship towards me.

"You're right, Kai! I would rather we remain friends if that's at all possible. I'm not making any promises, but I'm willing to try."

I nodded in agreement, and with that we walked back to my kol and spoke of other things. He told me that he was in a relationship with a young woman right now, and that he was hoping that they would soon be married. I told him all about Tihanna and Nymadawa, although; I still didn't have a clue where they both were right now.

We continued to talk until it was time for him to leave with the rest of his party. I was purposely avoiding bumping into the Italians again, so I waited in my kol until after they'd all gone. The dust from their horses' hooves hadn't even had a chance to settle before my father had turned up to ask me if I was feeling a little calmer now. I replied that I was, but I didn't think that I was ever going to be able to handle being in the company of these Italians after what had happened. My father seemed to understand this, and resting his hand on my shoulder he said:

"Let's just take this one step at a time shall we. Nobody's going to force you to act against your better judgement Kai…just give yourself some time."

I reluctantly agreed to comply with my father's wishes, but inside I knew that it wasn't time that I needed – but the complete exclusion of all these so-called Italians from our village.

18

No Holds Barred

The very next day my father decided to check in on me after my rather unexpected, and some-what upsetting encounter with the Italians the day before. I could see that he was holding something in his right hand which was wrapped in a piece of faded blue hemp cloth.

"I think this belongs to you," he said, gently placing it on my bed.

"We can talk later if you like," he said, before swiftly leaving again.

Picking up the neatly wrapped bundle, I untied the knot in the leather cord which had been tightly wound around it several times, and carefully un-wrapped the cloth from around the golden Akinakes which I had returned to him the day that I'd left Scythia.

"Hmm," I said, smiling to myself. He must have been waiting for just the right moment to give it back to me, and I guess he thought that this was it.

I attached the Akinakes to my belt before setting off to see if Merren and Aptien were anywhere to be found. I really wanted to ask them if either of them had known anything about the Italians coming here. It didn't take very long before I'd managed to find them, as they were both over at the training area where Merren was currently involved in a bare-knuckle fighting contest. Apparently Merren used to take part in these no holds barred competitions quite regularly at one time, and he'd managed to gain himself quite a reputation in the process. There was quite a gathering, and perhaps not surprisingly, Aptien was to be found right at the very front of the crowd whole-heartedly engaged in cheering Merren on, who just like his opponent, was on his third fight after having won two fights already. It was very difficult to tell who was actually winning this fight, as both Merren, and his unfortunate opponent, who was called 'Trita' both looked as though they were desperately in need of urgent medical attention by this stage. There were men and women loudly cheering for Merren, while others were loudly cheering for Trita, and I soon found myself forgetting what I'd come here for, and began whole heartedly joining in with all the cheering for Merren instead. There 'was' a referee…well…if you could have called him that. He was mainly there to try and prevent the fights from resulting in someone's death. The winner was either determined by a knockout, or one of the fighters not being able to continue and forced to give up. It was always the same with Scythian warriors, if they weren't busy fighting an enemy, they would either be busy making weapons in preparation for fighting an enemy, or busy fighting each other; be it in a so called friendly fight such as this one…or for real. Although looking at the state of both Merren and Trita I don't know if there was actually any difference. I must admit, you wouldn't have got me in there, as although I may have been very agile, I would have been no match physically for the likes of Merren, who was at least 6ft 2in and powerfully built.

Trita eventually gave up as he was unable to carry on, and was duly helped out of the enclosure by a few friends who would most probably take him straight to a healer or an Agari priest to patch him up again. Trita had put up a good fight and he was not dishonoured in any way. Scythians believed that it's a fool who knows that he is beat but continues anyway, and a wise man who can gracefully admit honourable defeat in the face of a greater opponent.

That was also enough fighting for Merren for at least the time being. So with bloody knuckles, a split lip, two black eyes, and a broken nose, to name but a few of his obvious injuries, Aptien and I escorted him back to their bachelor kol. His face was a mess, and when we helped him to take off his tunic, I could see that the rest of him wasn't much better either. I used the Agari skills that I had already acquired to tend to his cuts and bruises. There wasn't much that I could do about his nose, as he'd had it broken so many times before, that as long as he could still breathe through it was all that really mattered. But I was a bit worried about the bruising on his chest, and the way in which he was holding himself.

"I think you might have a couple of broken ribs there Merren, all I can say is that I hope that the winning was worth it, because by the looks of things you might be laid up for a little while. I'm going to go and fetch you some bandages and something for the pain, In the meantime just try to stay out of trouble…I won't be long."

When I arrived at Garenhir's kol, Sai was there busying himself with the preparation of some Agaricum fungi, which was just one part of the several ingredients needed in the making of the hallucinogenic mixture, which would soon be used during the coming Agari ritual. I explained to him about Merren, and he agreed that it did sound as though he may have at least one broken rib…maybe even two.

"Do you want me to come and have a look at him?" he asked me.

I knew from experience that Sai was an excellent physician, and he was far more qualified than I was to make this diagnosis.

"Yes, I'd appreciate your opinion on this. But first – I'm going to fix him something for the pain, as I think he's probably going to need it by the state of him."

"Sure," he said with a nod of his head, "You go ahead and sort that out first, and then I'll walk back up with you."

I proceeded to make up a potent pain killer, which amongst other things contained Opium as this was also good as a muscle relaxant as well as a pain killer; as if it turned out that Merren did have a couple of broken ribs as suspected, the muscles around his rib cage would soon go into spasms as they tightened around his damaged rib cage, causing excruciating pain.

Sai watched me prepare the mixture, and he agreed that this would have been the very same mixture of opium, anti-spasmodic, and anti-inflammatory herbs that he would have used. So after pouring the mixture into a little bottle which I then placed it in a small leather pouch, we made our way to Merren and Aptien's kol where we found them both patiently awaiting my return. "I've brought Sai along for a second opinion, so I hope you don't mind if Sai takes a look at you?" I said to Merren.

Although he tried his best to hide it, I could tell that Merren was obviously in a lot of pain, so I immediately gave him some of the opium mixture to drink.

"What's in this stuff?" he asked me.

"Something for the pain – just drink it," I replied.

Sai carefully studied Merren's movements, and he asked him if he could stand up. Merren just about managed to stand, but not without obvious discomfort. "Do you mind if I examine you?" Sai asked him.

"Yeah, but no funny business now," said Merren, trying his best to raise a smile.

"Don't worry – you're not my type," responded Sai, humorously blowing him a kiss. Oh boy, Sai could really camp it up when he wanted to. I gave him a look that would have soured milk, and he obviously found my reaction to his behaviour very amusing, and carried on with his role play until I just couldn't stand it any longer, and I made a sarcastic comment to the fact.

"Now don't get jealous Manu Kai – you know I only have eyes for you," said Sai, with no attempt to keep a straight face.

At this point I really felt like strangling him, but I just stood there shaking my head and coldly glaring at him disapprovingly instead. Merren and Aptien didn't know him like I did, and I don't know why, but I was afraid that they were going to totally get the wrong impression of him, as he wasn't normally like this at all. As usual Aptien found all of this hilarious. And poor Merren was pleading with us all by now to cease with our theatrical travesties, as it was just too damn painful for him to laugh right now.

"Well – do I get to examine you or not?" asked Sai, once again.

"Yes, of course…please do, I was only joking," said Merren, who was clearly regretting ever having made the errant remark in the first place.

Sai sat down next to Merren, and he carefully felt his rib cage, and asked him if he could take a few deep breaths. This he was obviously unable to do without causing himself a fair deal of discomfort. Sai then gently put his ear to Merren's chest, and he listened carefully.

"I think your initial diagnosis was correct," said Sai, looking up at me. Then turning his attention back to Merren he continued: "I can feel two broken ribs, but you're very lucky as they're both still in place, and there doesn't appear to be any internal organ damage, not as far as I can make out any way…just bruising. So the best thing that we can do is to strap you up, and keep you as comfortable as possible for a couple of weeks, and that means resting up and not doing much for a little while. And maybe in the meantime you could consider finding yourself another slightly less harmful hobby."

Pulling out a couple of linen bandages from Sai's bag, I began wrapping them tightly around Merren's chest.

Aptien had watched fascinated during Sai's examination of Merren, and now curiosity had obviously got the better of him.

"So what exactly are you then Sai…are you a Shaman, or an Agari priest?"

"I'm both," said Sai, now turning his attention to a rather nasty looking cut near Merren's eye. Sai's filed teeth hadn't gone unnoticed by Aptien either. "Have you noticed Sai teeth?" Aptien asked Merren.

"It's kind of difficult to see much at all at the moment," said Merren, peering up at him through his half closed and swollen eye lids.

Aptien then turned to Sai and said: "Show Merren your teeth Sai."

Sai grinned at Merren, and he stuck his forked tongue out at him just for good measure.

"Whoa…Have you seen his tongue?" asked a rather astonished Merren.

Sai turned to Aptien without being asked, and he poked his tongue out at him too.

"Impressive – I should imagine that must have stung a bit," said Aptien, raising his eyebrows. "Would you like to find out?" responded Sai, with a slightly wicked grin on his face.

"Not likely," answered Aptien. "I think I'd much rather drive an arrow through my hand. But thanks for the offer."

"It doesn't really matter whether you're a priest or a shaman, you seem to know what you're on about, so that's the important thing I guess," said Merren, resting himself back down again.

"I've only seconded Manu Kai's original diagnosis that's all – he'll look after you now," said Sai, standing up to leave.

"Well, thanks for stopping by anyway…I really do appreciate it. Oh, and by the way…I really should apologise for my comment earlier, about the 'no funny business' thing, I really didn't mean to cause any offence by it."

"That's OK! No offence was caused…or taken. But I still meant what 'I' said; you really aren't my type at all…Sorry! See you soon," replied Sai, with that slightly twisted grin of his.

And with a wave of his hand he left us, and made his way back over to Garenhir's kol in order to carry on with whatever it was that he was doing before I'd disturbed him earlier.

Merren carefully lay down on his bed. And peering at me through his half open eyes he said:

"Your Agari friend there is a bit of a character Manu Kai, but he knows his stuff well enough…that's for sure."

"Yes, he does…and you're right; he's certainly a character, and as you've seen for yourselves, he can really wind me up – but you have to hand it to him…he is an excellent Shaman," I said, thinking back to when he'd helped me to find the answer to my question.

I allowed myself to muse for a few moments before noticing that Merren and Aptien were both looking at me rather strangely.

"What?" I asked, frowning at the pair of them.

"If we didn't know any better, we could easily be led to believe that you're somewhat smitten by our Shamanic friend there," said Aptien, with one slightly raised eyebrow.

"Well…you do know better. I just admire him for his skill's that's all. Is there something wrong with that?" I retorted sharply.

They both just continued to sit there staring at me, and I could feel my face starting to burn, so trying to hide my embarrassment I quickly stood up and began clearing away a few things that had been left on the table. However I could still sense their annoying curiosity. "Would you both just get off my case?" I said, beginning to feel harassed.

"No problem, Chief…no problem at all," replied Aptien, with an expression on his face that told me that he knew me far too well for me to be able to fool him that easily.

"Look…I really didn't mean to embarrass you. You should know that it wouldn't make any difference to us even if you were…well you know! It's quite a well-known fact that a fair few Shamans and Agari priests tend to have…Uhm…complicated sexualities, and you are an Agari priest after all," said Aptien, with a certain air of feigned indifference.

"Well…not all Shamans and Agari priests are the same; so will you just quit harassing me, and bloody well leave me alone," I said, beginning to feel more than a little annoyed.

"Sorry, Chief…I really didn't mean to touch a raw nerve," said Aptien, raising both eyebrows at Merren, who was just lying there quietly taking it all in.

I'd had just about enough of this, so I quickly poured out another dose of the opium mixture, and placing it loudly on the table, I instructed Aptien that he was to give it to Merren at sundown if he felt that he needed it, and that I would be back later on that evening to see how he was doing, and then I left them both to get on with it.

Feeling more confused than ever, the only thing that I could think of to do was to have a chat with Garenhir about this, so instead of heading straight home, I decided to take a detour to Garenhir's kol and see if he was back yet. My feelings for Sai were beginning to become a problem for me. And although I didn't regard myself as being bisexual, the Hun part of me had a real problem with the possibility that I might be. I just couldn't deal with this, so I would need to be on my guard and quickly learn to suppress any feelings of this nature that might arise in the future. I loved Tihanna – I was straight…and that was all there was to it!

When I arrived at Garenhir's kol, I called out from outside before entering, but instead of Garenhir; who still hadn't returned, I found Sai who was just finishing up with what he'd been doing earlier. Fuelled by the events of earlier, I marched right up to him and stood directly facing him with my arms folded somewhat indignantly – but also protectively at the same time.

"Did you really have to act so camp with Merren and Aptien?" I asked him outright.

With a genuine look of surprise at my obvious disapproval at his behaviour earlier, he said:

"No, I didn't have to. Why…did it bother you?"

"Yes, it did, and I'd prefer it if you didn't do it again," I said rather harshly.

And with that I turned and walked straight back out again.

But just before I left, I caught sight of just a little hint of a smile on his face. I was well aware of the fact that he already knew the truth about how I really felt, and he also knew that I knew – so I didn't really care how this might have come across to him. I wasn't going to act on any of these feelings, and as far as I was concerned 'that' was the important thing, so he could just carry on and look as smug as he liked.

19

Initiation

The day had finally arrived for my initiation into the outer circle of the Agari. I had seen twenty winters, and since my return to Scythia I had studied hard and passed all the trials, and during this time…I hadn't killed anyone. So today I would be accompanied by Garenhir, Sai, and six other Agari Priests to the mountain cave where my initiation was to take place. Sai had already gone through the first and final part of the initiation process into the Agari, and as such he was already a fully initiated member of the brotherhood.

Garenhir instructed me to go and take a bath, and to make sure that I washed my hair. And as soon as we were all ready we set out and headed for the Agari's sacred cave.

To get there we had to cross two rivers, and pass a very strange tribe of people that all shaved their heads and painted themselves blue. They didn't live in kol's like ours, but made their dwelling places out of animal skins secured to trees. And although they had a reputation for being cannibalistic, they never caused us any problems, so we always passed them by with quiet respect. When we finally reached the cave, we were immediately met by several Agari priests who had arrived a little earlier than us, and had already begun making the necessary preparations for our three day stay. Garenhir asked me to follow him into the cave, and the first thing that I noticed was a large fire which was happily burning away in a fire pit in the very centre of the cave. There were scented oil lamps which had been lit and placed all around the edge of the cave wall, which had the effect of illuminating the mystical and occult symbols which had been painted on the walls, and the heady scent of hemp oil and frankincense filled my nostrils and had the effect of having a slightly intoxicating effect on my senses. Some of the Agari were presently sat around the fire, and were chanting something in varying tones, which had the effect of making it sound quite musical. It all felt quite overwhelming, and I couldn't help but wonder what I had let myself in for. I didn't even recognise some of these Agari priests, and I wondered where they could have all suddenly appeared from.

"Don't look so worried – you'll soon get used to it all…I did!" said Sai reassuringly.

Garenhir told me to go and sit down by the fire, and just listen to the vibrations of the chanting for a while. I did as I was instructed, and sat down cross-legged on one of the cushions that had been placed around the fire, and after a short while I began to feel a lot more relaxed as the deep vibrational resonance of the powerful chanting of the priests, seemed to reach deep within my very core being and struck a strangely familiar but unrecognisable cord, which seemed to call out to me from a long ago distant memory of another time and place. I felt a strange sadness arise within me, and a deep longing for something…but quite what it was I knew not! So I allowed myself to be carried along by the powerful chants of the Agari priests, and very soon I found myself falling into a deep trance like state of meditation. Even when the priests had finally stopped chanting, I was still hard pressed to return to normal waking consciousness, and apparently Garenhir had quite a job calling me back again. And when I did finally return, it was to the sound of some kind of disturbance which appeared to be taking place over in one of the smaller adjoining caves.

"What's going on?" I asked Garenhir.

"Hmm…I'm afraid we've got a bit of a problem Manu Kai. It's what's been holding things up. It turns out that one of our Agari brothers has rather unwisely been experimenting with certain dark energies, and he has obviously allowed himself to attune to something quite malevolent, as it has managed to attach itself to him, and it has now chosen this particular moment in time to possess him. I must be completely honest with you Manu Kai; we are having real problems getting rid of it right now. I didn't really want to tell you if I didn't have to, as I know that you've had problems with negative entities yourself in the past, and I didn't want to alarm you. We all thought we would have been able to deal with this by now, but whatever this entity is, it's proving to be quite a formidable opponent, and so far none of us has successfully been able to get rid of it."

"Oh! – can I take a look?" I asked him.

"Yes, you can Manu Kai, but whatever you do don't listen to anything that this entity has to say to you. Remember it's not our brother talking, and don't try and approach him."

Garenhir escorted me over to the small adjoining cave where the incident was taking place, and as I took a peek inside, I could see Sai, who was leaning on the wall along with several other Priests, with the possessed Agari brother sitting right in the centre with his hands and feet bound together; obviously as a precautionary measure to prevent him from causing any harm to himself or to anyone else. As soon as he noticed me, the affected priest immediately reacted by calling me brother, and asking me to join him. Garenhir barred my way – strictly forbidding me to do so.

"Please let me try – I'm not afraid," I responded, confidently.

"Hmm...very well...but please...be very careful," said Garenhir, moving aside a little. The possessed priest immediately began to tell me that he was happy to see a kindred spirit, and that he and I were both on the same side. I replied that we were not. "Oh...but we are Manu Kai," said the entity, staring at me coldly through my brother's eyes.

"You're one of us – you've always been one of us. You're just fooling yourself...you don't belong here."

I didn't take any notice of this rubbish as I knew it wasn't true. But what was slightly more unnerving, was that the entity went on to tell me all sorts of things about myself that it couldn't possibly have known, it even told me that I was in denial about my own sexuality, and with both Sai and Garenhir standing there, not to mention all of my other Agari brothers who were also stood around listening to all of this, I wondered if I was going to be strong enough to see this through. I don't know what was guiding me that day or how I knew what to do, but suddenly the tables began to turn in my favour, as I proceeded to tell the possessing entity of the things I knew about 'it', I also told the entity that it was no match for me, and that I wasn't impressed by its ramblings. And in fact I was getting rather bored and I thought that it was about time it left as it was starting to look quite pathetic.

"Oh really...do you know who I am?" it asked me.

"No, and what's more – I don't care either," I replied sharply.

"Don't you want to know who I am?" it asked me.

"No...like I said, I really don't care," I replied, yawning loudly. "You're so pathetic – why should I give a damn who...or what you are?"

"Oh, really," it said with a malignant grin. "Well maybe this will impress you then."

And with that, the priest's face began to metamorphose right before our eyes; becoming grossly distorted, before changing into a hideously demonic abomination. The infernal image seemed to be imposed upon the face of the priest, and if I had reacted negatively in any way by showing any fear right now, I may have been in a whole heap of trouble, but as fate would have it, I'd already dealt with far worse than this, and I knew that fear was the real enemy, so I continued to calmly hold my gaze as I knew that whatever happened I had to remain calm and outwardly unfazed.

"Is that it?" I said, laughing out loud. "Was that supposed to scare or impress me? That was quite amusing actually."

I watched as the demonic face slowly receded, and the face of the priest was visible once again.

"Now it's my turn to impress you," I said, closing my eyes.

I took a couple of deep breaths, and focussing on a sense of inner peace, I began to visualise myself connecting directly into the active Cosmic Serpent Energy itself, and I could feel the positive forces of this omnipotent energy begin to flow right through me, and radiate outwards in all directions. I opened my eyes just in time to witness the priest, or at least whatever it was that currently possessed him, turn away with a look of absolute horror.

"Leave now and return to where you truly belong, and harm no sentient being on your way there, or else I'm going to have to fry your sorry arse," I said in an impressively commanding tone of voice.

Or at least I thought that I sounded rather convincing. It certainly seemed to do the trick, as the entity left immediately, and the affected priest who although disoriented was otherwise unharmed, and hopefully he had managed to learn a good lesson from this in the process. He was then promptly untied and given a drink of water before being led away to a quiet corner to recover.

"Hmm…that was impressive," said Garenhir. "But how on earth did you know what to do?"

"I honestly don't know Derkesthai. I just felt that if I could get the entity to show itself to me, and I held fast and showed no fear, I'd soon have it on the run. The rest just seemed to come naturally."

"Well, you've just managed to do what all the rest of us put together couldn't, so congratulations. It would seem that you're finally coming into your own Manu Kai, and that your specific talents are beginning to shine through."

The priest who had been possessed was allowed to continue resting outside the cave, while my initiation went ahead. It may have been a little later than was scheduled, but that didn't really matter. And after it was all over, Garenhir said to me:

"Although you went through the process of the ritual initiation, I tend to believe that your true initiation into the Agari was by removing that dreadful entity from our brother. And the fact that you are here today proves that you have already travelled very far on your journey. You still have a long way to go, but for now rejoice…rejoice at the progress that you've made Manu Kai, and ready yourself for the next part of your journey, as the path ahead can sometimes get a little rocky at times, and you will sometimes feel your faith tested to its limits. But you must never lose faith no matter how hard the going gets Manu Kai…you must never lose faith."

Garenhir spoke with such conviction, that I actually wondered if he had some prior knowledge about some of the things that lay ahead for me, but I knew that there wouldn't have been any point in asking him, as he wouldn't have told me even if he knew.

20
Complex Dualities

After my initiation into the outer circle of the Agari, I was allowed to be present at most of the Agari meetings, and I could even take part in some of the rituals. Although; there were still a few that I wasn't allowed to attend. Garenhir intensified my studies, as he told me that he wanted to see me initiated into the inner circle of the Agari before the seasons had turned full circle. This put a lot of pressure on me, as I had to dedicate almost all of my time to the meditations, concentration and breathing exercises and techniques; not to mention the practical application of ritual, daily prayers, mantras and salutations – which were all part of the process which led to becoming a fully initiated member of the brotherhood of the Agari.

There were also some very serious concerns of a political nature going on at the moment. Celts from the west were beginning to cause us major problems, mostly due to lingering past grievances, when they were apparently usurped from this land by our forefathers. However; they themselves had once laid claim to this land by usurping the inhabitants that were living here before them. While at the same time a kindred tribal people called the Sarmatians were busily causing more problems in the eastern part of Scythia – apparently for similar reasons. The old adage of: 'what goes around comes around' seems very appropriate here.

The Thracian's wouldn't ally with us against the Celts, for the same reasons that we wouldn't ally with them against the Huns. And although the Huns were allied to us, they were too busy fighting another rival Hunnic tribe that were attempting to make a claim to the ruler-ship of their land. So a great deal of political unrest was going on all around us right now, and it seemed to be gradually getting worse.

My father along with Merren and Aptien were currently away, engaged in a battle situation with the Celts; as were most of the able warriors in our tribe – which also included some female warriors amongst them. Only priests, shamans, women, children, crippled warriors, and the old, sick or feeble, were left at home. Oh…and me! Yes, I did come under the heading of priest, and as a result, I was excused from all the fighting. In fact it was actually forbidden for me to do so at the moment, and as much as my father needed every able-bodied warrior right now, thankfully he was very understanding of this fact. He knew that in order for me to gain my full initiation into the Agari, it was important that I didn't kill any one right now. So, I couldn't very well enter into a battle situation. And thankfully my uncle, who also knew of my present predicament, was equally as understanding about this. I suppose this was a blessing in itself, as how on earth I was ever going to have been able to choose between fighting alongside my father, and fighting alongside my uncle I just don't know. Even so, I found this whole situation very difficult to deal with, and it caused me a great deal of unrest at the thought that my father, uncle, and most of my closest friends and male family members, were away fighting in two separate battles while I was stuck at home. And even though I was a skilled and competent warrior – I was not there fighting at 'any' of their sides. How was I supposed to study and meditate when all that I could think about was what was currently going on within these battle situations? Being left behind was far more likely to end up killing me than fighting on the battle field ever would. The warrior in me was very strong and probably always would be, so it was not surprising that I finally got to the point where I just couldn't stand it any longer, and I would have rode off alone to join my comrades in battle for sure, except for the fact that Garenhir had already foreseen this very situation arising, and had managed to successfully hide all of my weapons while I was sleeping, and no matter how much I protested and caused a fuss, he refused to give them back to me; or to tell me where they were hidden. I felt as though my right arm had been cut off. Not since I was a small child had I gone without carrying some sort of weapon for this long. I even asked Tihanna if she knew what Garenhir had done with my weapons, but all she could tell me was that he had made a prior arrangement with her to sneak in when I was asleep and take them. I couldn't be angry with her for going behind my back on this, as I knew she had only been acting in my best interest. And so I resigned myself to staying behind, and made every effort possible to keep my mind on other things, and to not let this whole damn situation drive me to the brink of insanity. I repaired a pair of boots, and a leak in the kol. I spent quality time with Tihanna and Nymadawa, and I had a tattoo of a stag done on my left shoulder to represent the guardian of the forest and the warrior hunter. (This deity later became known as the pagan God Cernunnos.)

A couple of days later, Garenhir informed me that an emergency meeting had been arranged for all Agari priests that could get there on time, at the mountain cave five days from now. So on the morning of the gathering, Garenhir, Sai, myself, and several other Agari priests first prepared ourselves by taking a ritual bath, as cleanliness was always paramount with the Agari; after which we gathered all of the necessary provisions that we were going to need, and after securing it all to the horses, we were 'almost' ready to head off. Almost that is, as there was just one small problem. There was absolutely no way that I was venturing outside of our village unarmed, so I flatly refused to go unless I could at least take my swords and my bow and arrows. So eventually Garenhir had to cave in and hand them back to me, although he did insist that I gave him my word that I wouldn't be tempted to ride off. So after I swore a solemn oath that I wouldn't just ride off in the opposite direction at the very first chance that I had, we finally headed off towards the mountain.

Apparently it was a regular thing with the Agari to have these little meetings, so that they could keep up to date with whatever was going on. And any problems with anything or anyone that needed to be dealt with could be openly discussed between them. And either a decision for a possible solution would be reached, or if no viable solution could be found, then the matter would eventually be capitulated upon.

When we arrived, we were also joined by a few Agari brothers who had travelled from several neighbouring Scythian tribes for what was to be the usual three day stay. This was the first time I'd actually been present at one of these types of meetings, and I must say that I found it all fascinating. After certain formalities of prayer and Gnostic salutations had taken place, the meeting soon got under way, and just about everything that was going on around us at this particular moment in time was discussed, including the worsening political situation which appeared to be getting way out of control.

The Agari astrologers mapped out the planetary alignments, and then debated at great length upon how this was most likely to affect the possible outcome. No stone was left unturned, and every possible scenario was considered, and the most likely effect that each one would have on our respective tribal settlement and their inhabitants, and what…if anything could be done about it. This went on for two whole days, and on the third day a more relaxed atmosphere was

235

enjoyed between the brothers. It was a chance to socialise, and to get to know one another on a more personal level, and it was also a time to appreciate one another's individual skills or talents, as several of the brothers turned out to be quite talented musicians, and had brought their musical instruments along. One of the brothers played an instrument called a lyre, while two others played different types of stringed instruments that I didn't recognise, along with a variety of different types of drums and flutes. I'd learned to play a shamanic drum while living with the Hun, and a small mouth-harp, something like the Jews harp of today, which was often used by Hunnic Shaman during their rituals, and as I usually carried this with me wherever I went, I quite enjoyed the chance to join in and relax for a while. The sound we jointly managed to produce between us was surprisingly quite melodious, considering the fact that no one had previously come together at any time in order to practise anything.

Sai, and another Agari shaman from a neighbouring village, who were both excellent shamanic dancers, changed into one of their shamanic costumes which they had both brought along with them, and treated the rest of us to quite a graceful, thought provoking, and elaborate visual performance.

During this time, the Agari were not opposed to the use of a little cannabis or wine for relaxation purposes. And although some of the older and more experienced priests preferred to abstain, most of us indulged ourselves a little, although after saying that, Aptien had at some point seen fit to inform Garenhir that I'd developed a problem with alcohol during my time spent living with the Hun, so he was keeping his beady little eye on me, but even so, I still managed to get pretty inebriated by acting a lot sober than I actually was, until eventually I became too drunk to give a damn any more, at which point Garenhir stepped in and strictly forbid me to drink any more for the rest of that evening.

The evening's pleasantries continued well into the early hours of the morning, until one by one the brothers all slunk off to make their makeshift beds and to get their heads down for what was left of the night. And finally left alone to my own thoughts, they inevitably began to wander once more to my father, and to Merren and Aptien, and the rest of our warriors. I wondered how my uncle and the Huns were faring up against their rivals, and I wondered how many had either been killed or injured. It didn't bare thinking about, so closing my eyes, I said a silent prayer for them all. And no doubt aided by the effects of the alcohol I could feel my emotions beginning to rise, so I decided to go outside for a while to get some air, and was promptly followed by Garenhir and Sai, who obviously weren't letting me out of their sight for a moment – and especially now after I'd had a few drinks. They knew me only too well, but I really don't know what they thought I was going to do I'm sure. Perhaps they thought I might try and ride off, as it was certainly true that I did have a reputation for being somewhat impulsive and predictably unpredictable, but I swear that all I was going to do was to sit outside for a little while and gather my thoughts.

I told myself that I would completely ignore the fact that both Garenhir and Sai had followed me outside, but that was proving to be somewhat difficult, as I was immediately flanked by Sai on my right and Garenhir on my left, and when I sat down, they both followed suit…one on either side of me. I said nothing, so we all just sat there in silence until Garenhir finally asked me if I was OK. I could see the look of concern written all over his face, but for some reason I could only see the funny side of the whole damn situation.

"I'm fine," I said, struggling not to laugh. "I just needed some air…that's all. I wasn't going to make a run for it if that's what you thought."

Garenhir studied my expression for a few moments before resting his hand on my arm and leaning in towards me.

"Manu Kai – nothing you do ever surprises me anymore," he whispered, "I've learned that it's best to keep a watchful eye on you when you're like this…just in case."

"Look…I swore an oath that I wouldn't ride off the minute your back was turned didn't I? And I'm not about to break that oath; so you can relax and go and get some sleep," I said, looking him straight in the eyes.

"It's OK, Derkesthai," said Sai. "You can go and get some rest, I'll stay with him."

"Very well, Sai," said Garenhir. "But don't let him out of your sight for one moment. It's not that I don't trust you Manu Kai – it's just that given the current circumstances…plus all of the alcohol that you've obviously managed to consume this evening, I don't think you're capable of thinking straight right now, so I think it's probably a good idea that someone keeps an eye on you…just for now."

Garenhir winked at me before rising to his feet and wishing us both a very peaceful night, and then he turned around and headed back to the cave to get some much-deserved rest. I looked at Sai who was still sat there cross legged next to me.

"Are you sure you're OK?" he asked me.

I just couldn't help myself and laughed out loud at the irony of it all.

"What do you think Sai? And to be honest – you're all I need right now – but for fucks sake…you probably already know that too…don't you?"

Sai looked down at the ground, and closing his eyes for a moment, he smiled to himself before taking a deep breath.

"Yes, I suppose I do. It looks like we're beginning to understand each other just a little bit better, so I guess we don't need to worry…do we?"

"God give me strength…if you understand me so bloody well you'll already know that it's that very fact that makes me so damn uncomfortable in the first place…"

"Hmm," he said, quickly changing the subject. "I'm thinking of growing a beard…what do you think?"

"What planet are you on? Do you really think I give a damn what you choose to do with your facial hair."

"Hmm," he said with such a thoughtful and understanding look on his face, that he made me want to hit him…hard!!!

I guess the alcohol must have given me the courage to open up to him about how I really felt, as I suddenly turned to face him, and looking him straight in the eyes I said:

"Sai, will you please do me a favour and stop understanding me so damn well. You say you understand me but I honestly don't think you have any idea how you make me feel? Even when I was a small child, and I was confronted by a Hun warrior who told me that he was going to kill me, I wasn't as afraid of him as I am of you right now. You really need to know how you make me feel…you terrify me Sai…you really do! There…I've said it now!"

As we both sat there just looking at each other, time seemed to stand still, and I began to feel strangely vulnerable and exposed. I felt as though he was able to penetrate straight through my protective shield, and see right into the very depths of my soul. I think Sai must have somehow picked up on my thoughts, as he suddenly averted his gaze and stared down to the ground for a few moments, before raising it again.

"Maybe it isn't me you're actually afraid of Kai – but yourself," he said, looking me squarely in the eyes.

I knew that he was probably right – and the realisation of this, and the undeniable energy that existed between us was enough to make me tremble, so I turned away and buried my head in my hands and silently prayed for inner strength and guidance. In an effort to comfort me, Sai rested his hand on my shoulder; it felt strangely reassuring and familiar somehow. I unburied my head from my hands, and turning once more to face him, I allowed myself to study his face for a few moment while he just continued to sit there silently looking back at me.

"There really is no reason to feel afraid you know," he said, while very cautiously moving a piece of hair away from my face.

Within the sheer intensity of that moment, he had skilfully managed to read the whole situation, and very cautiously he edged himself a little closer next to me, and gave me a single kiss on the mouth, and after gently running his hand down the side of my face, he completely withdrew his advances and awaited my response.

I must admit to feeling quite intoxicated by the sheer depth and passion that was contained within that single kiss, and I knew that in my somewhat alcohol induced state of mind, I could have easily allowed myself to be carried away by the heat of the moment, but at the same time I was once again torn between the two opposing sides of my nature. It would seem that I did have a conscience after all, and morally this all felt so wrong to me. I couldn't help thinking of Tihanna, and I realised that I just couldn't go through with this.

"Sorry, Sai, but I just can't do this," I said, raising myself from the ground and quickly heading back in the direction of the cave entrance.

Sai immediately stood up and followed me, he'd promised Garenhir that he wouldn't let me out of his sight, and one of the many things you could say about Sai was that he was always true to his word. I found a suitable place to make my bed for the night, and after throwing a few sheepskins down onto the ground, I removed my boots, and placed my weapons close by the side of me, and after pulling a sheepskin blanket right over the top of my head, I soon shut out the world and drifted off to sleep.

I awoke early the next morning, and the very first thing that I needed to do was to answer the call of nature, and looking all around me, I could see that most of the brothers were still fast asleep. I couldn't tell which one if any of them was Garenhir, but I wasn't at all surprised to find that Sai had made his bed right next to mine; no doubt so that if I had got up for any reason in the night, I would have had to disturb him, as he'd made quite sure that I would have had to clamber right over the top of him.

The embers of the fire although very low now, were still managing to give off a warm orange glow. And a few shafts of sun light had also managed to permeate the darkness of the cave by penetrating through the little gaps all around the edges of the heavy sheepskin blanket, which was still securely fastened to the cave entrance. Dazzling rays of sunlight struck the cave walls at every angle; illuminating the Occult symbols which had been painted in ochre's of red and burnished amber. The rays of light seemed to reflect off the uneven surface of the cave wall, creating a crisscross effect of radiant beams of light all around the cave.

As I quietly pulled on my boots, I continued to watch the beams of light as they seemed to shimmer and dance their way through the gentle rising smoke of the fire, when suddenly I noticed that my weapons were no longer where I'd left them the night before. Someone had obviously managed to take them without waking me, and no doubt they had also hidden them from me…again! And although I tried very hard not to wake Sai as I stepped over him, I should have known that I was never going to get past 'him' without him knowing about it.

"Going somewhere, Kai?"

I stopped dead in my tracks. "I'm just nipping outside to answer nature's call that's all. I'll be straight back you don't have to worry."

"I've promised Garenhir that I wouldn't let you out of my sight," said Sai, sitting upright. Just then I heard Garenhir's voice, which seemed to be coming from one of the adjoining caves just about two metres away from where we had both been sleeping.

"Don't worry, Sai – you can relax…he's not going anywhere. I've got his weapons."

Sai lay back down again, and I was entrusted to go outside all by myself. I shortly returned, and as it was still very early, and mostly everyone else was still sleeping, I stepped back over Sai who had crawled back into his makeshift bed, and I crawled back into mine.

Unable to get back to sleep, I just lay there and thought about my life and the craziness of it all. I really didn't know who I was any more, and I was beginning to wonder if I was going to be strong enough to deal with all of this. I found myself wondering who I could have been in my last life, and what I must have done to have brought me to this point in this life. I was becoming increasingly aware of the two very distinct aspects of my personality, and the ever increasing need to bring these two opposing sides of my nature together into some sort of harmony, as I was beginning to think that I was in danger of going mad. I decided to have a heart to heart with Garenhir just as soon as we got back. I was just going to have to be honest with him about what was going on with me right now. I knew that this wasn't going to be an easy thing for me to do, but I also knew that if Garenhir could have found it within himself to share his buried secret past with me, then I'm sure I could find it within myself to step down off my pedestal and bury my pride for a while, and open up to Garenhir about the certain aspects of my personality that were making me feel very uncomfortable right now. The strange thing was that I knew Garenhir was probably already fully aware of the very parts of me that I found so difficult to talk to him about. I really needed his help right now. I had reached yet another crisis point, and I was lost…again!

21

The Power of Attraction

After we returned to our village, we were all quite surprised to find out that our warriors had already returned from battle. This of course meant that the battle must have taken place practically on our own doorstep, and although I found this rather unsettling, I was relieved to find out that my father had escaped totally unscathed this time; unfortunately Merren and Aptien had not been quite so fortunate, as both of them had sustained injuries. Their injuries had already been dealt with by the one of the two remaining Agari physicians, and luckily their wounds although serious, had not proved fatal, and now they were both currently laid up in their kol.

Many of our warriors had sustained serious injuries, and we had already lost 57 warriors from our tribe alone. Some tribes had lost more than this, with an estimated total loss of around four hundred men and women.

Along with the two remaining Agari physicians, there had been enough healers and shamans in our village to have tended to the wounded while we were away, but no sooner had we arrived, Garenhir and all of the other Agari immediately set to work, which gave the village shamans a much-needed rest.

As soon as I found out that both Merren and Aptien had been injured, I instantly forgot about my own problems, and asked Sai if he wouldn't mind coming along with me to go and see them, just in case there was anything further that could be done for them. Sai of course didn't hesitate, so we both made our way over to their kol as quickly as we possibly could.

I called out to them from outside their kol, and then patiently waited for an answer before entering out of respect. I heard Merren shout out for me to enter, so we let ourselves in and found them both laid up in their beds. Aptien had sustained the worst injuries, with the loss of two fingers from his left hand, and a rather nasty gash to his forehead, but his most worrying injury of all, was a very deep sword slash to his left leg. Merren had been hit by two arrows; one to his right forearm, and one in his left foot. Both arrows had been successfully removed, and he was managing to hobble around with the aid of a stick. Aptien however was finding it very painful to move much at all at the moment. Neither of them needed to say a single word, I could see by the looks on their faces that the battle had been a hard one. Our opponents were obviously formidable warriors, and maybe we'd made the mistake of underestimating them. I asked them how our adversaries had fared, and Merren said that they had probably lost more warriors than we had, but it offered very little consolation as even though our warriors had been successful in preventing them from making any solid gains by forcing them into a retreat; there were no outright winners in this battle. They had obviously calculated their losses, and had wisely concluded that the cost was far too high to warrant them continuing.

"Would you like us to have a look at your wounds?" I asked them both.

"If you don't mind, that would be very much appreciated," responded Aptien weakly. It was a fact that there was no better healer in whole village than Sai, and as Aptien was obviously in a worse state than Merren, he decided we should start with him, so I began removing the dressing from Aptien's hand, while Sai removed the dressing from his leg. It was quite clear that there was nothing more that could be done about his hand, as his fingers had been sliced clean off. He had managed to stem the bleeding himself while he was still on the battle field, so now it was just a matter of keeping the wounds clean until they had healed, but his leg was a different matter entirely, and would need very careful attention if it was ever going to heal properly. But even though it was a bad wound, he had still been extremely lucky as the main artery had not been severed, or the chances are that he would not have survived. The wound across his forehead was also quite deep, so Sai decided to put a couple of stitches in it for him. He didn't do the same with his leg, as it would need time for any dirt, or anything else that may have got into the wound to work its way back out again. So after Sai had packed his wound with an antiseptic poultice, and applied fresh dressings, I gave him something for the pain. We did our best to make him as comfortable as we possibly could, before we set our attentions on Merren, who had already begun removing his own dressings.

After both Sai and I had taken a look at the wound in his arm and foot, we both agreed that the Agari physician who had taken care of him had undoubtedly done an excellent job. And both of his wounds were looking clean and free from any infection. So after I'd cleaned and redressed his wounds, I asked him if he needed anything for the pain.

"Well, it wouldn't hurt…would it?" he said, raising his eyebrows at me.

"No it wouldn't hurt," I said smiling, and I poured him an equal dose of what Aptien had been given.

Sai told them both to drink plenty of water, and to periodically add some kind of herbal medicinal concoction that he'd given them both. He said that due to Aptien's blood loss he would feel weak for a few days, but that he would soon recover with adequate care and plenty of rest, and that he would pop in to see them both in the morning, after which he left to go and see if he could be of any further assistance to the other wounded warriors. I remained with Merren and Aptien for a while in order to prepare the food that I had brought for them.

After making sure that Merren and Aptien had everything they needed, I left them for a while and joined Sai in tending to the rest of the injured. Our dead had all been brought back to our village, and preparations were already under-way for their funerals. They would all be buried with the full honours that were always given to every fallen warrior, and the funeral rites were set to go on for many days. The mournful cries and laments of the bereaved family and friends of these slain warriors was a stark reminder of our own mortality, and could be heard for many weeks to come. I eventually managed to make my way to my father's kol, where I found him being fussed over by my mother and sisters. I hadn't seen my brother since I got back, but apparently he had also managed to escape injury. My father was currently resting as he was understandably exhausted, but was nevertheless obviously pleased to see me, as he made a special effort to stand and greet me as I walked in.

"How are you, Father?" I asked him.

His face was strained with the mien of one so battle worn and heavy hearted, that he looked at least ten years older than he actually was. Sighing heavily, he looked me straight in the eyes and just shook his head. He didn't have to say another word his eyes told a tale that a thousand words could never hope to do; a tale of a leader who although battle hardened, was becoming increasingly weary of burying his friends and comrades…and for what?

I walked over to where he stood and embraced him warmly.

"I should have been there fighting at your side," I said to him.

"Ahhh…don't worry too much Kai, I don't think badly of you for not being there," he said with a sigh, as he sat back down again. "Garenhir and I had already spoken on this subject, and we both agreed that it was right that you should stay behind this time."

"That may be," I said thoughtfully. "But all the same, I'm never doing it again; it just didn't feel right to me. I know that you're tired, so I'll go now and let you get some rest…I'll see you tomorrow!"

Before I left my father in peace to get some much-needed rest, I kissed my mother on her forehead, and blessed each of my sisters as was in keeping with my standing as an Agari priest, and then I headed off to go and look for Garenhir.

With all of the wounded taken care of for the day, Garenhir had returned to his kol and was now busily preparing the necessary compounds and medicinal concoctions that would be needed for tomorrow. The doorway to his kol was slightly open, so I didn't bother to announce my arrival and just walked straight in.

"Ah, Manu Kai," said Garenhir. "I was wondering when you were going to turn up. You can give me a hand here if you like."

"Yes, of course," I said, as he thrust some tree bark into my hand.

"Here…you can grind this into a fine powder if you like," he said, pointing to a mortar and pestle which was stood on the table at the far side of the kol. "And after you've finished, pour a little alcohol over it and leave it to steep for a while."

"Where's Sai?" I asked him, as I began to grind up the tree bark.

"He's busy helping with preparations for the funerals…why?"

"I really need to talk to you about something, and I know that this isn't really the best of times, but if I don't get this off my chest soon I think I'm going to go mad, and I don't want Sai to overhear what I have to say."

"Hmm," he said thoughtfully. "I can't say that I'm surprised Manu Kai, I've been waiting for this."

As I continued to grind the bark into a fine powder, I proceeded to explain to Garenhir all about the current situation between Sai and myself, and how difficult and confusing I was finding it all. I told him how torn it made me feel; as one part of me wanted to give into my desires, but another part of me fought very hard against them – as morally it all felt very wrong to me, as not only did I know that if I gave in to these feelings, I'd be betraying the love that I felt for Tihanna…and she for me, but the homosexual intolerant Hun half of me – and the more tolerant Scythian half of me, were currently battling it out with one another, and the inner conflict that it was causing me was slowly but surely…driving me insane!

Garenhir sighed, and after he put down the things that he had in his hands, he picked up a stool and sat himself down opposite me.

"Put that down for a minute Manu Kai, and look at me, what I'm going to say to you is very important."

I did as I was told, and he proceeded to explain.

"Manu Kai, please understand that there could be many reasons why you're going through what you're going through right now. Perhaps there are lessons to be learnt from this situation, but I tend to believe that there is a distinct possibility that you and Sai are connected in some way…most likely from a past life, which would go a long way in explaining your feelings for each other. I would have liked to have had a chance to have compared your birth charts, but unfortunately Sai's time of birth is unknown to us so that's impossible. Of course there may be other reasons why you are experiencing these feelings, and although this is far from being typical, there have been other Agari priests that have experienced similar feelings for each other. But I shouldn't worry too much if I were you, as sexual attraction is a thing of the body, and it does not affect who you are spiritually. Garenhir stood up and after removing a small cauldron of boiling water from the fire, he asked me if I'd like a liquorice and honey drink. I said that I would, so he made us both a hot drink, and after handing me a cup containing the liquorish and honey tea, he sat back down again.

"Well, that really is all I'm prepared to say on this matter of whatever is going on between you and Sai," he said, placing his cup down by the side of him.

"Thank you Derkesthai, I was seriously beginning to wonder if I was going insane. I feel a lot better now. It really helps to know that there may be several possible but hidden reasons for all of this, and that I'm not going mad after all. Perhaps now I know this, I can learn to deal with it a bit better…although…it's still not going to be easy."

"No – it's not going to be easy Manu Kai, but then life isn't meant to be easy," he said with a sigh. And I understood exactly what he meant.

I'd never thought to question Sai's background before, and I realised how little I actually knew about his lineage. All I knew is that he'd been adopted by a shamanic couple who had taken him in when he was very young, and now he lived alone in his own kol. But I knew nothing about what happened to his real parents, and it suddenly occurred to me that I'd never even been to his kol.

"Garenhir…Can I ask you a question?"

"Of course."

"Who were Sai's real parents?"

"It's not for me to tell you Manu Kai, if he wants you to know – he'll tell you himself." I suppose he was right, so I didn't question him any further on this, and I decided that I'd just have to ask Sai myself…when the time was right of course!

Garenhir stood up, finished off his tea, and continued on with the business of preparing a variety of different compounds and preparations. I'd finished grinding the tree bark into a fine powder, and added the alcohol as instructed, so I left it on the table to allow it to steep for a while. Garenhir then handed me a bag of mixed roots, and instructed me to add a little alcohol and pulverise them to a paste. We continued working until all of the preparations had been made, after which I popped in to see Merren and Aptien, just in case they needed anything, and to give them both another dose of medicine for the pain. And then completely worn out by the trials of the day, I finally returned home for the night.

Tihanna was still awake when I got back, and she said that we needed to talk, but I was so exhausted by now that I found it practically impossible to stay awake. She could obviously see this, and not really knowing if I was awake enough to hear her, she softly whispered in my ear…

"Kai – I'm pregnant."

"You're what?" I asked, half awake, and not quite sure if I'd heard her correctly.

"I'm pregnant," she repeated once more.

"That's wonderful," I said, just managing to give her a hug just seconds before I fell asleep. The next morning I arose early, and not wanting to wake Tihanna or Nymadawa, I quietly got dressed and went straight to Garenhir's kol to collect the dressings, herbal poultices, antiseptics and medicines, that would be needed for the seven injured warriors who had been placed under my own personal care by Garenhir. Although I was a fairly competent healer, I was not yet a fully initiated member of the Agari, so I was appointed the least seriously injured. I found it ironic that although I was technically the least qualified, it was a great honour for the wounded warriors to be treated by me due to my high status within the tribe, but as far as the Agari were concerned, it didn't matter who I was, as any status that I, or anyone one else may have held, was completely irrelevant to them, and received no recognition within the brotherhood whatsoever.

Due to the serious nature of Aptien's injuries, Garenhir had appointed Sai to take care of him and Merren. But it didn't stop me from popping in a couple of times a day, just to make sure they had everything they needed and to bring them little treats. Aptien was particularly partial to smoking cannabis for one thing, while Merren thought he'd try his luck, and knowing that it was well within my power to get it for them, he asked me for a whole slaughtered sheep. I had to admire his audacity, and I arranged to have one slaughtered and cooked for them as soon as I left their kol. My oldest sister, who I called Trisha, had recently become very interested in healing, and she asked me if I'd mind if she accompanied me on my rounds to tend to the wounded. I could see no reason why this should be a problem, and I was happy to have her as company as we always got on very well. She was very strong willed and reminded me of myself at times, and she could aim an arrow and ride a horse equally as well, if not better than most of the male warriors here. I found that I actually enjoyed teaching my sister how to clean and dress a wound, and her sheer joy at being able to spend some time with me, coupled by her thirst for knowledge surprised me. So I decided to have a word with Garenhir, as although she wasn't allowed to train to become an Agari priest, I wasn't aware of any rules that may prevent her from being instructed in the practical application of the healing arts. But before I could go ahead with this, I would need to get Garenhir's permission as my Derkesthai. Garenhir said it was fine for me to teach her all the necessary skills for her to become a healer, and he gave us both his blessings for Trisha to 'unofficially' become my pupil.

The very next day after I had finished tending to my patients, I wanted to pop in and see Merren and Aptien, so I asked Trisha who had accompanied me on my rounds as my newly acquired assistant, if she'd like to come along too. Although Trisha knew who Merren and Aptien were, she'd never actually been officially introduced to them, so after arriving at their kol, I shouted out to them from outside and waited for a reply before entering as usual, but before going in, I asked Trisha to wait outside for a few moments, so that I could inform them of her presence first.

"My sister Trisha is waiting outside," I said, quickly clearing away some of their mess. "She's been with me most of today and she'd actually like to meet you both, I can't imagine why," I said humorously. "Is it okay if she comes in?"

The remaining sheep carcass had been broken up into manageable-sized pieces, and left in a large cauldron which was hanging over the central fire pit to keep warm. I was happy to see that Aptien was looking a little better, but as he was still finding it very difficult to move about very much, he still had to rely heavily on others to care for him right now. Merren on the other hand was making a remarkably speedy recovery, and was now doing most of the caring for Aptien.

"Yes, of course, go and ask her to come in," said Merren, kicking his dirty dish under a pile of firewood.

I walked back outside and informed Trisha that it was okay for her to go in and meet them. I hadn't realised that Trisha might actually be feeling a little nervous about meeting Merren and Aptien for the first time, but just as we were about to walk in through the entrance to their kol, she held onto my arm tightly, and I must admit that I found this quite amusing.

"You're not nervous are you?" I whispered in her ear.

She dug her finger nails into my arm before allowing me to lead her inside...I was still rubbing it as I introduced them to each other.

"What's wrong with your arm?" asked Merren.

I just rolled my eyes in my sister's direction, and Merren just nodded knowingly and said no more.

Aptien made a brave effort to sit upright, but Sai had strapped his leg in a large splint to prevent him from moving it so that the damaged tendons would have a chance to knit back together again, and he was obviously finding this a bit of a struggle, so both Merren and I immediately went over to help him. Aptien politely asked Trisha to find herself somewhere to sit while Merren and I helped him to make himself half presentable. Trisha looked all around the kol for a few moments, before finding herself a suitably uncluttered space to sit.

Aptien had obviously taken a shine to her, and he was soon winning her over with his charismatic charm and wit. I hadn't really paid all that much attention before as she was my sister, but Trisha was actually very pretty, and it was obvious that this hadn't gone unnoticed by Aptien, and they were soon chatting away like they'd known each other all their lives. They seemed completely oblivious to the fact that both Merren and I, were just sat there watching the pair of them openly flirting with each other.

"I don't believe this," I said, very quietly to Merren. "My sister is flirting with Aptien. I've got to get her out of here. You can tell Aptien I'm going to have a quiet word with him later."

"Trisha, It's time to go," I said, as I quickly ushered her away from Aptien, and out through the doorway of their kol.

Just before joining her, I sharply pointed my finger at Aptien with a very serious expression on my face...he would know well enough what it was about, and just as I turned to leave I saw him look at Merren and grimace.

After walking my sister back to my father's kol, I made my way straight back to Merren and Aptien's, and letting myself in again, I immediately walked over to Aptien and carefully sat down on the edge of his bed, so not to cause him any unnecessary discomfort.

"What were you thinking? Has all the medicine that I've been giving you dulled your senses – or have you just completely lost your mind?" I asked him, still feeling bewildered by his unashamedly inappropriate behaviour towards my sister.

"I'm sorry Chief; I just got a bit carried away that's all. I didn't mean any harm. She's so pretty...I just couldn't help myself," he said, looking so severely castigated and helpless right now, that I couldn't help but to forgive him.

"Well...just watch yourself that's all, you don't exactly have a very good reputation with your 'love them and leave them attitude' towards women...do you? And if my father ever catches you flirting with my sister – it'll be no good telling him that you couldn't help yourself when the crows are helping themselves to your liver."

Several weeks had passed, and slowly but surely Merren and Aptien recovered from their injuries, as did all the wounded warriors. And no doubt due to Sai's excellent healing skills, Aptien's leg had healed well; although he still walked with a slight limp due to the severity of his injury, he was very lucky not to have lost his leg, or even to have died. And the loss of two fingers didn't seem to bother him very much at all.

I also received the good news that my uncle had been successful in his stance against the beleaguering rival Hun tribe that had tried to take their land. And although they had lost twenty-seven warriors during the five long days and nights that they were under siege, their rivals had finally decided to retreat, so for now at least their land was safe. However, our battle with the Sarmatians had proved very costly for both sides, and due to possible repercussions it had resulted in several Scythian tribes accepting partial defeat, and deciding it may be wise to uproot and move further inwards.

Three months later and Tihanna's bump continued to grow, and for a short while things seemed to settle down a little. But it wasn't long before the political situation between ourselves and the Thracians, which was already very fragile due to both nations being allied with the other's enemies, began to become heated again, and it was probably only going be a matter of time before we would be declaring war on each other...again! These were very troubled times for sure, and although it was all I'd ever known, I did wonder sometimes what peace would be like, and if it was even possible. I'd genuinely had more than enough of all the killing, and at least the peaceful interlude that we did have, gave me some time to concentrate on my studies. Garenhir was obviously suitably happy with my progress, as he informed me that I was to take my final initiation into the Agari before the next ritual of the Sacred Serpent.

In the meantime I continued to instruct Trisha, on how to prepare the basic compounds that were mostly used for healing wounds, and for easing pain and fever; when one day while I was right in the middle of explaining to her how to apply a poultice...she suddenly blurted out...

"Kai – I need to tell you something...Aptien and I have been seeing each other."

"What? ...I'm going to kill him if he's...Have you? ...Don't even bother to answer that...I'm going to see him right now."

"No, Kai, please don't," she pleaded with me.

But I was already half way through the doorway.

Reaching Merren and Aptien' kol, I was so angry that I didn't even bother to call out from outside, and I marched straight in to find them both quietly making arrows by the fire. They looked quite shocked to see me standing there looking so angry, but I think they both had a good idea what it was all about.

"I think we need to have a little chat Aptien," I said, glaring at him.

"Ah!" he said, dropping the arrow that he was making to the ground. "I 'was' going to tell you...honest!!! I was just waiting for the right moment, so don't kill me before I've even had a chance to explain. Please, Kai...just calm down and let me explain." I sat down on Merren's bed and buried my head in my hands.

"You know I'm not going to kill you Aptien, but what in the name of the Gods do you think you're doing? She's my sister and the daughter of the Sha Pada of our tribe. Have you finally lost your mind?"

251

"It's not what you think, Kai, I know I don't have a very good reputation with women and all that, but this is different. You've got to believe me Kai…I really believe she's the one."

Merren, who was doing his level best to look as though he was minding his own business, just shrugged his shoulders, and continued to fletch the arrow that he was making.

"Listen to me very carefully Aptien, if you are genuinely interested in marrying Trisha, then before this goes any further, you 'must' go and speak to my father, and ask him for his permission to court her. You come from a noble bloodline, so if my father refuses you it won't be because of your lineage, but if by chance he does refuse you, I think you know only too well that you'd better just accept it, or I really don't fancy your chances of survival. Oh…and I'm only going to ask you this once so you better give me an honest answer. Have you…you know what I mean."

"No…we haven't," said Aptien, shaking his head. "And I will speak with your father, and I'll ask him for permission to court Trisha. I intended to do it soon anyway, but I'll go and see him tomorrow…you have my word."

Aptien was as good as his word, and he spoke to my father the very next day. Oddly enough my father had no hesitation in giving Aptien his blessings to court his daughter. I guess he must have thought that if he was brave enough to come and ask him for his permission, then he must be genuine, as he knew his neck would be on the line if he wasn't. Apparently my father had asked him if he was willing to marry Trisha, and luckily for Aptien he'd answered that he truly loved her, and he would marry her tomorrow if he could. I don't think he'd still be standing if he'd given any other answer. Although Aptien was one of my closest friends, I'd never bargained on having him as a brother in law. It's strange the way things work out sometimes.

22

Initiations and Tribulations

The time had come for my second and final initiation into the Agari Priesthood, and although I would only be away for a few days I didn't really want to leave Tihanna alone right now as she was getting very close to her time. But the Artim Derkesthai (Celestial Dragon Master) of our village had decreed that this would be a good time for my initiation, so I didn't really have a great deal of choice in the matter. Trisha had offered to stay with Tihanna until I returned, which made me feel a little better at least. So after all the members of the Agari who would be joining us had made the necessary preparations, we headed off to the sacred mountain cave.

When we finally arrived at the cave, Garenhir was surprised to find that it had already been prepared in advance for the once yearly ritual of the Sacred Serpent, by several priests from a neighbouring settlement who had arrived several days early. Also present were two other candidates for initiation who had also arrived early, and had travelled from two separate neighbouring tribes, one of which was an eight-day trek away. Apparently it was very unusual to have more than two new disciples present for any initiation, as sometimes years could go by without a single one. I didn't know why this day was particularly special, or why Garenhir had pushed me so hard in order to have me initiated on this day, but it looked as though I hadn't been the only one.

Garenhir asked me to go and join the other two candidates who were presently sat together outside the cave. Along with all the other Agari from our village, Garenhir and Sai then disappeared inside the cave; leaving the three of us alone to get acquainted. So after introducing myself, I sat down and joined them.

"I'm Teshken," said one of them.

"And I'm Kerkeren," said the other.

We weren't outside for very long when a high priest, who was dressed in a long heavy looking deep blue robe, which was tied at the waist with a golden sash, appeared from inside the cave and called us in, so all three of us immediately stood up and followed him inside. Everyone except for Sai was wearing similar robes, and the only difference between them was that the symbols for their own particular special talent's or abilities were delicately embroidered on the right sleeve of their robes.

Sai was dressed in the most magnificent shamanic finery that I'd ever seen. I must admit that when I saw him standing there looking the way that he did, it didn't do anything at all to help my plight.

"Here you are," said Garenhir, handing the three of us a pale blue robe each. "Now go into one of the adjoining caves, remove all of your clothes, and put on your robe. And after you've done that – come straight back here again."

He told us that we were allowed to keep our boots on for now as the bare cave floor was very cold on the feet. So after we had changed into our robes, all three of us walked back out into the main cave together, where we were then immediately escorted to another small adjoining cave by three high priests, who told us to stand in the centre of a star within a circle which had been brightly painted on the cave floor. One of the High Priests then proceeded to anoint each one of us in turn, by making a symbol of the cross on our foreheads with special oil, while all the time reciting words of purification and protection.

Another high priest then painted a symbol on our foreheads which symbolised our spiritual awakening, and as the three of us were also experienced warriors, a swirl was painted on each of our cheeks. This showed others that we could also be fierce and brave warriors if necessary. We were then asked to take our boots off, and more magical symbols were then painted on our hands and feet. One of the high priests then asked us to wait for a little while before putting out boots back on again in order to give the painted symbols time to dry. Although not permanent, the paint dyed the skin and could last for up to a month, or sometimes even longer. It was the same concentrated plant dye, mixed with a certain blue fungus that was sometimes used by warriors to paint each other's faces before going into battle.

One of the high priests then asked us to follow him back into the main cave and over to a large roughly made wooden table, where Garenhir was already stood waiting for us. Placed upon the table on a pure white linen cloth where several ritual items, along with a neat little pile of linen bandages. Garenhir told

254

us that a few drops of blood would be needed from each of us, and he pointed to a very sharp looking ritual knife and a golden receptacle.

"Draw your blood, and allow a few drops to fall into the receptacle," he said, picking up the knife and holding it outwards towards us.

All three of us hesitated, but as I was the only one out of the three of us who was Garenhir's pupil, I felt somehow obliged to be the first to take it from him, so reaching out, I took the knife from his hand and quickly made a small cut on the side of my left hand, after which I placed the knife back on the table. I held my hand over the solid gold receptacle, and allowed a few drops of my blood to drip into the cup.

"Here you are," said Garenhir, handing me one of the small bandages that had been placed on the table.

"Thank you," I said, quickly winding it tightly around my hand in order to stem any further bleeding.

Teshken and Kerkeren both followed suit, after which we were all instructed to go and stand in the middle of a protective circle which had been painted at the far side of the cave, and to remain there for the whole duration of the ritual, and on no account should we leave the circle until we were told that it was safe for us do so by one of the high priests.

All of the other members of the Agari each added a few drops of their own blood to the grail, after which the other ingredients of snake venom and alcohol were added, along with a very potent concentrated mixture made from hallucinogenic plants and fungi, including the famous fly-agaric mushroom, the name of which is too similar to the name of 'Agari' to be just a coincidence. And, finally, a few spoonfuls of melted honey was also added to the mixture, as not only did it disguise the bitter taste, but the Agari regarded bees as being little incarnated nature spirits, and the honey they produced was considered sacred. The concentrated mixture was then brought over to us, and we were then instructed to drink just one measure each from the cup, after which it was passed to all of the other initiates who were already seated around the fire in the very centre of the main cave, all that is except for one of the high priests, who had already left the main cave and entered into one of the smaller adjoining caves. He was to act as the overseer, and his job was to remain in a normal state of consciousness; just in case someone who was unaffected by the hallucinogenic mixture was needed for any reason. And if his requisite skills were not required, he would have to remain there until the ritual was complete.

The ritual went ahead, and thankfully all three of us were successful in passing the final trial which also marked our initiation into the inner circle of the Agari. I'd made it against all the odds, and I was now a fully initiated member of the Agari.

We returned home the next day, and as we rode back into the village, I noticed that a few Thracian horses had been tethered at the back of my father's kol, so it was pretty obvious that he was playing host to a party of Thracians right now. Evidently they had decided to make an impromptu visit while we were away; no doubt to discuss the present political situation. I was quite happy to be excluded from all of this senseless drivel right now, so I surreptitiously hid myself away in my kol, as I knew only too well of the likelihood that this meeting would turn out to be a very tense and volatile affair, as it was inevitable that sooner or later a breakdown in communication would arise, as neither party was ever going to be willing to bend to the will of the other.

I was busy making myself useful by giving Tihanna a hand with a few mundane chores, when I heard a familiar voice call out from outside. It was my Thracian friend Gaidres, so I called out to him to enter.

"How are you my friend? It's been a while," he said, pulling back the doorway flap and letting himself in. "You're looking well I must say."

"Yes, I'm keeping well…and you?" I replied.

"Very well, thank you. Ha…and I see that you are soon to be a father for the second time," he said, suddenly noticing Tihanna's bump.

I smiled and nodded, and with a gesture of my hand I beckoned him to join us.

"Come – sit down. Would you like some water or tea…or something a bit stronger maybe?"

"Honey and fruit tea would be good…if that's not too much trouble."

Tihanna immediately stood up and began preparing the tea using a mixture consisting of several different types of crushed dried berries, herbs, and some dried root powder which tasted a little like ginger. Gaidres and I engaged in small talk for a while, and amazingly enough we both completely managed to avoid mentioning anything about the present political situation.

Tihanna brought the tea and a couple of small cups over to us, and neatly set it all down on a small table in front of us. I proceeded to pour some of the tea into the cups from the small pitcher that Tihanna had made it in, and then I left them to cool for a little while. Gaidres picked up one of the little cups containing

256

the tea and took a few sips before placing it back down on the table. He asked me about the design that was painted on my forehead.

"Oh that," I said, having almost forgotten that it was there. "It's to do with my initiation into the Agari."

"Well...I must say that I'm impressed! So what does that make you now? Some sort of Holy warrior priest maybe! Or does this mean that you're not allowed to kill anyone anymore?" he asked me with a rather peculiar look on his face that was somewhere in between sceptical and cynical. "Ah...but wait! I see that you still carry weapons, so I guess that answers my question then doesn't it?" he said with an obvious tinge of sarcasm in his voice.

I hadn't been back very long, and I hadn't bothered to remove my throwing knives which were still strapped to my legs, or the Akinakes Dagger that presently hung from my belt, so I couldn't blame him for his slightly disparaging comments, so I didn't allow it to get to me.

"Hmm...As an Agari priest it is preferable that I don't kill anyone, as it's very hard to be a killer one day and a healer the next. But after saying that, I am allowed to fight to protect others from those who would wish to do them harm, so yes...I suppose you could say that I 'am' some sort of warrior priest. Although; I certainly wouldn't call myself holy, as I'm far from being holy that's for sure," I answered, ruminating over my somewhat tainted past.

I didn't know why, but I was beginning to feel very uncomfortable in his company. However, it didn't take much longer before I understood the reason for this.

"I was wondering if you're still in contact with the Hun," he suddenly asked out of the blue.

"Why?" I asked, beginning to feel a sense of deep unease beginning to rise.

"Well, I won't beat about the bush. We need to know exactly where they are and the layout of the place, and also the degree of protection that they have in place around their settlement, and I want 'you' to get me in there. They trust you, so if I was to dress as a Scythian warrior and go there with you...they wouldn't suspect a thing."

I just sat there for a few moments blankly staring at him, and struggling to take in what I'd just heard. Was he actually asking me to betray my uncle, and to co-operate with the Thracians in a bid to destroy my own people? I felt the blood rush to my head...and in a split second I'd stood up and delivered one of my throwing knives right between his feet. It made a loud 'Thuck' sound as it

257

penetrated the matting on the floor and stuck in the ground beneath. Gaidres quickly rose to his feet, and I responded by drawing my Akinakes dagger from its sheath.

"Look at me, Gaidres…I'm half Hun…or have you failed to notice? My own mother is a Hun…and you know that. How could you ask me to betray my own people?" I yelled at him angrily.

Gaidres just stood there staring at me.

"I was right – it's just as I suspected," said Gaidres, beginning to make his way towards the doorway. "Please don't throw one of those Hun knives of yours at my back as I leave. I'll see you around, Manu Kai."

I was enraged, he'd gone out of his way to provoke me, and then acted as if I was the one who'd been at fault. Yes, I did throw a knife, but it was aimed at the ground and not at him, and I did draw my weapon, but that was entirely a reflex action of a warrior who felt threatened. He knew exactly what he was doing, and he had managed to push just the right buttons, and to trigger a precipitous reaction from me that given the circumstances, was not an unreasonable response.

Lifting the flap of the kol, Gaidres paused for a moment, and then turning to look at me he said: "Oh yes…I almost forgot. You should have killed all those Italians in the forest back when you were living with the Hun. One of the men you allowed to escape was here a while ago, he must have got a good look at you back then Manu Kai…he recognised you."

Picking up the small earthenware pitcher from the table, I hurled it at the doorway in anger. It hit the wooden inner structure and shattered, sending pieces of broken pottery flying in all directions. Gaidres had obviously anticipated my anger as he had made damn sure that he could make a hasty retreat before saying any more.

"Please, Kai, sit down and try to calm yourself," said Tihanna, doing her best to try and get me to calm down.

"Why did he do that? – What does he want from me?" I exclaimed angrily. "He knows I'm half Hun. By the almighty will of the Gods…what was that all about?"

I felt bewildered and overcome. I knew that I probably deserved this, but I didn't know how on earth I was supposed to deal with it. If what he'd said about the Italian recognising me was true, it could turn out to be very problematic for me. But how could he possibly know about it if it wasn't true, as I'd never actually told him about that part. The Thracians and Italians must either be in very close contact and have obviously openly spoken of this. Or this surviving Italian must have personally spoken to Gaidres. Either way, it didn't look too promising right now. It would seem that my violent past was beginning to catch up with me, ironic really, as now all I really wanted was to live a peaceful life. "Try not to let it get to you so much," Tihanna said, rubbing my shoulder.

I know that she only meant well…and as I didn't want to upset her any more than had already been done, I took a few deep breaths, and just quietly sat there until I'd eventually managed to calm down again.

As soon as the party of Thracians had left, I walked over to my father's kol where he was still discussing the outcome of the meeting with my brother and a handful of his right-hand men, and it didn't take me very long to work out that once again it was a stalemate. Nothing had been resolved, and nothing had changed. But at least a declaration of war had been avoided…for now at least. But even so, I couldn't help wondering how much longer it was going to be before the situation had finally reached boiling point.

"You decided to turn up then," said my brother sarcastically.

Completely ignoring his stupid comment, I turned instead to my father who was presently helping himself to some Agari wine that I'd specially brought down from our sacred cave for him to sample…

"Do you remember when I told you all about the party of Italians that we massacred in the forest back when I was living with the Hun? Well…there was something that I didn't tell you. In fact, I've never told anyone, and as far as I know neither has Merren and Aptien, who as you know, were also there that day…but we purposely allowed a couple of them to escape so that they could live to tell their story, and hopefully never dare to return. But here's the thing…somehow Gaidres knew all about it, and he told me that one of the Italian's who had been here previously, was one of those who we allowed to escape, and unfortunately…he recognised me."

"Ah!" said my father, cringing. "Yes, I can see how that could turn out to be a bit of a problem, as we're expecting them back again for talks in a few days' time. The Thracian envoy is also acting as envoy through an interpreter to the Italians, and has brought word that we can also expect a visit from the Italian envoy in just three days from now."

"Just great," I said with a long drawn out sigh.

"Don't worry...we'll take care of it – whatever happens," he said, resting his hand on my shoulder.

"You're such an idiot," said my brother, sneering at me. "I hope you can see now father what a great mistake it would be to allow 'him' to become Sha Pada."

"Hold your tongue," responded my father sharply. "You may leave now and go about your business."

My brother had hated me from the very day that I was born, but never had he hated me more than on the day that my father had informed him that preparatory measures had already been put in place, to ensure that if anything was to happen to him, I was to take his place as leader of our tribe. And although I knew that my brother would happily kill me if he ever had the chance, I still couldn't hate him. In fact, if anything I actually pitied him, as all his hate for me had ever managed to achieve, was to turn him into a twisted and bitter man. For years he'd gone out of his way to make my life as unpleasant as he possibly could, but long gone were the days when he could vent all his hatred out on me by constant taunts and bullying. And now the mere fact that he knew I was still breathing was enough in itself to cause him immeasurable suffering, while all he was to me was a slight irritation.

A few days later, Tihanna gave birth to a baby boy. We named him Kern, and for a while at least I was happy. Well, as happy as anyone could be considering the unstable environment that we lived in.

Meanwhile, Aptien and Trisha's relationship continued to deepen, so my father decided that the time had come for them to marry. And after a suitably auspicious day for their marriage ceremony was determined – the marriage went ahead. My father had arranged for a kol to be erected ready for them to move straight into, and as a wedding gift, he'd had it adorned with beautiful wall hangings, and hand-woven rugs which covered the floor. There was no doubt left in my mind that they were made for each other, and I was happy for them both. Aptien had finally met his match in Trisha, and I couldn't have hoped for a better brother in law. Merren joked that he was glad to have their bachelor kol all to himself. But I knew that he was going to find it an empty space now that Aptien had moved out. They'd been tied to the hip since I'd first met them all those years ago, when they had accompanied me on my stay with the Pa-ra-lati. Aptien and I both agreed that we were going to have to find Merren a good woman to look after him now. Not that he was actually on his own all that much, as he was either in my kol or in Aptien's, and the three of us often rode out on hunting trips together, so I suppose things hadn't really changed all that much.

23

The Sentence

The only way that I was ever going to find out for sure if what Gaidres had said was true was to face up to the situation. So I decided that it might be a good idea for me to be present at the forthcoming meeting, and then I'd have a pretty good idea if the soldier in question was also present by the way he looked at me. I would then wait until the end of the meeting, and through the aid of an interpreter, I'd ask him face to face if he knew who I was.

So when the day of the meeting arrived, I proudly took my place at my father's side as the next in line for the position of leadership of our people, and although I appeared every inch the sharp witted and sagacious warrior, I was actually finding it really difficult to focus on what was being said; as all correspondence between ourselves and the Italians had to be through an interpreter, as none of us had learned to speak one another's language at this point in time. And although I didn't recognise the soldier in question, I felt confident that I knew who he was, as during the meeting, I noticed that he kept looking at me a lot more than any of the other soldiers. So after the meeting had come to an end, I asked the Greek interpreter to tell this soldier to meet me privately outside my father's kol, and to act as an interpreter between us, after which I walked outside and patiently waited for the soldier and the Greek interpreter to join me. Thankfully I didn't have too long to wait before they both emerged from my father's kol, and seeing me standing there, they both headed over to where I was waiting for them just a short distance away. Of course the interpreter had absolutely no idea what this was all about, but I think the Italian who I would later learn was called Cornelius had a pretty good idea, as he started to fidget uncomfortably as he now stood directly facing me.

As we just stood there staring at one another, I could see the anticipation of what was about to enfold captured in the soldier's expression, and I wondered what I was going to say to him, as now that we were actually stood face to face, words didn't come as easily as I'd anticipated. "Ask him if he knows who I am." I said without breaking my fixed stare upon the soldier. The interpreter relayed my question to Cornelius, who without taking his eyes off me for a second, replied to my question in his own language. The interpreter then turned to me and spoke in Scythian.

"He says that you are one of the Huns who took part in the massacre of the unit of Italians that had lost their way in the forest, he says that he knows this is true, as he was one of the three soldiers who had managed to escape."

So it looked as though what Gaidres had said 'was' true after all.

"Yes, it is true that I took part in the massacre of your unit," I said, folding my arms. "But you only escaped because we purposely allowed you to, and we would never have attacked any of you if you hadn't attacked and killed two of our small party of eight first. We were on a friendly hunting mission, and we showed you no hostility, and we would certainly have gone peacefully on our way if only we had been allowed to do so."

The interpreter stopped me for a moment, so that he had a chance to interpret what I'd just said, before signalling me to continue.

"Ask him what else he knows about me," I said to the interpreter.

After the interpreter had relayed my question to Cornelius, and he had received an answer, he turned to me and said:

"He says that you're the son of the tribal leader here…and the next in line."

As I continued to stare with sullen enmity at Cornelius throughout the whole of this translated exchange of dialogue, the atmosphere grew with ever increasing intensity.

"Ask him if he's also aware that in addition to this, I happen to be the nephew of the leader of the party of Hun warriors in question, and one of the young men that his party attacked and killed was my cousin, and also one of my best friends, and the son of my uncle…Yes, that's right! Tell him his lot only managed to kill the next in line, and the son of the leader of the Huns. Ask him if he knew that. And also ask him if he knows that due to this…I'm now also next in line for the position of Khan…which if he doesn't know…is the title given to the leader of several united tribes of Huns."

The interpreter just stood there staring at me open mouthed, and before he'd had a chance to relay the message, I bared my teeth angrily at Cornelius and said:

"We meant you no harm. Yours was a totally unprovoked and unjustified attack, and your lot got exactly what was coming to them."

And quickly turning to the interpreter, who was by now looking decidedly flustered, I said:

"And make sure you tell him exactly what I've said."

And with that, I strode off and left them both standing there looking quite shocked by my little revelation. I felt charged with the emotion at what had just taken place, and I quickly marched off and headed straight for the security and privacy of my kol. However, I hadn't managed to get very far when I heard a voice behind me shout…

"Wait!"

Turning to look behind me, I was surprised to see that it was the Greek interpreter who had apparently been struggling to catch up with me. He was obviously not a fit man, and rather stout from too much easy living no doubt. But he was a learned man, and obviously one with a conscience, so as I stood there patiently waiting for him to catch his breath after his rare exertion. I thought that whatever it was that he had to say to me must be quite important for him to have made such an effort to chase after me.

"You walk very fast my friend…it was difficult to catch up with you…but I really need to talk to you," he finally managed to blurt out.

"Please walk to my kol with me, we can talk there," I said to him.

He smiled gratefully, and after he had caught his breath a little more, we continued to walk until we had reached the privacy of my kol, but before going inside, I asked him to wait for a minute or two, while I went inside and gave Tihanna prior warning that I was about to bring a stranger into our kol. I then went back outside and asked him to follow me inside.

"Thank you, you are very gracious," he politely replied.

As he stepped inside, he suddenly stopped in his tracks and began looking all around him, I couldn't blame him, my home was lavishly furnished with some very fine things, including some beautiful Mongolian wall hangings, solid gold trinkets which were made by our finest craftsmen, and beautifully woven rugs from here and from afar.

"What a beautiful home and family you have," he said, smiling at Tihanna.

"Thank you for your kind comments. Please…sit down. Would you like some refreshments?" I asked him.

"Some water will be fine – thank you."

Tihanna fetched him some fresh water, after which I immediately pulled up a stool so that I could sit directly facing him, as I was very eager to hear what he had to say.

He appeared a little nervous, and I realised that he was probably feeling quite vulnerable right now, as although he had visited our village on several occasions before, and had spent a fair amount of time living with other Scythian tribes in order to learn to speak our language, he was just a little out of his comfort zone right now.

"Please don't be afraid to say whatever it is that has brought you this far, I guarantee your safe keeping, and I will personally make sure you return to your party unharmed," I said, reassuring him of his absolute safety while in my keeping.

"Thank you," he said with a warm smile. "My name is Kavtios. And as you know I am interpreter between your people and the Italians, and I generally uphold the rule of confidential impartiality to whatever information may pass through me as acting translator, as I'm paid well and it suits my purpose to do so. But I'm afraid to say that your private conversation earlier with the Italian soldier Cornelius has left me in no doubt that there are certain times, when it may be appropriate to break that rule. You see, your account of what happened, and the accepted account that was given by Cornelius and the other two surviving men, who had belonged to the fifty or so members of the Italian cohort that had been left to guard camp, and if I should be so bold as to say…shouldn't have even been in the woods in the first place, is quite different. And it sheds a whole different light on the whole situation. And considering the importance of the current political situation, I think that I have a moral duty to make sure that the whole truth of this matter is recognised, as it has potentially far reaching consequences."

I'd never once given a second thought to the possibility, that the true story of why we had taken such a bloody revenge on those men was never really fully understood. And now it would seem that the truth of what had happened had been covered up, and the three surviving soldiers had obviously given a false account which has stood its ground right up until now.

Kavtios drank the water down in one go, and then looking me straight in the eyes he continued: "You should know that the story which was given by the three surviving Italian soldiers was that they were ambushed and brutally set upon and massacred by yourself, and the party of what we now all know to have been Huns, and in a totally random and unprovoked attack."

I just stood staring at him for a few moments until the full impact of what he'd just said had hit me like a smack in the face.

"What?" I exclaimed, completely taken aback by what Kavtios had just told me.

I wasn't sure if I should feel angry or shocked. Kavtios could obviously sense my rising anger.

"Please…I ask you to not get very upset by this. You may rest assured that I'm going to make sure that the truth behind what went on is known…you have my word on that. Please…I must ask you to leave this to me. I promise you that this isn't the last you shall hear of this. You will definitely be hearing from me very soon. I must get back now, as people will be wondering where I've disappeared to."

Although his Greek accent was heavy, his knowledge of the local Scythian dialect was very impressive, and my higher senses told me that his actions were those of a man driven by some sort of personal moral code, and that he could be trusted. So taking him at his word, I was quite happy to see him safely back to my father's kol, where the party of Italians were rather impatiently waiting for him to show up, as not a further word could be spoken between Italian and Scythian without him.

During the meeting with the Italians, it was clear that they were very keen to establish a secure link with the Scythians and their trading posts, and they really didn't want anything to upset the apple cart at this rather strategic moment in time, and as the news of my link with the Huns, and of my involvement in the massacre in the woods was well known by now, it was a real thorn in the side of the Italian console, as they also knew that I was next in line to my father, and obviously the whole future of successful communication rested solely upon whether a solution could be found concerning the present situation regarding my grievances with the Italians. But what they didn't know quite yet was that I was also next in line for the title of Khan. I think if they'd known that, they would have probably given up right there and then, as the Huns were now sworn enemies of the Italians, and it would have taken a miracle to have changed that, and I was certainly not in any hurry to try and alter the situation as I had absolutely no time for them at all. I hated them coming to our village, and I was deeply suspicious of their motives, and I trusted them even less.

The Greek translator Kavtios proved to be as good as his word, and had obviously returned to Italy, and had presented my side of the story of what had happened in the forest to the Italian senate, as it wasn't even a full cycle of the moon before we received another message, giving us prior notice of yet another impending visit in just a few days' time.

The day had arrived for the meeting, and unfortunately the Italians kept their appointment.

There were more of them this time, including a high-ranking officer and a member of the senate. The Greek translator Kavtios was amongst them, but this time he was accompanied by another Greek translator, as someone had obviously realised that one interpreter wasn't really enough. It turned out to be more like a court setting than a meeting, as I had to give my side of the story via interpreter to everyone there present. After which, Cornelius was called to give his. He actually surprised me by admitting that what I'd said was true, but that in his own defence he wasn't guilty of lying, only of withholding the whole truth. As when they were initially questioned as to what had happened, the other two surviving soldiers, knowing that they were already in trouble for disobeying a direct order by leaving their camp in the first place, had decided to lighten the blow by omitting the fact that they had been the first to engage in hostility, thus resulting in a revenge attack by the Huns which had incurred the loss of close to fifty men. And because they feared reprisal if they told the truth, they had decided to give the false account that they had been the innocents in all of this, and that they were brutally set upon and massacred in a totally unprovoked attack. Cornelius said that he chose to remain silent, and to go along with what the other two men had said, as he was afraid of the implications had he gone against them and done any different.

It was clear to everyone concerned, that this whole thing had very far reaching consequences, as this situation had already resulted in the Italians having made a deadly enemy in the Hun, and could even compromise any hope they may have had of ever stabilising successful trade links with the Scythians, and of any future utilisation of Scythian skills into the Italian army.

Unfortunately, the other two surviving soldiers had been stationed too far away to be able to be physically present to answer to any of this. So for now at least – Cornelius was going to have to take the full rap for the problems which had resulted from the actions of that ill-fated unit, of which he had once played a very insignificant part.

The acting member of the senate was obviously very eager to sort out these annoying little problems, and set them to rest once and for all so that the more important business of securing trade links with the Scythians could continue unhindered. So he asked my father what it was going to take to put this situation right. My father answered quite correctly, that nothing could put right the death of the son of the Khan, and although his own son, 'namely yours truly' – 'did' have strong links with the Hun, I had no power to influence any grievances that the Huns now held towards the Italians.

The Italian consul just sat there during most of the meeting just eyeing me up and down. I would have loved to have permanently wiped that look of arrogance off his face.

"Fair enough," said the Italian consul. "So what would you have us do to set matters straight again with yourselves?"

My father paused and thought for a few moments.

"We'll gladly have this soldier executed if it pleases you," said the Italian Consul.

"Hmm – I don't know if that will do any good at all," said my father, turning his attention to me.

"What do you think, Manu Kai? Would you like to see this man executed?"

All eyes were presently fixed in my direction, but Cornelius' eyes were the most firmly fixed of all. His rapid breathing was shallow and laboured as he stood as if frozen in time, barely able to maintain his self-control as he awaited my final verdict. I had the power to take his life with a single word if I so wished. But luckily for him I saw no justice in having him executed. I'd killed enough men already, and it would bring me no satisfaction whatsoever to end this man's life.

"No, Father, I don't see any point in executing this man, as it won't change what's already happened. However, I am so sick of having to speak through an interpreter, that if we are expected to continue with this verbal exchange on a regular basis, I think that it's only fitting that at least one of them should learn to speak our language. So, I propose that instead of Cornelius being executed, he should live amongst us until he has learned to speak our language, and to a standard that we're happy with. After which – they will be able to speak to us directly…through him."

The Greek interpreters both turned to look at one another, and Kavtios nodded to his fellow interpreter to signal that he would be the one to translate what I'd just said. Cornelius breathed a sigh of relief at hearing that he was not going to be executed, which was immediately followed by an open-mouthed expression of astonishment, which was of course directed at me.

All the Italians present nodded in agreement, and the console then said something which was translated as: "If that's what you wish, then it shall be done. Cornelius shall forthwith stay with you until he has learned to speak your language."

"Well, I have to hand it to you," said my father, nodding his head approvingly. "That's a damn good idea."

"Thank you, Father…your approval is very valuable to me," I said with just a hint of a smug smile.

I then politely asked my father for his permission to leave, as I needed to make all the necessary arrangements to accommodate Cornelius, and I had just the right men in mind for him to stay with during his time spent living amongst us. They were three of the most battle hardened and brutal warriors that I knew, and they all shared a bachelor kol together. All three of them stood well over six-foot-tall, and would have towered over Cornelius, who would have barely reached up to their shoulders. If ever there were three more intimidating warriors than these, I certainly didn't know of any. Poor Cornelius…I almost felt sorry for him.

And so it was arranged that Cornelius should live amongst us until he'd learned to speak our language. Not an easy task for an Italian to learn to speak the Scythian language either I might add, as the languages were very different, and some of the guttural pronunciations of Scythian words were almost impossible for the Italian tongue to master. But I wasn't looking for perfection…just close to perfection would do.

Of course the question now was just 'who' was going to act as his teacher, as no one here was going to be able to communicate with him. I thought about this for a minute or two, and I decided to ask the Greek interpreter Kavtios if he would consider a position of employment by us as teacher to Cornelius. He would be well paid, and of course accommodation and food would be provided to the highest standard we could offer. He'd lived amongst Scythians before, so he was well used to our ways and customs, and as far as I could see, he seemed to be the perfect candidate for the job. I was absolutely thrilled when he accepted the position. So arrangements were quickly made for Kavtios to move in amongst us too.

Things soon got under way with Kavtios schooling Cornelius for up to five or six hours each day. After which, each man's time was his own, and as you can imagine, this was spent quite differently, as Kavtios was shown every courtesy and respect by the Scythian people, while poor Cornelius was not. His stay here was not going to be a pleasant one that was for sure, so it fared him well to get on with the task in hand so that his duration here would be as short as possible. But unfortunately for Cornelius, he found the Scythian language very difficult to master, and the weeks turned into months, and throughout the whole time, the three warriors that he was sharing a kol with were making his life hell…and not by my request I might add. They taunted him and teased him, and made his life an absolute misery. They intimidated him, and treated him as their personal slave. They had him doing all of their chores, and all of the cooking. In fact, he was made to do absolutely everything around the kol that needed to be done. And not content with that…they stole his blanket at night, often hid his boots, and they did absolutely everything in their power to be as annoying and as aggravating as was humanly possible. The only thing that I'd forbidden them to do was to physically harm him in 'any' way, as this would have been counterproductive. The only rest he ever got from them was when he was being tutored by Kavtios, or when he was outside chopping wood. In fact rather than stay inside the kol and get bullied and intimidated by his personal tyrants, he started to wander around the village more and more, offering his assistance here and there, and generally making himself useful. This also gave him a perfect opportunity to practice the Scythian that he'd learned on the locals. And even though I appeared to keep my distance, I kept a very careful watch over him during this stage by having someone follow him around wherever he went – mainly for his own safety. And I was happy to see that he seemed to be knuckling down and taking everything in his stride. If nothing else, I had to respect him for his steadfast and indomitable spirit, as it would be fair to say that many men would have cracked by now under such constant duress. So it came as no surprise to learn that one day he'd obviously reached the end of his tether, and had bravely stood up to his three aggressors, and in no uncertain terms he had told the three of them just what they could all go and do with themselves…and in perfect Scythian. Apparently he had stood in the middle of the three of them, who were all stunned into silence by this sudden and unexpected turnaround of attitude and said…

"Just get on with it and do whatever it is you're going to do to me. Kill me if you wish…in fact death would be a luxury compared to living with you lot. All I ask is that you just make it quick." But rather than cause them to get angry with him, strangely enough it actually had the opposite effect. Here was this little Italian standing his ground against three very formidable Scythian warriors, and telling them all to go and **** themselves. Apparently the three of them just nodded to each other in approval and gave him a pat on the back. By standing up to them he'd actually managed to gain their respect; after which they all stopped picking on him and left him alone – with my blessings.

It took Cornelius nearly a year and a half in total to master the Scythian language, but by the end of it he'd learned far more than just a new language that was for sure, and had also managed to earn his self some respect in the process, including the respect of yours truly. I still had no love of the Italians, but at least I'd managed to overcome my intense hatred of them, and this was largely due to the rather unusual relationship, born out of the mutual respect that had slowly developed between me and Cornelius.

I had made quite sure that my uncle was made fully aware of this situation, as I'd ridden out with a party of warriors to inform him of exactly what was going on. At first he got angry with me, and questioned my loyalty to him. But after I'd explained that I was not being disloyal at all, and neither was my father. We were simply taking advantage of the situation to learn as much as we could about our enemy, as the more that we knew about them, the more of an upper hand it gave us. As to know your enemy well, is to know your enemy's strengths and weaknesses. And my father being a wise leader and a wily warrior, knew only too well of the wisdom in keeping your enemies close at hand.

By the time Cornelius had left to return to his people, he had become more Scythian than Italian, and he was to become a familiar sight in our village. In time he progressed through the ranks of the Italian army, but due to his knowledge of our people, and the fact that he was able to fluently speak our language, he would often act as delegate, and was the only Italian who had ever managed to gain my respect.

The time had come once again for the once yearly ritual of the Sacred Serpent, and those of us who would be taking part had been busy preparing for the journey to the mountain cave. And on the morning that we were due to leave I arose early, and after bathing, I packed all the necessary provisions that I was going to need, including my weapons – as I was still very much a warrior as well as a priest, and even now I still refused to go anywhere without them. And finally last but not least, I packed my neatly folded deep blue ritual robe and white sash, which had been presented to me after I had successfully completed the last trial that marked my full initiation into the Agari proper. So after I kissed Tihanna and my children farewell, I left my kol to meet up with Garenhir, Sai, and three other fully initiated Agari from our village. There were to be no new initiates this year.

As soon as we were all ready to leave, we set out at a gentle pace and headed for the mountains. We had given ourselves plenty of time to get there so we didn't have to rush. The journey was relaxing and pleasant, and so by the time we actually arrived we felt suitably calm and reposed. We weren't the first to arrive, as it had already been previously arranged for three priests from a neighbouring tribe to arrive two days before the rest of us, especially to prepare the cave in advance, as the fire needed to be kept burning for at least two days, in order for it to achieve just the right quality and ambience which was required for the ritual itself. So after we had taken a little time to refresh ourselves, and to make sure that our horses had all been taken care of, we got on with the task of helping to make all the necessary preparations for the ritual at sundown.

24

The Ritual of the Sacred Serpent

Part 1

Meanwhile back here in our present time line, I was preparing to once again attempt to access the so called 'Akashic records' and induce a past life regression. Unfortunately, Seren was convinced by now that I'd completely lost the plot. I suppose I couldn't really blame her, as night after night I continued to lock myself away in the spare room until the early hours of the morning. I tried to reason with her that it wouldn't be for much longer, but I guess she'd had enough of spending every night alone with only the TV for company, and so she finally gave me the ultimatum that either I gave up all this nonsense, or she would be forced to leave me. I really didn't want to lose her, but I didn't want to be forced to give up something that was really important to me either, and I would probably only end up resenting her for it if I did. So standing my ground, I pleaded with her to just be patient with me for just a little while longer, but to no avail, as she proceeded to inform me that she had already packed two suitcases earlier on that day, and that she had already made arrangements to move back into her parent's house until she'd found herself somewhere more suitable.

"I'll be back to get the rest of my things when I can," she said coldly, as she walked out the room.

Of course, I felt sad that she was leaving me, but if I'm honest…also a little relieved, as now I could just get on with what I knew I had to do without being made to feel guilty all the time, and Seren would have the company which I just wasn't able to give her at this moment in time. I knew that it was the best thing for both of us right now, and after helping her load her suitcase into the back of the taxi, I told her to call me if she needed anything. There was no shouting – no angry voices, just an amicable parting of the ways. I watched as the taxi reversed out of the driveway, and then finally disappeared from view altogether, and with a sigh I turned to head back towards the house; it was only then that I noticed one of my neighbours; the lovely, if not a little dishevelled looking, prince of darkness himself, who had been standing on the front porch watching us the whole time.

"Missus just left you, did she?" he barked. "Yeah…mine left me a few weeks ago…bit of a shit, as I had to do all my own washing after she left, and then she had the bloody cheek to turn up with her new fella and take the fucking washing machine …so I have to use the laundrette now. You don't happen to have a washing machine that I could use now and again do you mate?" That was the very first time that he'd ever bothered to speak to me, even though I'd often politely spoken to 'him' on numerous occasions. And although I didn't want to appear as rude as he had been to me, I was in no mood for his 'polite' conversation right now, so I just nodded and walked straight back into the house…locking the door behind me.

It was beginning to get quite late by now, so after closing all the downstairs curtains, I made my way up to the spare room where I walked over to the old Victorian bay window and began gazing upwards towards the night sky. It appeared unusually clear tonight, and the full moon looked almost surreal as she shone her effulgent ethereal light down upon the earth below her. The vast expanse of the universe was ablaze with stars…so many stars! And I wondered how many of those stars supported some kind of sentient life just like our own Sun does. I was truly in awe at the sheer hypnotic beauty before me, and after standing there for some time, I finally forced myself to close the curtains; making sure that they were pulled tightly together, as if shutting out all outside influences; after which, I picked up the little Scythian artefact which lay on the bookshelf where I'd placed it the night before, and sat down in the peaceful silence of my room. And after making myself comfortable, I closed my eyes and took a few deep breaths before proceeding to still the internal dialogue within, and then with a clear intent, I began to focus my attention on the task in hand.

Before very long, I began to feel as though I was travelling through a long twisting tunnel, through amazingly beautiful and ever-changing isometric shapes and geometric patterns and colours, and then suddenly I saw a blinding white flash…

At first I felt disorientated, and I couldn't see very much at all, but then slowly things began to come more and more into focus, until I realised that I was actually gazing downwards into water. I could also hear voices which appeared to be coming from somewhere nearby; although I couldn't understand a single word that they were saying, as they were very quiet and muffled. Then slowly the voices became louder, and clearer, until I was able to make out a single word here and there, until finally...I could understand what the voices were saying. Raising my eyes upwards, I began to look all around at my surroundings. I could see that I was sitting just outside the cave entrance which was used to practice the Agari's sacred rituals, meetings, and initiations.

This all felt very different from my usual past life visions, as everything appeared so vivid and real. This wasn't just an induced memory, or a matter of simply gaining access to the 'Akashic records', this was far more interactive, and I actually felt as though I was really looking straight through the eyes of 'Manu Kai', just like I had done thousands of years before.

Looking back down towards the water that I'd just been gazing into, I could see that it was actually being held in a large round golden vessel of approximately a foot in diameter...and quite deep.

"Manu Kai," someone shouted over to me. "Bring the vessel over here."

This sudden demand for my attention had the effect of startling me into full conscious awareness, so quickly standing up I looked across to see where the voice had just come from. It turned out to be one of my Agari brothers who was known as 'Goshan', and he was presently just stood there staring at me as if to say...'What are you waiting for?'

Looking back down at the golden receptacle at my feet, I could see that there was a handle on either side of it. Just then another initiate who was known as 'Athwiya', walked over to the golden receptacle and grasped one of its handles; so firmly gripping the other handle I helped him to carry it over to Goshan and gently place it down on the ground by his feet. Brother Goshan then proceeded to empty the contents of a small leather bag which consisted of the sun-bleached bones of various small forest herbivores, into the water contained within the golden vessel.

A container of slightly warm melted fat was then brought over by another Agari brother, who very slowly and carefully poured it onto the top of the water so that it didn't sink. It soon solidified once it hit the cold water, and once it had hardened, a few dried leaves and herbs were sprinkled on the top, after which it was set alight. Athwiya and I then proceeded to carry it to the back of the cave, and place it onto a natural stone shelf that had been kindly provided by the cave itself. Inside the cave there was a large circular fire of approximately a metre round, which had been kept continuously burning for a couple of days and nights in a fire pit in the centre of the cave. So it was now burning low but steady, and was currently giving off a fair amount of heat.

The cave had already been prepared ready for the ritual, and several ornately painted lamps had been lit and placed within the natural crevices in the walls of the cave structure, and were now burning brightly all around the perimeter of the cave.

One of the brothers was busy placing sheepskins all around the centre fire pit, while someone else was going behind him, and placing small ornately embroidered sitting cushions, which had been stuffed with wool on the top of those. There was a heavy scent of burning incense, which consisted of a mixture of crushed hemp seeds, tree resins, oils, and frankincense. The heady aroma seemed to bring me into a conscious awareness of what was going to take place here this summer's evening, and of the part that I was about to play in it, and I was suddenly so overcome with a powerful sense of deja-vu that I began to feel a little dizzy. The filed away memories of this sacred ritual that we were about to perform, that in my present incarnation had up until now remained shrouded in mist, had now begun to magically unfold itself before me like some mysterious sacred scroll, and the words that it contained which had been held frozen in time, and written in some kind of esoteric invisible ink, had now chosen this moment to reveal themselves to me…and I suddenly remembered! I could now remember that this was to be the first time that I would actively take part in the once yearly ritual of 'The Sacred Serpent', since my initiation into the inner circle of the Agari Priesthood the previous year, so this was to be a very important ritual for me; a sort of rite of passage if you like, and perhaps quite understandably – I began to feel a little nervous.

Although I hadn't been an active participant in the sacred ritual last year, I 'was' present for the whole duration, and my initiation had been encompassed within the ritual itself, as I, along with the other two candidates for initiation, had been made to stand apart from the main circle of fully initiated brothers within our own protective circle, and we had to prove ourselves worthy by successfully completing a sacred trial. So I was already familiar with the set up and the ritual itself, but this was going to be the first time that I would actively join my brothers as an equal. I was about to take my place amongst an ancient Sacrosanct brotherhood of Agari priests, that had remained immutable and single minded for centuries before us, and all the many patient years of wise teachings by my

'Derkesthai' (Dragon master – or – The one who sees clearly) had prepared me for this time. I looked around to see if the other two new initiates were amongst us this evening, but I couldn't see either of them. I hoped that they were both doing okay…wherever they were. An appointed Overseer, who had been chosen some days earlier, was busy preparing a circle of protection in one of the smaller adjoining cave structures. I realised it was Garenhir, and I watched fascinated as he cast his circle, and then proceeded to throw a few sheepskins along with one of the ornate cushions and a blanket into the centre of the circle. He then returned to the main cave where the ritual was to take place. His job this evening was to remain in a discreet and sober state of presence, just in case there was any particular need for someone to be in full mental clarity of mind. Meanwhile, Sai was busily preparing his Shamanistic finery for the forthcoming ritual. He glanced across at me before gathering all of his gear together, and then walked off into another of the smaller adjoining caves to change into his Shamanic garments. He had seen twenty-five winters, so he was not all that much older than I was, but he had already managed to build himself a reputation for being an extremely talented seer, healer, shaman, and Agari priest.

Garenhir suddenly called us all to attention and asked if we were all present and ready to begin the Ritual, and after we had all responded that we were, he then asked us to all go and change into our robes, after which, he along with two other priests walked over to the cave entrance, and began to fix a large heavy blanket which was made from sewn together deerskins over the cave entrance, and then held it in place by weighting it down with large stones. I watched him fascinated as he began to walk all around the inside of the cave while reciting powerful words of protection, and casting holy water as he went. After which, he activated the Guardian of the entrance to the cave. (The Guardian of the cave was an active semi intelligent thought form, which had been jointly created by the wills of several Agari Priests, and was regularly re-charged by the same Priests. It had been programmed to carry out certain tasks, under certain conditions, and there were very clear warnings of this painted near to the entrance of the cave. If any intruders didn't fully understand the warning, or chose to simply ignore it and had dared to enter into the cave, I very much doubt if they would have hung around for very long.)

Garenhir then took hold of a large wooden staff which was made of a branch from the willow tree. It had been beautifully carved with two intertwining snakes, which continued all the way from the base to the top, which then split

277

outwards into two small wings. One snake was painted white and the other one was red. There were many other symbols carved and painted into the wood, and the whole thing represented the awakened Serpent energy of the winged messenger Mercury.

Garenhir then proceeded to invoke the elemental forces of the four corners of North, East, South and West, and loudly and purposefully thumped the staff down hard onto the ground three times. Garenhir then leant the staff against a large wooden table, and he picked up two metal discs and clanged them together three times, after which he rang a small bell.

"Would you please all take your places," said Garenhir in a powerful and commanding tone of voice.

After first removing our footwear, we all made our way over to the centre fire pit, and randomly sat down upon one of the cushions with our bare feet resting on the warmth and softness of the sheepskin rug beneath us.

Garenhir picked up a stack of small wooden bowls from the table, and then proceeded to place one in front of each of us; including the empty seat that was still to be taken making twelve in total, which he then filled with fresh water from a large pitcher. Garenhir then walked back over to the large wooden table, and picked up an expertly crafted solid gold ritual cup; with its long slender handle and graceful receptacle, it had been purposefully created just for this particular ritual. Garenhir then proceeded to walk over to each of us in turn; offering the ritual receptacle out towards us with one hand, and an ornate razor-sharp ritual knife in the other. And then one by one, we each took the knife, and after nicking the small finger on our right hand we allowed a few drops of our blood to drip into the cup before tying a small bandage around the cut in order to stem any further bleeding.

Garenhir then carried the cup and the knife over to the table and placed them on a clean white linen cloth, and no sooner had he done so, Sai suddenly appeared in his full Shamanic apparel, and walking straight over to the table, he picked up the knife, and proceeded to add his own blood to the cup. He then added the previously prepared secret mixture of hallucinogenic ingredients, and mixed it all together with a long solid gold ritual spoon, and after casting his right hand over the cup three times, he walked over to the seated initiates and began handing the cup containing the potent mixture to each of us in turn. All of us including Sai drank one single mouthful each, before Garenhir carried the cup containing the remaining mixture over to the large golden receptacle containing the fat, water, and bone mixture, and cast its contents into the fire. It spat and fizzled for a moment or two before returning to its previous state of…just being.

Garenhir then left the main cave, and there he would remain for the rest of the duration of the entire ritual, unless of course he was needed for any reason.

Sai picked up his Shaman's drum, which had up until now been leaning up against the cave wall, walked over to a pile of specially prepared sheepskins which had been placed a short distance away from the main circle and sat down. He began to beat out a slow but constant rhythm until he suddenly rose to his feet, walked over to where I was sitting, and promptly handed me his Shamans drum. Thankfully I immediately realised that I was meant to continue to beat out the same rhythm as he had been doing.

We all began to sway to the rhythm of the beat, and every now and then, Sai signalled to me to pause the beating of the drum, as this was the signal for everyone in the circle to take a deep breath, which was directed towards the centre fire.

Sai then stood up and began to perform a Shamanic dance, while I continued to beat out the same rhythm. The rhythm of the drum beat was designed to call to attention the wild forces of nature, and the spirit of the untamed forest. His movements were precise and intelligently applied, and the effect was very hypnotic.

Sai's Shamanic costume was brightly coloured with red and gold, and several different shades of blue and green, and was quite stunning to behold. It was embellished with intricate embroidery, and carefully chosen appliqués and talismans; there were highly polished gold and metal plates of different sizes which cleverly acted as reflective mirrors. The smaller ones were attached to the arms of the coat, and the larger ones were attached to the front and back of the coat, and jangled about as he moved. There were bird of prey feathers, painted animal bones and teeth, small dangling pompoms that were made of animal fur, and the tails of all manner of beasts.

The light from the flames of the centre fire pit, and from the golden vessel illuminated the gold and metal plates on Sai's coat, and reflected little beams of light, which darted outwards in all directions as he moved, illuminating the cave walls, and creating a kaleidoscope effect of colour and form. I think the hallucinogenic mixture was starting to kick in at this point, as I kept seeing Sai's face metamorphose into the faces of animal like apparitions; which although a little unnerving, was totally fascinating to watch. His filed teeth and forked tongue added to the overall effect, and he really was an impressive sight to behold and a master of his art for sure.

I could really feel myself becoming one with the energy, which was being created here. It was a raw primordial energy, and the very essence of nature, and of the wild beast and bird of prey. It was a sharp slightly edgy feeling, and it gave me goose bumps and made me feel as though I wanted to emulate and to act out this sensation, and to become one with the wild beast, and of the lone baying wolf calling out to the moon: "Hear me...I am here...Listen...I am wild and free...I am wolf." Suddenly I felt as though I could actually see things from a wild cat's perspective; I was looking straight through its eyes and seeing what 'it' was seeing, and feeling what 'it' was feeling. I really felt as though I was experiencing the excitement and the anticipation of a cat lying in wait; silently watching its prey from some hidden vantage point; every nerve and sinew charged with the anticipation of the leap...aimed with single minded focus upon my unsuspecting prey; with claws bared, I was ready to...

I was completely losing myself in the primeval energy of the natural killer, and I was thankful that I couldn't see my reflection anywhere. I wasn't quite sure where this ritual was supposed to be going with this at first, but then I remembered Garenhir telling me once that there was a part of the ritual which symbolised the emergence from the lower animalistic state, into the awakening mind of the higher principles and consciousness of mankind. He said it was a very ancient ritual, and not even he knew where it originated.

Careful to avoid making eye contact with anyone, I looked upwards towards the roof of the cave, but to my surprise it appeared to have completely disappeared...or at very least, to have become transparent as I could see an eagle soaring high above me...and then in a flash, I was actually looking straight through its eyes, and with my incredible magnified eagle-eyed vision, I could peruse all on the ground below me. I could see right through the solid rock of the cave, and all of my brothers sat around the fire. But what was really odd was that I could also see myself sat amongst them.

I could really feel the cool uplift of the wind under my wings as it lifted me higher and higher, and I found myself wondering if I was ever going to come back down again. I could still clearly see Sai, who for some reason suddenly looked upwards, and as he did, he appeared to change into the form of a giant eagle, which had the strange effect of instantly drawing me back down to earth again. And with my consciousness now returned to my earthly body, I could really feel this raw, basic, fundamental energy coursing through my very being, and I only had to take one look at my brothers to know that they were all experiencing a similar thing.

There could be no doubt that Sai had been successful in achieving the desired result, so ceasing with his shamanic dance, he turned to relieve me of the Shamans drum, and commanding my attention with his eyes, he held me frozen with his stare. I knew damn well that he wasn't just looking 'at' me but deep into my core being…searching! He had managed to gain the upper hand by successfully catching me completely off guard, and I felt powerless to stop him.

"Hmm," he said withdrawing his gaze.

And with that slightly twisted smile of his, he put his finger to his lips in a gesture of silence. Sai took the drum from my hands, and setting it down out of the way, he turned to glance back at me, and with a slight sideways nod of his head he gave me a look as if to say…later! And even though he had continued to walk right around to the other side of the fire, and had taken his place in the empty space directly opposite me, I could have sworn that I faintly heard him say: "Interesting!" There was no doubt in my mind whatsoever that Sai was somehow aware that there was something else going on with Manu Kai this evening; via future reincarnated Manu Kai – yours truly! But how could he know. I felt as though he'd just read me like a book – and I felt as transparent as a glass window. Could he really see into my inner being?

As Sai began to quietly remove his outer regalia; setting it down on the cave floor behind him, he turned his head to look at me once more, and this time, I clearly heard him talk to me without speaking.

"Yes, I see you…but you don't have to fear. I'm your friend…do you remember, Manu Kai?" Quickly looking down at the cave floor, I purposely avoided making any eye contact with him. I felt very confused…was he actually able to get inside my head now? I decided the best thing to do was not to react and pretend that I didn't hear him, and so I just continued to stare down at the ground.

For some reason, I began to recall the many events that had not yet come to pass in this life. It was not something that I particularly wanted to remember right now, so hoping to distract my thoughts away from the subject; I raised my eyes from the ground…only to be met with Sai's. He was now looking at me with a very questioning expression on his face. I knew that I was going to have to be very careful, so quickly looking back down at the ground – I tried very hard not to think much…of anything. This hallucinogenic stuff was incredibly strong…we could even hear each other's thoughts.

This was starting to get a little freaky…even by my standards, and for a moment I thought about terminating the whole experiment, but I'd gone far too deeply into this by now, that it would most probably have taken every ounce of my will power just to bring myself out of this; besides…I didn't really want to…not unless I had no other choice of course. I'd always known that Sai was an unknown quantity, and although I came to know him very well, there were many things about him that I still didn't fully understand. No one…except perhaps for Garenhir knew what he was actually capable of, and it was probably just as well that they didn't.

Sai finally sat himself down amongst the rest of us, and no doubt sensing my unease he spoke to me directly into my head once again.

"You can relax…I'm just interested that's all!"

I decided that if he could do it…so could I, and so I directed my focussed will in his direction, and clearly speaking in internal dialogue I responded in kind.

"How do you know?" I asked him.

"Manu Kai," he said, raising his eyebrows, "How could I not know?"

Well, that told me absolutely nothing, but it did feel reassuring, and at least I felt a little more at ease now and safe enough to continue. This was all very strange indeed, and it was getting to be one hell of a road trip – in more ways than one. Somehow I'd managed to transfer my present time-line consciousness to my past life time-line consciousness, and I was actually really here, but the best part of it was, I had no idea how I'd managed to do it.

By now the effect of the hallucinogenic mixture was getting much stronger, and the centre fire pit was beginning to look like an explosion in a paint factory. I could clearly see the fire elementals as they fed on the energy from the flames, which contorted and danced like insane ballerinas, and turning to look at the brother who was seated to the left of me, I wasn't at all surprised to see that he was also looking straight back at me, and with a smile that would have lit up the night sky.

"I think we are all as one now," he said to me without speaking.

And although I was a little surprised to learn that he could also talk to me without speaking, I knew exactly what he meant. And then before I'd had a chance to respond, he suddenly leaped to his feet and headed straight over to the golden cauldron containing the water, fat, and bone mixture, and just stood there staring into the flaming receptacle for a few moments, before plunging his hand straight through the fire and into the water. And then completely unaffected by the flames, he pulled out his hand which was now holding one of the little bones, carried it back to his place by the fire, and sat back down again. I watched him intrigued as he just continued to sit there staring intently at the little bone for a short while, before he suddenly stood up and immediately threw it into the centre of the fire pit.

I'd already previously undergone the process of this trial of fire, as a necessary stage in the lead up to my final initiation into the inner circle of the Agari, and so I was quite familiar with what I had to do here, but I didn't have a clue as to what I was actually supposed to do with the little bone once I had retrieved it. So hoping to pick up some sort of clue, I purposefully allowed everyone to go before me. But even after carefully watching every brother go through the very same process, I was still none the wiser. So feeling a bit like an Arab trying to build an igloo, I walked over to the fire, and began to study it very closely. I could clearly make out the little fire elementals, and I watched them as they seemed to dare and entice me to touch them. But before I did; I knew that I had to first form a special connection with the fire before it would be safe enough for me to put my hand through the flames. So focussing my absolute attention on the active intelligent elemental principle within the fire itself, which is not an easy thing to do I might add...especially when you're 'tripping your block off' ...as the saying goes, I began to call upon all the years of training that I'd undergone in this life which had prepared me well for times like these, and before very long I was able to centre myself and remain focussed on the task at hand. I soon began to feel as though the fire and I were as one, and I watched entranced as the flames slowly appeared to change from the fiery red and orange colours that we have come to associate with fire, to beautiful translucent shades of blue. And then right at that very moment, I knew that it wouldn't burn me; that is...I absolutely knew, and not just simply 'thought' that it wouldn't burn me. There is big difference. And so, just as my brothers had all done before me, I plunged my hand straight through the flames, and proudly retrieved my small bony reward which had once been part of the hind leg of some little forest critter. And then with my prize in hand, I promptly returned to my place around the fire pit, and then mimicking the actions of my brothers, I proceeded to rest my somewhat altered state of vision upon the tiny bone, in the hope that whatever it was that was supposed to happen…would!

And all the time I was increasingly aware of the ever-watchful presence of Sai.

As I continued to focus my eyes upon the little bone that lay there in the palm of my hand…or at least I did my level best to – as it was definitely getting much harder to focus on anything anymore; I suddenly became aware of the presence of some very impish looking creatures of very strange appearance, that were all currently having enormous amounts of fun running rings around us all. These little fellows belong to the astral realms, and were affectionately known as the cave Jinn, and in our normal state of consciousness most of us wouldn't have been able to see them, but right now we could all see them, and for me at least they were proving to be very annoying. They were everywhere, and one of them was even sitting on my boots; while several others were sitting in a circle just like we were and mimicked our every move; while another one of them appeared to take great delight in pulling a grotesque face at me every time I looked at him, and believe me, it was impossible not to look at him. I could even hear them giggling in merriment, delighting in the fact that we could see them, and for the opportunity that this gave them to taunt and to tease us. In fact I could see to be no other reason for them to be here, other than to be as annoying as possible and to disrupt our sacred ritual in any way they could; although of course to them it was simply just a game…a bit of harmless fun. I guess the protection thing wasn't designed to ward off these harmless, but somewhat irritating little cave critters. So I tried my best to just ignore them, and to focus instead on whatever it was that I was supposed to be doing. But unfortunately they proved to be just too much of a distraction, and I really felt like running over towards them and booting them into another less accessible dimension…like a large black hole maybe. This was no good at all, and as they were obviously intending to stick around for a while, I was just going to have to try harder to block them out. So with steely determination I fixed my eyes with such a cold tunnel vision stare upon the object lying there in the palm of my hand, that it would have rivalled Medusa's on a bad hair day. And as I continued to stare downwards at this tiny appendage in such a way that you would have thought my very life depended upon it…and at this moment believe me…it felt as though it really did, I realised that it might be a good idea if I tried to relax a little, as I'd become increasingly aware of the pain from my finger nails from my other hand; especially the one on my little finger that I kept long and sharply filed, which was now digging deep into the palm of my hand. I had allowed myself to become so side tracked by the local astrally challenged resident cave dwellers that I was practically on the verge of losing control…which was obviously not good. So taking another deep breath, I closed my eyes for a few moments, and then I counted to ten 1 – 2 – 3…10. Right! I was ready to start all over again.

I opened my eyes and began to gaze at the little bone far more gently this time, and in a much more relaxed state of mind, and I watched in silent fascination as it began to glisten and then change into a multitude of different forms, but I almost dropped it in shocked surprise when it suddenly began to grow a mouth and spoke to me.

"Just get on with it," it said to me. "Our beards are beginning to grow."

Instinctively, I looked straight towards Sai, who just so happened to be staring back at me and grinning from ear to ear. My face must have been a picture, and I just knew that he was somehow responsible for the mouth thing, but how he actually did it I have no idea.

Sai folded his arms, and still staring at me, he raised his eyebrows and began to twirl at his long hair with his fingers, and after tossing it back out of his eyes, he looked straight up towards the roof of the cave, and began to act as though he was deeply engrossed in the study of its internal structure.

There were a few muffled chuckles coming from the other brothers, and I just had to smile. He really was a star, and I thought to myself how hard I was finding it to remain at a safe and composed distance from him, and not betray the secrets of things not yet come to pass that I knew I must keep safely hidden within. Thousands of years have gone by…but I kept my promise, although; not in a million years could I ever have guessed that it would turn out to be like this, and as I sat there watching him blatantly pretending to act naturally, I spoke to him internally, but not really expecting him to actually hear me…

"The answer to your question of do you remember is yes, I do remember you Sai…I've never really forgotten."

Sai suddenly looked across at me with an expression of deep intrigue…Whoops! I quickly lowered my gaze once again, and I felt slightly annoyed with myself for forgetting how naturally psychic and intuitive Sai actually was, especially in this heightened state of awareness. I would need to remain on guard at all times; I really couldn't afford to make too many mistakes like that. I decided I'd better get this thing over and done with, and now in a completely different state of mind, and feeling much more focussed and level headed, I got on with the task in hand, and it wasn't long before I saw something quite remarkable.

As I gazed upon the little bone still resting in the palm of my hand, I saw that both my hand and the bone appeared to be engaged in an interchange of energy, and I could see that it was forming some kind of a vibrational link with me. It suddenly dawned on me that there was some kind of Alchemical process going on here. The bones, my blood, and the blood of all my brothers, and all of the ingredients that were in the mixture which had been thrown into the fire receptacle, had somehow through the Alchemical process of trial by fire, which we had all participated in earlier, undergone an Alchemical change on a deep sub atomic level, and were now all vibrationally in tune with each other. And now this little bone was connecting with me. "EUREKA!" I finally got it!

And now to complete the final process of this part of the ritual, it must be thrown into the centre fire pit. I completely forgot myself for a moment and I shouted out loud: "YES!" and I threw the little bone into the fire. I'd successfully completed my final rite of passage, and cemented my initiation into the Agari, and everyone applauded in respectful accord.

Each one of us seated around the fire then picked up the bowls of water that had been placed before us at the beginning of the ritual, and taking one mouthful, we all simultaneously spat it out into the centre of the fire pit; after which, we all began a prolonged state of chanting. The cave was becoming alive with a positive force of electromagnetic energy, which was increasingly building up within the cave structure, and I could clearly see the waves of charged energy in the ether all around us. And then without really knowing why…everyone suddenly ceased chanting, and we were all mercilessly thrown into a sudden and indescribable silence that was almost deafening…

Phase one of the ritual was now complete.

The next part of the ritual was considered to be highly dangerous, and everything depended upon the solidity of our unity, skill, and understanding. We were our own protective circle, and it was imperative that under no circumstances should it be broken.

I suddenly became aware that the cave Jinn were all gone…

25

Ritual of the Sacred Serpent

Part 2

I watched fascinated as the glowing embers of the fire seemed to constantly change in colour and form. Their flickering light danced around the uneven structure of the cave walls, creating strange and slightly demonic shadowy forms, which although a little disturbing, were hypnotic to the senses. You certainly needed a strong head about you in order to keep a firm grip on your imagination, or the powerful effects of the hallucinogenic mixture could very easily run away with you.

As I looked around at all the brothers who were taking part in this ritual here this evening, I could feel the deep connection that existed between us. The very air that we breathed seemed fuelled with the anticipation of what was to come. It was a moment of inner reflection for us all, and it also gave us a little time to prepare ourselves for the next stage of the ritual.

Closing my eyes I inhaled deeply, breathing in the essence of all that this was. I became so lost in the moment that I wasn't sure who I was any more, and I felt as though I was flashing back and forth through time and space. I could remember events that had occurred both in this life, and in my present life, and it all felt very surreal like a strange and lucid dream; except of course that this wasn't a dream.

Right at the beginning of this whole experience, when I'd caught a glimpse of my reflection in the water, it felt so very strange to see the face of Manu Kai looking back at me again. It had been a very…very long time, and a lot of what I was going to have to deal with in this life had not yet occurred, and at the same time it already had, and thousands of years ago at that. Yet this was as present tense as any feeling of 'now' I'd ever felt before. I felt a tightening in my stomach as confusion and anxiety began to take a grip, and I found myself wishing that I could forget all about what the future had in store for me in this life for a while. I knew that I needed to try and focus my thoughts on something else right now, as my thoughts had become too tightly wrapped around the concept of time, and of the reality…or perhaps more fittingly the 'non reality' of it. I wished somehow that I could find a way to change the worst of what I knew was to come. But I also knew that all of this was somehow written in the so-called sands of time, and it would be a complete waste of effort right now, to even try to understand what was just too deep to fathom. Time had ceased to have any meaning for me anymore. There was only the omnipotent sense of the eternal and ever present now, and I could feel a deep resounding and timeless echo pulse through my very being. This extraordinary planet of ours was indeed the greatest mystery school of all.

Glancing across at Sai, I wasn't at all surprised to see that he was looking right back at me.

"Are you okay?" he mouthed in silence.

I nodded that I was. He had obviously been watching me and picked up on my anxiety. He just winked at me and smiled. I don't know why but this immediately had a calming effect on me. Looking around at all the brothers here today, I wondered how well they all actually knew one another, as there were several here today that I didn't even recognise. But I suppose it didn't really matter, as the higher aspects of our selves transcended such trivia. We were bound together by an invisible thread of brotherhood, and of mutual trust and single-minded purpose, and I couldn't remember a time that I'd ever felt so close, or more connected to my fellow human beings than I did right now.

Don't ask me how…but I just knew that the time was now right for us to begin the second stage of the ritual, and as if by unspoken command we all stood up, and reaching out to one another we all took hold of the brother's hand standing next to us in unity, and the circle was sealed. One of the brothers called upon the spirits of the mighty elemental forces of Air, Fire, Water, and Earth, and of the fire Goddess Tabiti to make her presence known to us. He then recited an invocation calling upon the mighty presence of the Sacred Serpent.

We all took a very deep breath, and as we did, we mentally drew in the surrounding energy, and then focussing with an effort of our unified will, we directed our outward breath containing the concentrated energy into the centre of the fire, and this we repeated several times in unison. The water that was held in the golden vessel containing the bones and fat mixture began to vibrate, and a barely tangible but discerningly present trembling could be felt in the earth below our feet. We all remained perfectly calm and continued to focus on our breathing, as we were all becoming increasingly aware of the awesome power which was about to manifest.

A sound resembling the soft whispering of the wind was now quite audible, and seemed to be coming from all around us. The glowing embers of the centre fire began to glow noticeably brighter, but being trained to take such things in our stride, we continued to remain quite calm and unfazed, and continued with our unified breathing, until that is, our trance like state was abruptly brought to an end by an unearthly and impossible to describe deep resonant sound, which had even deeper under tones. This was then immediately followed by a sharp rising in the level of the tone, and then very suddenly it felt as though the air was being sucked outwards from the centre of the fire. It was so powerful that it almost knocked us off our feet.

Steadying our footing on the ground below us, we all focussed our attention on the strength of our unity, and then...we waited!

Instinctively I began to scan the inside of the cave...for what? – I really wasn't sure, so I was quite amazed to see that right above the fire pit, near the very top of the dome shaped cave roof, was what I can only describe as a manifestation of electrical discharge, which was currently creating such an incredible display of light and colour that it was quite breath-taking to behold. The electrical phenomena then began to act like a vortex, and it began to spin around and around like a whirling dervish. Then suddenly there was a bright flash of light, quickly followed by another powerful gust of wind...inwards this time, and straight into the centre core of the fire. And once again, the sheer force of it nearly knocked us off our feet.

The flames of the fire suddenly rose violently upwards from the centre of the fire, completely engulfing the swirling multi coloured whirlwind for a moment or two before it suddenly receded again, revealing two separate and very discernible, serpent like apparitions which were coiling and twisting around one another, and which seemed to emerge from the very centre of the fire pit. One was an orangey red colour, and the other was a translucent silvery blue. The two serpents then rose up high above us, but still remained connected to the centre point of the fire.

I continued to watch in awe as suddenly they began to blend together into one giant serpent, and then slowly transformed itself into the tangible shape of a woman. At first it was more half human and half serpent, but then slowly the process of transformation became complete. And there before our very eyes stood this figure of indescribable grace and beauty. She literally glowed with a multitude of iridescent shimmering colour, which was more beautiful than anything I'd ever seen before, and she moved with such graceful hypnotic presence, that it was like watching some unearthly 'symphony fantastique', and I felt completely overwhelmed by her presence. As one by one she acknowledged the presence of each of us in turn, I was moved to such a depth by her blessing that I had tears running down my cheeks. She just smiled gracefully, and then in a swirl of light she suddenly transformed herself into a silvery blue Serpent.

Suddenly there was another outward gust of wind from the fire, and the silvery blue serpent leapt out from the centre of the fire pit, as if projected by the fire itself, and began to fly around the cave, twisting and contorting with a display of iridescent silvery blue light.

It was impossible to describe the sight before us, sometimes the serpent would swoop down right up close to us, picking one or another of us out, and just a few inches from our faces would hold fast our attention with its eyes, before swooping away again.

Then all at once there was another gust of wind – inwards this time, and the serpent like form returned to the centre of the fire pit along with the inward rush of air, and in another swirl of light, it completely disappeared downwards through the cave floor and into the earth. There was a slight rumbling sound which was followed by…silence. It was a silence so profound in nature that it was almost deafening.

Not a word or a glance was exchanged between us; as no one wanted to be the first to break this unutterable feeling of inner silence, but eventually someone would have to answer the call of nature, and so it was. The sacred ritual of the Serpent was over for another year, and Garenhir was now free to return amongst us.

The effect of the hallucinogenic mixture was beginning to wear off a little by now, but none of us were in any fit state to ride back, so we would stay the night in the cave and ride back again at day break. The horses had been left with food and water, and had been tethered safely out of sight around the side of the cave ready for the morning, but for now it was time to rest, and maybe even try and get some sleep.

As most of the brothers began settling down for the night, I thought that it was probably a good time for me to return to my present time line. So pulling on my boots, I stood up and grabbed the sheepskin that I'd been sitting on.

I was feeling pretty thirsty, so after helping myself to a drink of water from the water jug, I retrieved my weapons and walked over to the cave entrance. The heavy sheepskin blanket was still firmly in place, so moving it aside a little, I stepped outside into the crisp summer night's air. I soon found myself a suitable place to shelter from the elements, so pulling the sheepskin tightly around myself – I huddled into the secluded alcove in the rocks. This would be a perfect place for me to drift off to sleep, and on awakening I would be returned to my present body consciousness, and my criss-crossed timelines would all return to normal again. Well…that was the plan anyway.

Making myself comfortable, I sighed deeply and gazed out upon the wide-open plains which seemed to stretch endlessly before me, and only the sound of a gentle breeze that carried the whisper of the wisdom of the universe could be heard. The night sky was ablaze with stars here too, and the moon was also full here tonight and looked so close. I felt as though if I were to reach out I'd be able to touch it. However, I wasn't there for very long before soft but noticeable footsteps of someone approaching had disturbed my quietude. My eyes were immediately drawn to the direction of the footsteps, and I was not at all surprised to see that it was Sai; who had also seen me and was now heading straight towards me. I should have expected this, I'd been doing my level best to avoid him all evening, but it was painfully clear that he wasn't going to let me get away with this so easily.

"So…what's going on?" asked Sai, positioning himself directly opposite me.

"I have no idea what you're talking about," I answered, defensively.

"You know exactly what I'm talking about," said Sai, folding his arms and raising his eyebrows. I knew that I had to be on my utmost guard not to give too much away, but at the same time I wanted so much to reach out to him and tell him everything he wanted to know, but I also knew that this would most probably be the wrong thing to do.

"Please, Sai," I pleaded. "Don't push me on this."

"Fine…I won't push you…much! All you have to do is tell me what I want to know and I'll leave you alone," he responded, with that slightly crooked grin of his.

I decided that the best approach was probably to respond to Sai's questions with a question of my own. I'd learnt this technique by watching political debates on the television.

"So go on then…What is it exactly that you want to know?"

"Well…to be honest…I'm not quite sure," he said with a sigh. "You're still you…but different somehow. Your aura is different for one thing, and it's as if you're connected, but not quite completely attached. It's very difficult to explain. My senses tell me that you're somewhere else, and yet you're here at the same time. Well…am I right? What's going on with you, Kai? Don't make this difficult, just tell me…I really need to know, and you should know me well enough by now to know this."

I could see that this was killing him, and I had to hand it to him, he was bloody good! How was I supposed to respond to that?

"Hmm, pretty close…spot on actually!"

"I knew it! So now that we've cleared that up, will you just tell me what's going on? In the name of our ancestors Kai…just tell me?"

I knew that he was far too wise to try and fool, and I had far too much respect for him to even try, and so I explained briefly what had happened while he just stood there staring at me in amazement. There were a few moments of silence before he finally responded.

"That's just incredible!"

"Yes, I know," I said, pulling the sheepskin blanket right over the top of my head.

Sai then began to bombard me a whole heap of questions, one after the other, and although I could completely understand his curiosity, I just didn't feel able to deal with this right now. "OK…will you please just cease with all the damn questions," I said, re-emerging from under the blanket. "I'll tell you what, I'll answer three questions…and that's it. So make sure you choose very carefully. And after I've answered your questions, you must promise to leave me alone so that I can get to sleep, and then hopefully when I wake up again, the Manu Kai that you know will be back. There are a couple of things that worry me though…the first thing being…what if I'm not supposed to answer your questions."

Sai nodded and thought to himself for a moment or two before answering.

"Kai – if I really wasn't supposed to know, I don't think that it would have been possible for me to have seen so much already."

He had a very good point I suppose, so nodding my head in agreement I continued…

"The second thing is, I don't know what…if anything, I'm going to remember of any of this, so you're going to have to be prepared to deal with any possible aftermath of all this. And if I don't remember anything, it will probably be for a very good reason, so you must never tell me anything about what I'm about to tell you. You have to promise me Sai…and I…oh…I don't know."

"Yes, of course, you don't need to worry. Are you sure that you're alright?" he asked me, looking a bit concerned.

"Yes, I'm fine!" I said, taking a deep breath. "So come on, let's just get this over with…what do you want to ask me?"

Sai thought for a few moments before asking his first question.

"So apart from being here…Where are you right now?"

"I'm living across the water now, in a land called Don, which is…I mean…will be, called South Wales in Britain."

"Ahhh…I've heard of such a place, I think that's where Garenhir originally came from. OK…Question number two: So who are you now?"

"I'm a Celt," I replied.

He began to laugh, "You're…a Celt?"

"Hmm, I suppose it does sound funny given the present circumstances."

"I've heard that all the Celts are bi-sexual – so do you find me a little more attractive now?" he asked, striking a seductive pose and blowing me a kiss.

"Back off you idiot," I said, trying hard not to laugh.

"Not even a little bit?" he asked, with raised eyebrows.

I was never going to admit it to him here – but I was feeling attracted to him, but he probably knew that anyway.

"You have one more question left," I said with a forced serious expression on my face.

"OK – such a damn shame though," he said, composing himself once more. "How in the name of my ancestor's breath did you ever manage to pull this one off?"

"Sai – I'm sorry but I genuinely have no idea. Right…I'm tired and I really need to try and get to sleep now, so you're going to have to keep to your side of the bargain and leave me alone now." My defences were weakening by the second, and I was finding this whole situation between Sai and myself very difficult to deal with.

293

"OK, if it's what you wish," he said, turning to leave.

"Sai," I called out. "Before you go…please…come back a minute." I knew damn well I shouldn't be doing this, but I just couldn't help myself.

Sai came to a sudden halt, turned around and looked at me for a moment, before returning to the exact spot where he'd been standing earlier.

"Yes?" he said with a puzzled expression on his face.

"God help me but come here," I said, rising to my feet.

Sai took a few steps towards me, and to his obvious surprise, I pulled him closer and kissed him.

"Don't even ask!" I said, releasing him from my grip, "Just something I needed to do that's all. And now I really do need you to leave me here alone, before I say, or do something else that I'll 'really' regret."

Sai didn't say a word; he just stood there staring at me. He was obviously totally confused by my uncharacteristic behaviour, and taking one step backwards, he hesitated for a moment as if he was desperately searching for the right thing to say, but whatever it was – I guess he must have thought better of it, and then with a heartfelt sigh he just winked at me before turning and walking away.

I stood and watched him walk away from me until he was completely out of sight, and with a sigh, I sat back down again and pulled the sheepskin blanket tightly back around myself and closed my eyes. I was completely overcome with tiredness by now, and it didn't take very long before I fell into a deep sleep.

The next thing I remember is waking up again to the familiar sight of the spare bedroom of the house that I had been renting with Seren. The memories of the night before spared no time at all in flooding back, as if to remind me of the high price I had to pay for all of this, but then…just for a brief moment…I thought I heard the distant echo of Sai's voice, and the deep and esoteric mystery of time resounded so very deep within my soul once more, and I just knew that I had to follow this whole thing through to its final conclusion no matter what the personal cost.

Even though my body here had been resting, I still felt totally exhausted, and it wasn't very long before the need for sleep finally overtook me, and I drifted off into a very deep and timeless sleep.

The very next evening, I continued on with my quest…the whole story wasn't finished yet, and I was determined to see this thing through till the very end.

26

Classified Information

Meanwhile back in Scythia, the morning light had come all too quickly, and I awoke as Manu Kai to find that Sai was sat directly opposite me. He was leaning up against the wall of the crevice where I'd fallen asleep the night before. I held my hand up to my eyes in an attempt to shield them from the glare of the newly risen sun which was presently sitting uncomfortably low on the horizon, and through squinted eyes I strained to look around at my surroundings in an effort to figure out exactly where I was.

"Good morning," said Sai, with a warm smile.

"How did I get out here?" I asked him.

"You walked here – last night, don't you remember?" he asked, briefly looking up at me before going back to focussing his attention on the repair that he was currently making on his boot.

"No...I can't remember. In fact, I can't remember much about last night at all. Everything feels kind of hazy...like when you've just had an important dream but it all feels very vague and distant. I didn't mess up...did I?"

"Don't look so worried. You didn't mess up; in fact you did really well. Can you remember anything about last night at all?" he asked, with an upwards glance of his eyes.

"No...I can't! I'm glad that I didn't mess up at least," I said with an exaggerated wipe of my brow. "But why can't I remember anything?"

Sai took a deep breath, and sighing deeply; he shook his head and gazed out towards the horizon.

"Manu Kai, there are times when I realise the incredible possibilities that lie before us, and the vast and incomprehensible wonders of the universe and everything that we are, and last night was one of those times. If you don't remember what happened last night then it's probably for a very good reason, and when its right for you to remember, I'm sure that you will, but for now at least, you just need to know that you did nothing wrong."

"Nothing happened between us last night...did it?" I asked him, fearing that it possibly may have, as with my present case of amnesia I couldn't be absolutely sure that it hadn't.

"No nothing happened between us...unfortunately. Well, not much anyway."

"What do you mean...not much? Come on, Sai – you'd better tell me what happened. You'd better tell me the truth...now!"

"Hmm...like I said, it was nothing much – you just kissed me that's all. It was a good kiss too!" he said smugly.

"I did what? You're just messing with me aren't you?"

"Nope! Are you ready to go back into the cave now?" said Sai, holding his hand out towards me.

Although I was feeling confused and surprised by my apparent behaviour, I reached out and took Sai's hand and allowed him to pull me to my feet. I figured that as long as I hadn't done anything worse than kiss Sai then things were OK. I knew in my heart that he wasn't lying; so if he said I'd kissed him, then I guess I must have kissed him. There were far worse things that I could have done. I could live with having kissed Sai, and maybe the memory of exactly what had happened last night would return to me in its own time.

I picked up the sheepskin and my weapons which were still lying on the ground where I'd left them the previous evening.

"Did you sleep out here too?"

"Yes! Come on...we'd better go," he said, grabbing a hold of my hand again.

We walked back into the cave hand in hand as it was perfectly acceptable for men to walk around holding hands in Scythia; it didn't carry the stigma that it does in our modern day western society, and quite often you'd see heterosexual men holding hands as a mark of their friendship. Back in the cave, everyone was busily tidying up and packing everything away. The fire had been completely extinguished, and the fire pit had been meticulously cleaned out ready for next time. Garenhir was sat over on the far side of the cave cleaning some of the ritual items which had been used the night before. He immediately noticed us as soon as we entered the cave; as did everyone else by the look of things, as there were a few subtle sideways glances in our direction by some of the other brothers. I hadn't realised up until now how this must have looked to them.

"Ah…The two wanderers return," said Garenhir, beckoning for us both to come and join him.

"Is everything all right, Manu Kai?" he asked me, with just a hint of concern in his voice.

"I'm fine. But for some reason I can't remember anything about last night…that's all," I said awkwardly.

"Well…as long as you're quite sure that you're OK," Said Garenhir, holding my gaze for a few moments. "We can talk about it when we get back."

Garenhir and Sai both looked at each other and nodded. I couldn't help feeling as though they both knew something that I didn't, and that they were keeping it a secret from me.

"Did I do anything wrong last night Derkesthai? …I really need to know."

"No, Manu Kai, you really didn't do anything wrong last night…not that I'm aware of anyway. So please stop worrying and do something far more useful by giving me a hand by cleaning that instead," said Garenhir pointing to the large golden receptacle which had been used during the ritual.

Sai walked off into one of the small adjoining caves, and began packing away his shamanic finery, leaving me to get on with the task of cleaning the cauldron.

I suddenly realised that I was still wearing my ritual gown, so I walked off into the adjoining cave where I'd left my clothes the night before, and after untying the white sash from around my waist I removed my robe. I'd managed to get it quite dirty, so it was going to need extra washing to get it clean again, and as each member of the Agari was responsible for washing their own robe, I wasn't even allowed to let Tihanna do it for me.

After the cave had been swept clean, and everything had been neatly packed away and fastened to the horses, we all bowed to the mountain and gave thanks to the spirits that dwelled there for allowing us to hold our sacred ritual inside the cave, after which, we all respectfully bowed to each other before heading back to our respective Gers. (Dwelling places).

Arriving back at our settlement, I was surprised to see several Thracian horses. It really did seem to me that whenever I'd been away for a couple of days on Agari business, I always returned home to either Thracian or Italian visitors, or occasionally even a few Grecians who came to 'share' with us their philosophy and religious beliefs. They never seemed to get the message that we really weren't in the slightest bit interested, so we'd just carry on with our business as usual and completely ignore them, as we knew that it was only a

297

matter of time before they'd give up and eventually go home again. They were lucky, as my Scythian ancestors would have had them executed on the spot and been done with it. And I know for sure that the Huns wouldn't have tolerated them for more than a few seconds.

I rode straight up to my father's kol where the gathering was obviously taking place, and after dismounting, I covertly peered in through a small gap in the doorway to try and see who was in there. I could see that Gaidres was sitting in amongst a party of Thracian's, but unfortunately I wasn't being quite as covert as I thought I was, and he noticed me peering in at him. With my attempt to take a sneaky peak without being seen now compromised, I immediately moved back away from the doorway, but within a few seconds I watched as Gaidres lifted up the flap of the kol and tentatively emerged. I just stood there indignantly staring at him with my arms folded; wondering to myself what delights he might have in store for me this time around. "Can we talk?" he said, looking at me with a slightly worried expression on his face. "Why?" I asked him, fearing that it would be just another ploy to try and get at me for being half Hun again.

"Look, Kai, I'm sorry for what I said to you the last time we met, I was out of order – I know that now, and I really don't want to make an enemy of you. And despite what I said…I really do value your friendship. I just wanted to apologise to you…that's all."

I wasn't really expecting an apology, but I figured that we all make mistakes – and life is just too damn short to bare ill will against someone you had once called a friend. So relaxing my fortified stance a little I said:

"Well, as it turned out you actually did me a massive favour, but you must promise me that you'll never do anything like that again. You made me very angry…and that's not usually a good thing for 'anyone' to do. I'm willing to forgive you Gaidres, but perhaps the bigger question is can you forgive me. I'm not going to deny that I've killed Thracian's in the past…what's the point…you know I have, but then…so have you!"

The look on Gaidres' face instantly dropped from pleasantly confident to absolutely mortified. "Yes, Gaidres – I know about your 'little secret', but you don't have to worry – your secret is safe with me."

"Shhh…keep your voice down. Do you think we can we talk about this somewhere else. How on this earth could you have known about that?" he asked me, grabbing my arm and swiftly pulling me further away from my father's kol.

Gaidres suddenly came to an abrupt halt, and in those few moments of awkward silence where neither of us really knew what to say next, I realised that I was as much taken aback by what I'd just come out with as he was, as I had absolutely no idea how I knew that Gaidres had killed Thracians either, but I could tell by the expression on his face that what I'd just said was true.

"Oh – and there's just one more thing that I have to say on this matter," I said, finally breaking the silence. "I really can't change the fact that I'm half Hun Gaidres, so if you think you can just get past that, I really think we might have a chance of repairing our friendship."

"Yes," said Gaidres, engaging me in a firm embrace. "I think we can work this out…in fact I'm sure we can…eh! Brother Kai."

I had detected just a tiny hint of sarcasm with the 'brother Kai' thing, but I just let it go as I really didn't want to upset the apple cart all over again over something so trivial.

The truth of the matter was that I didn't have a clue how I knew that Gaidres had killed Thracian's, or where, when, or in what circumstances. But somehow as we were talking it just seemed to filter into my mind. It was as if I was actually picking up on his thoughts somehow. Hmm…this was new! I already knew from my own personal experience that thought transference was possible during altered states of consciousness between two people who were very much in tune with one another…so to speak!!! But this was something entirely different. I didn't hear Gaidres speak to me in my head, as I'd heard my Agari brothers speak to me while we were under the influence of a strong hallucinogenic, I actually just 'felt' this information filter through into my conscious mind – and I just knew. The trouble was I wasn't quite sure what it was that I actually did know. Confused? Well how do you think I felt? But whatever it was that I had accidently stumbled upon, was obviously something that Gaidres wanted to keep hidden – and this I found very intriguing. But it would wait, as all I wanted to do right now was to relax and forget about everything for a little while.

"How long are you staying here for, Gaidres?" I asked him, changing the subject entirely.

"Two days…why?" he asked curiously.

"Good! Then let's celebrate our newly rekindled friendship. Sometimes a few of us have a little get together in the evenings – just to smoke a little cannabis and have a few drinks, and I think tonight is a good night for such a gathering.

In fact I think I'll go and organise something right now…so I'll see you outside my kol at sun set."

It would seem that Gaidres didn't really have a lot of choice in the matter other than to agree, as I hadn't actually asked him if he'd 'like' to join me for the evening, I'd just gone ahead and assumed that it was my God given right to practically command him to do so. I suppose that I'd just got used to using my position to get my own way with just about everything, and I would defy anyone in my position of potential power, (even though I didn't actually want it) – not to become affected by it to one degree or another, and at this point in time I couldn't possibly have seen the early signs of how my position was slowly beginning to affect me. I had no craving for power, glory, or riches, so if someone such as I could be affected, you may begin to understand how and why a megalomaniac is created.

It is a truism that those who crave for control over others, and who actively seek to take positions of power are always the ones that are totally unsuitable for the job, and should be automatically disqualified and prevented from attaining such a position. And those who would be completely suited to the task of holding a position of immense power would usually prefer not to have to touch it with a barge pole. And here lies the irony of it all.

It was a fairly mild day, and the sky certainly looked clear enough, so hopefully the conditions would be perfect for an outdoor gathering. But before I began making the arrangements to kick start the whole process into being, I decided to spend a little quality time with Tihanna and my children first, as if I'm honest, I hadn't really seen a whole lot of them of late. So after a pleasant morning of family fun and frolics, I kissed Tihanna and my children farewell for the rest of the day…and most probably well into the night, and I dropped by to see if Merren and Aptien were up for some drunken revelries later, and as they both unsurprisingly seemed pretty keen on the idea, I roped them both into giving me a hand to spread the word that there was going to be a large gathering tonight. I also asked them to go and organise enough fire wood for a huge fire and to drag a few dead tree trunks around the fire for people to sit on.

I wondered if I should ask Sai if he wanted to join us. He didn't really socialise very much, and I thought it might be good for him. He already knew Merren and Aptien, and although I knew that this sort of gathering may not exactly be his scene, I thought that maybe with a little gentle coercion from me, he may actually enjoy himself. I figured that at least I should ask him, and then if he says no, well at least he couldn't make the excuse that he wasn't asked.

I knew that there wouldn't be any point in asking Garenhir as I was 100% sure what his answer would be. Of course you didn't need an invite in order to be able to join our little gathering, as everyone was welcome, but I knew that if I didn't personally ask Sai myself the chances were that he wouldn't bother. So without further ado I set off to go and see if I could find him.

I tried Garenhir's kol first to see if he was in there, but Garenhir said that he'd left some time ago, and as far as he was aware he had gone back to his own kol. I'd never actually been to Sai's kol before, but to be quite honest, I'd never really had any reason to up until now. Sai's kol was about a ten-minute walk away, so I decided to take a little stroll and find out if he was at home.

It didn't take much effort to work out which kol was Sai's, as it was instantly recognisable by the Agari and Shamanic symbols that were painted on the doorway and all over the main body of the kol itself.

Walking up to what I assumed was Sai's kol, I tugged twice at the red and green cord which would have been attached to seven little bells which would certainly have been dangling on the inside of the kol, and I waited for a response.

"Who is it?" I heard him call out.

"It's Kai," I replied, taking a step backwards.

"Kai – Oh!" he said, sounding surprised.

The heavy woven hemp doorway of the kol opened to reveal Sai, who just stood there for a few moments looking a little surprised to see me.

"Kai…it's you. Well…this is a surprise. Won't you come in," he said, holding the doorway ajar to allow me entrance.

Stepping inside, I could see that Sai already had company. His name was Tagitus and he was a well-known soothsayer in our village, as well as being known for his openly gay behaviour. Tagitus instantly stood up to greet me, and after we had exchanged greetings I turned my attention to Sai who was obviously finding it a little difficult to disguise his awkwardness.

"Sorry…I didn't know you had company. I can't stay anyway…I only popped over to ask you if you wanted to join me at the gathering later. You're welcome to come along too Tagitus," I said, as I stepped outside closing the flap behind me.

"Well…that was a bit awkward," I said out loud to myself, before briskly heading back again.

I didn't know why but I felt strangely put out by the fact that Sai might be having a relationship with Tagitus. I knew that I had absolutely no right at all to feel like this. I guess that seeing him with Tagitus had just taken me a little by surprise that's all, and I really hadn't expected the feelings that I had for Sai, which I'd tried so very hard to deny, to suddenly leap out and slap me straight in the face…and with so little warning at that. I did wonder why Sai had chosen to keep this a secret from me though, or maybe it wasn't so much that he was keeping it a secret, but more a case of me just wrongly assuming that he had remained single all this time. I just couldn't believe how naive I could be at times. So yes, it did come as a bit of a shock, but I also knew that it was something that I was going to have to learn to deal with as I knew that these feelings were misplaced and that I was just being ridiculous. Yep! I was definitely being completely ridiculous. I continued to walk back to the area of the forthcoming gathering, and forcing the whole thing to the back of my mind, I carried on with the preparations, and the task of making sure that there would be sufficient amounts of everything we needed for the coming evening.

Gaidres was smack on time, and as soon as it began to get dark, Merren lit the fire, and before very long people began to gather around and help themselves to the fermented mare's milk, which was usually in plentiful supply. I'd had it brought over from the store house, as although it was kept near one of the trading posts with the other things that we had on immediate offer for trading, fermented mares milk was not something that was greatly popular with outsiders, although we occasionally traded it with passing nomadic tribes, who still preferred the nomadic way of life to the more settled ways of the majority of the Scythian people by this time.

Women were also welcome at these Scythian fireside gatherings, unlike the Huns who preferred that 'their' fireside gatherings be an exclusively male affair, but even so, Tihanna didn't really enjoy the avid revelries and loud drunken enthusiasm of many of the Scythian male warriors, who could sometimes get a little 'too' carried away; completely forgetting their usually commendable and impeccable manners. So I couldn't really blame her for choosing to steer clear, as did most of the women to be honest. And if news ever managed to reach outside our settlement that we were going to be having one of these social gatherings, you could almost guarantee that we'd have a visit from a group of pa-ra-lati prostitutes from one of the neighbouring settlements, and if there was enough time for them to get here, even further afield than that. These women…and even some men, would come and flaunt themselves in front of our warriors, and try to tempt them in whichever way they could. And, of course, in their drunken state of mind, some of our warriors could be quite easily persuaded, so there was always good business to be had. I'd seen both Merren and Aptien disappear with one or two of these women on more than one occasion, but I'm glad to say that since marrying my sister, Aptien seemed to be behaving himself. I'm not saying that in a less sober state of mind, I'd never felt tempted by the lure of their erotic charms myself, but not quite enough to have ever actually gone off with one of them.

As darkness descended and the revelries of the evening commenced, Gaidres and I talked about many things, and inevitably the conversation turned to the issue of what I knew about him killing Thracian's, and how I'd actually come by this information. I knew he wasn't going to allow me get away with making such a statement without justifying it, but the trouble was, I didn't really 'know' anything at all, but even so…I was damn sure that I was right all the same. So I was just going to have to be honest with him, and then if he wants to tell me the truth of the matter…he will!

I stood up and looked all around to see if Sai was anywhere to be seen…but he wasn't. Too busy 'entertaining' his guest I should imagine. Oh well!

"Who are you looking for," asked Gaidres, obviously curious as to why I intermittently kept scanning the area.

"Oh…no one in particular," I answered with a sigh.

"So are you going to tell me what you know?" he said, demanding my attention once more, and I couldn't help smiling to myself at the irony of it all.

"The truth is, I don't really know much at all, or even how I know what little I do. You probably won't believe me, but I actually just picked up on your thoughts."

Gaidres shook his head and gave me a little smile. He picked up the pitcher and poured himself another drink before turning to face me again.

"Hmm – Oddly enough I do believe you. I've heard people say that you can do some pretty weird stuff, and back when I made you really angry that time, I wasn't just worried about those Hun knives of yours that might have been heading in my direction. Look Kai, I know that I joke around and call you 'brother Kai' and all that, but I'm not stupid, I know that what you lot get up to sometimes is some pretty serious stuff, and regardless of what you might think – I actually have a great deal of respect for you and your strange religion."

Leaning forward, I rested my hands on my knees and stared downwards at the ground through the gap between my legs.

"Well…if I'm honest, I don't actually know what you did Gaidres…or why," I said, sitting upright again. "But if you want to talk about it, you can be sure that it'll never go any further, and you have my solemn word on that as an Agari priest."

"I know you're good for your word, Kai, but it's a very long story," he said with a deep and troubled sigh.

"Well…I don't have any plans for the next couple of hours…what are you doing?" I asked him, adopting a cross legged position on the tree trunk that we were both currently sat upon. Folding my arms, I raised my eyebrows in a gesture of giving him my full and undivided attention, and awaited his response.

"Hmm…If I tell you, you must swear to me that you'll never repeat it to anyone."

"I already have…but yes, I swear. I'll even swear it in blood if you want me to."

"No, it's okay – you don't have to cut yourself just for my entertainment. If you can't trust a priest who can you trust? Ay brother Kai," he said with a wry smile.

"Well – that all depends on the priest I suppose," I replied, with raised eyebrows.

Gaidres gave me a knowing smile, before he began to tell me a tale that began with a small family group of about twenty five ethnic nomadic Thracian's, who had most probably originated from Dacia, and who called themselves 'The Daos' which means: 'People of the wolf.' (Daos was their Deity, and was said to take the form of a wolf)And once a year they held a religious ceremony in honour of this Deity; which oddly enough was also recognised by the Scythians. Sometimes the Daos nomads would even seek to join with the Scythians in celebrating this particular day, as the Scythians were very well known for celebrating their religious celebrations in grandiose style. Dancers called spirit dancers, or ghost dancers would always put on an impressive performance at these occasions. And dancing around a giant fire, they'd skilfully pretend to take on the form of a wolf and become 'Neuri', and then playfully chase people down the street; sometimes suddenly jumping out, and pretending to attack people.

(The myth of the Neuri was quite similar to the myth of the werewolf, which has been carried down through the ages, and through many civilisations right up

304

to modern day. This was the day that the veil between the spirit world and the physical world was thought to become very thin, and if by chance you are Pagan, you will recognise this day as 'Samhain', or if you are unfamiliar with the Pagan term you will know it as Halloween', and to those of a Christian faith it has become more commonly known as 'All hallows eve'.)

The Daos were very similar to Gypsies, and they travelled from province to province mainly because they found it very difficult to settle for very long in any one place. Not for them were the constraints of living amongst so many people, being taxed, and having to abide by a harsh and restrictive hierarchical rulership. They preferred their freedom of choice, and because of this, they were classed as low life and unclean, and generally ostracised and made to feel like second class citizens. Wherever they went they were regarded with a certain amount of suspicion, but oddly enough even though they were generally looked down upon, many people would come seeking their advice and to trade for the herbal remedies that they made; while others would gather around and listen to their wonderful tales of magic and mystery, which had been handed down through generation to generation, and had been retold word for word for hundreds of years. People would also throw coins at the feet of the women as they danced to the sound of a flute and the beat of a drum. The little bells that they wore around their ankles and wrists would jingle and jangle, and they'd rattle the small cymbals that they held in each hand, and sometimes clatter them together in the air above their heads.

The Daos had been camped out on the southern border of Thracia, as this was within a reasonable distance from the forest that they often visited to gather the herbs and roots that they used in their medicines. Unfortunately this was also quite close to where the Italian military garrison was stationed. The Italians and the Daos were obviously aware of one another's presence, and didn't really bother one another…that is, until one fateful evening.

The Daos were sat around their camp fire preparing what was to have been their evening meal, when they were visited by seventeen Italian soldiers, who demanded that the Daos share their food with them. The Daos had no other choice it would seem other than to comply, and the Italian soldiers greedily helped themselves to the food that the Daos had prepared, while the poor Daos could only look on helplessly. Needless to say – the Daos all went hungry that night.

This wouldn't have been quite so bad if it had just been an isolated incident, but it was to become an increasingly regular occurrence, so much so that the Daos had finally had enough, and they went seeking help from the Thracian authorities. But unfortunately their pleas for help fell upon deaf ears, and they were hastily turned away and left to get on with it. And so it would seem that they were left with no other alternative but to devise a cunning plan of their own. They were going to have to teach these thieving Italians a lesson that they were never going to forget.

So the very next time that they saw this same group of Italians making their way towards them, with the sole intention of stealing the food from their children's mouths once again, one of the women quickly added a mild poison to the large pot of meat and forest roots which was left hanging over the fire, and after giving it a good stir, she quickly sat back down again and waited for the Italians to rudely help themselves as usual, and as usual they greedily wolfed down the lot before leaving an empty pot behind them. An hour or so later they were all violently ill. They told their comrades that the Daos had purposely poisoned them, and even though it had been the soldier's fault for steeling the Daos' food in the first place; around thirty or so Italian soldiers immediately set out to wreak their revenge on the Daos. They flogged the men, raped the women, and kidnapped two of their female children. The children would have fetched an excellent price on the slave market, and this they saw as fair compensation for the hospitalisation of seventeen men.

Once again the Daos went to the Thracian authorities, and desperately pleaded with them this time for assistance in getting their children back. But they were told that it was their own fault, and once again they were coldly turned away and left to themselves to sort out their own problems. They knew that there was very little hope of ever seeing their children again, but they were certainly not finished with these Italians yet. Even though they were very few in number, they swore that they would not rest until they had taken their full revenge, as although they may have been responsible for the hospitalisation of seventeen Italian soldiers, if they hadn't stolen their food in the first place – They would never have been poisoned. It wasn't as if the Daos had actually given it to them. So after moving the women, remaining children, and the two elderly men to a secret and reasonably safe location, they double backed on themselves, and using the cloak of darkness as cover, they patiently waited for an opportunity to pounce upon a lone soldier who for one reason or another, had allowed himself to become separated from the rest, and after gagging their victim into silence, they very quickly dragged him off into the night. The Daos didn't kill their victims outright, but what they did was to devise the most horrible of tortures…and I'll give you just one example of this so that you can get a fairly good idea of what they were actually capable of.

The victim was taken to the forest, stripped naked, hog tied and gagged. Boiling honey was poured over his private parts, and then he was thrown on top of an ant hill and left to his own fate. The Daos had several other delightful ways to make a man sorry that he was ever born, and most of them died a horrible and lingering death, and this the Daos continued to do for a couple of weeks, until unfortunately for the Daos, one of their victims had finally managed to escape, and after making his way back to camp, he was able to explain away the mystery of what had happened to the missing soldiers.

Needless to say that after this – security was tightened, and there were no more opportunities to capture any more victims. So the Daos left the area and re-joined their families. They knew that they would have to get as far away as possible now, as it would only be a matter of time before the Italians would come looking for them. So they decided to head on up to a place known as the forbidden land, which lay just below the mountains; near to where a strange tribe of people that shaved their heads, painted themselves blue, and had a reputation for cannibalism lived. I knew this area well, as I along with my Agari brothers would have to pass through this area to get to our sacred cave, and we often saw these 'so called' cannibals. They didn't look at all threatening to me, but even so, this whole area had a reputation for being a terrible place, and was filled with superstition and dread, and was carefully avoided if at all possible by Scythians and Thracians alike.

Very few people ever dared to venture there for fear of either being eaten alive, or attacked by the evil spirits that were said to reside there, so I guess the Daos thought that they'd be pretty safe living there.

I can actually remember seeing the Daos camped quite close to where the blue people lived when we were on our way up to our sacred cave one day, and I had actually made a comment to Sai about the reputation that the blue people had for eating people, and how I thought that it was most probably greatly exaggerated, as the Daos hadn't been eaten, and if anything, it looked as if the blue people might have actually been helping them. Of course, none of us passing Agari priests had any idea 'why' the Daos were there at this point in time, and we unwittingly spoke openly amongst ourselves, and to our families and friends of these people, who then in turn spoke openly to others about them being camped where they were. And before very long, it was common knowledge amongst the Scythian people that a small band of Daos were camped very near to the blue cannibals. Unfortunately due to the close contact between Scythians and Thracians, the Thracians soon got to know where they were too.

The Italians had asked the Thracians if they knew where the Daos were hiding out, and they were told that they were rumoured to be camped near a place inhabited by cannibals, and had most probably been eaten by now. The Thracians were then asked by the Italians if they would take them to this place, but they were told in no uncertain terms that the whole area was cursed, and no Thracian in their right mind would ever dare to set foot anywhere near the place. So if they wanted to go and find these people, they were just going to have to do it alone. When the Italians complained that they didn't know how to get there, they were politely but firmly told: "Tough!" Needless to say they got a similar response when they asked the Scythian people to help them in the same way.

The terrible reputation that this area had managed to gain for itself suited the Agari just fine, in fact we even helped it along a little, as it was a perfect way of safe guarding our privacy, and keeping away any of the curiously minded. It also ensured that the chances of anyone ever discovering our sacred cave was very slim. Although after saying that, on several occasions we had been met by the sight of offerings of fine wine and fresh fruits which were very rare to this area, and also some of the most beautifully made pottery that I had ever seen. So someone obviously knew where we held our meetings and rituals…and exactly on which days. We never found out who was responsible for leaving the offerings…or why.

As Gaidres continued to tell me his story, I actually remembered him asking me about the blue people some time ago, as he obviously knew that as a member of the Agari, I would have had to pass that way in order to get to our sacred cave. I told him that I really didn't think that they were half as bad as their reputation, and I can remember asking him why he'd asked me. He just said that he was simply curious that's all.

Gaidres stopped for a moment and took a really deep breath, and I noticed that he shifted into a slightly more defensive position before going on to tell me that he had been asked by one of the Italian consulate, if he would like a position working in Italy teaching Italian soldiers how to ride a horse and take care of it, as equestrianism wasn't exactly a strong point with the Italian army at this moment in time. He said that he was told that he would be amongst five other well-chosen Thracians, and that he would be much better paid than he was now, and he would also receive many benefits. And later on, he would even be in with a chance of obtaining a good position within the future Italian Auxiliary forces. I noticed that Gaidres appeared to be purposely avoiding making any eye contact with me.

"Kai – I was going to tell you anyway – but I've already accepted this offer, and I'll be leaving for Italy in the turn of two moons."

I was really taken aback by this, and I found it impossible to hide my disapproval which was obviously plainly written all over my face, as before I had a chance to say a single word he said:

"Yes, I knew that you wouldn't approve of this, but unfortunately I'll just have to live with that. But you haven't heard the worst of it yet. So please…before you say anything…please, hear me out. You see…there was just one condition attached to all of this, in order to qualify for the position, the six of us had to prove our loyalty to the Italian army by leading them to the area that the Daos were said to be staying. At first the other five men said that they wouldn't do it, as they didn't fancy getting eaten for one thing, but I asked the Italian senator for some time to talk amongst ourselves, after which, we would be able to give him our definite answer before the sun had set."

Although what Gaidres had just told me caused me to feel very uncomfortably for a moment or two, I soon settled down again as he continued to explain to me that he'd told the other five Thracian's that an Agari priest who regularly travelled that way, and had seen these blue people on many occasions had told him that essentially the stories of the blue people being cannibals were obviously greatly exaggerated, and if anything they were a peace loving people who just didn't want to be bothered by their more aggressive neighbours, and they had obviously discovered that by looking the way that they did – and keeping themselves to themselves – the stories about them grew ever more terrifying and larger than life, and subsequently guaranteed them non-interference from outsiders, and total freedom and exclusion from all the political chaos and the squabblesome behaviour of their neighbours.

So now it would seem that I'd unwittingly managed to have some involvement in whatever this was going to turn out to be too. I suddenly felt a cold chill run up my spine, as I just knew that whatever Gaidres was about to tell me was going to be something pretty damn awful.

"We decided to take the Italians to where we thought the Daos had most probably made camp," said Gaidres, hesitating for a moment or two before continuing. "But as we obviously knew that the Italians intended to kill them all, and none of us particularly wanted the blood of women and children on our hands, we decided to make a deal with the Italians; telling them that we were prepared to lead them to the Daos on the condition that they'd spare the women and children. This they agreed to; saying that instead of killing them – they would spare their lives, and they would be taken to Italy to be sold as slaves instead."

(The Thracians had their fingers in the slave trade themselves, as did the Scythians, so no one would have had a problem with this, so in the circumstances, this would have been seen as an acceptable alternative.)

Gaidres continued to explain that the six of them had headed out with thirty Italian soldiers who had borrowed Thracian horses for the journey. None of them could ride a horse properly, or even use a bow, so if they had been attacked at any time during the course of their journey, the Italians would have been totally useless, and the only real value that they would have had would have been to unwittingly act as decoys, thus giving Gaidres and the other five Thracians, a very good chance of riding away to safety. He said that their journey was a long, slow, and difficult one, which was mainly due to the ineptitude of the Italians who just weren't used to riding horses, and who moaned constantly, especially about how cold it was during the night. They also had major problems crossing the river, and they were always going on about how much pain they were in. He said that on a couple of occasions he had felt like killing them himself.

"Kai…If I knew then what I know now – I would have just turned around and headed straight back home again. We did eventually catch up with the Daos, but how we managed it with thirty whinging Italians in tow I'll never know. But the fact is – we did, and what followed was an immediate and brutal execution of all the male Daos. This we were expecting, but not the subsequent plan to first have their 'fun' with the women and children, before executing them too. This wasn't part of the original deal, so we stepped in and reminded the Italians that the deal was that the women and children were to be taken back with us unharmed. They all seemed to find this highly amusing, and it soon became very clear to us that they never had any intention of honouring this deal. So to cut a long story short, in order to save the women and children from the horror of what the Italian soldiers had in store for them, three of us jumped into one of the wagons that the women and children were huddled in, and three of us jumped into the other, and very quickly ended their lives; thus saving them from any further suffering. And even though I know we probably did the best thing that we could have done given the circumstances, I will be forever racked with guilt, as I know it never would have happened if we hadn't led the Italians to them in the first place."

It wasn't like me to be lost for words, but all I could do was to nod my head in agreement. "Well Gaidres," I said, finally finding my voice again. "I thought that 'I' carried a lot of guilt for some of the things that I've done in the past, but that beats anything that I've ever managed to do. It's pretty bad, and I'm not trying to make you feel any better by telling you this, but I'm feeling pretty guilty myself right now for telling you that the stories about the blue people were unfounded in the first place. But in my own defence – I didn't know that what I'd told you was going to contribute to the massacre of innocent women and children."

I proceeded to pour us both another drink which we both downed in one go, so pouring us another, I quickly scanned the immediate area to see if Sai had bothered to show up...he hadn't! I have no idea how I got back to my kol that evening, but when I awoke, I was safely in my bed. So obviously someone must have managed to get me there, and had also managed to remove all my weapons and my boots, but oh boy...did I have a hangover!

27

A Cruel Twist of Fate

Tihanna was already up and dressed, and seeing that I was conscious she scowled at me and said:

"You were very drunk last night."

"Was I…? I don't remember. How did I get back?"

"It was just like old times, Merren and Aptien had to carry you back," she replied sharply.

"Oh!" I said, struggling to remember. "Do you know what happened to Gaidres?"

"Apparently he was in just as bad a state as you were…a couple of men had to carry him to your Father's guest kol."

Forcing myself to sit upright, my head felt as though it was about to explode, so abandoning any plan I may have had of actually getting out of bed, I instantly laid back down again.

"Ugh…my head hurts," I moaned.

"Well, it serves you right for getting so drunk in the first place. I hope you're not going to start drinking heavily again," Tihanna responded unsympathetically.

"Here," said Tihanna, handing me some boiled water with honey. "Drink this, and I know it's a stupid question…but I don't suppose you'll be taking us to the forest today to gather roots and berries now either…will you?"

I'd completely forgotten about the planned trip to the forest. I'd usually accompany Tihanna and some of the other women on their little fruit gathering trips to the forest, but my head was pounding and I just felt too rough.

"Tihanna – I'm really sorry but the answer is obviously no. I honestly forgot all about it, we'll do it tomorrow instead?"

Tihanna marched off muttering something under her breath; she grabbed our son and roughly pulled a tunic over the top his head.

"No we cannot!" she snapped at me angrily. "It's already been arranged for today, and if you won't take us, then I'll just have to find someone else who will."

"You're just being awkward now," I said, pulling the sheepskin blanket up over my head.

"There's no good reason why we can't just go tomorrow." "And you're just being selfish…as usual," she retorted.

"I don't want to go either," piped in Nymadawa.

"Fine…then you can stay here and take care of your father," said Tihanna crossly, and grabbing our son on the way out, she marched out through the kol doorway.

Daring to peer from under the relative safety of the covers, I was met by the sight of Nymadawa staring back at me.

"Be a good girl," I said with a sigh. "Everything's fine…Papa's not feeling very well that's all, so you can go outside and play if you want to…but make sure you stay close to the kol."

"Yes, OK Papa," said Nymadawa standing up and heading for the doorway.

I pulled the covers back over my head so that I could get back to sleep, and hopefully sleep off the worst of my hangover.

I don't know how long I'd been asleep before I suddenly awoke with a start. I'd had a bad dream that Tihanna was calling me: "Kai…wake up…we need you…help us." And in my dream I saw her running with our son in her arms. She was trying to get away from something, or someone, but I couldn't see who…or what it was.

Leaping out of bed, I quickly pulled on my boots and grabbed my weapons. I didn't need to get dressed as I still had my clothes on from the night before. I just knew that something was terribly wrong…I could just sense it. What had I done? I should never have allowed her to take our son and go into the forest without me. So quickly grabbing Nymadawa, I asked a neighbour to watch over her before hurriedly gathering together around twenty or so warriors, after which we all immediately headed straight out towards the forest at full gallop.

As we approached the forest which seemed to loom before us just a short distance ahead, I was suddenly overcome by an indescribable feeling of dread. So powerful was my anxiety about what may lie ahead, that it caused me to pull so tightly on my horse's reins that he almost stumbled.

"Are you OK?" asked one of my men, pulling up alongside me.

"I've got a really bad feeling about this." I said, giving my horse a sharp kick and riding full pelt towards the forest.

As we finally reached the edge of the forest, we cautiously entered at a slow walking pace, and I made everyone remain in complete silence while I listened intently to see if I could hear anything unusual. But all I could hear were the rustling of the leaves blowing in the breeze, and the shrill cry of a falcon somewhere high above us. I gave a silent hand signal for my men to continue to follow me, and with extreme caution we moved a little deeper into the forest, while constantly scanning the area with our eyes and ears as we went. My senses were so incredibly heightened right now, that I could even hear the sound of a beetle as it crawled across a fallen leaf on the ground. I could hear the beat of my own heart, and my breathing was so shallow right now that the air in my lungs seemed to choke me. I could feel the presence of a dark foreboding heaviness in the atmosphere, which seemed to be building up all around me, and I felt as though my rib cage was about to crush under the sheer pressure of it at any moment.

We hadn't got very much further, when our eyes were confronted by a vision so unimaginably shocking, and so terrible to behold, that it was enough to make several of us physically sick. I immediately jumped down off my horse and collapsed in a broken heap on the ground, as there before us lay the mutilated bodies of the small party of our women, children, and the four inexperienced young warriors who had volunteered to accompany them.

As I knelt down next to the body of Tihanna, I could see that she had obviously been raped and her throat had been slit, and it looked as though all the women had experienced a similar fate. My young son lay just a short distance away…his throat had also been slit, and so brutally that he'd been practically decapitated. I covered Tihanna's half naked body with my cape, while some of the other warriors did the same for the other women. I wasn't the only one to lose loved ones here today.

I could feel a loud wringing in my ears, and everything felt strangely distant and began to fade in and out of focus. So forcing myself to my feet, I left Tihanna and walked over to where my son's body lie unnaturally contorted and motionless on the ground. For a few moments I just stood there gazing down upon his little face. His pale blue eyes that were so full of life just a short time ago, now just stared blankly upwards, and I wished with all my heart that I could take a look through his lifeless eyes just for a few moments…even for just one second would do, just so I could see the burnt in image of the very last thing that he would have seen…the face of the twisted evil excuse for a human being who had robbed me of my only son with this cold blooded and twisted act of depravity.

Kneeling down by his side, I gently rested my hand on top of his little face and closed his eyes.

And bending down low, I kissed him on his forehead as I said goodnight to him for the very last time. I told him that I loved him, and I almost expected him to respond by saying: "I love you too Papa." But his little body just continued to lie there motionless and devoid of all life. I found myself wishing that this was all just a bad dream and I would surely wake up at any moment. But of course it was real, and as I stroked his blood-stained hair…willing him to come back to life somehow; I noticed that the ground was still wet with his blood, and he still felt warm to the touch. And jolted by the sudden realisation that this must have all happened just a very short time ago, I realised the murdering scum who had done this couldn't be all that far away.

Why couldn't we have got here sooner? What cruel twist of fate was this?

Tears wouldn't come, as I was too numb with shock, but I know that part of me died in that forest along with them that day. I was about to stand up and shout out a command to track down whoever it was that was responsible for this atrocity, when suddenly I felt the top of my head begin to tingle, and although it was very faint, I heard my sons voice say: "Papa…look!"

I wasn't sure if I'd really heard the voice, or if my mind was just playing tricks on me, so I could hardly believe my eyes when there…standing just a few metres away from me, was the slightly translucent image of my murdered son. He was looking down at the ground, and appeared to be pointing at something down by his feet. Instinctively I reached out towards him, but he was already beginning to fade. But just before he disappeared altogether – he glanced up at me and smiled.

I quickly rose to my feet, and I walked over to where I had seen the vision of my dead son, and I began to scrape around in the thicket where he appeared to have been pointing. It didn't take me very long to uncover a buckle of the type that was worn by the Italian soldiers. It told me everything that I needed to know. So armed with this valuable information, I ordered two of my men to go back to our village, and tell my father what had happened, and that I'd gone to hunt down the perpetrators, and also that I intended to personally kill every last one of them myself. We had no time to lose if we were going to stand a chance of catching up with them. We were just going to have to come back for the bodies later, as we needed to track down these monsters while the trail was still fresh. We had an excellent scout amongst us, and those responsible for the brutal murder of my wife and son couldn't have got very far, especially if they were on foot, so if we hurry we should be able to track them down.

So leaving the bodies of our loved ones in the forest, we rode out onto the open plain to search for clues as to which way the murdering cowards were headed. Of course the obvious course to follow would have been to head in the direction of their base, but we couldn't just assume that they were headed in that direction – we needed to be absolutely sure.

As we searched for some clue to the direction that they were headed, I could just about make out in the distance a large band of warriors who were presently heading straight towards us at full gallop, and I was glad to see that it was my father who was accompanied by a band of around fifty or so warriors. It would seem that the two men that I'd sent back to inform my father about what had happened, had actually met my father and his men head on, as they were already heading in this direction. My father told me that they had immediately set out to look for us after he had received word that I along with a small band of warriors had gone to the forest looking for my wife and son, as I'd apparently had a gut feeling that something was wrong. My father knew me well enough to know that I didn't get these feelings for nothing. So he'd decided that he had better come looking for us.

Merren and Aptien were also right up there in the front alongside him, but surprisingly…so was Gaidres. They didn't need to ask, as they could see by the expressions on all our faces that the news was not good.

"They're all dead," I said, looking straight into my father's eyes. "I already know it was Italian soldiers that killed them, and their bodies are still warm, so I know they can't be very far from here, and when we find them I swear by the spirits of our ancestors that I'm going to bathe in their blood."

My father raised his eyes and his fists up to the sky before spitting at the ground and cursing at the Gods for allowing this to happen.

"Why? Damn you!" he said bitterly, before turning to face me once more. "Tell me how you can be so sure it was Italians, Kai?"

"We don't have enough time right now for me to explain, so I must ask you to trust that what I say is true. We need to find them before they get back to their base, or we'll never be able to get to them after that."

"So do you know which way they're heading?" he asked me.

"That way," said our scout, pointing to a north westerly direction.

My father immediately gave the signal, and we all headed off at some speed in that general direction.

It hadn't taken very long before we spotted some smoke which appeared to be coming from behind the brow of a hill just a little way up ahead of us, so proceeding at a slow walking pace, we continued to make our approach in relative silence, as we weren't entirely sure who was actually responsible for the smoke yet. So before we all went riding in, and terrifying the wits out of a handful of innocent travellers, we sent a couple of warriors up ahead on foot, so that they could check out the situation first.

While the rest of us waited in silence, the two warriors quietly approached the area that the smoke was coming from, they were very careful to stay low to the ground so that they wouldn't be seen, and on their return they were able to confirm that it was a group of between twenty-five to thirty Italian soldiers. As soon I heard this I immediately turned to my father and said:

"I want them captured and not killed…that pleasure has to be mine."

After making sure that this was understood by every warrior, my father gave the signal to attack by sounding out the battle cry. Everyone immediately began to psyche themselves up by whooping and sounding the war cry. Some of them even hit each other on the legs with their horse whips in order to get the adrenalin really flowing, and to make each other feel even more angry and aggressive. I needed nothing to prepare me for what I was about to do, as I'd already switched myself into a state of mind that I called my warrior mode. I had become cold and calculated, completely devoid of any anger or fear. My senses where heightened to an incredible level, and I was like a finely tuned killing machine, ready to unleash my wrath upon the monsters who had destroyed my family and had just taken away two of the most important people in my life, and whom I just happened to have loved very much.

Although they had obviously heard us approaching, they were hopelessly outnumbered, and we were able to quickly overpower them. They had been about to cook two small wild boar which they had obviously hunted in the forest, which would also explain why they were in there in the first place. It was such a shame they weren't going to get a chance to eat them.

After forcing them to strip naked, we made them all kneel down before tying their hands behind their backs. And after we'd burnt all their clothes, we gathered all of their weapons and armour ready to take back with us, as we would melt it all down and re-use the metal for making weapons and armour of our own.

Gaidres had obviously learnt to speak a little of their language during the times he'd spent living with these Italians, as I saw him whisper something to one of them as he was tying his hands behind his back. So walking up to him, I asked him what he'd just said. Gaidres looked uncomfortable and pale in the face as he grabbed my arm, and turning his back from everyone else he said very quietly:

"I know some of these soldiers. They were amongst the ones that I told you about yesterday...the ones that I'd accompanied to find the Daos. And that one," he said, pointing to the man he'd just tied, "was one of the main instigators in the plan to rape and torture the women and children. I just told him that I wouldn't want to be him right now." He paused for a few moments before continuing..."Kai...I don't believe this is actually happening, we were only talking last night...about the...the uh..."

I could see that Gaidres was obviously struggling to find the words that were needed to finish his sentence, so I just nodded, there was no need for words, I knew only too well what he meant, but I was in no mood right now to discuss the stranger side to all of this.

"No, you're right, Gaidres. You really wouldn't want to be him right now! Drag 'him' over here," I said loudly, pointing to the soldier that Gaidres had just spoken to.

Two of my father's right-hand warriors immediately responded to my command, and grabbing the Italian they threw him at my feet. My father took two steps backwards and bowed to me as a clear indication that he was handing me full command of this whole situation. Merren and Aptien stood close by the whole time, while skilfully still managing to retain a respectful distance. "Ask him what happened to the women, children, and the four young warriors in the forest," I said to Gaidres.

Gaidres said something in Italian, and the Italian soldier then blurted something out in response.

"He said he doesn't know what you're talking about," said Gaidres.

"Oh really," I said reaching into my leather pouch and pulling out the little buckle that the spirit of my dead son had pointed out to me, and I threw it at the ground in front of him.

"Now ask him again, and tell him that if he doesn't tell me the truth this time, I'll cut out his tongue, and then I'll go on to the next man, and if he doesn't tell me the truth, I'll cut out his tongue too, and I'll continue to do this until someone tells me the truth. In fact – just tell them all." Gaidres immediately did as I asked, and the Italian soldier began to babble on and on, until Gaidres eventually had to stop him so that he had a chance to accurately relay to the rest of us what he had just said.

"He said that they only meant to have a little bit of fun, but they got a bit carried away. He says that he's very sorry for what they did, and if you spare their lives, he'll show you where a huge pile of gold is hidden."

I turned to look at my father, who just shook his head in utter disbelief that this piece of scum thought that we could be bought by the promise of hidden treasure.

"Tell him he's already told me everything that I needed to know, and no amount of gold could ever replace the people that they brutally tortured and killed. Tell them that one of them was my wife, and another was my son. Tell them they can keep their gold as we already have enough of our own, and that I would prefer their payment to be in blood, and you can also tell them that if they want mercy they'd better start praying to their Gods to come and save them."

It's not necessary to go into the gruesome details of how I chose to deal with these men, it should be enough to say, that they all experienced a slow and horrifically painful death, the nature of which was enough to make even the most hardened warriors amongst us cringe. I carried out my final act of revenge by covering myself from head to foot in their blood. I said that I was going to bathe in their blood – and I meant it.

We left their mutilated bodies to the vultures. I wanted to chop off their heads and throw them over the wall of their base, but my father forbade me to do this, so after returning to the forest to pick up the bodies of our loved ones – we began the ride back home. Except…I didn't really feel as though I had a home any more. I still felt numb at this point, but as we continued to ride back, the reality of what had happened slowly began to sink in, and a dreadful thought occurred to me – I didn't have anything to go back to now!

I know that I was never the perfect husband to Tihanna, and I was often away for long periods of time with the Huns, and even if I was closer to home, I was either off hunting or involved with Agari business, but I'd always managed to remain faithful no matter how long I was away, and that wasn't always an easy thing to do, as I had plenty of opportunity to be unfaithful time and time again. My pretty boy looks seemed to be attractive to women, as well as to some men. But Tihanna remained the only woman I had ever slept with, and I just couldn't believe that she was gone, and my little son…I never even had the chance to teach him how to use a bow, or to take him hunting as my father had done with me. He'd never even ridden a horse on his own yet. He was still a baby!

What kind of evil lurks in the body of a man that can coldly take the life of one so young? Yes, what I'd done to those men was pretty horrific, but as far as I was concerned by removing them from the face of the planet, I'd prevented any chance of them ever doing anything like this again, as it was highly likely that they'd re-offend if the opportunity ever came their way.

Our collective mood was as black and as sombre as the darkest night as we arrived back into our village, and as the bodies were immediately taken to a special place where they would be prepared for burial, I refused to utter a single word to anyone throughout the whole miserable process, and after I had made it quite clear that I didn't want to be disturbed by anyone, I walked off and headed straight towards my kol.

Stepping inside, I felt my heart suddenly sink low within the cavity of my chest. It felt as heavy as a stone, and I really didn't care if it chose to stop beating altogether right now. I just stood there for what seemed an age, before literally having to force myself to continue to walk right into the very centre of the kol right next to the fire pit. And there within the echo of the deafening silence of my pain, I gazed around through half glazed eyes at all the many things around me. The cup of honey and boiled water that Tihanna had brought me just this morning was still by the side of my bed where I'd left it, and the wooden figures that Kern had been playing with just a few hours ago now lay there redundant upon the ground. The very structure of the kol itself seemed to echo with the sound of their voices. I knew that it would be impossible for me to live in this kol anymore; the memories of Tihanna and Kern would be far too overpowering for me to bear, but the funeral rites were not for two days, so I would have to wait until after then to decide what I should do.

The blood of the Italian soldiers that I wore as a gory medal for my revenge, had become caked and dry, and was already beginning to flake off my hands and face, and as the reality of losing my wife and son, and the terrible way in which they'd been killed began to deepen, the enormous guilt that I felt at not having been there to protect them both, and for not preventing Tihanna from going to the forest in the first place was slowly beginning to rip me apart. If only I'd made more of an effort to stop her...but it was too late now, I'd never have that chance again. At that moment in time I would have given anything to have been able to go back in time and put things right, but that was never going to happen, and I really wasn't sure right now if I was going to be able to live with this heavy burden of guilt that weighed down upon me so heavily right now, that I felt as though every bone in my body would soon snap under the sheer weight of it all. It felt bad enough after Altan had been killed, but this was worse...far worse. But suicide wasn't an option for me either, as this was against everything that I believed, as I knew that this would be the worst thing for me to do, as I would still have to face this awful burden on the other side, only it might even be in more wretched conditions than this.

Just then I heard someone call out my name from outside the kol, it was my sister Trishanna, so jolted from my place of hellish solitude, I walked over to the doorway, and lifting the flap, I just stood there blankly staring back at her. The look of total concern on my sister's face was clearly evident as we stood facing one another in the doorway. I was still covered in dried blood, and it would have been quite obvious to her that I really didn't want any company right now, so seeing this she said:

"Kai, I've just come to let you know that I've taken Nymadawa to come and live with me and Aptien for the time being, as I think it's probably best for her right now. I don't think you're going to be able to deal with her grief as well as your own, so I just need to come in for a minute or two and collect some of her things...is that all right?"

Taking a step backwards, I allowed her to enter, and I stood silent and motionless as she quickly gathered together as many of Nymadawa's things as she could carry, and with her arms overflowing she proceeded to head straight towards the doorway, but then she suddenly stopped and paused for a moment.

"Aptien and I truly share your grief right now, Kai, and if there is anything at all that we can do, or anything that you need, you know that we're both here for you."

I hadn't said a single word to anyone since returning to our village, and I still had no words that I wanted to speak, so with a slight nod of my head, I turned my back on her and walked over to the bed that I'd shared with Tihanna just the night before and sat down. Trishanna walked over to a nearby table, and after placing the heap of Nymadawa's clothes that she was carrying on top, she walked up to me, and despite all the blood she reached out to give me a hug, but I immediately recoiled away from her, I didn't want to be touched by anyone, in fact I really didn't want 'any' human contact at all right now. Trishanna realising her mistake, immediately backed off and just gave me a knowing look, and without saying another word, she picked up the bundle of Nymadawa's clothes again and left me to my sorrow.

I really didn't want company…but I couldn't stand the terrible silence either; it became so deafening that I thought I would go mad for sure. I even put my hands over my ears in a vain attempt to drown out the empty silence, but it seemed hell bent on making me listen despite my attempts to drown out its piteous lamentations, so suddenly in a fit of madness and despair, I leapt to my feet and began violently smashing up the contents of the kol; when suddenly I was halted in my tracks by the sight of some of Tihanna's clothes which were still lying at the foot of the bed where she had left them this morning. So instead of smashing up the kol, I calmly walked back over to the bed, and sitting back down again, I picked up Tihanna's dress and held it up to my blood-stained face. The sweet smell of her skin seemed to comfort me, so I looked around for something that my son had worn, and there by my feet was a little pair of Kern's trousers. Tihanna had been planning to repair them before she washed them as they had a split in the knee. Kern was at that age now when he was always wearing the knees out of his trousers. Tihanna said that she was going to make him some new ones very soon anyway. I don't know why she spends so much time making clothes when she can get everything she needs made for her. No…I hadn't lost my mind; not yet anyway. I knew full well that they were never coming back, but it gave me some comfort to pretend to myself that they were. I picked up Kern's trousers and lifted them up to my face, and if I closed my eyes, I could almost imagine that he was standing right there in front of me, and clutching both articles of clothing tightly to my chest, I lay down and curled up into a foetal position and prayed that the gods would have mercy on me and take me too.

28

My Shamanic Angel

As I continued to lay there still clinging to the clothes that had so recently been worn by my wife and son, I could hear the muffled voices of people talking outside. I really didn't want to be bothered by anyone right now, and I wished that they would all just go away and leave me alone. I heard Gaidres' voice call out to me from outside, but I reasoned that if I didn't answer him he would soon get the message and leave again, but obviously he didn't…as I watched as the doorway flap slowly opened to reveal Gaidres intrusively peering in at me.

"I've just come to say goodbye Kai," said Gaidres, taking a few steps inside. "I'm going to be leaving very soon, and I just wanted you to know that my thoughts will be with you."

I hadn't invited him in, and I really didn't need this kind of shallow sympathy right now. If I'd wanted him to enter I would have asked him…so making my feelings clear, I very rudely turned around and faced the other way.

"Hmm…perhaps you shouldn't be alone right now," he said, before disappearing back outside again.

Five minutes later and I hadn't heard him enter, but something made me turn around and open my eyes to the sight of Garenhir, who was sitting on the bottom of my bed holding a cup in his left hand.

"Drink this, Kai – it'll help you," he said, offering me the cup.

I just lay there staring at him. I could hear him…but it was as if he was all foggy and far away, and I couldn't quite connect to what he was saying to me.

"Come on, Kai…I want you to sit up and drink this," he said firmly.

Placing the cup down on the ground for a moment, Garenhir began to help me to sit upright. I didn't fight against him, and finally releasing my grip on Tihanna's dress and Kern's trousers, I allowed him to help me into an upright position. Garenhir picked up the cup and handed it to me, and once again he ordered me to drink it.

Staring blankly into the cup, I asked him what was in it. Garenhir proceeded to explain to me what was contained in the mixture, and by today's standards, it would certainly have been classed as an illegal substance, but of course, these kind of opiates were used back then by the Agari for medicinal use, but even so they were still not yet widely available, and usually only accessible to the elite few. The potent mixture had been mixed with a genuine helping of honey to mask the unpleasant taste.

"I haven't had any of this since I got a horse whipping from my father, I didn't even know we had any," I said, drinking it down in one go.

"No, well, I usually keep some just for emergencies," he said, removing some of the shattered pieces of pottery that had landed on my bed from my emotional outburst earlier.

I made sure that I finished off the few drops that were left in the bottom of the cup before handing it back to him.

"You're going to be okay you know," he said, removing the cup from my hand.

"How come none of us were able to foresee this? I can see things…but I didn't see this until it was too late. How come you or Sai didn't see it either? – I don't understand."

"Manu Kai, there are some things that just seem to be written in stone, and no matter what we do we can't change them. Sometimes there are things that we may be allowed to see, while others we are not. I can't tell you why none of us were able to foresee any of this, but I do know that there must be a very good reason, even if it makes no sense to us right now. We weren't given the opportunity to prevent it, therefore, for whatever reason it must have been meant to happen."

"I'm sorry, Derkesthai, but I can't do this anymore…I quit! …I just can't accept that the senseless murder of my wife and son, along with all the others was just…'meant to happen'! As of now I'm resigning from the Agari, and please don't try to talk me out of it. I don't think I was ever meant to be a priest. Has anyone told you what I did to those men…well…have they?" "Yes, well, at least some of it. Your father has already told me what took place Kai, and I can totally understand why you were driven to do what you did. Don't get me wrong…I'm not condoning what you did – but I do understand…truly I do. I won't try to talk you out of leaving the Agari – but I would just ask that you don't try and make any definite decisions while the balance of your mind is upset.

You're not in any fit state of mind right now to be able to make that decision. You need time to come to terms with what has happened."

The narcotic that Garenhir had given me was already beginning to kick in, and although nothing was going to take away the terrible anguish that I was feeling right now, it had managed to have taken the edge off it a little; so a little shakily at first, I rose to my feet and walked over to where I'd left my weapons and began gathering them one by one. I looked across at Garenhir who was still sat on the edge of my bed.

"What I really need right now Garenhir is solitude. So please don't take this the wrong way…but at this very moment in time, even though I have the deepest respect for you and I always will, I'm going to need a lot more than your words of wisdom can offer me. I'm more than feeling a bit lost this time Garenhir…and right now I don't think I'm ever coming back."

"Manu Kai…Please…I know it's hard but you must listen to me…I told you right in the beginning when you were only twelve winters of age, that the path you were about to tread was not going to be an easy one, and that it may be full of trials and tribulations that may push you to your very edge of reason. Of course, back then I didn't know the form that these trials were going to take, but it would seem that for you in this life time they are proving to be particularly difficult, and regardless of what you may think, I really do understand that what you're going through right now may seem impossible to overcome, but one day you'll be able to look back on all of this and tell others your story, just as I was able to tell you mine. Please don't give up Manu Kai, this might feel like the end of your world right now, and I know that you don't think that you'll ever get over this…and maybe you won't, but I promise you that as time passes it will become easier to bare."

"Maybe I deserve all of this for all the terrible things I've done in the past. What if I really do belong to the Caverns of Gehenna (Hell) Have you thought of that?"

Without giving Garenhir a chance to respond, I picked up my horse harness which was lying on the ground near the doorway, and quickly walked out of my kol leaving Garenhir still sitting alone on my bed. My horse had been taken to the paddock, and I had to pass several people to get there. I still hadn't changed my bloody clothes, or even washed the blood off my hands and face, and my long-braided hair was so caked with dried blood that my normally dark brown hair was now a reddish brown. Everyone stared at me as I passed, but no one dared approach me. I guess the look in my eyes must have said it all.

On reaching the paddock, I quickly harnessed up my horse and rode straight out of our village. I wasn't sure where I was headed and I didn't care, I just needed to get away from people for a while. I allowed the reins to fall from my hands, and holding onto my horse's mane I gave him a sharp kick, and shouted out at the top of my voice:

"Yit, yit…Yeearrrrhhhh."

The sudden rush of cool air against my face almost took my breath away and caused me to inhale deeply. I had given my horse complete freedom to choose our destination, and quite frankly…I really didn't give a damn where he was headed right now. If he actually galloped straight in through the gates of Gehenna, it couldn't be any worse than where I was right now. And if the Gods decided to take hold of his reins and lead me straight to my death…then so-be-it. I was ready to accept whatever my fate had decreed.

I must have continued to ride this way for several hours, only slowing down periodically to allow my horse time to rest. He seemed to be heading in the general direction of the sacred caves, maybe he thought that's where I wanted to go, but at this point – I truly didn't care; although, I felt pretty certain that he was heading towards the caves after we had reached the first river crossing, as he even remembered to cross at the shallow point of the river, and then without any encouragement from me, he carried on across to the other side before galloping off again.

At last we had arrived at our destination at the base of our sacred mountain cave. So respectfully dismounting, I continued to make my way up the rocky incline on foot with my horse now following on behind me. It was beginning to get quite dark by now, and although there was a little light provided by the half-moon, I knew that the cave itself was going to be pitch black inside, and I wasn't going to be able to see clearly enough to light a small fire by using my fire stones which I always carried in my pouch. I was just going to have to light a fire outside the cave, as it was beginning to get very cold as well as dark right now. It was only then that I realised that in my haste to leave, I had left my utility pouch containing my fire stones back in my kol.

My horse shook his head and whinnied as if to show his disapproval, before trotting off and disappearing around the side of the cave where there was a natural stream which disappeared underneath the mountain, only to reappear again from a large crack in the side of the mountain as a spring, which then continued to snake into the river down below. I guessed that he most probably needed a drink after our journey, I was pretty thirsty myself so I decided to join him, and as we both drank from the cool mountain spring, I could see the reflection of the moon in those deep dark brown eyes of his shining back at me.

"Why here?" I asked him out loud.

He just continued drinking from the little stream that ran down the craggy rocks, so I sat down with my back resting up against a large rock, and stared up towards the heavens high above me. "Why here?" I asked him out loud once more, as it seemed so ironic that out of all the places he could have brought me…he chose here.

The wind was beginning to pick up a little now, so leaving my horse to his own devices, I stood up and walked over to the cave entrance, but before I stepped one foot inside I asked the guardian for permission to enter, as even though I'd told Garenhir that I'd resigned from the Agari, I still held a deep respect for its members and everything that it stood for. Just because I was too weak and unworthy to remain a member, didn't mean that I held it in any less esteem.

Stepping inside, I was immediately engulfed in darkness, I knew the layout of the cave pretty well, and even in almost total darkness I was able to make my way over to the far side of the main cave. I was totally unprepared for an overnight stay, and I didn't even have so much as a blanket to sit on, so sitting down on the cold damp cave floor, and pulling my knees up tightly to my chest, I huddled myself into as tight a ball as I could in an effort to try and stay warm.

Blankly staring through the cave entrance and out into the world outside, I tried very hard to imagine that the cave entrance was collapsing in on itself, trapping me inside forever…but it didn't happen. I guess my powers of concentration weren't quite up to that task. It was probably just as well they weren't, but even so, I thought I'd give it just one more go…Still nothing! But at least it took my mind off my situation for a few minutes.

As I continued to sit there in the darkness of that cave, I prayed for death to take me before the sun rose again in the morning exposing my sorrow to the world once more. I began to tremble either from cold or shock, or maybe a bit of both, and I felt a sudden wave of such utter helplessness and sorrow, that I could no longer contain it, and crying out in the darkness I cursed the air, and the rocks, and the stones. I cursed the rivers and the trees in the forest, and the beasts and the birds, and the rain and the snow, and every living thing on the planet just for being there, and then I retracted it all, fearing that I may have done something too terrible to comprehend. And in the darkness of my solitude, I cried out again…and I cursed each breath that I took for keeping me alive, and I cursed myself most of all for being me.

I had never felt quite so alone and isolated in my life, and when tears finally came, I wept solidly for at least an hour, and then completely exhausted, I lay down on the cave floor, and curling myself tightly into a ball, I prepared to die of either hypothermia or a broken heart…or both. As I continued to lay there in total silence inwardly praying for death to come swiftly, I thought I heard the sound of someone's footsteps outside the cave. My hearing was probably the most sensitive of my five physical senses, and I knew it wasn't my horse that I'd heard. I strained to listen…Yes, I heard it again. But who could possibly be outside the cave at this time of the night? So slowly and silently I reached out and picked up my bow and arrows. Whoever it was wouldn't be able to see me in the darkness, but if they stood in the cave entrance, I would be able to see their silhouette in the half moon light. So taking a half kneeling stance, I nocked an arrow ready to aim it at whoever was trespassing outside…and I waited…and I waited some more. But nothing appeared. Perhaps the cold was causing my mind to play tricks on me. No…there it was again. Why didn't they show themselves? I really couldn't stand this any longer, so deciding to investigate, I very slowly and silently approached the cave entrance, listening for any tiny sound as I went, but there was only silence now. I figured that whoever had been out there must have left; so cautiously I stepped outside…bow in hand, and an arrow knocked in readiness to take aim…just in case!

"You didn't think that I was stupid enough to stand in the entrance did you?" said a voice from right behind me.

I almost jumped right out of my skin, and spinning around I was shocked but relieved to see Sai, who was stood about a metre away from me. All I can say is that he was very lucky that I had such a steady hand. I immediately released the pressure and un-knocked the arrow.

"How in the name of my ancestors did you manage to creep up behind me like that?" I said, taking a sharp intake of breath. "What are you doing here anyway? And how did you know where to find me?" I asked, replacing my arrow in its Gorytos (quiver)

"I just wanted to make sure that you were going to be OK. And as for knowing where to find you, well…you know!"

"Do you realise I could have killed you just then?"

"You didn't though – did you?" he responded with a knowing smile.

"I left the village so that I could find some solitude. Can't I even be left alone to die in peace?" "Don't worry, I don't intend on disturbing your solitude, I've just brought you a few things to make your time alone here a little more comfortable. Wait here…I'll be back shortly."

I watched him as he walked around to the side of the cave and disappeared out of sight. I just stood there obediently waiting for him to come back. I was still slightly shaken by the fact that he was able to just creep up behind me like that. I was good…I was damn good! So how on earth he did it I really don't know.

It wasn't long before he reappeared again, and handing me a pile of sheepskin blankets he said: "I also took the liberty of going into your kol and finding you some clean clothes; it's probably best that you get cleaned up first before putting them on though, so I'll fetch those for you in the morning."

"Fetch them from where?" I asked him, wondering what on earth he was up to.

"From one of the bags that I've brought with me of course," he replied.

"I thought you said that you weren't going to disturb me," I said, not quite believing my eyes and ears.

"Oh no…I won't disturb you, I'll stay in the little alcove around the corner, I'll see you in the morning," he said, walking off.

"What…Sai wait. I just don't believe this," I said, shaking my head in disbelief. "You might as well stay in the cave now that you're here."

"Thanks! Well, if that's the case, would you mind helping me fetch a few things from outside?"

"What have you brought with you?"

"Just some things to last you for a few days, as that's how long I figured you'll probably want to stay here for."

I really didn't have an answer, so I just followed him to the alcove where he handed me a bundle of sheepskin blankets.

"There…you can carry those," he said, picking up another tightly bound bundle, and carrying it into the cave.

"Kai, you've been through a lot," said Sai, suddenly resting his hand on my forearm. "You should try and get some rest now. I'll light a fire, and tomorrow I'll cook you some food, and I'll even help you to get cleaned up, and then I'll leave you the rest of the food and I'll head back." "Hmm," I said thoughtfully, as I placed the bundle that I was carrying down onto the cave floor, and after unravelling a couple of the sheepskin blankets that Sai had handed me earlier, I threw them down onto the ground, and watched as Sai lit a fire and then prepared his bed for the night right over on the opposite side of the cave.

As I lay down on top of one of the sheepskin blankets, I closed my eyes and pulled the other sheepskin right over the top of my head, thus completely shutting out the world and all its sorrows for a while. I had prayed for death, and I was sent a Guardian Angel in the form of Sai instead. Exhaustion soon overtook me, and I must have quickly fallen asleep, as the next thing that I can remember is waking up to the light of day pouring in through the cave entrance. It was a cold crisp morning, and as I threw back the sheepskin blanket and stumbled to my feet, I shivered involuntarily, and I must admit that I was somewhat grateful to see that Sai was already up and busy with the task of re kindling the fire.

"Where are you going?" he asked me.

"To answer the call of nature, where do you think I'm going?" I replied in a surly manner.

"OK," he said nonchalantly, while continuing to build up the fire.

I returned just in time to see Sai about to hang a large cauldron of water over the fire.

"I'm warming some water so that you can wash all that filth off yourself, and then I'll make us some breakfast," he said with just a hint of a smile.

"Just make it for yourself…I don't want any breakfast," I retorted, climbing back under the sheepskins.

"Well, I'm making you some anyway," he replied.

I pulled the sheepskin right over the top of my head and wondered if starving yourself to death was classed as suicide, and if not, how long it would take.

"Come on then…let's get you sorted then shall we?" said Sai, tugging the sheepskin right off me.

I didn't care if I lived or died right now, so why would I care about how covered in filth I was, so quickly reaching up I grabbed a hold of the sheepskin and gave it a sharp tug. Having released it from Sai's grip, I stubbornly pulled it right back over my head again. But Sai wasn't having any of it, and with another sharp tug, he had managed to pull it straight back off me again, and with a certain air of determination in his voice he said:

"Kai – You really need to get cleaned up. Come on…I'll help you!"

"I know you mean well, Sai," I said, still lying on the ground but now minus the security of my sheepskin blanket. "But I really don't give a damn right now, so please…just go away and leave me alone."

"Look, Kai, I understand what you're going through, and I know that you want to be left alone right now, but I'm not going to stand by and watch you needlessly destroy yourself. So the longer you lay there, the longer I'm going to have to do this, so please, do us both a favour and get up and let me help you wash that filth off yourself."

Very reluctantly I forced myself into an upright position, and pulling my knees tightly up under my chin I began to glare up at him. He was just standing there with my sheepskin blanket in his hands. All I wanted was to be left alone…was that so damn difficult to understand.

"Just give me my damn blanket and leave me alone," I said, reaching up and attempting to grab the blanket again.

But unfortunately Sai was holding onto it far too tightly this time, so finally giving up my feeble effort of defiance, I just sat there scowling at him instead.

"How can you say that you understand what I'm going through? You have no idea what I'm going through, so don't pretend that you do. Why don't you just go back home to your boyfriend and leave me alone?" I retorted rather sharply.

Sai's eyes narrowed, and throwing the sheepskin down onto the ground in front of me, I saw the closest thing to a flash of anger that I'd ever seen in Sai.

"Fine!" he said, marching over to the fire. "Here…have it your own way."

Sai removed the cauldron of water from the fire and carefully set it down onto the ground, before sitting down on a little carved wooden stool with his back to me.

I realised that what I'd just said had obviously upset him, and I knew I probably shouldn't have spoken to him the way that I had. He was only trying to help me after all.

"Look…I'm sorry," I said apologetically. "I shouldn't have said that."

Sai didn't respond. Something I'd said must have really got to him for some reason. I felt bad about upsetting him, so I stood up and walked over to where he was still sitting with his back to me. "Sai, I'm sorry! You win...I'll get cleaned up – just please don't sulk. I really can't stand it when people sulk."

Sai turned around and gave me a little smile. "Good!" he said heartily. "And no matter what you think...I really 'do' understand Kai, and after we get you cleaned up I'm going to tell you a little story. I'll give you a hand to get cleaned up first though. Come on...you can sit on this stool."

I wasn't sure if it had all been just one big act to get me to respond, or if I'd genuinely upset him, but whatever it was, it certainly did the trick, as before I knew it, I was already sat on the stool and he was unbraiding my hair. He helped me to wash all of the dried blood out of my hair using a special kind of soap, which was made out of boiled seaweed which he'd brought with him. It took a whole cauldron of water just to get my hair clean, and then after waiting for another cauldron of water to warm up, Sai gave me a hand to carry it into one of the smaller adjoining cave structures, where I stripped naked and washed my body clean again. Sai handed me the clean clothes that he'd brought with him, and after getting dressed again, I walked back out into the main cave and sat close to the fire to warm myself and dry my hair. Sai picked up my soiled clothes from off the cave floor, and he set them to soak in another cauldron full of cold water. He then went and fetched a little more wood from the huge wood pile that was always stored ready in case of emergencies in another one of the smaller adjoining caves. And throwing a couple of small logs onto the fire, he then walked over to one of the bags that he'd brought with him, and pulled out four medium-sized fish that he'd previously prepared, before proceeding to cook them over the fire. The thought of eating anything right now made me feel quite sick.

"I don't think I can eat that, Sai," I said, wrapping my arms around myself and pulling a face.

He just ignored me and just carried on regardless.

"Ugh! You eat them," I said.

It hadn't taken very long for the fish to cook, and placing two of them on a wooden platter he held them out to me.

"Eat!" he said firmly.

"I don't feel like eating, I already told you," I said, shaking my head. Sai continued to hold the platter out to me and once again he said: "Eat."

"No!" I said, firmly pushing the platter away.

And once more, he held it back out towards me.

"Eat the damn fish."

Taking the platter from his outstretched hand, I walked over to the table and left it there, while I picked up my sheepskin blanket from off the cave floor, and carried it back to my makeshift bed.

"Look…I'm not going to eat that damn fish…so even though I appreciate your concern…will you please just leave me alone now, I've done what you wanted, and I really don't have the strength to deal with this right now."

Crawling back into bed, I pulled the blanket back over my head once more, and wished for nothing other than to be left alone to die. But I guess Sai had other ideas as I heard him pick up the stool and rest it down nearer to where I lay safely hidden from view.

"Hmm…I was going to tell you a little story wasn't I? I've never told you this before Kai; mainly because I haven't had any reason to until now, but Garenhir isn't the only one of us that isn't originally from these parts."

I already knew that Sai had been adopted when he was very small, but when I'd asked Garenhir what had happened to Sai's parents he wouldn't tell me, and all he said was: "If ever there is a time that Sai wants you to know, he will tell you himself." I had a funny feeling that this might be just that time.

"OK!" I said, curiously peering at him from under the security of my sheepskin. "You've managed to get my attention. So where are you from then?"

"Well…that's just it…I don't actually know. I was brought here when I was very young, and the Scythian warriors who rescued me aren't really sure either. But I've been led to believe that I'd most probably belonged to an ethnic minority group of travelling Dacians."

He'd seriously got my attention now, so sitting up into a cross legged position I began to study his body language and the serious expression on his face. I could tell by his whole demeanour that he was uncomfortable with talking about this, so obviously there was a lot more to this story. I think he must have realised that I'd picked up on this as he said:

"Yes, I have a story too, Kai. Do you remember when we were down by the river and I gave you that strong Hallucinogen, so that you could cross over into the realm of perception?"

"Yes!" I answered.

"And I stopped you from looking too deeply into what I kept hidden inside, and I told you that there were things about me that I wasn't ready to share with you just yet?"

"Yes!" I said again, deeply intrigued.

Sai rubbed his face with his hand and paused for a minute, and after gazing out into empty space for a few more moments, he rubbed his face with his hand again before turning to face me, and I wrapped my arms around myself as if to shield myself from…whatever it was that he was about to share with me. He nodded as if he understood, and then he began to tell me his story…"I don't know who my parents were, but I do remember them. I was around two winters of age when it happened. I don't know why we were travelling, where we had come from, or where we were headed, but I can remember being inside a wagon with my mother, and other people that I knew, but I don't even remember who they were. All I remember is that we were attacked, and my mother made me get down on the floor of the wagon, and told me to stay there, and not to move or make any sound at all, no matter what I may hear, and then she threw a blanket over me. It was the last time that I would ever see her alive. The next thing I heard was my mother and the other people screaming, and being dragged out of the wagon, but I did exactly as my mother had told me to do, and I remained totally still and silent. I just lay there listening to the screams of my mother and the others for a while…until finally…all the screams fell silent. But then I could hear that something else was going on, but too terrified to move, I remained hidden under the blanket that my mother had thrown over me. The very next thing that I can remember after that, is feeling the blanket being pulled off me. I didn't know it at the time, but a small troop of Scythians had coincidentally been passing that way and had chased off those marauding scum, and on searching the wagons they'd found me. The Scythian warrior who had discovered me spoke to me, but at the time I obviously couldn't understand a single word of what he was saying, so he just scooped me up and carried me to his horse. He tried to cover my eyes in order to spare me from the horror of seeing the mutilated bodies, but as I didn't understand what he was doing, or why, I tried to struggle free, and in doing so I caught sight of my mother's half naked body lying on the ground. She'd been raped and then killed. And the terrible shock of seeing my mother stripped and covered in blood had had a very deep and lasting psychological effect on me, and my mind couldn't cope with the sheer horror of it all, and reacted by temporarily erasing all memory of what had happened. I couldn't even remember my name, and apparently no one could get me to say a single word either, so not even the language that was spoken by my people could be identified.

"As time went on the memories of the event resurfaced little by little, and as a result, I experienced terrible nightmares. I'd completely forgotten my own language, and by the time I was able to speak again, Scythian was the only language that I knew. I'd been placed in the care of an elderly couple of herbalists, who were never able to have any children of their own, and they renamed me 'Sai', which as you know means wise. They were wonderful people, and were incredibly patient with the deeply troubled child that they had willingly taken on. They showed me the meaning of love and compassion, and they brought me up as their own son, and when I began to show unusual abilities, they took me to Garenhir. Sadly my adopted parents who were both blessed to have lived to a very old age passed away within one winter of each other, and although I was deeply grateful to them for the love they had shown me, and for the time that I had spent living as their son, I was still not quite twelve winters of age, and still too young to be able to fend for myself, so Garenhir took on the role of my guardian, and he's been like a father to me ever since. So you see Kai – I really 'do' understand."

I didn't know any of this, and I just sat there with my chin resting in my hands staring up at him. I felt completely blown away by his revelation, and I really didn't know what to say to him. He just nodded at me and gave me a little smile and such a heartfelt and genuine look of deep understanding, that he made me feel ashamed at my own self-pity. So taking a deep breath in order to centre myself, I stood up and walked over to the table that I'd placed the platter of fish that he'd cooked for me, and I picked it up and walked back over to my makeshift bed and sat back down again.

Without saying anything, Sai stood up and walked outside. I just continued to sit there feeling very humbled, and even though I struggled with every single mouthful, and I wasn't at all sure how long it was going to stay down...I ate that damn fish.

29

A Moral Code

Sai had been gone for ages, and I was beginning to wonder if he'd actually left and headed back home again. I couldn't really blame him if he had. I wasn't exactly an easy person to deal with sometimes. 'Like father like son' as the saying goes.

I walked over to the cave entrance and stepped outside into the crisp morning air, it was so peaceful here. It was such a far cry from the all the horror and turmoil of my life that I felt as though I must be on another planet. There was still no sign of Sai, so I sat down on the ground which was still slightly damp from the morning dew, and as I stared outwards across the lowland plains that stretched out before me, a tiny little mouse suddenly appeared from underneath some clumps of long grass which was growing in between a few large rocks about two metres in front of me. He didn't seem at all bothered by the fact that I was there, or perhaps he just hadn't noticed me yet, but whichever it was, he just carried on with the business of doing the things that mice do, and I thought to myself how lucky he was not to have to face some of the hardships and sorrows that people have to…when suddenly out of the blue, a hawk swooped down and pinned the terrified little critter to the ground. It wriggled and squealed a couple of times before it fell limp and silent. Having succeeded in killing its prey, the hawk suddenly turned to observe me still sitting there watching it for few moments, and after it was quite satisfied that I didn't seem to pose any real threat to it; it proceeded to consume its morning meal, and as soon as it had finished, it took off again leaving me feeling slightly stunned by the whole dramatic performance.

Nature can seem very cruel sometimes, but nature only takes what it actually needs to survive. Only man has the capacity to kill for entertainment, pleasure, gain or revenge. I thought of the fate of Tihanna and Kern, and how I'd taken my own revenge upon the low life scum that had so cruelly taken them away from me, and although I felt no remorse for killing them; as I genuinely believed that by killing them I had prevented anyone else from ever having to suffer a similar fate at their hands…ultimately it didn't actually make me feel any better. I'd expected to feel some sense of satisfaction in torturing and making those men suffer such slow and painful deaths, but any satisfaction that I may have felt at the time was very short lived, and had only served to add weight to the scales, and to tip the balance in favour of the darker side of my nature which was very rapidly beginning to take the upper hand.

I drew one of my throwing knifes from its leather sheath which was strapped to the outside of my leg, and rolling up the sleeves of my tunic, I began to draw the razor-sharp edge of the blade across the back of my arms. The scars were still visible from the last time I'd done this after the death of Altan.

I watched as my life blood began to trickle down my arms in little streams, and slowly dripped onto the cold damp earth, and even though I knew it was wrong, as Garenhir had told me that blood should never be given up as an offering to the Gods, I was passed caring, and so I asked the Goddess Apia to accept my life blood as an offering, and to have mercy on my wretched soul and to ease the passage of my suffering.

Laying face upwards on the ground with my arms outstretched like some unholy sacrifice, I waited for the blood to congeal, when suddenly I became aware of the sound of distant approaching footsteps, but instead of hiding and lying in wait for whoever it was to appear, I chose to remain exactly where I was and to place my life in the hands of the Gods instead. So surrendering to my fate, I closed my eyes and listened intently to the approaching footsteps, until I became aware that whoever it was had stopped walking, and was now standing very close to my feet. Of course…curiosity eventually got the better of me, and I slowly opened one eye to the sight of Sai looking down at me with two large hares slung over his left shoulder.

"Hmm…Stay where you are…I'll go and get a couple of bandages," he said, quickly disappearing into the cave.

Relieved that it was just Sai and not some dark assassin after all, I sighed deeply and rose to my feet, and after placing my knife which still lay on the ground back in its sheath, I followed Sai into the cave.

I could see that Sai was presently preoccupied with rescuing the fire that I'd allowed to almost go out in his absence, so I just sat on the pile of sheepskins that were still lying on the ground from the previous night and waited. Sai then grabbed one of the bags that he'd brought with him and pulled out a piece of linen cloth, and after tearing off a couple of strips he knelt down in front of me and asked me to hold out my right arm. I watched in silence as he proceeded to neatly wrap the bandage around it, after which – he repeated the process with my left arm. And then without so much a single word having been exchanged between us, he stood up, picked up the hares, and carried them outside. I noticed that he seemed to be purposely avoiding making any eye contact with me. This intrigued me, and I wondered why he was behaving this way. Did it have something to do with what he told me this morning? Or was there another reason? I didn't know why this was getting to me…but it was. So with both arms now covered in bandages I followed on after him. He hadn't gone very far, and was just outside busy gutting one of the hares on a large flattish rock a short distance away from the cave entrance.

"Ahhh…what kept you?" he said. "Give me a hand here will you."

"Are you playing some kind of mind game with me, Sai?" I said striding up to him, "because if you are – you can stop now!"

I was beginning to realise that he'd been able to manipulate me into doing what he'd wanted me to do, by using a very clever mind control technique of some kind. Probably in order to gain the upper hand over me. And this, coupled with his exceptional mental agility had up until now been having the desired effect.

Realising that he's been rumbled, Sai stopped what he was doing and closed his eyes for a moment.

"OK – but it was worth a try though eh? How else was I ever going to have any chance of taking control of this whole damn situation? Try and put yourself in my position for a moment, you're a very strong minded individual, so I hope you'll forgive me for trying to get the upper hand over you…even if I did only have your best interest at heart. But to be fair I should have known that you'd soon realise what I was up to, but hay it was worth a go. I'd still appreciate a hand in skinning these hares though."

I wasn't angry, I knew he was only acting in my best interest, so I just nodded and gave him a hand to skin the hares. After we had finished preparing the hares, Sai picked them up and began heading back towards the cave entrance, but just before he went inside he paused for a moment and looked back.

"Well…are you coming or what?"

I gingerly followed on after him, and once inside the cave, I sat down on a round wooden bench that was situated on the far right hand side of the cave, and as Sai skewered one of the hare's and set it to cook over the fire, it suddenly struck me that in all the years that I'd known him, I didn't really 'know' very much about him at all. I didn't even know anything about his background until this morning, and I certainly didn't know anything about his private life. And what of 'Tagitus' who was sat in Sai's kol when I paid him a visit that time. I'd presumed he was Sai's lover, but maybe I'd always 'presumed' too much before actually knowing any of the facts. I'd struggled with my feelings for Sai for many years, and after failing to convince myself that these feelings didn't really exist, I'd fought very hard to conceal and to suppress them, but as I watched him carefully placing a few pieces of wood onto the fire, there was no denying what I was feeling right now. I think he must have picked up on something because he looked across at me and gave me a knowing smile, and the expression on his face told that he'd caught me good! He just seemed to know, and I felt flustered and embarrassed, and I stood up and quickly walked out of the cave.

"Kai…Stop!" he said, jumping up and grabbing me by the shoulder. "It's OK…Please come back inside."

"No, Sai…It isn't OK…nothing is OK. I'm really screwed up and I can't take this…I can't trust myself right now…or you!"

"Hmm…Look, Kai, I understand that you're feeling very vulnerable right now, but do you really think I'd stoop so low as to try and take advantage of this situation? You should know me better than that by now."

"Yes, I 'should' know you well enough by now…but I'm beginning to wonder – as in all the years that we've known each other Sai, you've always known everything that there is to know about me, but I really don't know much about you at all…do I? For a start, you've managed to keep your private life completely hidden from me, and you've never even told me anything about your past until this morning. I don't know you Sai – I really don't know you at all."

"Hmm," he said again, dragging his fingers through his hair. "OK…let's just get inside, and I promise to tell you anything you want to know."

We walked back into the cave, and Sai immediately began attending to the hare that was slowly roasting on a spit over the fire, while I sat back down on the wooden bench.

"So, what is it that you want to know about me? Go on – you obviously have a few questions that you'd like to ask, so now's your chance," he said, while continuing to add a few small pieces of wood to the fire.

"I don't have any questions," I replied brusquely, while struggling to untangle the knots in my hair.

"If you didn't have any questions, then you wouldn't have come out with what you did outside the cave. So go on…don't act shy all of a sudden – just ask me."

I suddenly felt really awkward, as it just didn't feel right to just start asking him personal questions about his private life, but I must admit that curiosity did eventually get the better of me, so I thought I'd start with the question that had been niggling away at me for some time.

"OK, if you insist…so what's the deal with you and Tagitus?"

"Hmm…I was wondering when that one was coming," he said, poking at the fire and sending sparks flying in all directions.

"Well?" I prompted, determined to get the answer I'd been promised.

What do you want me to say Kai? You already know what the answer is going to be. Yes…Tagitus and I 'did' have a relationship.

"Did?"

"Yes, did! And although it didn't last very long, we still remain very good friends."

"How long did it last?" I found myself asking.

"Less than three moons," he replied with a sigh.

"No…that's not very long," I said, still tugging at the knots in my hair.

"Would you like me to help you untangle your hair?"

"No! I can manage my own damn hair at least!"

Sai smiled at my indignation. His smile was contagious, and I found myself responding by seeing the humour in the situation and smiling back.

"Can I ask you a very personal question, Sai?"

"I've already said that I'd tell you whatever you wanted to know, didn't I? So go on…ask me."

"How many relationships have you actually had?"

"Hmm," he said, poking at the fire again. "Seven…no sorry…eight," he said, counting on his fingers.

"You have to be kidding me," I said, somewhat taken aback by this. "See what I mean? – I really don't know you at all do I Sai? I bet you know how many relationships I've had though don't you?" "One," he replied, throwing a couple more pieces of wood on the fire. "Yes, right first time. And were they all with men?"

"Yes," he said, stabbing at a log in the fire.

"Were they all sexual in nature?"

"Yes," he answered, taking a deep breath.

"Have you ever felt attracted to a woman, Sai?"

"Yes, actually I have, but that's another story."

"Go on…I'm listening. You said you'd tell me anything I wanted to know."

"Well, I suppose I've only got myself to blame for promising to tell you anything you wanted to know in the first place," he said, before continuing: "While you were living with the Hun, I began seeing a girl; she was very pretty, and around the same age as me, and one evening when we were alone in my kol, we began to get…well you know…a little amorous and all that, and with very little encouragement from me, she removed her clothes and lay down on my bed. But what happened next was something that I could never have foreseen; as she lay there naked, I suddenly had a flashback of the half-naked body of my mother lying murdered on the ground, and I totally freaked out and ran outside. Needless to say – that was the end of that relationship, and since that day I've never been able to look that way at another woman again. So there you are…now you know all 'my' dark secrets, well…most of them anyway. Do you mind if we have a break from questions for the time being, I think the hare is cooked now," he said, removing it from the fire. "Well, Sai, I've managed to learn more about you in one day, than in all the years that I've known you, or should that be, 'not' known you as the case would seem to be."

Sai took the hare off the spit, and cutting it roughly in half he placed the pieces onto two wooden platters and held one out to me. I walked over to where he sat, and taking the platter from his hand, I walked back over to the bench and sat back down again. We both ate in total silence; I still couldn't quite get my head around what Sai had just told me. So what did this actually tell me about Sai, or my own self for that matter? Was I really that naïve? – I guess I must have been. But what was really odd was how shocked I felt at learning that Sai had slept with all those men. But I still had just one more question.

"Are you in a relationship now?" I found myself asking him.

"Apart from this crazy one with you…No!"

His answer was very clever, as it was secretly what I wanted to hear – and he knew it! So after that, I just shut up and continued to eat the meal that he'd prepared for us.

It still felt as though my head had been shredded into tiny pieces, as everything that I'd believed in, loved, or had any faith in, had either been taken away from me, destroyed, or held up to question, and I felt as though I had nowhere left to turn. And even my Shamanic Angel was suddenly looking a lot more human and flawed. I needed something to numb my pain, and I knew that copious amounts of strong wine was stored in one of the small adjoining caves, so I decided to take a little wander over to the Agari alcohol preserves. But of course, I'd have to wait for Sai to leave the cave for some reason first, and so I patiently waited for the right moment before I seized my opportunity.

However, I didn't completely get away with it, as Sai wasn't gone very long, and when he returned I was still busy drowning my sorrows with copious amounts of Agari wine. There wasn't any point in trying to hide how much I'd had, as very soon it was going to become glaringly obvious anyway, so I just carried on drinking as Sai just stood there glaring down at me.

"I can't trust you to be left on your own for one minute can I?" he said glowering at me. "I'm guessing that you've probably had more than enough of that already."

He was right of course, and marching straight over to me, he removed the pitcher from my hands and placed it back onto a small table which was situated right next to the large earthenware jars containing the wine. I tried to use the table as a support to help myself stand up, but unfortunately the table wasn't quite where I thought it was, and my hand completely missed the table, which resulted in me landing in a rather undignified heap back down onto the floor of the cave again.

"Oh boy…well that's just great," said Sai, realising just how drunk I'd actually managed to get in such a very short time.

"Come on, I'll give you a hand," he said, standing behind me and linking his arms through mine. And with surprising strength he pulled me straight back up onto my feet, before helping me back into the main cave and over to the old wooden bench.

"Sorry," I said, as I slid back onto the bench. "It was there…I wouldn't have drunk it if it wasn't. Oh what the hell – I just needed a drink that's all!"

"Yes, well, all I can say is that it's a good job I'm here to pick you up off the floor," he replied. Sai picked up the pail of water that he'd previously fetched from outside, and proceeded to pour half of its contents into the cauldron, which he then hung over the fire to warm.

"I'm sorry to put you to all this trouble, Sai; you don't have to do this you know."

"No, I know – but someone has to," was his some-what reassuring reply.

Sai then walked over to where my blood-stained clothes had been left to soak in cold water, and he began to wring them out before using the seaweed soap that he'd brought with him to scrub them clean. I watched him the whole time, and I thought how quick I was to judge him after I found out about all the relationships that he'd had, and I thought of all the things that I had done. Sai had never killed anybody, all he'd ever done was care for the sick or injured. How many people had I actually killed to date? I'd lost count a long time ago, but if I was to be totally honest the number would probably be in the hundreds by now. Yet, I'd actually felt quite shocked by Sai's confession this morning that he'd had sex with eight men. But isn't it true that we all tend to judge others by our own standards, and it's very hard not to condemn the actions of another based upon our own personal perception of what we think is morally acceptable. And compared to me…Sai was a saint. And even though I was drunk, I realised that I had no right at all to judge him for what he'd done in the past, and maybe if it had been anyone else but Sai – I wouldn't have so much as batted an eyelid, but because it was Sai, I felt genuinely shocked. I began questioning myself and why I'd reacted the way that I had, and I wondered how deep this whole thing really ran between Sai and myself. Had we been lovers in a past life? I deeply suspected that we may have been.

I wasn't doing it on purpose, but my staring was obviously starting to bother him.

"Do you realise that you're beginning to make me feel uncomfortable," he said, momentarily pausing from hanging my clothes to dry near the fire.

The alcohol may have succeeded in numbing my senses, but it also appeared to have numbed my sense of what was appropriate behaviour given the present circumstances. "Don't you like me looking at you?" I asked him.

"This is difficult enough as it is, Kai, so please don't play games," he said, looking uncomfortably serious.

"Who said I was playing games?" I said in a slightly flirtatious manner.

Sai immediately left what he was doing and marched straight over to me, and standing directly in front of me he said:

"Kai, I know that you're drunk, but let me tell you something before you say anything else that you may regret later. You've got no idea how difficult this is for me. I worship the very ground that you walk on, but you already know that don't you? And I might as well come right out and say it. I'm in love with you, but you probably know that too; so let's just be honest with each other, as if truth be known I could so easily go along with this right now, but I promised myself that I would make sure that you're OK…and that's it! I have wanted you so much in the past that I thought it might kill me. But I'm telling you right now that nothing's going to happen between us while we're here, because if it did, you'd most probably end up blaming me for taking advantage of your vulnerability, and then you'd hate me for it, and then I'd hate myself. And I don't want you to hate me, and I really don't want to end up hating myself. So any feelings that you think you might have for me right now…I'm asking you Kai for both of our sakes…please, just keep them to yourself…at least for now…eh." And with that he very gently touched the side of my face and marched off again.

I was stunned speechless, and I didn't really know how to respond to that. Sai always did have very high morals, and I respected him for that. I may not have been able to trust myself – but I could certainly trust him. I began to see the dark humour contained in the irony of this whole situation, and then I remembered why I was here, and with a solemn heart I stared down at the dried bloodstains on the ground, which were still plainly visible from my lacerated arms.

"I'm really glad that you're here, Sai – I'd probably be dead by now if you hadn't turned up."

"Hmm!" he said, throwing a couple more logs onto the fire.

30

A Leap of Faith

I'd eventually crawled off to my bed of soft sheepskins to sleep off my alcoholic binge, and I didn't awake until some hours later. It was obviously dark outside by now, as I could see that Sai had lit a few lamps which he had placed around the cave. The fire was burning steadily, and the rocks that were placed around it were now extremely hot, and helped to promote maximum heat. Sai was sat upright on the opposite side of the cave on his own makeshift bed of sheepskins. He had a sheepskin blanket wrapped all around himself, and he seemed to be in a deep state of meditation. I didn't want to disturb him, so I very quietly helped myself to a drink of water before sitting down on the old wooden table that had been part of the furnishings of our sacred cave for so long now that it had almost taken on the appearance of a stalagmite. The anaesthetising effects of the alcohol had been replaced by the cold hard chill of reality, and once more I found my thoughts beginning to wander to the Agari wine reserves. There was so much of it that it wasn't as if anyone was likely to miss it. So as silent as my own shadow, I crept into the little side cave and helped myself to another drink…swiftly followed by another. And before very long I was soon suitably numbed once more. And as quietly as I possibly could, considering my inebriated state, I crept back into the main cave, and sat back down again on the wooden bench.

Sai had been too deep in meditation to have noticed what I was up to, so I just quietly sat there with only the occasional crackle coming from the fire to disturb the silence, and as I stared into the hypnotic flickering light of the flames, I began to reminisce about Tihanna, and how we'd fallen hopelessly in love right from the very first time our eyes had met, and what we had gone through in order to be together…and for what? She would have been far better off if she'd never met me, and probably still very much alive and happily living out her life with the Pa-ra-lati. Everything seemed so pointless, and nothing made any sense to me anymore.

Removing the bandages from my arms, I reached out for one of my throwing knives that I'd left on the large wooden table that stood right next to me, and once again I proceeded to cut myself, but this time I did it across the inner part of my forearms, and even though the cuts were superficial, they must have looked worse than they were, as by the time Sai had returned from his meditation I'd already managed to make at least fifteen or so cuts.

Realising what I'd done, Sai immediately jumped to his feet and within a second he was standing directly in front of me, and looking at me sternly he held out his hand towards me. "Kai – you've been drinking again haven't you? Never mind…just give me the knife," he said holding out his hand towards me.

"Yes, I've been drinking again," I said, standing up in a show of defiance. "And no…I'm not giving you the knife."

Still holding out his hand he asked me more sternly this time.

"Kai…give me the knife."

"No, I'm not going to give you the knife, so just back off," I said rather aggressively – blood still dripping from both arms.

"Hmm," he said, making a sudden lunge to grab my wrist. But even under the influence of alcohol I was still far too quick for him, and before he could grab the wrist that was attached to the hand that was holding onto the knife, I'd already successfully tossed it into the other hand. I could see the look of sheer frustration in his eyes, and for some reason I found this amusing.

"You should know me better by now than to try and take a knife off me, Sai," I said, remembering the conversation of earlier on in the day.

The very next thing that I can remember is getting a hard slap across the face, which managed to stun me just long enough to enable Sai to grab a hold of my wrist, and quickly wrestle the knife from my grip.

"Kai…please just sit down, and I'll go and get some fresh bandages," he said, quickly gathering up any other knives that were left lying around, and then depositing them at the far side of the cave.

"You just slapped me!" I said astounded, but at the same time ever so slightly impressed by his ingenuity.

"Yes, I know! Please don't make me do it again," he replied with a very serious look on his face.

After tearing off a couple more strips from the piece of linen cloth, Sai walked back over to where I was still stood in partial shock from the slap that he'd just given me. There was no need for words, so I sat down on a sheepskin rug on the ground and held out my right arm for him to bandage.

"Some of these cuts are very close to being a little too deep Kai," he said, kneeling down in front of me, "so enough of this Scythai (to cut) nonsense now…do you hear me?"

I could tell that he was a great deal more serious this time. In fact he looked more serious than I'd ever seen him look before…but what was I supposed to say?

"Yes, of course, I can hear you, but I'm not making any promises, Sai."

"Then may the Gods give us both strength that's all I can say," he said, shaking his head in dismay.

And for the first time, I could clearly see how deeply concerned he was for me, and how badly all of this was affecting him, and I was suddenly hit by a feeling of guilt for having put him through all of this. So feeing very culpable I said:

"I really can't promise anyone anything right now Sai…but I will try…okay?"

"You've got to do better than that Kai, the next time you do this…it could be the last, you know what I mean, and you know what you're doing. So I need you to give me your word that you won't do this again."

Our eyes met and I realised just how selfish I was being. Here I was wallowing in my own self-pity, when so many people around me depended on my strength and aptitude. And for the first time I realised this wasn't just about me…I had responsibilities. We stared into each other's eyes for what seemed like an age. Time appeared to stand still, and it felt as though our minds were almost becoming one. The sensation grew so strong at one point that I began to feel slightly afraid, and for a few moments I had to avert my gaze. There was a slight look of satisfaction on his face.

"Yes, well done," said Sai. "You've finally got it!" And with that, he proceeded to bandage my other arm.

I knew something very odd had just transpired between us, but what it was – I had absolutely no idea, so I just watched him as he finished bandaging my arm.

"Yes, I think I have. What did you just do?"

"Nothing…and that's what's so good about it!" he said, grinning at me.

"Ouch," I said, flinching with pain from the damage that I'd managed to do to both of my arms.

"I'll give you something for the pain, and hopefully it will calm you down a bit too," he said, walking over to his little bag of tricks…as I called it!

Sai pulled out a little leather flask and poured some of its contents into a small drinking bowl before adding a little water.

"Here – this should do the trick," he said, handing it to me.

I didn't bother asking him what was in it, I just drank it straight down in one go and handed him back the empty bowl. And after carefully wiping it clean, he placed the bowl neatly back in the pile, and then sat back down on the round wooden bench next to the fire.

"I'm really sorry for all the trouble I'm causing you Sai," I said, still feeling very apologetic. "Don't worry – it's no trouble. Someone has to look after you, and I'd rather it be me than anyone else," said Sai warmly.

"I can remember Merren saying something similar to me many moons ago; it does seem to be that way doesn't it? Some great leader I'm going to make…eh!" I said with a sigh.

Sai threw a couple more pieces of wood on the fire, and with an upwards glance in my direction he said:

"Hmm…I'm sure it'll all make sense one day."

"Will it? I don't know, Sai, Sometimes I think I'm not going to live long enough for it all to make any sense."

"Why do you say that?" he asked curiously.

"Because ever since I was a small child, I've had prophetic dreams, and lately I keep having a reoccurring dream about being killed in a battle of some kind. Not that it actually worries me. You know I don't fear death Sai, and right now I think I'd actually welcome it." I said wearily. Sai said nothing, and began tending to the fire. He was obviously giving some thought to what I'd just said before responding. Then laying down the fire poker he turned to face me.

"Maybe your dream is actually warning you against being in a situation that you have the power to alter, or why else would you keep getting the same dream over and over again, unless it was trying to warn you ahead of time."

"I'd never really thought of it like that before," I said, resting my hand on the bench in order to steady myself.

Whatever he'd given me had obviously began to kick in, as I suddenly felt incredibly tired, and my limbs felt so heavy that I almost keeled over.

Seeing this, Sai jumped to his feet and quickly ran over and stood directly in front of me – ready to catch me if necessary. He could obviously see that I was finding it a bit of a struggle to remain in an upright position.

"Don't worry…you're just very tired that's all, and also, what I gave you to drink is beginning to take effect. I think you'll sleep well tonight. Come on let's give you a hand," he said, holding out his hands towards me.

"Ha! – You crafty three-eyed snake. You certainly made sure I wasn't going to get up to anything tonight didn't you?" I said, realising what he'd done.

Sai helped me to get to my feet, but as I could barely stand up never mind walk, he put his arm around my waist and told me to hang onto him. And with his help, I was just about able to make it to my bed of soft sheepskins. And doing his level best to prevent me from landing heavily on either one of my lacerated arms, Sai carefully lowered me down, and then covered me over with a blanket.

"Yep…I feel pretty confident that you won't be getting up to anything you shouldn't be tonight," he said with a rather smug look of satisfaction.

He then placed a bowl of fresh water, and old pitcher down by the side of me.

"There's some fresh water if you need a drink, and if you need to pee…go in that," he said, placing an old wooden pale by the side of me. "I'll see you in the morning."

And with that, he walked back over to his side of the cave and settled himself down for the night.

I awoke the next morning to the smell of something cooking, and peering out from under my sheepskin blanket, I could see that Sai was sitting on the round wooden bench next to the fire.

"Good morning," he said cheerily.

"Is it?" I replied, with a yawn.

"Hmm," he said. He always did that when he couldn't think of anything else to say.

"What's in the pot?" I asked him.

"It's the other hare with a few dried figs, and a bit of this and that thrown in just for good measure," he replied, giving it a good stir around.

"Well…it smells good anyway," I said, rubbing my eyes.

"You can go back to sleep – I'll let you know when it's ready."

"OK," I said, pulling the sheepskin blanket back over the top of my head.

349

However; the call of nature demanded that I emerge from the warmth of my bed, so I reluctantly threw off the blanket, and quickly stood up and made my way to the cave entrance.

"Where are you going?" Sai demanded to know.

"For a piss…where do you think I'm going?" I answered sharply.

It was quite cold this morning, so I didn't hang about; I did what needed to be done, and I quickly made my way back into the cave and stood next to the fire warming myself.

"It's cold this morning," I said, shivering.

"Here," said Sai, offering me a cup of something.

"Ha! You're not catching me like that again. What's in it?" I asked him suspiciously. He gave me that little twisted smile of his and said: "It's a hot drink of liquorice and honey that's all…it'll warm you…Here!"

"What on this earth did you give me last night?" I asked, taking the liquorice drink out of his hand.

"Ah! Well now…that would be telling. Let's just say that it's my own special mix," he said with a wink of his eye.

"Well, it's pretty powerful stuff that's all I can say."

"Yes, I know," he said, raising his eyebrows and giving the hare and fig stew a thoroughly good stir. "And that's why I'm not telling you what it is. It's going to be bad enough dealing with your problem with alcohol."

"What do you mean? Do you think I have a problem?"

"No, I don't think you have a problem, Kai – I know you do."

I wasn't stupid, I was aware that I may have had a 'slight' problem with alcohol, but I guess I just didn't want to admit it. My problem with alcohol had begun way back when I was living with the Hun, and for a while, aided by the invaluable support of Merren and Aptien, I'd managed to get a grip on it, but lately I'd been slipping back into old habits, and now that all of this had happened, I'd been catapulted straight back into the throws of using alcohol as an anaesthetic again; except that its deadening effects were very temporary, and I was well aware that in the long term it would only add to my problems and not cure them.

"Maybe," I said with a sigh.

Standing there soaking in the heat from the fire, I quietly reflected on what Sai had just said, I knew that sooner or later I was going to have to get my life

350

back on track again, it wasn't going to be easy, but I was going to have to try at least.

"You're right Sai, I've got to try and be strong. I've got to face going back some time, so if it's all right with you, I think I'd like to go back tomorrow."

"No one's expecting you to get through this on your own Kai…and I for one will be right there by your side. And I'm pretty sure Merren and Aptien will both be there for you as always."

"Yes, I know," I said, thinking about just how many times I'd been able to rely on both Merren and Aptien for their support in the past. "I may have the reputation of being a fierce and cold-hearted warrior, but I'm just not as strong as people seem to think I am Sai."

"Yes, you are, Kai, but there's a huge difference between being strong and being heartless, and I find it difficult to believe that you're cold hearted anyway."

"Forgive me for saying this, Sai, but you have no idea just how cold hearted I can be at times."

"Actually…I understand more than you think. I've watched you for a long time Kai, and I know how you struggle with the two opposing sides of your nature, and how potentially dangerous you can be. Anyway; I'm still here…aren't I?"

"Sometimes I wish I could just ride off to a place where no one knows who I am," I said with a drawn-out sigh.

Sai didn't respond, he just stood up and gave the contents of the pot another good stir and sat back down again.

"Maybe I should do just that," I said, walking back over to my bed of sheepskins. And picking one of them up off the floor, I threw it closer to the fire and sat on it. Sai still hadn't responded, so I proceeded to stare blankly into the flames until the hare stew was finally cooked. And after Sai had shared it out equally between the two of us, we both sat and ate in silence.

The hare stew was really rather good, and to be honest, it was the best meal that I'd had in quite a while. And apart from me commenting on that fact; very little else was said between us throughout the rest of that day.

The accursed light of daytime had slowly begun to fade to more sympathetic shades of misty grey, as finally this strange and emotional day had finally drawn to a close, and as it did, my mood began to rapidly darken along with it. The impending night loomed heavily on my soul, and once again I found myself engulfed in a wave of uncontrollable sorrow. Sai decided to give me another dose

351

of his special mix; although not quite as much as the previous evening; so it didn't quite knock me out this time, but was just enough to keep me calm and controllable.

"I think it might be a good idea for me to stay with you for a little while when we get back, just until I can be sure that you're going to be all right on your own. Unless of course you'd rather someone else stays with you…I really don't mind! But someone should do it."

I knew that he was probably right, as I just couldn't be trusted to be left on my own right now, I'd probably end up killing myself one way or another.

"Yeah, maybe," I said, crawling off into my bed for the night.

The next morning I felt well enough to give Sai a hand to clean up the cave and tidy everything away again, before we both went out to try and locate our horses. I hadn't even bothered to tether mine when I arrived here, and neither had Sai, so we couldn't be absolutely sure that we still had any horses. Luckily, neither of them had wandered very far, and we found then both happily grazing together just a short distance away. So after rounding them up, we secured what had to be taken back with us equally between the two horses – and then we headed off home again.

Finally arriving back into our village, Sai immediately escorted me straight to my kol. It was obvious that someone had been there in my absence, as not only had they tidied it up, but they had also removed all of Tihanna and Kern's clothes and possessions. I guessed that whoever had been in here must have thought that it would be far better for me not to have to face all of their things lying around when I got back.

I just stood in the middle of the kol looking all around me, and for a split second I thought I saw Tihanna and Kern out of the corner of my eye, but when I turned to look…they had both disappeared. It felt like just one more twist of the knife which was firmly embedded in my heart, and the cold stark reality that they were never coming back suddenly hit me like a landslide, and I immediately fell to my knees and broke down again. Sai decided to wait outside for a while in order to allow me some private time to adjust to being back, and also to prevent anyone else from bothering me for a little while.

However; word had soon travelled that we were back, and it wasn't very long before people were turning up to see how I was bearing up. Sai made sure to inform everyone who enquired about me that he would be staying with me for the time being, and everyone seemed to agree with him that it was in my best interest that he did.

After I'd had a little time to myself, Sai allowed my close friends and family, and of course Garenhir and the rest of the Agari, to come and pay their respects and to offer their condolences for my loss.

Trisha and Aptien brought Nymadawa to see me, and as soon as she saw me she ran into my arms. It was obviously very hard for her too, as she'd just lost her mother and her little brother. I knew that she was far better off living with Trisha and Aptien, as I wouldn't be able to look after her now, but I'd always be her father, and I only wanted what was best for her, so it was decided that she should continue to live with Trisha and Aptien on a permanent basis. So I helped Trisha collect the remainder of Nymadawa's belongings, and Aptien helped her to carry them back to their kol. The funeral rites of all the victims including Tihanna and Kern were held the very next day, and the official rites of passing went on for many days and nights. And due to the fact that two of the dead were akin to the tribal leader of our village, their bodies were taken to a special place that was reserved for those of high status, and Tihanna and Kern were buried together in a special tomb called a Kurgan.

Sai was as good as his word, and he was a rock of support to me throughout this whole time.

He barely left my side which seemed to have my father's full approval. Sai was well respected as a healer, and as an Agari priest within our village, and he was not far off from earning himself a reputation on par with Garenhir, so my father was more than happy to know that Sai was keeping such a careful watch over me, but of course he had no idea at this time of the feelings that Sai and I shared for one another. But in the many weeks that followed, not once during the whole time that Sai had shared my kol, did he say, or do, anything out of line, and in the end it was me who made the first move. I admit that I had been drinking and inhaling cannabis that very same evening…Sai wasn't able to keep track of me all of the time. But don't get me wrong…I'm not using that as an excuse, I knew exactly what I was doing.

I'd sneaked off to join a few other warriors for a few drinks etc, but I was careful to leave before I was too drunk to walk. So feeling a little tipsy, I made my way back to my kol where Sai was sat near the fire waiting for me. He didn't say a word…he didn't have to, as the look that he gave me was quite enough.

"Oh come on…cut me a bit of slack will you," I said, sitting myself down on an ornately carved wooden bench.

Sai just gave me another one of his cold stares, and his expression of unbending disapproval made me laugh. He just tutted at me, and jabbed at a large chunk of wood on the fire sending sparks flying in all directions. He still hadn't said anything, and I wondered how he still managed to say everything without uttering so much as a single word.

The flickering light of the fire reflected in his eyes, and seemed to accentuate his face and the outline of his body, and in my tipsy state of mind, my thoughts soon began to wander…I must have been pretty obvious as he said:

"Kai…please don't…I've told you before."

Undeterred, I walked right over to him and sat down by his side.

"It's okay," I said, moving a piece of hair that was dangling in front of his face, and then to his obvious surprise, I very boldly kissed him on the mouth.

"No Kai," he protested. "This is not okay. I'd do anything for you…you know that, but I meant what I said in the cave."

"If I remember rightly, you said that nothing was going to happen between us while we were in the cave."

And putting my hand up to his face, I leant in and kissed him again. This time he didn't resist, and pausing for a moment I said:

"Isn't this what you've wanted all along?"

"Yes, and more than you'll ever know, but only if the time is right," he said, taking a deep breath.

It was getting a little warm in that kol, and it had nothing to do with the heat that was coming from the fire.

"Kai…don't do this. I'm not going to be strong enough to resist you, and I'm so afraid you'll end up hating me when you've had some time to…"

"Shhh," I said, putting my finger to his mouth. "Don't worry – I'm not going to hate you. I want this just as much as you do."

I'd struggled with my feelings for Sai for so long, but this was far too strong now for either of us to fight against. The energy between us was electric. And now that the tables had been turned, and 'he' was the one who was fighting against his feelings for 'me' – it had only made me want him more.

"Are you absolutely sure you want to do this? Because I really don't think that I can fight this any longer, he said."

"Nor me," I replied. "And yes…I'm absolutely sure."

And looking deeply into my eyes, he asked me again: "Are you really sure?"

I just nodded this time, and he stood up and held out his hand towards me. And taking his hand in mine, I allowed him to lead me over to my bed.

"You can still change your mind, Kai," he said, pausing for a moment.

"I'm not going to change my mind…"

We became lovers for the first time that night, and when the morning came, I didn't hate him, and may the Gods hear me…neither did I have a single regret.

31

Time to Come Out

Well, there was no going back now! It had taken years of soul searching to finally admit to myself that I really did had these kind of feelings for Sai, and it was the tragic loss of my wife and son that had ultimately brought me to this point. I guess the biggest question now was where would we go from here? I couldn't escape the fact that I was still closely affiliated with the Hun, and this coupled with my duty to my uncle, had been a major factor in my inability to come to terms with my sexuality in the first place. I realised that if my uncle ever found out about my intimacy with Sai, it would be extremely detrimental to my relationship with him, and probably with the Huns as a whole. And as for my position as future Khan…well…I could just forget all about that!

I knew that whatever happens, I had to keep my relationship with Sai a secret from my uncle. It wasn't that I craved the position of Khan; far from it in fact, and the thought had even crossed my mind that if my uncle ever did find out, he would most probably withdraw my position as next in line, and in doing so, take a whole load of responsibility off my shoulders. But my moral code demanded that I show him more respect than that by continuing to stand up to the task of being what he expected me to be. Besides, I still felt partially responsible for the death of Altan, and that was another reason why I felt obliged to take Altan's place, even though the ironic truth of the matter was that Altan had been homosexual. But even so, if my uncle had ever found out about Altan's sexuality when he had been alive, he would have possibly faced public humiliation or even exile. And now here I was following in Altan's footsteps, but now with the perfect understanding of the terrible burden that Altan must have been carrying. I really wished that the Hun didn't regard homosexuality or bisexuality as such a huge crime. It must have been extremely difficult for Altan, as I know how much I'd struggled with my feelings for Sai. And now I had another problem…who to trust with this, as it was going to be really difficult for me to hide this from everyone.

Sai knew only too well of my predicament, and of the dilemma that I now faced, and that's one of the reason he had struggled to keep his distance for as long as he could; fearing that a relationship with him right now would only add to my problems and I'd end up hating him for it. Of course he was right on one score…it did add to my problems, but he was wrong on the other, I certainly didn't hate him for it. It was inevitable that something would eventually happen between us, and it was only ever going to be a matter of time. It was a good job that Sai was so understanding about the position that I was currently facing, as I had to ask him to keep our relationship a secret, and not to tell anyone except for Garenhir, as I needed some time to think about who I trusted enough to finally reveal the truth concerning the true relationship between Sai and myself, as I had absolutely no intention of ending it.

Obviously the first two people that I decided to tell were Merren and Aptien, so I arranged to meet them both privately in my kol. I'd always been able to trust them with my secrets in the past, and I'd shared mostly everything with them that didn't involve any Agari business, but even so, I was a little bit worried about how this might affect our friendship, but as it turned out I needn't have been, as thankfully they both seemed to just take it in their stride. Merren told me that they both had their suspicions for some time anyway, and now that I'd actually confirmed it to them, he wasn't really all that surprised. But he still couldn't resist having a little dig at me by saying that although he had no problem with it, if I ever came onto 'him' he'd knock me out cold, and although he said it light heartedly; I knew that it was his way of letting me know where we stood. "Don't worry, Chief," said Aptien. "Nothing has changed – In our eyes you'll always be the same son of a bitch that you've always been, and we still have exactly the same amount of respect for you, I'm just never sharing a bed with you ever again that's all." And with that they both burst out laughing.

"Do you realise how difficult it was for me to sit here and tell you this, and all you can do is laugh," I retorted, feeling just a little bit peeved off by their apparent 'lack' of respect for me. "Come on chief…lighten up. We already knew this was blowing in the wind anyway. Nothing about you ever surprises us anymore. I was just trying to add a bit of humour to the situation that's all," said Aptien, shrugging his shoulders.

I should have guessed that they'd find the funny side to it, and I realised just how much I'd missed their wry humour of late. The expression on Aptien's face was the same old expression of friendship and loyalty as always. Merren just widened his eyes, and raising both his hands palm upwards he looked at me and said:

"So, you've finally been brave enough to crawl out of your hidey hole, and admit to us something that we already knew anyway. So what did you expect me to say?"

"Hmm – I guess I was just a bit worried that you'd both think of me differently…that's all."

"Surely you can both understand that."

"Don't worry, your confession hasn't changed my rather warped opinion of you in the slightest," said Merren, appearing slightly amused by his own banter.

"Me neither," added Aptien.

"Thanks guys – I feel like a massive weight's been lifted off my shoulders…despite your mockery!!!" I said, raising my eyebrows. "Your friendship means a lot to me."

"Who else knows about this?" asked Aptien.

"Only Garenhir – not even my father knows yet. So I won't need to tell you how important it is that you keep your mouths shut about this. I wouldn't have said anything to either of you if I didn't trust you."

"Don't worry – your secret is safe with us Chief," said Aptien, raising a finger to his mouth in a gesture of silence.

Eventually, the conversation moved away from my sexuality and my relationship with Sai, and onto other subjects. And apart from the occasional wise crack here and there, everything remained the same as always. I didn't mind the wise cracks as they were done in a genuinely humorous and light hearted manner, and as long as neither of them did it in front of anyone else, I didn't have a problem with it. I just felt relieved that they didn't appear to regard me any differently, and that they were both just as loyal as ever.

After they had both left, I was about to leave to tell Garenhir that I'd just informed Merren and Aptien about Sai and myself, when my father turned up out of the blue looking flustered.

"Sit down Kai, I need to talk to you," he said very seriously.

As I sat down on my bed I was immediately joined by my father, who wasted no time at all in getting straight to the point. "Kai…I've received word that the

Italians know what happened to their soldiers…and why. And apparently several more of them have been attacked and killed on different occasions since then…and as far as I know, those attacks didn't have anything to do with us. They know they're not welcome here, and they're currently thinking about packing up and leaving, but before they do, they'd like to hold a meeting with us to express their deep regret at what's happened."

I just sat there trying to remain calm while the reality of what my father had just said sunk in, but unable to contain my anger any longer, I felt a sudden surge of rage rise up and take control of my senses.

"I swear that if any of them dare set one foot inside our village…I'll kill them." I said, rising to my feet in protest. "So don't say I didn't give you fair warning."

Just then Sai who obviously hadn't realised that my father was here, walked straight in through the entrance. There was an awkward moment of silence before Sai realised that there was obviously something pretty serious going on between my father and me right now. So without saying a single word he about-turned to leave again.

"Sai wait! – I want him to stay," I said, firmly looking my father straight in the eyes.

"Fair enough," he replied.

Stopping dead in his tracks, Sai turned around and walked over to the far side of the kol and tentatively sat down on a gilded chair that had been a present from my uncle. Although Sai had seen me upset, he'd never actually seen me quite this angry before.

"Tell Sai what you just told me," I said to my father angrily.

"Please Kai just calm yourself and listen to what I've got to say first," said Father, still managing to retain his steely composure.

"TELL HIM," I yelled at him.

"OK – calm down. I knew this would happen," said Father, turning to face Sai.

My father proceeded to tell Sai what he'd just told me at my request. Sai just gave a slight nod of his head and said: "Ah…I see!"

"I 'will' kill them," I yelled, kicking a low standing table flying across the kol before angrily marching out.

I was immediately followed by Sai, who quickly caught up with me and grabbed a hold of my arm. But in my blind fury, I reacted by violently freeing myself from his grip, and promptly marching off again.

"Kai...STOP!" he shouted out. The tone of command in his voice did seem to have an effect on me – and I did stop. And folding my arms indignantly, I defiantly stood there staring at him. I was incensed, and certainly in no mood for anyone to try and placate me.

"You've got to learn to control your temper, Kai," he said, walking over to me. "Don't let this get the better of you. Be the warrior that we all know you are, and go back in there and face your father and deal with this situation. He's only doing what he believes is the right thing, so pull yourself together and act like that great leader of men that people are hoping you'll be one day."

Dropping my act of defiance, I took a long deep breath, and stared up towards the sky above me.

"Come on, Kai, let's go back inside," said Sai, holding out his hand towards me. I took another deep breath, before allowing him to walk me back into the kol.

My father had calmly remained exactly where he was, and as I walked back into the kol with Sai, I reticently glanced in his direction, before sitting back down again in the same place as before, but with Sai sat right next to me this time.

"Right...I don't blame you for reacting the way that you did, but you have to listen to what I have to say," said my father, obviously doing his best to remain as calm as possible.

"OK! I've calmed down now...go on I'm listening," I said somewhat reluctantly. "The thing is Kai – no one can ever rectify the terrible things that were done, and the perpetrators of that horrendous crime have already paid for it with their lives. It should never have happened, and it wasn't by command of their leaders that those debased individuals carried out their vile act of depravity. They've all stayed well away from us since then; obviously for fear that we'll kill them, but I've received word that one of their leaders would like to come here and offer us his condolences, and make an official apology for the unforgivable conduct of the murdering scum in question. Obviously this won't put things right...nothing will, but I think we should at least let them come and say their piece."

There was a moment of silence as he hesitated for a moment before continuing:

"Obviously they are going to need reassurance from us that they won't be harmed in any way if they do come here. So I have to have your word Kai, that you won't make any attempt to kill them while they're here. Oh…and there's just one other thing…they would like you to be present for this."

Shaking my head in disbelief, I turned and looked at Sai, but he wasn't giving anything away, not even the slightest hint of what his thoughts were on all of this.

"You actually expect me to do this…don't you?" I asked my father somewhat diffidently.

"Yes, Kai…I'm afraid I do," he said wearily. "As a leader of men, you're going to have to do many things that you don't want to do, and undoubtedly some of these things will deeply cut across the grain, but you just have to put aside your personal feelings, and focus on what's right for the welfare of your people. And not only do I expect you to do this…I expect you to do it well."

Hoping for some feedback on how I should react to this, I turned to Sai, but he just continued to stare firmly down at the ground. But if Sai thought he could stay out of this by remaining silent he was sadly mistaken, as his behaviour had obviously not escaped my father's notice, as he decided to ask Sai himself:

"So tell me, Sai…you've been sat there listening to all of this. Do you think that Kai should do this…or don't you?"

"Yes, sir…I do!" said Sai, raising his eyes for just a moment.

"Yes, of course you do, that's because it would be the right thing to do," said my father nodding in approval. "Well, there you have it, Kai, your wise friend here agrees."

"Of course he agrees; you've just put him in a really awkward position. He's got no choice but to agree with you," I complained.

Sai then surprised both me and my father by actually speaking up at this point.

"Actually, Kai…I do have a choice. Sha Pada Herian has asked me for my honest opinion, and I've given him my honest answer. I really do think that you should do this."

"Well, then it would seem that I don't have much of a choice then doesn't it?" I said petulantly.

"Thank you," said my father, standing up and arching his back. "Your co-operation on this matter is very much appreciated Kai. I'll let you know when the meeting has been arranged. And thank you also brother Sai for your valuable assistance, and for your very honest contribution to this discussion."

And with that he made his way over to the doorway, and was about to let himself out when he paused for a moment.

"Will you step outside with me for a moment Kai? I need to ask you something…in private." I obliged by following him outside, and as soon as we were out of earshot he turned to me and said:

"I'm going to ask you a question, Kai, and I want you to give me an honest answer. Just a yes or a no will do for now."

I felt a sudden wave of apprehension sweep over me, as I had the awful feeling that I knew what the question was going to be…and I was right. As usual – he didn't beat about the bush and just came straight out with it.

"Are you and Sai lovers, Kai?"

"No!" I bluntly answered.

"Are you going to tell me the truth, Kai?" he asked with raised eyebrows.

I knew that there wasn't any point in trying to keep this from him any longer, he wasn't stupid and he was going to find out sooner or later.

"OK! Then yes we are!"

"I knew it!" he said with a sigh. "How serious is it?"

"I don't know?" I lied, not really wanting to elaborate any further on the subject of my relationship with Sai.

Rubbing his chin, my father shook his head and sighed deeply, and looking down at the ground he spoke in a furrowed voice.

"Kai…You know this isn't what I wanted to hear…if your uncle ever finds out about this…."

"Yes, I do know that! But before you say anything else…I'm not going to end it."

"Hmm…OK, we can talk about this some other time," he said, briskly walking off back in the direction of his kol.

I immediately returned to my kol and flopped down onto my bed right next to Sai who was just sat there awaiting my return. I didn't feel any anger towards him for taking my father's side; after all, he was only being honest, so I just let out a long sigh and stared blankly up towards the roof of the kol.

"My father knows about us."

362

"Oh! How did he find out?" asked Sai, obviously quite taken aback by my somewhat abrupt and unexpected announcement.

"He's smart, and he obviously had his suspicions. He just asked me straight out. I denied it at first, but he didn't believe me – so I had to tell him the truth."

I could tell by the expression on Sai's face that he was obviously very worried. "How did he react?"

"He wasn't too bad about it actually; he's just understandably worried about my uncle finding out."

"Yes, I'm sure he is. Look, Kai – if you want to end this I'll understand," he said, placing his hand on top of mine.

"Why…do you?"

"No – of course not, but then I'm not in your position am I?"

"Then neither do I," I said, reaching towards him and gently moving a wave of hair that had fallen down across his face.

"I was about to go and see if Garenhir was available for a chat before all of this. Do you want to come with me?"

"Just ask me if you want me to come."

We both made our way over to Garenhir's kol, and I was glad to find that he was at home busy with the task of hanging up some herbs to dry.

"Ah…the fated lovers," he said light-heartedly.

Garenhir asked us if we wouldn't mind giving him a hand with some preparations he was about to make. We of course obliged, and got stuck straight into the grinding up of this, and the pulverising of that.

"How are you, Manu Kai?" he asked me.

"Bearing up," was my simple but honest answer.

"Good – as I was wondering if you were ready to re-join us yet," he asked, with a warm smile. "Well, that was one of the things I wanted to talk to you about actually Derkesthai – I really need more time."

"That's fine," he said, resting his hand on my arm for a moment, "I do understand, but all the same, it would be really nice if you popped by a little more often, as I could really do with more help around here you know."

I knew that Sai had been keeping him up to date with how I was coping, and he'd obviously informed him that we were now lovers, but Garenhir obviously wanted to keep in close contact with me himself, so that he could monitor me, and hopefully prevent me from wandering into dangerous territory…again!

"Yes, of course," I said, smiling back at him.

Sai and I were able to relax in Garenhir's company, as we didn't have to hide the fact that we were lovers. Garenhir wasn't bothered by our occasional show of affection for one another, and he was the only person in whose company I felt relaxed enough to behave in this manner, as although Merren and Aptien may have known the truth, they hadn't even seen the two of us together as a couple yet, so that was going to be interesting. And I certainly wouldn't show any affection towards Sai in front of those pair…can you imagine?

I explained to Garenhir that I'd already told Merren and Aptien about Sai and myself being lovers, and he asked me how they both reacted when I told them. So I told him what they had said to me.

"Good!" said Garenhir. "You're going to need good friends, Manu Kai. Yours is not an easy path."

I didn't need any wise teacher to tell me that!

"Oh – and my father also knows," I said casually.

Garenhir stopped what he was doing for a moment to clear his throat, and trying his best not to appear overly concerned, he then carried on with the process of pouring a concoction of some sort in an earthenware jar before placing it on the shelf.

"Oh…what did he say?" asked Garenhir.

So I told him the same thing I'd told Sai earlier.

"Yes, it's a tough one…that's for certain," was his short but poignant reply.

We didn't dwell on the subject, and I was soon able to relax and just be myself. And for now at least – I could forget about the consequences if certain people ever got to learn the truth about Sai and me for a while.

The time soon came around for the meeting with the Italians, and both Garenhir and Sai had helped me to mentally prepare myself for this day. So when I turned up to my father's kol I was calm…well…reasonably calm anyway. And outwardly I appeared reposed and confident as I walked in through the entrance to my father's kol and took my rightful place at his side. I was a little surprised but pleased to see that the Italian who had lived with us for some time 'Cornelius' was acting as interpreter, and even more surprised to see that Gaidres was sat in amongst them. I had to sit there in silence throughout the whole damn charade, and listen to some Italian official as he droned on and on in a language I didn't understand. I found it difficult not to fidget as I began to ponder about how nice it would feel to end this torment right now by delivering an arrow right between his eyes. And if my father hadn't had the foresight to insist that I leave all my weapons in my kol, I think I may have put an arrow in his skull right there and then. And if that wasn't bad enough, I then had to listen to Cornelius interpret the long drawn out apology concerning the 'unfortunate incident.'

As soon as it was over I didn't hang about, I walked straight over to Cornelius and I asked him to meet me outside, after which I just walked straight out of there without so much as a single glance or a word spoken to anyone else present.

Within seconds Cornelius had joined me, and as I didn't want to be there any longer than I really had to, I got straight to the point.

"You'd better tell that lot in there that I'd been 'forced' to sit and listen to that crap against my will, but for as long as I live they won't be welcome here, and I'm going to make it my personal business to make it as difficult for them as possible to continue to trade in this area. Did they really think that a 'sorry' was going to make everything all OK again."

Cornelius raised his eyes to meet mine for a just a split second before looking away again. I could see that he was genuinely too ashamed to look at me right now. I know that he didn't have anything to do with the deaths of my wife and son, or the other members of our tribe, but I guess it was all too painfully reminiscent of the time when he'd stood here on trial – accused of being a part of the cohort of Italian soldiers who'd killed Altan and Chinna.

"I will tell them," he said, allowing his eyes to meet mine again for just a moment.

Having said all I needed to, I immediately withdrew and made my way to the privacy of my own kol. Sai had been sat inside waiting for me; just one look at me and he didn't need to ask me how it went…and it was all that was needed for him to fix me one of his special mixes to help me calm down a little. Sai was all too well aware that my weapons were now very much at my disposal, and the Italians were still very much within my somewhat volatile reach. I hadn't been sat there for very long when I heard a familiar voice calling to me from outside…it was Merren, so I called out to him to enter. Aptien was also with him, so they both let themselves in and promptly plonked themselves down on my bed.

Sai played host by offering them honey cakes and refreshments, something I had never done, as in the past they just helped themselves to anything they wanted, Sai would soon get to realise this after a while. I wasn't really in the mood for talking, so the four of us just sat in silence for a little while until Aptien finally broke the silence.

"So how's it all going between the two of you then?"

You had to hand it to him; he certainly knew how to lighten a situation.

Merren gave him a sharp dig in the arm with his elbow. Grimacing in pain, Aptien scowled at him and rubbed his arm.

"Ouch! What was that for? I was only asking…that's all."

"We're doing just fine…and thank you for asking," said Sai, who was obviously finding this situation a little amusing, as I could tell that he was doing his level best not to laugh right now. We all just continued to sit there in total silence, until I just couldn't stand it any longer.

"Look this is ridiculous. I've known all of you for the biggest part of my life. You are three of the closest people to me on this planet, so why do I feel so damn awkward right now. You all know me, and probably better than I know myself, so please will you all do me a big favour and help me out a little here."

Just then I heard another familiar voice calling to me from outside…it was Gaidres. I shouted back to him to enter, and he walked in and sat down on the wooden bench by the fire.

"I'm not intruding on anything am I?" he asked, obviously sensing the tension.

"No – you're not intruding, Gaidres. I wanted to talk to you about something later on anyway," I said with a sigh.

"Oh…nothing bad I hope," he said, looking a bit worried.

"That will all depend on how you look at it," I replied somewhat indifferently.

Talk about an awkward situation, I felt so uncomfortable that I was actually about to stand up and leave, when Merren, Aptien and Sai began engaging in light conversation. Aptien said that he was about to build a store house, as he needed the extra space to store the stockpile of sheepskins that he had recently began using to trade with, and he was supposed to pick some wood up from the wood cutter today, but he needed to borrow a cart from someone in order to go and fetch it. "I have a cart that you can borrow. Would you like to come and get it…now?" asked Sai, as a hint for the three of them to leave.

"Yes, that would be great!" replied Aptien, enthusiastically.

"I'll come and give you a hand," said Merren, also taking the hint.

I waited for the three of them to leave before focussing my full attention on Gaidres.

"Do you mind if I talk to you openly, Gaidres?"

"No, of course not," he said, obviously intrigued by the very serious manner in which I'd approached him.

"Firstly I'm only going to ask you this once. Was it you who told the Italians that it was me who killed the men who murdered my wife and child?" Gaidres had no hesitation in replying.

"Yes, it was Kai…someone had to, and I was there, so I knew the real truth. I did it on your behalf, so that there wouldn't be any misunderstandings this time around as to why you'd done what you did."

"Hmm…well that's fair enough I suppose, I should thank you then…if that's the case," I said, relaxing a little.

"The other thing that I wanted to tell you is, well…you know the Agari priest who was here just now?"

"Yes," he said, in a questioning tone.

"Well, you might as well here it from me first…he and I are lovers."

"You're kidding me…right?" he said, looking slightly shocked.

"No, I'm not kidding you."

"Well, well, I would never have thought that about you. You're a bit of a dark horse aren't you brother Kai?"

"Yes, I suppose I am. But I hope that by telling you this, it hasn't affected our friendship at all."

"No…not at all. But just so that you know – I'm not attracted to men…at all!"

"Don't worry Gaidres – I don't fancy you," I responded with a little smile, "You're really not my type anyway."

"Well – that's all right then. In that case I don't have a problem with your sexuality. You're not the only friend I have who leans in that direction you know," he said, smiling to himself.

"I just wanted you to know that's how it is with me now. Anyway…enough of all that. How do you fancy some sword practice?" I asked, changing the subject entirely.

"Yeah – why not," he replied heartily.

So we both made our way over to the practice area, and although he'd never managed to disarm me yet – he certainly gave it a fair go.

"I think you've improved," I said, secretly impressed.

"I've been practising," he responded smugly.

I suddenly noticed that a couple of Italians were stood not too far away watching us.

"You can't do this though can you?" I said, drawing one of my throwing knives from its sheath and throwing it at a wooden post about a foot away from where the Italians were standing. It stuck in the post with a satisfying 'Thuck' sound.

"Phew...for one moment there I thought that you were...actually going to..." Gaidres began to stumble over his words, as he began to wave his hands at the Italians in an effort to get them to leave.

"Hmm," I said, folding my arms and menacingly glaring at the Italians, who just very slowly backed away until they had safely removed themselves from the whole area.

32

Gehenna

My relationship with Sai continued despite my father's disapproval. I guess he knew better than to try and interfere this time around. I think that he hoped it would just fizzle out in its own time, and that I'd eventually find myself a good woman, re-marry, and produce a couple of sons, but as time went on I think it was gradually beginning to sink in that this relationship between Sai and me was more than just a passing phase, and like it or not – he was just going to have to accept it.

He did make several attempts at 'trying to talk some sense into me', as he put it, but of course his words always fell upon deaf ears. He even told my mother about my relationship with Sai, and asked 'her' if she could try and talk some sense into me instead. At first I was annoyed with him for doing this, as I knew she'd be upset to learn that her only son was having a relationship with a man, as her upbringing as a Hun meant that she believed such relationships to be wrong, and she knew only too well the consequences if my uncle ever got to hear about it. She pleaded with me to end it for all our sakes, but I told her that although I didn't want to hurt her, I was not going to end my relationship with Sai, and that despite my sexuality I was still her son, and that she would have to try and accept the situation.

Of course, I still missed Tihanna and Kern, and I kept in close contact with Nymadawa and made sure that she had everything she needed. And I'm glad to say my relationship with Merren and Aptien remained as solid as ever. They still continued to make the odd humorous wise crack here and there, but in their defence – they were always very discreet and careful not to do it when there was anyone one else around. In fact, I actually found our friendly exchange of banter quite amusing, and I became so good at returning their banter, that Aptien said my words were becoming as fast and as sharp as my knives.

Garenhir continued to try and talk me into re-joining the Agari priesthood, but I just didn't feel that I had it in me anymore. I was already a battle-hardened killer of men, and I still hadn't recovered from the deaths of my wife and son…and probably never would. My many physical scars that were either acquired during battle or self-inflicted were plain to see, but the inner scars that I carried had cut much deeper and had refused to heal. And although Sai was my rock, and our relationship went very deep, many the time he'd turn up to find me either very drunk, or ever more frequently out of my head on opium. In fact my opium habit eventually got completely out of control, and had become so bad at one point, that Sai decided to plan an intervention, and unbeknownst to me, he had enlisted the assistance of Merren and Aptien into giving him a helping hand with the not so easy task of trying to get me straightened out again.

So one day Sai had tricked me into going to his kol for some reason, and when I arrived, Merren and Aptien were already there waiting for me. I was then forcibly held against my will by the three of them and made to go cold turkey. This was kept a careful secret from my father, who although aware that I indulged in this way – had no idea as to the extent. Sai had, of course, already informed Garenhir of his plan, and he along with several other Agari priests remained very close at hand…just in case I began to display any undesirable occult abilities during this time, as this was also an added risk which had to be taken into consideration. Luckily their assistance wasn't needed as I barely put up a fight. I knew that my chances of outsmarting these three were very slim. They had managed to outsmart me, and I knew I wasn't going anywhere, so I might as well just lie down and accept whatever was coming to me.

By the second day my withdrawal symptoms had really begun to kick in, and it was nearly a week before Merren and Aptien felt confident enough to leave me in the safe keeping of Sai. Garenhir often checked in on me during this time, and he'd sit and talk with me for a while, which gave Sai a well needed break.

After that, I actually managed to remain sober for a little while, but unfortunately it didn't take long before I began to slip back into old habits, and before too long I was right back where I'd started. And if that wasn't bad enough, due to my addiction and depressive state of mind, I began to feel drawn towards the dark forces that were patiently waiting for me to slip back into shadow once again, and very foolishly I even began to experiment with those dark forces.

Sai was only too aware of what I was up to, but despite this, he remained faithfully by my side and desperately tried to get through to me instead. He even enlisted the help of Garenhir who also tried to make me see the terrible mistake that I was making, but all to no avail. It seems that history was repeating itself, and I was gradually descending further and further into shadow.

During this time we were engaged in another head on battle with the Celts, and I fought with such ferocity that I felt as though I was invincible. My father was now convinced that I was indeed destined to become a great leader, so much so, that I even began to believe it myself. I demanded the respect of all those around me, and people soon began to fear me, and to pander to my every wish. Even Merren and Aptien began to fear that the Manu Kai that they once knew and loved was gone for good this time, and a stranger had slowly crept in and taken his place. It seemed as though nothing was ever going to be able to reach me this time. And still throughout it all, Garenhir never gave up on me. But even he must have wondered if the darker side to my personality had finally gained the upper hand.

There was no attempt by Garenhir and the Agari to try and forcibly intervene this time, as the dark forces that were now working through me would be too difficult to challenge outright, so all they could do now was to watch, wait, and pray for the positive forces of light to penetrate the dark place that I had descended into. And yet – Sai 'still' remained by my side, enduring my angry outbursts and dark moods. In fact as strange as it may sound, our relationship continued to be as solid as ever. He referred affectionately to me as, "My dark lord," a phrase that he had coined many years ago which had annoyed me at the time, but now I didn't care, as it was finally fitting. One day, I was out leading a hunting party in the forest, when I felt something sting me on the back of my leg. It wasn't as painful as a wasp or a bee sting, and I hadn't given it much thought until later on that evening, when I noticed a raised lump on the back of my leg where I'd felt the sting earlier on that day. I showed it to Sai who said it didn't look right, and he immediately prepared something to put on it. However, by the morning it was much worse, and the whole area of the mysterious bite was now red and inflamed, and my leg was beginning to feel very stiff and painful. Sai said that he'd never seen anything quite like this before, so he went and fetched Garenhir who after taking a look at it, said that it was obviously badly infected, and that he was going to return to his kol to prepare a poultice to try and draw out the infection. When he returned, he immediately began a process of administering a form of natural magnetic healing to the affected area, before applying the hot herbal poultice; after which he bound it with a clean positively charged linen bandage. He also gave me a herbal drink which he said contained anti-inflammatories and a natural antibiotic. He then told me that I should rest for the remainder of the day.

Later on that evening, Garenhir returned to my kol in order to remove the poultice, but it was quite obvious that it hadn't worked, and the infection had continued to spread with incredible speed, and now the whole top half of my leg had become very red and swollen, and also felt very hot to the touch. By now I was beginning to have difficulty walking, and both Garenhir and Sai were becoming increasingly worried, and were obviously at a complete loss of what to do. They had already attempted to administer every healing technique that was known to them, and nothing seemed to make a scrap of difference.

Garenhir ordered me to strip off and get into bed, and to remain there while they tried to figure out what else they could to do. Meanwhile Sai began to wipe me down with lukewarm water in an attempt to bring down my temperature, as by now I was also burning a fever. Garenhir said that he would go and inform my father that I was ill and that he would be straight back, and when he returned my father was by his side. Garenhir had already told him about the strange bite on my leg which had become badly infected, and was now rapidly spreading upwards which could possibly be life threatening if they couldn't do anything to stop it, as the redness caused by the infection had already reached my groin.

Taking my father to the side, Garenhir had obviously forgotten about the sharpness of my hearing, as even though I was burning a fever, I was still able to overhear him.

"I've never seen anything like this before, and I'm going to be honest with you Herian, I really don't know what else we can do."

The pain was so bad by now that I began to vomit, and it was painfully clear to everyone present that I was rapidly deteriorating. I felt as though I was burning up, and I could see strange little astral creatures all around the kol. They were all just staring at me, which I thought was very rude.

"Isn't it ironic?" I said to Sai, "It's going to be a damn insect bite that's going to get me in the end."

"Not if I've got anything to say about it," he said, hurrying out of the kol.

"Where are you going?" Garenhir shouted after him.

"Don't worry, I'll be back very soon," he shouted back from outside the kol.

I felt a loud ringing in my ears, and my eyes felt so heavy that I was forced to close them. I could hear the sound of my own heart beat pounding in my ears, and everything became very distant. I could hear a strangely foreboding echoing sound, and I began to feel as though I was falling backwards into an empty void. And as darkness enfolded me, I was gripped by a deafening silence which dulled my senses…and then…nothing!

I don't know how long I was unconscious for, but when I came around again, I was immediately struck by the fact that I no longer seemed to be in my bed, as the ground below me felt abnormally cold and hard. Slowly I began to open my eyes, but there was nothing but pitch blackness, so staring blankly into the darkness, I struggled to rationalise with myself that it must be night time, or perhaps I was in a dark cave…but how did I get here? It was then that my senses were besieged by a foul smell which seemed to permeate the air, and the very atmosphere felt thick and heavy, and had a very oppressive feeling about it.

Forcing myself to sit in an upright position, I pulled my knees up under my chin, and wrapping my arms tightly around my legs, I waited for my eyes to adjust to the darkness, until little by little, I was able to make out a grey shape here and there, until I could finally make out the shape of my hands as I held them out in front of my face, and then…to my horror, I realised that I appeared to be trapped on a very narrow ledge half way down a sheer cliff face, and as I tentatively inched myself closer to the edge and peered over into the endless void below me, I wondered how in the name of the gods did I ever manage to get here. There was a massive drop which seemed to go on forever, below me was another ledge, and looking up there was another ledge above me. Things gradually began to come more into focus, and I could now clearly see what appeared to be another cliff face directly opposite me some distance away; it had many ledges similar to this one, and craggy rocks and winding pathways, which appeared to come to a sudden end and disappear into enormous caverns which looked very much like monstrous gaping mouths. I could see something moving on one of the ledges opposite, and as I stared at it I could hardly believe the sight before my eyes. This was like nothing I'd ever seen before. The top half of this creature's body was vaguely human in appearance. It had a head, and what looked like eyes, a nose, and a mouth. It also had arms and a torso, but the bottom half of its body was like a giant grub of some kind, and it dragged itself along the ground by its elbows. And as more and more of these ugly monstrosities slowly came into focus, I began to realise that there were many of these strange and terrifying creatures all around me, and it began to dawn on me that I must be in some lower astral realm. I must have formed a vibrational link with this awful place shortly before I'd...I was going to say 'died'. Was I dead? Was this place my 'Gehenna' (Hell) would I have to stay here as a punishment for all the wicked things I'd done? And if so, how long would I have to stay here? And what was going to happen to me after that? I had so many questions; yet there was no one here to answer them. In fact, apart from all the many crawling, slithering, mind-bending abominations, there didn't seem to be anyone else here but me. There was no way up, and there was no way down. I was trapped on a narrow ledge that precariously dangled over the entrance to the Abyss.

Filled with a sense of utter hopelessness and despair, I realised that the most pitiful creature in this God forsaken place right now was undoubtedly me. And just as I thought that things couldn't possibly get any worse than this, my eyes beheld the most terrifying sight of all; as there standing on one of the ledges on the opposite side of the abyss, was the same hideous demonic entity which had appeared to me once before, and had tried to possess me all those years ago. I immediately averted my gaze and prayed that it hadn't seen me. I thought about praying for help, but then I began to think that it was probably way too late for that now, and that nothing was going to hear me anyway, and even if someone or something did hear me, I probably didn't deserve any help, or I wouldn't be here in the first place.

I finally came to the conclusion that it couldn't do any harm to at least try, and so with heartfelt longing for redemption from my pitiful plight, I began to pray to the God of the Sun for just one more chance, as deep down I knew that I wasn't really a bad person, I just had a lot of issues that's all...either that, or just put me out of my misery for good, as I would rather not exist at all than have to spend just one whole day and night in this terrible God forsaken place.

It didn't appear that my prayers had been heard as nothing had changed; so still not daring to open my eyes, I huddled closely to the ground and curled as tightly into a ball as I possibly could – I couldn't even pray for death to take me, as I was obviously already dead.

As I continued to lay there in my hellish torment, just for one moment I thought that I heard Sai call out my name. At first I thought I must be imagining it, but I heard it again. Was this some cruel trick to make my torment even more unbearable?

"Kai...look up," said the voice once again.

I opened my eyes, and fearing what hellish creature I may see peering down at me, I forced myself to look up, and there looking over the ledge above me…was Sai.

"Kai – grab my hand," he said, reaching down towards me.

Was this a trick? – It must be – it just wasn't possible that Sai could be here, so reasoning that this was all part of my torment, I curled back into a ball again.

"Kai…For pity's sake…it's me Sai…now will you please grab hold of my hand. Come on…we don't have much time."

Although I was sure that this was nothing other than just a cruel trick, I couldn't resist looking up again, and there he was…still reaching out his hand to me. I thought how much it looked like him, and if this was a trick – then I just didn't care, so standing up, I reached out my hand towards him, and grabbing me firmly by the wrist he said:

"You've got to climb up here…grab on to the ledge and I'll pull you up."

I reached up with my other hand, and with Sai's help, I was able to hold onto the ledge that Sai was on above me. He was then able to secure a very firm grip on me with both hands, and with one almighty effort on his part he managed to hoist me up. I just sat there staring at him; I couldn't believe that he was actually here.

"Is it really you Sai?" I asked, reaching out to touch him.

"Yes, it's really me, but I don't have enough time to explain to you right now, I'll do all that another time. Listen carefully Kai, I'm going to get you out of here, but you must trust me and listen carefully to everything I say, or we will both die. Do you understand me?"

"Yes," I answered, still in a state of bewilderment.

"We really don't have any time to lose, so all you need to know for now is that when you wake up, 'I' will still be unconscious, and you have to make sure that I'm given the antidote to what I've taken in order for me to be here. It's in a little blue bottle in my bag that's lying next to me, and if I don't get it pretty soon it will be too late. It took me quite a while to find you, so let's get out of here shall we?"

Sai stood up and held out his hand towards me, I didn't have a clue what he intended to do, but grabbing his hand firmly I quickly clambered to my feet, and just stood there staring at him, still hardly daring to believe that it was really him.

"Kai – I'm afraid that there's only one way to get out of here…we have to jump off this ledge," he said, pointing down into the abyss.

"But there's nothing down there…it's just empty space," I said confused.

"We really don't have any time for this," he said, turning to face me. "Kai…do you trust me?"

"Yes, of course I do," I answered.

"Do you have faith in me?"

"Yes, you know I do."

"Then consider this a leap of faith," he said, gripping onto my hand tightly.

Our eyes met, and I knew without any doubt in my mind that I could trust him. He'd done more than just follow me to the ends of the earth; he had even followed me into the great caverns of Gehenna.

"Are you ready?" he asked, tightening his grip on my hand.

And staring into the darkness of the void that spanned out before us, I nodded that I was.

"Right," he said. "At the count of three, $1 - 2 - 3 - $ JUMP!"

As we leapt off the edge of the precipice and into the darkness of the abyss still holding onto each other's hands, I was plunged into the empty folds of blackness once more…

I became aware of the sound of muffled voices, and as I opened my eyes, I had trouble focussing, as everything around me was blurred. Slowly things began to come into focus, and I could just about make out a hazy figure peering down at me, it was Garenhir, and as I continued to look all around, I was surprised to see that the room was full of people; my mother and father was there, Merren and Aptien, and several Agari priests to name but a few. Suddenly I remembered what Sai had said to me just before we leapt into the abys, and I grabbed Garenhir by the arm and tried to force myself into an upright position.

"Whoa – steady!" said Garenhir, as he prevented me from almost falling out of bed.

"In Sai's bag by the side of him, there's a blue bottle, it's the antidote to what he's taken – you've got to get him to drink it Garenhir…or he's going to die."

"Right," said Garenhir, immediately leaving me and going over to Sai who was still lying unconscious on a pile of sheepskins.

Garenhir began to root around in Sai's bag until he found the little blue bottle, and after removing the lid, he asked one of the Agari priests to raise Sai's head a little, while he slowly began to pour the contents of the little blue bottle into his mouth. It seemed to take forever before the bottle was finally empty, and all anyone could do now was to wait, and hope and pray that it wasn't already too late.

My father, who had been stood at the bottom of my bed, walked around and sat down next to me.

"Welcome back, son," he said, resting his hand on my shoulder. "We all thought that we were going to lose you for a little while there, but Sai said he thought that there was more going on with your illness than met the eye, and all he would tell us was that he was going to take something that would help him to find you and bring you back again. But he refused to tell anyone what he was going to take, and he said nothing of the fact that it could kill him…not even to Garenhir. And he certainly didn't tell anyone about the little blue bottle in his bag that contained the antidote, so how could you have possibly known about it?"

"I was in Gehenna, it was the most awful place that you can imagine, but Sai found me…I don't know how he did it…but he did. He got me out of that place, but before he did he told me about the little blue bottle, and that I had to make sure that he was given its contents straight away or he could die."

I was determined to sit up so that I could see what was going on with Sai, and on seeing this, Aptien rushed over to help my father to raise me to an upright position, and despite being told not to, I insisted on trying to stand up, but as I was still far too weak, my legs just buckled from under me, but luckily for me, both my father and Aptien had been poised ready to catch me if I stumbled. They both tried in vain to convince me that I needed to get back into bed again, but I refused saying that if they didn't help me I would do it myself. So seeing that there was going to be very little point in arguing with me, they helped me to pull on my trousers, and then they half carried me to where Sai was still lying unconscious and on the brink of death. I knelt down next to him, and I had to bite back the tears as they welled up in my eyes – he'd done this for me.

"Sai…please come back, I can't do this without you," I said, not caring who was around to hear me. "I need you Sai…so please damn you! Don't you dare leave me here like this."

I began to shake him out of shear frustration, and incredibly…his eyelids began to flicker before he opened his eyes and looked right at me…he was back! I just couldn't contain my tears of joy, and looking around at everyone's faces, I could see that I wasn't the only one who'd been moved to tears.

"Hello, Kai," said Sai croakily.

"Hello!" I replied. "That was some freaky journey eh!"

We both needed a little time to recover after that episode, but it left me with a whole different perspective on life. It had been all too easy to get caught up in the madness, and to lose sight of the truth that was hidden behind all the glamour and the craziness that was all around me. I asked Sai why he hadn't told Garenhir about the antidote in his bag, and he said that if he had, Garenhir may have tried to bring him back too early. He said he knew that if he failed to find me, he would most probably have died too, but it was a risk that he was willing to take.

"But how did you ever manage to find me in that awful place Sai?" I asked him.

"Well…to be honest I couldn't at first, there was so much darkness that I didn't think I was ever going to find you. Many terrifying entities tried to stand in my way and block my path, and I was beginning to lose all hope, when suddenly I heard your voice, you were asking for help, and all I had to do was to link into your prayer, and I suddenly found myself looking down at you from a ledge. I realised that none of it was what it appeared to be, and that it was really some sort of a test for both of us – but in different ways. I knew that there was something not right about that insect bite right from the start."

I re-joined the Agari shortly after that, and once again I threw myself right back into my studies. My father was very grateful to Sai for what he'd done, and he showed his appreciation by richly rewarding him. Sai couldn't refuse my father's gifts, as that would have been seen as an insult, so instead he gratefully accepted, and he was able to use some of the gold that my father had given him to trade for rare herbs and opium, which were turned into medicines, and made freely available to the Agari priesthood, who in turn administered it to whoever needed it, and so what was given to Sai, was ultimately made of benefit to all.

And my higher self said unto me: "I will enter into the abyss of darkness for pre-adventure. For there will I find the light!"

33

Farewell Garenhir

As time went by, my relationship with Sai continued to remain strong, as did my dedication to the Agari brotherhood. The political situation between Scythia and Thracia had continued to remain reasonably stable, and for a while at least, life was pleasantly quite peaceful for a change; that is until we received word that several Scythian settlements which were situated on the far eastern border towards India, were once again engaged in yet another all-out pitched battle situation against the Sarmatians. This time more Scythian tribes had been called to assist them. But our tribe was excluded, as we were required to stay on constant alert to what was going on towards the western side of Scythia, as we were also expecting another attack from the Celts any time now. The battle with the Sarmatians was fierce and brutal, and both sides had incurred heavy losses. But this time Scythian losses were far greater, and several Scythian tribes had been forced to uproot once again, and move even further inwards, resulting in the Sarmatians gaining a foothold in the furthest eastern provinces of what had once been Scythian territory, and if this wasn't bad enough there was even worse news to come. It was quite late in the evening when I received the message from Garenhir that he wanted to see me in his kol right away. It was unusual for Garenhir to summon me so late, and when I arrived, I could see by the look on his face that whatever the reason for him calling for me at this hour couldn't be good.

"Sit down, Manu Kai, I have something very important to tell you," he said solemnly. I did as requested, and Garenhir immediately sat down directly opposite me.

"Manu Kai, I'm afraid that what I'm about to say to you pains me very deeply. The thing is, I've have had a premonition concerning the future of our people here, which has foretold a tale that I wish I didn't have to repeat. Basically I can see a time of great suffering for our people here. Many battles will be fought, and some of them will result in great loss. Please pay particular attention to what I am about to say to you. I can see many of our people moving to other lands, and although this isn't going happen overnight, or will it even happen in your life time...'if' you should choose to remain here. But it's timely that some of us should leave now, and pave the way for those who in time must surely follow. I regret to have to tell you this, but I and several other Agari high priests, will be leaving for my homeland very shortly. I've already made contact with the Chieftain of the Siluries there, and he's agreed to accept us into his settlement where we will be able to continue very much as we are now under the wise council of the Druids, who as you already know, were my original teachers. We will also be taking all those who would like to come with us, and I would very much like you to consider joining us."

I just sat there staring at him; I was completely stunned by what he'd just said, and I couldn't take it in...Garenhir was leaving? I must admit that my first thoughts on the matter were very selfish in nature, as I instantly thought about how I was ever going to cope without him. He'd been there for me since I was a very small child. Someone who I could always depend upon for wise council and sound advice, and I found the thought of him leaving quite distressing.

"Does Sai know yet?" I asked him.

"Yes, I told him this morning," he replied.

"I haven't seen Sai today. He probably wanted to wait until after you'd had a chance to tell me before facing me. Have you asked him to go with you?" I asked, apprehensively.

"Yes, just as I've asked you, but I do know that he's not going anywhere without you, so the decision as to whether you both come or stay rests entirely in your hands I'm afraid."

I wanted to go...but how could? I had a duty to my father – and to my uncle. I couldn't just up and leave whether I wanted to or not. I thought of all the times in the past when I would have given anything for the opportunity to begin a new life somewhere else, where I could be free from the heavy burden of being who I was here. But now that I had that opportunity, I realised that it wasn't really that simple.

"Have you told my father yet?" I asked him.

"No! I thought it best to talk to you first. I intend to inform your father before the day is out though, and I want you to give some very careful consideration to the possibility of you coming with us. I understand that this may be a very difficult decision for you to make, but I honestly think it's in your best interest, or I wouldn't have asked you in the first place. But I also understand that you may feel very tied to your duties and responsibilities here in Scythia. But please think very carefully before you make your decision, it has serious consequences for the direction that your life will take."

I was still reeling in shock at hearing this sad news, but I agreed to consider the possibility of leaving Scythia and journeying all the way to Britain. But the truth of the matter was that I already knew that I was never going to be able to go with him, as my responsibilities here would morally prevent me from doing so.

I left Garenhir's kol in a daze, I would have dearly loved to have gone with him, but unfortunately I'd already made the decision that my path ahead lay here, and whatever direction my life was going to take, it was going to have to take it in Scythia. It grieved me deeply to think of how much I'd miss having Garenhir around. But at the same time, I knew that I felt incapable of just casting my responsibilities aside and joyfully riding off into the sunset. It just wasn't going to happen, and in making that decision I had already signed and sealed my fate, and life had already decreed to me its final absolution.

Arriving back at my kol, I found Sai was already there and waiting for my return. Our eyes met, and neither of us needed to say a single word. So with a heavy heart, I just walked over and sat down next to him on my bed. We both just continued to sit in complete silence for a while, before Sai finally broke the silence by asking me if I'd like some liquorice and honey tea. I nodded that I would, and with that he immediately stood up and proceeded to make us some.

"You don't have to stay just for me," I said to him.

"Yes…I know," he said, while continuing to make the tea.

"I know that you want to go with Garenhir Sai…and so do I, but I can't – you know that. But you can, and you shouldn't stay here just because I have to."

"You know full well that I'm not going anywhere without you Kai, so please just shut up," he said, handing me a cup of liquorice tea.

"It's hard to imagine Garenhir not being here," I said, standing up and adding an extra dollop of honey to my tea.

"Yes, I know what you mean…he's been like a father to me," said Sai, plonking himself back down on my bed. "He said that if I choose to stay, I'll become the Derkesthai here, but I don't think I'm ready for that title yet Kai."

"If ever anyone deserved to be made Derkesthai, it's you, Sai. You're more than qualified for the job. You'll be fine!" I replied, forcing a smile.

"All I can say is that I hope that you're right…I really do!"

"You'll have to swear a moral oath of obedience to my father though. And just think…if I ever become Sha Pada, you'll have to swear an oath of obedience to me." I said, chuckling to myself. Sai's eyes narrowed as he turned to glare at me.

"Yeah, right…Don't kid yourself," he said, giving me a playful shove.

Word had soon travelled that Garenhir was leaving, and all the necessary preparations for the long journey to Britain were now well under way. In total there were seven Agari, around seventy warriors, and just as many women and children, who were ready to leave our settlement and accompany Garenhir back to his homeland across the waters. And although he said that he would remain hopeful that we will all meet up again sometime in the future, in my heart I knew that I'd never see him again in the flesh, and that this was truly goodbye. It made it very hard to put on a smile and wish them all a safe journey without betraying the sadness that I felt inside, and I knew that Sai felt exactly the same way that I did.

After Garenhir and his entourage had all disappeared out of sight, Sai and I walked to my kol, where we could both share each other's mutual sadness at the loss of the physical presence of our beloved teacher Garenhir.

"Oh well," I finally said to him, "You're the Derkesthai now – so how do you feel?"

"Probably very much like Garenhir must have felt when his Derkesthai left for India…very sad actually."

Shortly after that, Sai was officially ordained as the Derkesthai of our village by the remaining Agari, and I was appointed keeper of the Agari ritual grail, which had been Sai's appointed responsibility up until the time he had become Derkesthai, and now by tradition it had to be handed over to someone else. Sai was then almost immediately required to take his oath of obedience to my father in front of the whole village. After which; everyone just quietly returned to their respective kol's, and carried on with their business as usual.

In the process of becoming Derkesthai, and due to the fact that Garenhir obviously no longer needed it, Sai had also inherited Garenhir's kol and all that remained inside. So Sai traded in his own kol for three goats and a pile of furs, and moved all of his belongings into what up until very recently had been Garenhir's kol.

All things are in a constant state of motion, and all things corporeal are transient and subject to the cosmic law of change. This is a fundamental nature of the universe. But even though I knew and understood these truths, it didn't seem to make not having Garenhir around any easier to deal with. I seemed to miss him more with each passing day, and I knew that Sai was missing him too, but he seemed to be able to handle it better than I could, and I found myself leaning more and more on him for support instead. He was my rock, and he knew me better than I knew myself. I would have been lost without him, and although I'd never actually told him outright...I needed him.

Life went on, and even though I could talk to Sai about anything and everything, I still missed having Garenhir around to talk to. And although my two closest friends and right hand men, namely Merren and Aptien, whose strength and courage in almost any situation had stood as a constant reminder of the bravery, fortitude, and indomitable spirit, that was to be found within the very heart of humankind, and who had remained ever faithful, and were never too far away from my side whenever the sorrows of life became just too difficult for me to bear...I still pined for Garenhir. So I decided that it was probably high time that I paid my uncle a visit, as it would serve to take my mind off things for a little while. I hadn't visited my Hun family for a while now, so after informing Sai and my father of my intentions, I gathered some provisions and a few good men together, which included the ever faithful Merren and Aptien, and we all headed off towards Hun territory. I would have loved to have been able to take Sai along with me, as he'd never been to visit the Hun before, but of course that would have been totally out of the question...all things considered.

After a fair day's ride, we decided to set up camp for the night. It was beginning to feel a little colder at night now, so the first thing that we did was to make a fire using the dry wood which had been tied to the backs of the three extra horses which we had brought along with us, as it made more sense to carry provisions on un-ridden horses, rather than to laden down our own horses with heavy loads, so if for any reason we needed to ride at any speed, our own horses would not be weighed down with the extra weight.

It was actually some time since I'd travelled anywhere with Merren and Aptien, and it felt really good to be sitting around a camp fire with them once again. It also gave us a perfect opportunity to catch up with each other. Aptien had kept it until now to inform us that Trisha was pregnant, and the baby was due to be born in the early spring. This was wonderful news, and both Merren and I were really excited at the prospect of being first time uncles. Merren was not too distantly related to my father's side of the family, so oddly enough he was actually blood related to Trisha as well as to me. So as far as Merren was concerned this baby was going to be his nephew or niece too. Merren still remained a bachelor. He just couldn't seem to find a woman that he really clicked with. I guess the longer you remain on your own the harder it is to relinquish that freedom, even if part of you cries out for that special someone to fulfil the very human need for companionship. But I suppose that even loneliness has a very important lesson to teach us.

"So what about you, Kai – are you and Sai still going strong?" asked Merren, with what appeared to be genuine interest, and surprisingly enough with absolutely no hint of sarcasm.

"Yes, we're still strong," I said, looking him in the eyes, and wondering when the wise cracks would appear, but surprisingly…there were none.

"Good – glad to hear you're happy again," was his remarkably wise-crack free reply. "What…No light-hearted sarcasm?" I said with one raised eyebrow.

"No…you can have a day off today," he replied with a grin.

I just smiled back at him. I felt so blessed to have found friends like Merren and Aptien. They had stuck with me through thick and thin, even when I had stretched their friendship to breaking point. I think that the old adage of: "Love is not love that alters when it alteration finds," was probably more appropriate here than I have ever known before or since. Only Sai, Garenhir, and Tihanna have ever managed to equal that. But how rare is it to find 'one' truly loyal friend in a single lifetime – never mind five.

As we arrived at the Hun settlement, we were given a warm welcome, and our horses were immediately led away to the paddock to be given fresh food and water. So with our horses taken care of, we all proceeded to head straight towards my uncle's yurt. Word had travelled very quickly of our arrival, and had obviously reached my uncle who was already waiting outside his yurt ready to greet us. We embraced one another warmly before he asked us all to follow him inside. We had a lot of catching up to do – both politically and otherwise. So after we had all had a chance to refresh ourselves, the party of Scythian warriors who had accompanied me, all apart from Merren and Aptien that is; were all excused to go and have a little wander around, while a yurt was being prepared for us all to stay in. My uncle was naturally very curious as to my current relationship status, and as he was never one to beat about the bush, he asked me outright if I'd considered remarrying yet, as it had been two years now since the deaths of Tihanna and Kern.

Merren and Aptien just sat there pan faced, and not so much as a hint of an expression of any kind could be detected on either of their faces, and I had to hand it to them…that must have taken some doing…especially for them.

"No, it's still too soon. Do you know that my Agari teacher has left to return to his home land, and over 140 people from our village including 70 warriors have gone with him?" I said, trying to quickly deflect the conversation onto another subject.

"Well, that's all the more reason for you to marry and produce a few sons," he said, not allowing the conversation to waver one inch from its original course.

What was I supposed to say? I couldn't very well tell him the truth could I? So I told him the first thing that came into my head which was – that I just hadn't found any one who was suitable yet.

"Oh well, if that's all that's holding things up, I have two wonderful nieces that would be more than suitable. In fact I see no reason why you can't marry them both," he said enthusiastically. I on the other hand, was beginning to wish I'd stayed at home. How on earth was I going to get myself out of this one?

It was at this point that Merren stood up, and after politely excusing himself he quickly left. I guess it was just too much to expect him to be able to remain so pan faced any longer. I must admit that Aptien was the one I would have expected to have caved first. But he was still doing brilliantly. My cousins Chamuka and Nayan were a little younger than I was, and although they were both lovely girls, I really didn't want to marry either of them…never mind both of them, and try as I might, I just couldn't come up with any valid excuse to give my uncle for not wanting to marry them, and it would have been seen as a great insult to them and to my uncle if I'd refused to marry either one of them without a really good reason.

"It's not really common practice in Scythia to have more than one wife," was all that I could think of to say to him.

"Hmm…damn stupid practice if you want my opinion," he said, scowling at me.

"Then you will just have to choose between the two of them, and her sister will accompany her so that she has someone to keep her company during the times that you are away."

It was at this point that Aptien stood up and politely excused himself, before he also quickly disappeared out through the doorway.

Oh boy! I'd just been practically married off, and I don't remember actually agreeing to any of it. If my father had attempted such a thing he would have received the sharp edge of my tongue, but then my father already knows the real truth behind why I didn't want to marry, so I wouldn't have needed to hide anything. I didn't have a clue how I was going to get myself out of this one.

"So…which one are you going to choose to marry?" asked my uncle, quite determined in his effort to have me married off by the end of the day.

"Give me some time to think about it, they're both very beautiful," I replied, with a sigh. "Yes," he said thoughtfully. "This is why I think you should marry them both. It would be too difficult to choose between them. You're a Hun – there should be allowances made for this in Scythia. They should accept that we have different ways."

I could see that he'd obviously given a great deal of thought to all of this.

"This is true, but I'm also half Scythian, and I freely choose to live by Scythian rules. I won't take more than one wife while living in Scythia."

"Then you must choose which one you will marry, and which one will be your wife's companion. Please let me know before the end of your stay here, so that all the necessary preparations can be made. The wedding can take place here or in Scythia…I really don't mind, so I will leave that decision up to you."

On the face of things it would appear that I had very little choice other than to accept this situation, so I just nodded and obediently agreed to give him my decision concerning which one of my two cousins I was going to marry by the end of my stay. One of my uncle's men walked in through the doorway at this point, and informed me that a yurt had been prepared, and that all of my men were presently resting, so I stood up and after bowing respectfully to my uncle, I left with the Hun warrior so that he could escort me to the yurt.

When I arrived, everyone was either asleep or resting, all that is except for Merren and Aptien who were eagerly awaiting my arrival.

"Can we see you outside for a moment?" asked Aptien eagerly.

Without saying a word I immediately turned around and walked straight back outside again. Merren and Aptien quickly followed, and as soon as we were out

386

of earshot, Merren quietly asked me what my decision was going to be regarding my uncle's proposal to marry his nieces.

"Well…it looks like I'm getting married," I said, rolling my eyes.

"What…are you serious?" asked a very shocked-looking Merren.

Aptien just stood blankly staring at me. I really don't remember a time that I'd ever seen him look quite this worried before.

"Well, this is going to be interesting," he said, scratching his head. "But I suppose the obvious question here is what's going to happen with you and Sai after you get married."

"Nothing's going to change my relationship with Sai," was my resolute reply.

"This could get a little complicated, Kai – you're going to be marrying a Hun woman, and you have a male lover," said Aptien, spitting out the liquorice root that he was chewing. "I don't mean to sound doubtful and all that, but how on earth do you suppose you're going to carry this one off."

"Oh…I don't know – I'm just too damn tired to think straight anymore," I said, lifting up the flap to the entrance of the yurt and disappearing inside.

Merren and Aptien followed on after me. There was nothing more to be said right now, so after removing my weapons, I stripped off and climbed naked into the soft bed of furs that had obviously been meant for me to sleep in due to its location. But sleep didn't come easy that night, as I couldn't stop thinking about how on earth I was ever going to explain to Sai that I was getting married. I didn't even want to think about how he was going to react, and I wasn't looking forward to telling him either!

In the morning I awoke with the difficult decision of which one of my cousins I should choose to marry still weighing heavily on my mind. I knew that I'd have to make a decision pretty soon. But then did it really matter, as whoever I chose, the other sister was coming along to live with us anyway. I think that my uncle was hoping that by sending the other sister along, I'd eventually agree to marry her too.

It wasn't easy, but by the end of my stay I'd made my decision, and all that remained now was to inform my father of all of this, and to make all the necessary arrangements for the marriage to go ahead. Oh boy!

Before we got back, I asked Merren and Aptien to keep this between the three of us for now, at least until after I'd had a chance to speak with my father, and at some point I was going to have to confront Sai with this news…I was dreading it, as I had a really bad feeling that he wasn't going to take this at all well, and I couldn't have been more right.

When we arrived back, I asked Merren and Aptien if they didn't mind hanging around for a little while for some moral support. First stop was my father, and you should have seen the look on his face when I explained to him how my uncle had managed to manipulate me into agreeing to marry one of his nieces.

"That's brilliant news," said my father, with a huge grin on his face. "I can't wait to tell your mother – she's going to be thrilled."

And then pausing for a brief moment, he asked me what I planned to do about the current situation between Sai and me. Merren and Aptien walked over to the far side of the kol and quietly sat in the corner trying to remain as inconspicuous as possible, not something either of them was particularly good at, but I could see that they were both giving it their best shot. They were certainly getting plenty of practice of late that was for sure!

"I'm not ending it if that's what you mean," I replied firmly.

"Have you given any thought to just how you're going to be able to keep it hidden from both your new bride and her sister," he asked me with a sigh. "You don't need me to tell you that the possibility of them ever finding out that you're also having a relationship with a man, as well as being married to one of them just doesn't bear thinking about. For the sake of our ancestors Kai…please wake up! They are your uncle's nieces, and I hate to think how your uncle is going to react if it ever got back to him…can you imagine?"

"Yes, of course I can. But even so – I'm still not ending my relationship with Sai, so I'm just going to have to hope and pray that he never gets to find out then won't I?" I responded stubbornly.

Well…that was the easy part over with, and now for the part that I was dreading…telling Sai. So aided by the moral support of Merren and Aptien, I headed towards Sai's kol, but just before we got there I asked them if they wouldn't mind coming in with me, as I figured that if they were both present when I gave Sai my news, it might prevent him from over reacting. So before entering I called out to him to let him know that Merren and Aptien were with me. Sai must have wondered what on earth was going on, but he responded by asking us all to come on in. He must have known by the look on my face that I was not the bearer of good news. Merren and Aptien both quietly went and sat in the corner…they were getting very good at this.

"Sit down, Sai, I really need to talk to you about something," I said rather apprehensively.

"What's wrong?" he asked, looking understandably worried.

I began to explain to him what had happened with my uncle, and that I would be getting married very soon, but I was going to do my best to not let it affect our relationship too much. Sai just sat there listening intently until I'd finally finished speaking, after which he very calmly stood up and said:

"Well, I guess that's the end of our relationship then. What were you thinking, Kai; you can't marry your Hun cousin and still expect us to carry on as normal. I honestly didn't think you'd ever do this to me."

Sai turned to Merren and Aptien, and asked them if they wouldn't mind waiting outside. I could see that Sai was beginning to get upset. So I signalled to Merren and Aptien to leave, and they both stood up and immediately left the kol.

"Sai…Before you say anything else – I really had no other choice but to accept. What could I do? I couldn't very tell my uncle that I didn't want to marry his niece, as I was having a relationship with you now could I?"

"No…but I'm sure you could have come up with something – you didn't have to agree to it." "You don't know my uncle. He made it impossible for me to refuse. He'd got me so cornered that I just couldn't get out of it. Look Sai, I have to do what I have to do, and you're just going to have to accept the situation," I said, feeling irritated by his complete lack of understanding.

"Really!" he said, beginning to look equally as annoyed with me as I was with him.

"Unless you've forgotten – I chose to remain here with you when I could have gone with Garenhir. Maybe I should introduce myself as your lover to your new bride, and see how 'she' accepts that little gem then shall I. What if I don't want to be your little secret anymore? Perhaps it's about time that your uncle learned the truth. Let's see how accepting 'he' is when he learns the truth about you…shall we, Kai?"

I felt the blood rush to my head, and picking up an earthenware jar, I hurled it past him towards the stones surrounding the fire pit in the middle of the kol. Sai put his hands up to protect himself from the pot…just in case it was coming his way. I was really angry with him by now, and I yelled at him that if he ever dared to tell my new bride about us, or if my uncle ever found out because of anything that he'd said, I'd have it known that he used dark magic on me, and I didn't know what I was doing, and after having him branded as an evil sorcerer, I'd have him cast out of our village for ever.

Once again I'd managed to engage my mouth before my brain. I'm quite sure that I actually saw his eyes flash red, and the next thing I felt was the pain of his fist connecting with my cheekbone.

He'd hit me so hard – I literally saw stars, and I don't remember hitting the ground at all. The force of his punch was powerful enough to have split my cheek, and I felt warm blood begin to trickle down the side of my face. All the commotion had obviously alerted Merren and Aptien, who both burst in through the doorway only to find me still lying in a dazed heap on the ground, and Sai sat seething to himself over towards the far side of the kol.

"Whoops! I think you must have slipped and fallen there, Chief," said Merren, scraping me up off the floor.

"Whoa..." said Aptien, cringing. "That must have been one heck of a punch."

Sai had calmed down a little by now, and had come over to have a look at his handy work. He also cringed when he saw what he'd managed to do. My left eye was already beginning to swell up, and I was obviously going to have one heck of a shiner.

"Kai...I'm really sorry...I've never done anything like that before," he said, holding his hands to his head in utter dismay.

"You could have fooled me," said Merren. "You've got a damn good punch on you that's for sure."

"Yes, hasn't he just," I said, wiping the blood away with the back of my hand. Sai reached out to touch me, and I reacted by sharply pushing him away.

"Just get away from me Sai. That's it...it's over, we're finished."

"You'll be back," he said, walking back over to the far side of the kol.

I just wanted to get back to the privacy of my own kol. The trouble was...I didn't know what hurt the most, my cheek or my pride. It was embarrassing enough as it was, and as luck would just have it, I had to walk straight past my brother, who taking one look at my face said:

"Oh dear...had a fight with your boyfriend have you Kai? I'd stick to women if I was you – they won't hit you quite so hard when you manage to piss them off."

He began to laugh and chide me for my stupidity, and I really felt like giving him a matching cheek to mine, but Merren grabbed me firmly by the arm and stopped me.

"Ignore him, Kai – he's not worth it – you know that," said Aptien.

Both Merren and Aptien accompanied me back to my kol, and as soon as we got there, Merren found a piece of cloth and dipped it into a pitcher of cold water before holding it to my face. "I take it that Sai didn't take the news very well then," said Aptien, taking a closer look at the cut on my face.

"Good punch though…I'm quite impressed actually," said Merren, handing me the cloth. I just scowled at him as I wiped the blood off the back of my hand where I'd used it to wipe the blood off my face earlier.

Just then my father and brother walked straight into the kol without first calling from outside.

"What's happened Kai?" asked my father, staring at my swollen face.

"Just stay out of it – it doesn't concern you," I said sharply.

"Oh! – It concerns me all right! If it's got anything to do with you – then it's my concern. Now tell me what happened."

"I can sort this out myself, so if you don't mind…please stay out of it. You'll only make it worse," I said adamantly.

"His boyfriend beat him up," piped in my brother with a really irritating smirk on his face. "What's he doing in here anyway? …Get him out of here," I retorted, angrily pointing towards the doorway.

My father nodded to my brother to leave, so still smirking to himself, he slowly shuffled out through the doorway. He was obviously enjoying all of this, and I really wanted to knock that stupid smirk off his face, but I knew that if I allowed him to get to me, to the point that I hit him…it would only end up making things a lot worse for me.

"Right then Kai," said my father, obviously beginning to run out of patience. "If you won't tell me what happened, I'm just going to have to go and ask Sai."

"No, please don't do that! OK – I'll tell you. We had an argument…that's all."

"Yes, well…I've already gathered that much, Kai. You've got one last chance to tell me exactly what happened, or I'm just going to have to pay Sai a visit," he said, looking ever more irate by the second.

"I think you'd better tell him Kai," said Merren, nervously tapping his fingers on his knees.

I really didn't want this to escalate any further, so I reluctantly explained to my father what all the fuss was about, and the things that we'd each said to one another in anger, which had finally led up to the point of Sai landing me one.

"Right…now it's time to pay Sai a visit I think," said my father, heading straight towards the doorway.

"What? Please, Father, don't!" I pleaded.

"Don't worry – I'm just going to talk to him that's all," he said, quickly disappearing out through the door.

I just looked at Merren and then at Aptien, and throwing the rag that Merren had given me to the ground in frustration I said: "What am I supposed to do now?"

"There isn't much you can do. Don't worry! – he's only going to talk to him…that's all!" said Aptien, staring at a rather large spider which was presently scurrying across the floor.

"I only hope that you're right – I really do," I said, letting out a huge sigh of frustration. Meanwhile, my father had turned up at Sai's kol, and had respectfully called out to him from outside before entering. Sai who could have been in no doubt why my father was paying him a visit, asked him to come in, and after first thanking Sai politely for allowing him inside, he asked him to sit down as he wished to speak to him about what happened earlier. He then proceeded to tell him that although he had the greatest of respect for him, if he carried out his threat to say anything to my future bride about us ever having been lovers, or to say anything at all that would directly result in my uncle finding out about me ever having had a sexual relationship with him, it would force him to carry out the ancient law that was most befitting to one who betrays their leader by word of mouth, and he'd have to cut out that forked tongue of his. Sai assured my father that he hadn't really meant what he'd said, and that he'd never intended to carry out those threats as he'd only said it out of anger, as he got a bit upset when I'd told him that I was getting married.

Thankfully my father had been suitably pacified by Sai's response, and he returned to my kol and informed me that all was well, and that he'd had a little word with Sai, and he had assured him that he never had any real intention of ever carrying out his threats. I already knew that…he was just really upset that's all. But that was no excuse for having punched me – and I wasn't going to be the first to cave in and go around and see him. It was going to be up to him to come to me.

Several weeks later, and there was still no sign of Sai: I guess he could be just as stubborn as I was. My face, along with my dignity had mostly recovered. All that was left now was a little telltale scar, and I could have got that anywhere. It wasn't as if I didn't already have a few scars on my face anyway. During this time, all the necessary arrangements had been made for the marriage to take place between Chamuka and me. So along with my father, mother, sisters, Merren and Aptien, and about thirty or so of our warriors, I headed off to Hun territory to marry Chamuka.

After the very simple ceremony had taken place, there was much drinking and celebrating, at which time I did my best to mask my true feelings, and to appear outwardly happy throughout the whole occasion, but the truth of the matter was, I was beginning to wonder if I'd made a huge mistake in not going with Garenhir when I'd had the opportunity. Maybe if I'd made the decision to move to Britain, Sai and I would still be together. I really missed him – but of course I was far too proud to go and tell him this. And anyway – I was now married to a lovely woman, and it wasn't her fault that my life was in such a mess. I knew that I was just going to have to make the best of a bad situation, and do all that I could to ensure that neither Chamuka nor her sister Nayan suffered due to any of this.

Why – when all I ever wanted was a simple life – did things always have to be so damn complicated?

34

The Truth Will Out

After a couple of days, we all returned back home again to Scythia. My new bride Chamuka was accompanied by her sister Nayan, all of their personal belongings, and a large dowry which included a variety of animal furs and eight fine horses.

The very first thing that I had to do when we arrived back home again was to introduce Chamuka and Nayan to their new home and get them settled in. Merren and Aptien helped me to carry all of their belongings inside, and as you can probably imagine, my mother was absolutely delighted with the whole arrangement, as not only was she no longer the only full-blooded Hun living in our village, but my new wife and her sister Nayan were actually her nieces. My mother wasted no time at all in getting involved by making sure that their every need was taken care of. I was hugely grateful for my mother's support during this time as it took a lot of the stress off my shoulders, and as far as I was concerned she could carry on fussing over them as much as she liked. As it was Scythian tradition for wives to share a bed with their husband, Chamuka shared my bed with me, but I insisted on Nayan having her own bed at the far side of the kol, as regardless of what my uncle had cleverly worked out for me, I still remained adamant that I was not going to have two wives. So I helped Nayan to make her own little space over on the far left-hand side of the kol, as it was Hun tradition that the left side of the kol was for females, and the right side of the kol was for males. So by Hun tradition Chamuka should have slept over on the left side of the kol, and would only have slept in my bed when I requested that she should do so. But my mother had already explained to her that it was Scythian tradition that a wife should sleep with her husband in 'his' bed, so Chamuka had already been made aware of this.

Sai still remained perceptibly conspicuous due to his absence, and although I knew that he was purposely avoiding me, I couldn't really blame him given the circumstances. And even though I missed him badly, I remained adamant that I wasn't going to give in and go looking for him. A few days later I decided that it was time that I gave Chamuka and Nayan a full tour of our settlement, as so far they had barely dared to venture outside of the kol. They both seemed to find it all fascinating, and although I was pleased by their enthusiasm, if I'm honest, I found their constant chitter chattering quite draining, so after returning them safely back to my kol, I decided to wander on down to the river to give myself a chance to unwind for a little while.

Stretching out on the cool grass, I allowed the gentle sound of the flowing water to mentally wash away all my troubles. But I must have grown a little too relaxed and drifted off to sleep, as when I finally woke up, it was already beginning to get quite dark. I was about to pick up my bow and arrows which were laying on the ground next to me, when I noticed that four symbols had been scraped into the earth close by. The first symbol was my own personal 'Tamga' – (a symbol that represented me). The second symbol was that of an arrow which was pointing in the direction of my Tamga. The third was the symbol for sleep, and the fourth was for death. In other words, the message was warning me that whoever had scraped these symbols into the earth, could have easily killed me using my own bow and arrows while I'd been asleep. There weren't many people who would have been able to creep up on me like that without me having heard them…actually there was only one person that I knew of…'Sai.' I quickly looked all around to see if he was still anywhere in sight, but he was nowhere to be seen. He had obviously seen fit to warn me of my carelessness in falling asleep alone like that. He was right! It was a pretty stupid thing to do considering my position and all that, but I couldn't help smiling to myself as I began to reminisce about the first time that we'd sat on the banks of this river, and my moral dilemma at having felt so deeply attracted to him. I touched the symbols that he had scraped into the earth, and with a sigh, I stood up and made my way back to my kol. It had been a very long day, and all I wanted to do now was to climb into my warm bed. I was so caught up in my thoughts about Sai that I almost forgot that Chamuka and Nayan were living in my kol with me now.

Pulling back the flap of the kol I quietly stepped inside, and relieved to find that both Chamuka and Nayan had already gone to bed; I quietly got undressed and climbed into my bed next to Chamuka and promptly fell asleep.

In the morning I awoke to find Chamuka still fast asleep by the side of me. I glanced across at Nayan and she was obviously still asleep too. I didn't want to disturb either of them, so as silently as was humanly possible, I pulled on my trousers, grabbed my tunic, boots, weapons, and a horse harness. And after untying the flap covering the kol doorway; I pulled on my boots and wandered down to the family paddock, harnessed my horse, and went for little early morning ride around our settlement. I suppose if I'm totally honest, I was half hoping that I might see Sai up and about somewhere, but when he was nowhere to be seen, I very nearly caved in and went to pay him a visit, but at the very last minute my stubborn pride managed to get the better of me yet again.

"No…damn him! He should come to me," I said out loud to myself.

And with that, I gave my horse a sharp kick, and galloped off again in the opposite direction. When I eventually returned to my kol, I found Chamuka and Nayan preparing breakfast in my absence. This still felt really strange to me, as although I'd known both of them for many years, one of them was now my wife…and I'm not sure what the other one was supposed to be. I nodded to them both as I quietly removed my weapons, and walked over to my bed and sat down. They both carried on making breakfast in silence, so after removing my boots I sprawled out on my bed for a little while. It felt so nice to be able to stretch out on my own bed again. I could feel them both watching me, so glancing across at them, I raised my eyebrows and I gave them both a little smile. They both smiled back at me in return and began to giggle. This new arrangement was going to take some getting used to.

Chamuka dished out my breakfast and carried it over to me, and then both of them went and sat down over on the left side of the kol to eat theirs. They had been brought up to do this, and still didn't realise that Scythian women usually ate with their men. This was going to take time…and a whole heap of patience.

Several weeks had now past, and my marriage to Chamuka still hadn't been consummated. I guess part of the problem was that I still thought about Sai, and another part of the problem was that both Chamuka and Nayan had taken to sleeping in my bed. So I was presently sleeping in Nayan's bed…alone! I think Chamuka must have said something to my mother about us not having consummated the marriage, and my mother in turn must have told my father; as one day he actually came right out with it, and asked me if I'd had sex with either one of them yet, and he'd done so in such a notably sarcastic manner that I was left in do doubt that something must have been said. And when I told him that I hadn't got around to it yet, he just shook his head and tutted disapprovingly.

"Well, you'd better get on with it, son," he said. "Your uncle will be expecting you to have both of them pregnant by the end of the year."

"Well, he can hope all he wants to; I'm only married to one of them, and that marriage will be consummated when I decide the time is right," I retorted back at him.

"Please yourself – but don't be at all surprised if he starts to get on your case," he said, walking off tutting to himself.

And so the situation continued, that is until Chamuka must have finally realised that if anything was ever going to happen, she would have to be the one to instigate it. So one night she quietly crept into what was supposed to be Nayan's bed and began cuddling up to me and…Well…let's just say I warmed to her advances, and so after almost three months of being married, our marriage was finally consummated. And although I have to admit that at first it was purely lust on my part, I began to realise that slowly over the course of time, I was actually developing real feelings for Chamuka, and dare I say it – I was beginning to fall in love with her.

And as remarkable as it may sound – not once during the whole of this time, had I seen or heard anything from Sai, I still missed him though, and I finally realised that he was never going to come to me…how could he in the circumstances? And I knew that if I wanted to see him, I was just going to have to swallow my pride and go and find him.

So one evening, I made my excuses to Chamuka, and I left under the cover of darkness with the full intention of paying Sai a visit. I didn't have a clue how he was going to react, and as I approached the entrance to his kol I could feel my anxiety levels rising by the second. So before calling out to him, I just waited outside for a few moments trying to compose myself, but it was no good…I felt so nervous that I almost turned around and walked away again, but somehow I managed to find my voice and I called out his name. There was no reply; so deeply disappointed I was just about to walk away, when he pulled back the flap of the doorway and just stood there staring at me.

"Well…can I come in," I asked him, still feeling nervous of what his reaction might be. Sai took a step backwards to allow me to enter, so edging past him I walked straight over to his bed and sat down. He followed on after me and also sat on his bed. He still hadn't said a single word, and I wished that he'd just say something…anything! As now that he was actually sitting here right in front of me, it was hard to find the right words to express exactly what I wanted to say.

"I …I just…I wanted to…" Our eyes met, and I really wanted to reach out and touch him. It had been just over three months since the last time that I'd seen him, and I could see that he'd lost weight during this time.

"I've missed you," was finally all that I could think of to say.

"I've missed you too," he said, wiping away a single tear which was just beginning to trickle down his left cheek.

"The truth is – I don't think I can live without you," I said, moving a little closer to him. "Or I you," he said, giving me that slightly twisted grin of his which showed off his filed teeth, and which for some reason, always seemed to have a very odd effect on me…if you get what I mean?

"I'm so sorry…for everything," I said.

"Me too," he said, reaching out and touching the tiny scar which still remained as a token reminder of when he'd lost his temper and had hit me.

"Is that from where I hit you?" he asked me, looking surprised.

"Yes, but it's nothing I didn't deserve," I said nonchalantly shrugging it off.

"No, you didn't, Kai, I'm so sorry that I lost my temper with you. I should never have lost control like that."

"It doesn't matter now – forget about it – it's all in the past," I said, resting my hand on top of his.

One thing had led to another, and several hours later, I realised that if I didn't want to raise the question of where I'd been all night, I would soon have to make my way back. Everything was a lot more complicated now. And if trying to keep my relationship with Sai a secret from my uncle hadn't already been challenging enough in the past, with things the way they were now, it was going to be even more difficult than ever before.

Reaching the doorway to my kol, I quietly crept in, got undressed, and slipped into bed next to Chamuka. She appeared to be fast asleep; so doing my best not to wake her, I gently tugged at the blanket until I'd just about managed to cover myself, and I finally drifted off to sleep.

The very first thing that Chamuka did come the morning was to ask me where I'd been last night, so I told her that it was Agari business and I couldn't say. Well…I wasn't exactly lying, was I?

Chamuka tutted to herself and walked off to help Nayan prepare breakfast. She was very sensitive, and I knew that it was going to be very difficult to keep my relationship with Sai hidden from her, and as I watched her place a skillet over the hot stones in the centre of the fire, I hated myself for having to deceive her like this.

"Merren came to see you last night. He asked us where you were," said Chamuka, leaving the skillet to heat up for a little while. "I told him that I didn't know; so he waited here for a little while, and then he left saying that he'd call back some other time."

"Did he tell you what he wanted?" I asked her.

"I think it would better if he told you," said Chamuka, obviously not wanting to give anything away.

"Fair enough," I said, modestly pulling on my trousers from under the cover of the blanket. "There's something else you should know," said Chamuka, sitting down by the side of me. "I'm pregnant."

"What? …Well that didn't take very long," I responded with some surprise; as it had only been a few weeks since we'd consummated our marriage.

"Are you sure?" I asked her.

"Yes, I'm pretty sure."

"Well, in that case, it's excellent news," I said, giving her a warm hug.

I was really curious as to what Merren wanted, and I was far too impatient to wait for him to come to see me, so I decided to go and pay him a visit instead. It would be a lot easier for us to talk in the privacy of his kol, and I could also inform him about my reconciliation with Sai, as well as Chamuka being pregnant all at the same time. So taking a brisk walk up to Merren's kol, I did the usual thing of calling out from outside.

"Come on in, Kai," I heard him shout back to me.

Merren who had been resting on his bed immediately sat up to greet me, and as we both knew why I was here, he wasted no time in getting straight to the point.

"What's your relationship with Nayan Kai?" he asked, rubbing his chin.

"Why?" I asked, intrigued by why he would ask me such a thing.

"Just curious that's all. Well…actually its more than just curiosity, I need to know because if you're not having a sexual relationship with her, and you don't plan on making her wife number two, then I'd very much like to start seeing her."

"Whoa…hold on for a minute, Merren…before you get any ideas. I know you…or had you forgotten! And anyway – it doesn't work like that. Do you realise that you're actually going to have to get permission directly from my uncle before you can even think of going anywhere near her, and then it's not just seeing her; you'd have to marry her. And no, I've not had sex with her…and even though she's a good woman, I don't plan on making her wife number two either."

"Hmm," said Merren thoughtfully. "The thing is, Kai, I've been thinking a lot lately that it's probably about time I settled down with a good woman, and who knows…maybe even have a few kids. It can get a bit cold at night, and sometimes I could really do with a good woman to keep me warm…you know what I mean. Nayan is very beautiful, and if you don't want her…then I do!" I had to admit that if Merren were to marry Nayan, it would certainly solve the problem of having her living in my kol. It wasn't that I didn't like her – she was a lovely woman. It just wasn't an ideal situation that's all, and one that I really didn't think was going to be very suitable in the long term.

"Well, if that's the case I suppose we'll just have to go and have a little chat with my uncle. There's a blood connection between us, so I can't see my uncle would have a problem with you marrying Nayan. Have you actually asked her yet?"

"Well no! Of course not. But I did tell her that she was very pretty, and if she wasn't with you, I'd like her to be with me."

"You did what? …Well, that explains the look that Chamuka and Nayan gave each other when I asked them what you wanted. It would have been all the same if I 'had' been planning on making her wife number two though wouldn't it?" I said, narrowing my eyes at him.

"I have to be honest with you, Kai – it beats me why you wouldn't. But there you go – everyone to their own I guess," he said, shrugging his shoulders.

"Which leads me on to the subject of Sai and me – we're back together again. Oh…and Chamuka is pregnant."

"I have to hand it to you, Chief – you don't do anything by halves do you?"

"Tell you what…why don't you call around later and ask Nayan if she'd like to marry you, and then if she says yes, I'll make all the necessary arrangements for us to go and have talks with my uncle."

Later on that evening, Nayan accepted Merren's proposal of marriage. So a trip was specially arranged so that Merren could personally ask my uncle for his permission to marry Nayan. My uncle appeared to be over the moon by Merren's request to marry his niece, and immediately gave Merren his blessings. And so the marriage of Nayan and Merren went ahead, and now finally, Nayan could settle down in a home she could call her own, and with a man who truly appreciated her.

Time went by, and Trisha eventually gave birth to a baby girl, and Chamuka bore me a son. We named him Altan after our slain cousin. And shortly after that, Merren announced that Nayan was pregnant. Everyone was thrilled by the news, and as you can imagine my mother was in her element. My father joked that if this kept up at the rate that it was going – there would soon be more Huns living here than Scythians.

Nymadawa continued to live with Trisha and Aptien, she was settled and happy to remain where she was, and as long as she was happy with the arrangement then so was I. She knew I wasn't too far away, and she often came around for a visit and a chat.

Just over a year later, Chamuka gave birth to our second son. We named him Garenhir, in honour of the wisest man that I'd ever known.

During the whole of this time, I continued to maintain a secret relationship with Sai, and I quite often stayed with him overnight. Sai had eventually grown to accept that my position required me to marry, and to have children in order to keep the blood line going, and I always told Chamuka that the reason for my staying out all night was Agari business, and she soon learned not to question me any further on this. It was not always easy to conceal my relationship with Sai, but I'd done quite well up until one fateful night when Chamuka had unexpectedly turned up at Sai's kol after Altan had developed a fever, and as she didn't know where I was, she went looking for Sai instead. And in her panic, she had forgotten all about the Scythian tradition of first calling out from outside, and had just walked straight in and caught us fast asleep in bed together. Well obviously there wasn't going to be an easy way of explaining this one away. Chamuka just stood there with a look of total shock on her face, and then after momentarily gathering her thoughts together, just long enough for her to be able to explain that our son had a fever; she marched straight back out again.

"Ah…this is not looking good!" said Sai, holding his hands to his head.

"Oh well, it looks like I've got some serious explaining to do," I said, jumping out of bed and quickly getting dressed.

I raced after her, and I just about managed to catch up with her before we reached our kol. The look of utter disgust on her face spoke more a thousand words could ever hope to, and I knew that there wasn't going to be any point in trying to deny what had been going on.

"I know you hate me right now – but let's just see to our son first, and then if you can stand to look at me we can talk later," I said, holding the doorway of the kol open just enough for her to walk through.

Thankfully Altan's fever wasn't serious. He'd picked up a chill, and although it didn't give rise to a great deal of concern, you could never be too careful with very young children, as they could be very susceptible to this type of thing. So after I'd given Altan something to help bring down his temperature, and he'd finally settled down and fallen asleep, I asked Chamuka to sit down so that we could talk. She was obviously very upset by what she'd just seen, and who can blame her, and it took quite a while before she calmed down enough for me to be able to finally talk to her. I wasn't going to lie to her any longer – there wasn't any point, and I knew that I was just going to have to tell her the truth, and then I'd face up to the consequences afterwards.

Chamuka asked me loads of questions including how long I'd been a homosexual, and how long this thing had been going on between Sai and me etc. I tried to be as honest with her as I possibly could, and I told her that although I did love her…and I meant it! I also loved Sai, and that our relationship had been going on for many years, and I had no intention of ending it. This she found understandably very difficult to accept.

"How can you love me and love a man at the same time?" she yelled at me angrily.

I tried to explain to her that I wasn't homosexual, and that although I'd never had feelings for any other man but Sai, I must be 'bi-sexual', and it was obviously possible for me to love a woman or a man, and that I didn't just suddenly wake up one morning and decide to start having these kind of feelings, but that I must have been born this way. But I could see that she was having real problems understanding all of this.

"Look…I'll understand if you want to leave – I won't try and stop you," I eventually said to her.

"Oh! And where am I supposed to go? I can't very well go back to the Huns, can I? It would bring great shame on us all. And besides that…I happen to love you," she said tearfully. She didn't deserve this, and I genuinely felt so sorry for her right now, and surprisingly she allowed me to give her a hug.

"So does this mean you're not going to tell our uncle about this?" I asked her.

"No…of course not…how can I?" she answered, bursting into tears again and pushing me away.

"Damn you, Kai – I really do love you – but how am I supposed to just accept that you're having a relationship with a man?"

I knew that it wasn't going to be easy, but I figured that if Sai had learned to accept Chamuka, then Chamuka would in time learn to accept Sai.

To say that the next few weeks were difficult would be putting it mildly. So I thought that the best way for Chamuka to accept Sai was probably to get to know him. So one day I asked him to come around to my kol and meet her. This would be the first time that Sai and Chamuka had actually met each other properly. I'd recently been giving Sai lessons on speaking the Hunnic language, and Chamuka's Scythian was improving all the time, so I was quite sure that the language barrier wasn't going to be a problem at least. Sai had his reservations about all of this, but after a little manipulative persuasion on my part, he eventually came around to my way of thinking and finally agreed to give it a go.

When Sai arrived, I asked him to come in and sit down. This was the first time that he'd stepped foot inside my kol since I'd married Chamuka, and he looked quite surprised to see how much the decor had altered since his last visit. Chamuka automatically did what was expected of her, and immediately brought him over some refreshments, and ungracefully plonked them down in front of him. Sai thanked her, and without acknowledging his thanks, Chamuka turned to walk away, with the soul intention of finding herself a little corner somewhere to quietly hide away in.

"Chamuka…please come and sit with us," I asked her.

Chamuka stopped in her tracks, and obediently walked back over to where Sai and I were sitting, and very awkwardly joined us. Sai wasn't exactly looking very comfortable with the situation either. I wasn't expecting miracles, but I thought that if we could just get this first meeting over with, then everything would be a lot easier the second time around, and a whole lot easier for me to deal with as a whole. But sometimes the best laid plans don't always go as well as you'd like them to, and this was a lot more difficult than I'd imagined it would be, as neither Sai or Chamuka really knew what to say to each other, and even though I tried my best to instigate a conversation between the three of us, and Sai even paid Chamuka a compliment by telling her that he thought she was very pretty, it was painfully obvious that Chamuka was having a real problem with this whole situation, so in the end I spoke to her directly in her own language.

"Look Chamuka, I know that this isn't easy for you to accept Sai, but Sai has had to learn to accept you, and believe me when I tell you, he wasn't exactly happy about the situation at first either…see this scar," I said, pointing to my cheek. "Guess who gave it to me…and why? So even though I know how difficult this is for you – please try and be nice…eh."

"Don't push her, Kai…this isn't easy for either of us," said Sai.

"No, it's not easy at all," said Chamuka in Scythian, while glaring at me coldly.

"I'll tell you what," I said, rising to my feet. "Why don't I leave you both alone together, so that you can get to know one another, and then you can say whatever you want to each other without me interfering."

And with that, I walked out of the kol and waited outside for a while in order to gather my thoughts together. I really didn't want to go back in, but I knew that I couldn't stand here all night either, so I decided to take a walk over to Sai's kol just to clear my head a little.

Arriving at Sai's kol, I stretched out on his bed, and before too long I had become so deeply immersed in thoughts about my crazy complicated life, that for the very first time, I actually began to look deep within myself for an answer to all of this, and I wondered what enlightened words of wisdom Garenhir would have had for me right now, and I also wondered if he missed all of us just as much as we all missed him. I'd been thinking a lot lately about what he'd said to me about the premonitions that he'd had concerning the fate of our people here, and that it wouldn't happen in my lifetime 'if' I decided to remain here. So did that mean that if I'd gone with him it 'would' happen in my lifetime? This sounded very much like a warning to me, and I really wished that I had questioned him on this when I'd had a chance to. But there would be no words of wisdom from Garenhir today, so I was just going to have to work it all out for myself. So with a sigh, I stood up and made my way back to my kol to see how Sai and Chamuka were getting along.

You can imagine how relieved I felt to find Sai and Chamuka sat quietly talking to one another.

The only thing that bothered me slightly was that they stopped talking just as soon as they noticed me. I suspect that after discovering just how much they actually had in common, finding a suitable topic of conversation wasn't going to be all that difficult, and I had the distinct feeling that the subject matter might have been me. No doubt they both felt a certain amount of satisfaction at having finally found someone to talk to who was genuinely understanding of their situation. Ironic really!

Neither of them said a single word to me as I sat down to join them, and totally ignoring the fact that I was there, they proceeded to engaged in trivial small talk, which was obviously just a cover up, due to the fact that I was intruding on their 'real' topic of conversation.

"I'm really glad to see that the two of you are getting on so well," I said, standing up again. "But I have some business to take care of, so…I'll see you both a bit later."

I was about to take a stroll down to the river when my eyes were beset by a vision so astonishing to my senses, that I could barely believe what I could see, as heading straight towards me was Gaidres dressed in the uniform of the Italian soldiers. Gaidres rode right up to me, and with a slight air of arrogance, and an obvious display of misplaced pride, he looked down at me from the height of a fine white steed.

"Ah…Kai, you're the very person I need to talk to, he said with a slight but noticeable air of arrogance."

Gaidres hadn't come here alone; he was accompanied by a troop of Italian soldiers, who were presently being entertained by my father. Their visit had been unexpected, and I certainly wasn't prepared for this. Seeing Gaidres sat on that horse, and wearing those clothes actually had the effect of making me feel physically sick. How could he do this knowing what the Italians had done? Here was a man who I had once trusted and called my friend, proudly dressed in the uniform of my sworn enemy, and displaying himself to me like a Stag during the rutting season. There are no words to adequately describe exactly how I was feeling right now, and how I managed to control the urge to vomit I will never know. On the outside I'd managed to feign the appearance of repose, but inside I could sense the rising of a tempestuous storm.

"Follow me," was all that I could bring myself to say to him.

Gaidres dismounted and followed me into the privacy of Sai's kol. I showed no outward sign of emotion or anger, nor did I question or show any interest in his new found status and choice of company.

"Sit down, Gaidres," I said to him coldly.

Gaidres sat down, and I immediately sat down facing him. I just sat there blankly staring at him with my arms folded, and patiently awaited whatever it was he wanted to say to me. And if seeing him dressed in the uniform of my enemy wasn't difficult enough, what he said next was even harder…

"Kai – we've been friends for many years now," he said casually. "And I understand that what happened in the past between yourself and a few miscreant Italian soldiers didn't set you off on a good start, but don't you think that it's about time that you got over the past and buried your old grievances once and for all. I'm not going to beat about the bush, I've been asked to come here today and have a chat to you about allowing the Italians access to your trading posts, as it would seem that you've successfully prevented them from trading from around fifteen separate locations. And if you agree to lift your restrictions, they are willing to offer you much in return, and you are also cordially invited to come to Italy as an honoured guest of the senate, and to become accustomed with some of the fine luxury that would be freely given to you as an ally of the Italian consul."

So they could slit my throat more like it. I could hardly believe what I was hearing. This wasn't the Gaidres I used to know; I honestly thought that he must have finally lost his senses, so I decided to play him along and see what else he came out with.

"Hmm…Well, I'll have to give it some thought," I said, all the while doing my level best to keep my real feelings safely hidden.

I decided that my best tactic was to continue to humour him for a little while, just to see where this was heading.

"Well…I must say you look a lot different to the last time we met. So how are you getting along with your new position in the Italian army?"

"Things have been going really well for me recently, and they could be for you too, Kai. Come to Italy – you'll see. They have so many wonderful things there, much better than what you have here – Join me!"

"Join him," he said. I would rather gouge out my own eye balls with a hot poker, than to sell myself to the Italians for a few shallow luxuries.

"Maybe," I said, knowing damn well that I had absolutely no intention of ever giving it so much as a passing thought.

"If I were you, I wouldn't wait too long to make your mind up," he said, in a really condescending tone of voice. "You won't get another offer like this again in a hurry."

Even if he had lost his mind, he was really beginning to seriously irritate me now, and I just wanted to knock some sense into him, and I knew just how to go about it.

"Enough of all that for now...how do you fancy a sparring session? – We haven't done that for ages. Let's see if your skills have improved since you began working for my enemy...sorry...I mean the Italians. Perhaps you've learnt a few new sword techniques that you can teach me."

"Well – I don't know if...if I should now that I'm..." But before he could finish, I interrupted him.

"Come on Gaidres – or aren't you allowed to spar with me anymore? Or perhaps being in the Italian army has turned you soft."

"Okay – come on then...I'll show you who's turned soft," he said, quickly standing up and walking towards the exit of Sai's kol.

I knew that his pride would eventually get the better of him. We briskly made our way over to the practice area where we removed all of our weapons, and placed them down on the ground over in the far corner just as we had done so many times before. Gaidres also removed the helmet that he was wearing, and placed it carefully down on top of his weapons. We each picked up a blunt practice sword, and adopted the traditional Scythian defensive stance facing one another.

"Come on then Gaidres – let's see what you can do then shall we," I said with a glint in my eye. As he lunged towards me with his blunted sword, I blocked his blow with some force, and as he stumbled backwards I quickly moved in towards him, hooked my foot around his ankle, and delivered a sharp blow to his chin with my right elbow. He went sprawling to the ground, and I stood poised above him with my practice sword pointing at his throat.

"Come on...get up...or is that the best that you can do," I said, giving him a little kick. Gaidres suddenly reached out, and grabbing me by the foot, he managed to unbalance me by kicking my other foot from under me. But unfortunately for him, this only resulted in me landing on top of him.

"Gaidres you'd be dead by now if this was for real," I said, pushing the edge of my practice sword against his throat.

I had made my point, and tossing the wooden sword to the side, I was just about to get off him, when he grabbed me by my braided hair and yanked me back down again. But this time I purposely brought my elbow down into his face bloodying his nose. And wrenching my hair free from his hand, I quickly jumped to my feet again, leaving him stunned and bloody, still lying there defeated and humiliated upon the ground. It was never my intention to cause him any physical harm, and I did feel a bit guilty about his nose.

"I'm sorry Gaidres, but you really did need to come down off that high horse of yours and touch the earth again. And you can tell your Italian buddies that they can all go and burn in the fires of Gehenna for all I care. They can't afford me, and I'm really not interested in their pompous shallow luxuries," I said, quickly gathering up my weapons and briskly walking off.

"You're going pay for this, Manu Kai," he shouted after me.

"I've already paid in advance," I responded, not bothering to look back.

35

Dreams and Visions

Several years had passed since then, and the icy grip of a cold dark winter was finally drawing to a close. For months now we had all been confined to the solitary prisons of our own kol's, and everyone was overjoyed to see the first signs that it was finally beginning to thaw. The conditions had been particularly harsh this year, and had caused a great deal of suffering for our people. The rivers had all frozen over making fishing very difficult, and the howling winds and biting cold, had made it practically impossible to go hunting for fresh meat. And even though during the more plentiful months, we were always mindful of the need to preserve and to store such things as grain, dried fruits, and dried and smoked meat and fish in our underground store house; with so many mouths to feed it was still not enough to carry us through, and as a result we had no choice other than to slaughter many of our live-stock; as not only did we need the meat, but we were unable to sustain large herds, as we only had a limited amount of grain on which to feed them, and our horses always took priority over the rest of our livestock; as without our horses we would never have been able to survive. The winters seemed to get harsher every year, and this one was without doubt the worst that I could remember.

The first rays of sunshine were just beginning to penetrate through the shadowy gloom of winter, and the snow was melting fast. You could hear the crackling of the ice as it began to break away from the side of the kol. One crack was so loud that it managed to wake me from my slumbers, so rising from the security and warmth of my bed; I tentatively peered outside from the protective cover of my kol. The sudden unexpected brightness momentarily blinded me, and forced me to close my eyes. The shrill cry of an eagle soaring high above me, sliced through the stillness of the morning like a hot knife through soft butter, and with shielded eyes, I gazed upwards and watched the eagle soaring high above me as she surveyed the ground below, hoping for a chance of spotting a meal; some little furry creature that was still a little woozy after having recently woken from a long hibernation perhaps. I suddenly felt an overwhelming urge to go hunting myself. The horses should be able to get through the snow now, and the denser parts of the forest would have remained relatively clear of snow due to the protective covering of the trees. So grabbing my clothes, I quickly got dressed and popped around to see if Merren was up for it.

"Wake up…lets go hunting," I shouted out to him. After which, I did exactly the same thing to Aptien, and to several other warriors in turn.

After having been forced to stay cooped up inside the protective warmth of our kol's for months on end, everyone was more than a little enthusiastic for the opportunity to get out and hunt again. We had all felt like caged animals for months, so we just couldn't wait for the first opportunity to escape. So after we were all suitably kitted out, we harnessed up our horses, plus several pack horses just in case, and headed straight off towards the forest.

As soon as we arrived, the very first thing that we did was to make a fire, to give ourselves a chance to warm ourselves and rest for a while, before splitting up into two's and three's for the hunt. Each of us ate just enough of the dried meat and dried fruit that we had brought along with us to sustain ourselves until later this evening. So after extinguishing the fire, we split into four small groups, and headed off in different directions. And using this spot as our point of reference, we would all return here later on; hopefully laden with the fruits…or should I say the 'meat' of our efforts.

I had obviously chosen Merren and Aptien as my hunting partners, so the three of us wasted no further time in engaging ourselves in hot pursuit of a herd of deer. This was no easy task, as their sense of hearing and smell was so acute, that you had to hunt them with the stealth of a wild cat coupled with the cunning of the wolf.

After about an hour of searching for any signs that deer had come this way, we finally found some fresh droppings, which meant that they couldn't be all that very far away. So not wanting to alert the deer of our presence; we all picked up some of the droppings and rubbed then liberally into our clothes skin and hair. This might sound like a pretty disgusting thing to do, but this was done to camouflage our scent, and when you are hunting for more than just the leisurely pleasure that some people seem to reap from killing animals just for fun, it was vital that you do everything you can in order to enhance your chance of success.

There was a narrow river that ran straight through the centre of the forest, and a natural clearing that suddenly appeared from a dense thicket of trees, and if the herd had ventured down to the river to drink, it would be the perfect place for us to catch them out in the open, while we lay safely hidden within the forests leafy camouflage.

After tying our horses to some trees, we crouched down as low to the ground as we possibly could, and very cautiously approached the edge of the thicket before peering out between the cover of the trees. And there…right down by the river's edge was a small herd of deer. I silently signalled to Merren and Aptien to go and flank them from the other side. So they both quietly slipped back into the forest and made their way a little further on down the river. Meanwhile, I knelt down on the ground, and focussed my full attention on the herd. They could suddenly head this way at any moment, and I'd need to be ready with the sharp aim of my bow if they did. I hadn't been sat there all that long, when I heard a voice behind me quietly say my name. I turned around fully expecting to see either Merren or Aptien, but standing right before me was a man dressed in a long white robe. I was understandably startled by the sudden and unexpected appearance of this stranger, as I hadn't heard his approach, which made me feel all the more uncomfortable.

"Who are you?" I demanded to know, pointing a finely aimed arrow straight towards him.

"Manu Kai, please put down your bow, I really don't mean you any harm, and I do apologise if I startled you a little there," he said with a warm smile. "My name is Sirim. Your Derkesthai Garenhir was once a pupil of mine; he may possibly have mentioned me to you."

I was very confused, but yes, I did remember Garenhir mentioning him on several occasions. I instantly lowered my bow, and I asked him how he got here.

"That's really not important, Manu Kai, but my message to you is – so listen very carefully as I don't have much time. You are presently the keeper of the Agari ritual grail, but very soon some young warriors from the Alani tribe will come seeking you. One of them is called 'Egil' his name means 'sword' and he will be fair of complexion and tall in stature. You must give him the Grail as it contains a secret inscription, and his task is to prevent it from falling into the wrong hands. He will know what to do with it. I don't expect you to just follow these instructions blindly and without question Manu Kai, so in order to prove to yourself you are doing the right thing, you must choose a question that only

411

you will know the answer to, and you must keep this question a secret, and tell no one either the question or the answer. And then when the warriors from the Alani tribe arrive, you must ask the one who comes seeking the Grail whose name is 'Egil' your question, and if he answers it correctly – you can be sure that he is the one who has been chosen to keep your grail safe from harm."

"Blessings be upon you, Manu Kai," said Sirim, raising his right hand out towards me. And then right before my eyes he slowly began to fade away.

"Wait! I need to ask you something," I said. But it was already too late, and his image continued to fade until he had completely disappeared!

There were so many things that I would have loved to have asked him – but I didn't even get the chance to ask one single question. So sighing to myself, I turned back around again to face the herd of deer down by the river, and before I barely had a chance to gather my thoughts together, I realised that the herd was now heading full speed straight towards me. I quickly drew my bow…aimed…and loosed my arrow. I'd managed to bring one down, quickly followed by another, and then another. I'd managed to bring down a total of three; which was pretty good going by anyone's standards. Merren and Aptien turned up shortly afterwards and nodded in approval.

"Job well done, I'd say, but I don't have a clue what spooked them into running in your direction, as it wasn't us. When they all took off and headed straight towards you, we were both hoping you hadn't fallen asleep," said Merren, scratching the back of his neck.

After gutting the deer, we dragged them over to where we had left our horses earlier, and secured them one to each of three of the pack horses. And feeling very proud of ourselves for having had such a successful hunt, we headed back to our point of rendezvous to find that some of our hunting party had also been lucky, and had returned before us fully laden with all manner of game, and in our absence they'd lit a very welcoming fire, with several wild fowl presently roasting away on spits. It had been a while since we'd tasted wild game, and the smell of them cooking was a real delight to the senses.

It was still bitterly cold for the time of the year, so along with Merren and Aptien, I joined our hunting comrades who were all huddled around the warmth of the fire. And as soon as the rest of our party had safely returned, we all headed back home again. None of us could wait for the chance to share our bounty with members of our family and friends, and as was the custom of our people, we also shared out a third of our bounty amongst those who for one reason or another, were unable to go out and hunt for their selves.

As soon as we returned home, I handed my personal share of the meat over to Chamuka, and lay down on my bed for a well-deserved rest. I'd obviously drifted off to sleep, as I suddenly awoke with a start after having a really strange dream in which Garenhir was telling me that I needed to remember to control my emotions, and not to seek answers from those who nurture the seeds of deceit. It was one of those dreams that you just know contains an important message, and I knew that I needed to take it very seriously. It wasn't the first disturbing dream that I'd had lately, and I knew deep down that these dreams were a warning of my impending death, but the fact that I was having these warnings in the shape of dreams, was also an indication that I was being given a chance to alter the course that my life was currently heading towards.

I was still feeling groggy when I heard my daughter Nymadawa calling to me from outside the kol. I called back to her to enter, and she lifted up the flap of the kol and walked inside.

"Father...there are three Alanic warriors in our village – and they're asking for you," she said, looking puzzled.

Remembering Sirim's words during the hunting trip, I said to Nymadawa: "Please go and direct them here. Tell them I'll be waiting for them."

"Uh-umm...they're already waiting just outside father. I don't know who told them where to find you."

"Oh...right! OK!" I said, quickly bringing myself to my senses.

Still feeling a little disorientated by my dream, I asked Chamuka if she wouldn't mind taking our sons over to Aptien and Trisha, and to remain there with them until I'd sent word for them to return.

Nymadawa gave Chamuka a hand to quickly grab our sons, after which they all made their way over to Aptien and Trisha's kol. I followed them outside, and was immediately confronted with the impressive sight of three Alanic Warriors on horseback; one of whom immediately dismounted and introduced himself as Egil. He fitted the description that Sirim had given me in the forest exactly. He had long – almost white blond hair, and very pale skin and pale blue eyes. He looked to be approximately the same height as Merren, so he must have been at least 6ft 3, and although I tried very hard not to notice...he was also strikingly attractive in appearance.

"I'm Manu Kai," I said, looking up at him.

"I know!" he said, holding out his hand in a gesture of friendship.

I reciprocated, and we both grasped hold of one another's hands to show that we already considered each other to be a friend. I asked him to follow me inside my kol, and he asked me if I minded if his friends joined us. I said that I didn't, so Egil spoke to his two companions in a language I didn't understand, and they both proceeded to follow us inside.

I suddenly remembered that I was supposed to ask him a question that no one but me would know the answer to, but instead of asking him the question that I had previously chosen, I decided to change it at the last moment.

"Egil – I'm supposed to ask you a question…So tell me my friend. What was the question I was going to ask you?"

Of course if he could tell me what my question was, that would also be the correct answer to the question itself. Egil smiled at me and said:

"The question that you were going to ask me was: 'What am I holding in my hand?' But you were unable to reach the object without me seeing, so you decided to ask me what the question was going to be instead."

"That's exactly right. Do you know what the object was going to be?" I asked him, curiously. "I would only have known the answer to that question, if it had been the correct answer to the question you actually asked me," he said, smiling.

"Hmm…impressive…would you like to know what the object was going to be," I asked him. "Yes, I must admit – I would be interested to know."

"It was going to be a lock of my murdered son's hair, which I'd cut from his head just before he was buried with his mother, after they were both brutally murdered by Italian soldiers," I said, turning away from him.

Egil immediately stopped smiling, and he gave me a look of genuine sympathy instead, and then turning to face his companions, he spoke to them in their own language, I knew that he had told them what I'd just said by the way they both looked at me.

"Please, sit down," I said, making a gesture of my hand. "I'll arrange for some food and refreshments to be brought to you."

As I stepped outside my kol, I almost walked straight into Merren and Aptien. They had obviously got word that there were three Alanic strangers here, and the pair of them were now hanging around outside – no doubt itching to know what was going on as usual.

"What's going on, Chief?" asked Merren concerned.

"Is everything okay?" – asked Aptien, while straining to catch a glimpse of the strangers through the slightly open flap of the kol entrance.

"Yes, everything's fine – there's nothing to worry about," I said reassuringly.

"What do they want?" asked Aptien…still straining to get a better look at them.

Although I understood their curiosity, I didn't really have time for this right now.

"Look…I really can't talk to you right now; we can have a chat later. But if you really want to help, you can go and tell Chamuka to come and prepare food and refreshments for my guests. Go…go!" I said, hurrying them on their way.

"OK! OK! And then we'll come straight back and wait outside just in case you need us for anything else," said Merren, blatantly staring in through the flap of the kol at my rather unusual guests, who were just sat quietly talking amongst themselves.

Merren and Aptien left to go and fetch Chamuka, and I was about to walk back into my kol when I noticed my father approaching in the distance. He was also accompanied by three warriors, so he'd obviously got word of the presence of my three unexpected visitors too, and was also understandably curious as to what was going on. So before I went back into the kol, I stood and waited for him to reach me.

"Don't worry…everything's fine," I said, seeing the concerned look on his face. "Believe it or not – this is actually Agari business."

"Oh…well, I suppose that means you're not going to tell me what's going on then. Do I at least get to know who they are?" he asked, curiously.

I really couldn't see what harm there was in letting my father know who they were, so I told him that they were Alanic warrior priests, and I had some Agari business to sort out with them, and that was all there was to it, so he really didn't have any reason to be concerned.

"I'll introduce you to them if you want me to."

"Yes, please do," he said, already heading for the doorway of my kol.

I quickly followed after him. My Alanic guests stood up as soon as we entered, and I proceeded to introduce my father to the three of them. Egil then translated what I'd said to his two companions, before the three of them respectfully bowed to my father, and Egil very eloquently introduced himself and his two comrades; saying that they were all very honoured to meet him, and I could tell that my father was suitably impressed by their impeccable manners, and he nodded approvingly before politely excusing himself and leaving me to get on with it. No sooner had he left than Chamuka arrived, so after first introducing her as my wife, I asked her if she wouldn't mind fixing them something to eat. And while she was doing that, I fetched them some fresh water, before asking them if they'd like a tour of our village while food was being prepared. Egil translated everything that I'd said to his two companions before giving me an answer.

"That would be very nice – thank you."

I proceeded to give them a guided tour, after which we all sat down together and ate the meal that Chamuka had prepared. I asked Egil if they intended to stay the night, but he said that he was very grateful for the offer of such kind hospitality, but they were planning to continue on with their journey shortly after we had taken care of the business that they had come for.

"Well, if that's the case, I suppose we had better get on with it then," I said, rising to my feet. Egil said something to his men, after which he turned to me and said: "They will wait for us here…I am the only one that's supposed to come with you to the place that you've hidden the Grail."

"Okay – well, you'd better ask them to wait outside then if that's the case," I said, sitting back down again.

I'd already asked Chamuka if she wouldn't mind leaving again after we had all eaten, so after Egil had asked his men to go and see to their horses, I walked over to a row of earthenware receptacles that were hanging loosely from the inner wooden structure of the kol, and I untied one of them and handed it to Egil. He stared at it for a few moments…and then…it suddenly dawned on him.

"You've covered it in clay. Ah…hidden in plain sight…I like it!" he said with a broad smile.

"Do you mind me asking you what you're going to do with it?" I asked him.

"I don't know what we have to do with it yet, but I do know that we have to travel to India, where we will be met by a holy man who will lead us to where we have to go. And just like the Grail – we must carefully disguise ourselves so that we don't attract any unnecessary attention, as looking the way that we do, I think we might stand out a bit."

"That's not a problem; we have plant dyes that can be used to darken your skin and hair, and if you want we can even make you look like lepers; no one's going to bother you then."

"Excellent idea," he said, "Lepers we are then."

I gave Egil a plain hemp drawstring bag, and after placing the grail inside, he tied it tightly before casually throwing it over his right shoulder.

"I'll let my companions know of the plan to disguise ourselves as lepers, and as soon as you can make arrangements for our transformation to begin…we will be ready and waiting."

"Egil…Do you mind if I ask you how you knew the answer to my question? And how on earth did you know to come here looking for me? Where are you getting you're instruction?"

"Probably from the same source as you Manu Kai – in visions and dreams, which I know I have to follow. I don't know the outcome, or why I've been chosen to carry out this task, or even what it's all about. All I know is that for whatever reason I must do this…so I will, and I'll do it to the best of my ability. I just have to trust that we will meet up with friends along the way…just like your good self, who will be able to offer us advice or assistance if we should need it."

"Let's hope so. Come on then, I think we'd better get on with turning you all into lepers. The Derkesthai here has a wonderful selection of plant dyes that can be used to colour your hair and skin, and he should be in his kol right now…so why don't you fetch your companions, and we'll take a stroll up to see him," I said, collecting all the dirty drinking cups and dishes into one pile. We left the kol, and met up with Egil's two comrades who were waiting outside, and the four of us took a stroll up to see if we could locate Sai. When we reached Sai's kol, I asked the three Alanic priests to wait outside for a moment while I entered alone. Luckily Sai was inside preparing one of his herbal concoctions, and he was currently involved with the task of grinding up some tree bark. He already had some idea of what was going on, as I'd already told him all about my vision in the forest, so all I had to do was to quickly explain to him what I needed him to do.

I asked the three warrior priests, who had been patiently waiting outside to come in, and after all the formal introductions had been made, Sai immediately set about preparing a mixture of plant dyes, that would ensure a good temporary light brown shade, to disguise our three Alanic friends very pale skin and fair hair. After which, we set about the task of transforming our three unusual guests from impressively attractive Alanic Warrior Priests, into miserable looking leper outcasts. And believe me – by the time we had finished with them, not even their own mothers would have recognised them. Then with the final touch of providing each of them with an old well-worn woollen blanket with which to wrap around themselves, and a few fake bloody looking bandages wrapped around their hands; they looked every part the unapproachable leper. No one in their right mind would ever want to steal a dirty old clay grail from a leper...

After Egil and his companions had finally left our village with the Agari ritual Grail, I flopped down on Sai's bed and sighed deeply.

"Kai, I need to talk to you about something," said Sai, sitting down next to me.

I could tell by the serious look on his face that whatever it was he had to say to me must have been pretty important.

"Yes, okay – go ahead – I'm listening," I said, intrigued by what he had to say.

Sai knew that I was probably feeling a little stressed out by what had just taken place, so he climbed up behind me and began to massage my shoulders.

"Kai – I've been having really strange dreams about you," he said, pausing for a moment. "I think you need to be really careful, there's no other way to say this, but I think there may be an attempt to assassinate you. I've had the same dream three times now, but I just can't seem to see who the perpetrator is. In each of my dreams the nationality of the perpetrator is different." "Hmm, I know, I've been having similar dreams too, and to be quite honest with you, if my time to die is soon...then so be it! I'm so tired of all the conflict, I could do with the rest to be honest, and talking of which...I really need to sleep now," I said, curling up on his bed.

As I closed my eyes, I forced every thought of today from my mind, and very soon I felt myself drifting off into a deep sleep.

36

My Final Nemesis

At last the cold spell was over, and we had just received a twice-yearly delivery of rare herbs and opium that had been brought to us all the way from China, which we paid for in gold nuggets. We collected the gold from our local river by securing sheep skins in certain positions in the shallower parts of the river, and then leaving them there for a couple of weeks in order to give them enough time to have gathered a goodly amount of specks of gold before removing them again. And then after hanging them to dry out for a few days, they would then be hung over large earthenware platters, and then one by one the sheepskins were sprinkled with oil and then set on fire. The little flakes of gold that had been caught up in the tangled wool, would then be released and fall into the dish; while the sheepskin burnt away to practically nothing. We could then gather up all the gold, and melt it into little nuggets which could then be used either for our own use, or for trade. There was quite a lot that needed to be done; the herbs and opium had to be either preserved or prepared in some way ready for use, and needless to say, Sai still felt a little uneasy about leaving me alone with the opium, but he really needn't have worried, as I'd managed to get my addiction to opium under control a long time ago, and there was no-way I was going back down the dark path of addiction again. But all the same – I could understand why Sai felt that it was still necessary to keep one of his beady little eyes on me.

Sai had really come into his own by now, and I'm sure Garenhir would be really proud of him if he could see just how far he'd come. Sai had turned out to be an excellent Derkesthai in every way, and he now had three young Agari apprentices of his own; plus, he was also teaching a young woman the healing arts; as he said she had very special and unique abilities, and he didn't think that it was fair not to help her to reach her full potential simply because she was female. And even though he couldn't take her on as a prospective member of the Agari, he could see no reason why he shouldn't teach her how to develop her latent skills. Apparently she had sought his wise counsel after becoming increasingly aware that she could see and hear things that others couldn't, and had asked him what he thought she should do. His answer was simply – "Become my pupil." One of Sai's pupils reminded me very much of myself when I was his age. His name was Aptya, and he was also very keen to learn the skills of a warrior, so I found it very natural to take him under my serpent wing…so to speak.

Although I had many eager young pupils who I regularly schooled in the art of the bow, sword, and even knife throwing, Aptya really stood out from the rest, and I could tell that he had the aptitude to become a great warrior one day, so I tended to push him a lot harder than any of the other children, not that he seemed to mind. I knew that he looked up to me as a role model, and although I probably pushed him a little too hard at times, he always took it in his stride and never complained. I think that even at his young age, he knew that I was only doing it because I recognised the potential in him.

Although my father was now in his early sixties, he was still a very fit man, and whatever the passage of time may have robbed him of in the way of physical prowess, it had surely been more than balanced by the ever-growing wisdom that age had bestowed upon him over the years. So he was quite happy and willing to continue to hold the position of Sha Pada.' And I'm glad to say that my uncle was doing equally as well, which of course suited me fine, as I could carry on with doing what I was really happy with, and that was being an Agari priest, and quietly teaching weaponry skills to thirty seven children of both sexes – including my own two sons, who I was always mindful to spend as much quality time with as I possibly could.

Things had quietened down as far as all the fighting was concerned, but I knew that this was most probably just another lull before the storm, as things could kick off again at any time. The only good thing about the very harsh weather conditions that we had been experiencing over the last few winters was that during this time, you could guarantee that there would be no attempts to usurp us from the land that our ancestors had once laid claim to hundreds of years ago…it was just too damn cold!

After spending several hours preparing a variety of compounds and tinctures, I gave Sai a hand to quickly clear everything away as one of Sai's pupils was due to arrive very soon, and I had promised that today I would take my two sons down to the river and teach them how to spear fish by wading into the shallower part of the river – standing very still until a fish swims up close – and allowing for the refraction of the sun light shining on the surface of the water, you would not aim directly at the fish, but slightly past it. This took a lot of practice, but it was a very useful survival skill to learn as your life could depend upon it one day. So I left Sai's kol to go and fetch my two sons who were most probably eagerly waiting for me by now, and sure enough, as I approached our kol they were both sat outside waiting for me. So after harnessing up our horses we rode down to the river, and then spent the best part of the afternoon trying to spear fish. I enjoyed teaching my sons how to hunt and fish, and they in turn enjoyed the opportunity to spend some quality time with me on these little trips of ours. So after a very pleasant afternoon, we returned home again to cook the fish that we'd all managed to catch. Well…technically speaking – neither of them had actually managed to spear one yet…but hay! It was a joint effort – they'd get the hang of it eventually. When we got back, my daughter Nymadawa was sat in our kol talking to Chamuka. Nymadawa had blossomed into a fine young woman over the years, and had recently married a young warrior called Tesyrian from our village. I was beginning to believe that she was never going to get married and settle down, so when Tesyrian had approached me for permission to court her, I gave him my full blessings. I barely had a chance to step through the doorway when Nymadawa jumped up and ran over to me, and then excitedly announced that I was going to be a grandfather. Well…that was one way of telling me that she was pregnant I suppose. I was really happy with the news, and I gave her a big hug. Chamuka took the fish outside to gut them, and Nymadawa's face began to slowly sadden, so I asked her what was wrong. "Oh! …It's nothing father!" she replied with a sigh.

"Well, something must be wrong…so come on…out with it."

"I just wish Mother could have been here to share my good news that's all. Auntie Trisha and uncle Aptien have been very good to me, and I really like Chamuka, but I can't help wondering what it would have been like if Mother and Kern hadn't gone to the forest that day," she said with such a sadness in her voice that I felt her pain like an arrow directed to my heart.

"It really doesn't do any good to dwell too much on what might have been Nymadawa. Things are as they are for a reason," I said, gently wiping away a tear that was trickling down the left side of her face. "A very wise man once told me this fact, but at the time, I found it impossible to accept what he was saying, as I could find no logical reason why your mother and your little brother should have been so brutally snatched away from us the way that they had. But over the years, I have come to understand that everything 'does' have a reason, and although it may be beyond our ability to comprehend that there really is no such thing as chance, it doesn't mean that it isn't true. Just because something is hard to understand Nymadawa – doesn't mean that it isn't so."

Nymadawa looked into my eyes and gave me a half smile, I held out my arms towards her and I gave her another hug.

"Your mother would have been very proud of you Nymadawa…almost as proud as me. I think you'll make a wonderful mother. It doesn't seem all that long ago that your mother told me that she was carrying you, and now here you are telling me the same thing," I said, reminiscing about the time that Tihanna had first informed me that 'she' was pregnant all those years ago, when she was still living with the Pa-ra-lati.

Meanwhile Chamuka had returned with the gutted fish, and she asked Nymadawa if she'd like to eat with us tonight as we had plenty to share, and if she did, to go and tell Tesyrian who was presently getting his first tattoo. Nymadawa said that she'd like that, so she walked over to where Tesyrian was having his tattoo done, and informed him that they'd be eating at her father's kol this evening. The tattooist had just about completed the first part of Tesyrian's tattoo, so Nymadawa waited there for him until they were finished for the day, and then made their way over to my kol together.

Sometimes Sai would join me and my family in the evenings, and he often ate with us. Sai was an excellent cook, and he regularly did the cooking for all of us, which suited Chamuka just fine, as in Hun tradition it was unheard of for a man to cook for a woman, so Chamuka enjoyed every minute of it. The arrangement benefited us all, as Sai genuinely enjoyed doing the cooking for everyone, and he truly appreciated the family atmosphere that being welcomed by Chamuka had allowed him to experience. My sons called him uncle Sai, but of course, they didn't really understand the true nature of our relationship, as I'd decided to leave any explanations until they were old enough to understand, and then only if it was ever relevant or necessary. Sai hadn't joined us this evening, as he'd been invited by the parents of one of his pupils to eat with them, and it would have been considered a great insult to them if he had refused without good reason.

After we had all eaten, and everything was washed and tidied away, it was already beginning to get quite late. So Nymadawa and Tesyrian left to make their way back to their own kol, while Chamuka began to get our sons ready to settle down for the night. I was feeling very tired after a long day, so after removing all my clothes I climbed straight into bed, and was just beginning to drift off to sleep when Chamuka lay down beside me and quietly whispered in my ear: "Kai – I'm pregnant!"

It took a few seconds for what Chamuka had just said to filter through, but when the reality behind her words had finally penetrated into my conscious mind I opened my eyes, and in the dim light of a single lamp which had not yet been extinguished, I turned to her and asked her if I'd just heard her tell me that she was pregnant.

"Yes, you did!" she said with a little smile. "I didn't want to say anything until Nymadawa had had a chance to tell you her news first."

"That's wonderful news," I said, snuggling up close to her.

However, I didn't sleep at all well that night, as I was plagued with vivid and disturbing dreams that once again continued to foretell my death. And although I kept seeing the same image in my dream over and over again, I was unable to make out any details, or to see the individual who would prove to be my final nemesis. It would seem that these details were to remain concealed from me. Death itself held no fear for me, so it wasn't dying which caused me so much concern. In fact, if truth be known – I'd actually welcome the rest that it would offer me. What really worried me was how my family might be negatively affected by my death…and now learning that there was yet another child on the way only heightened my concerns. Of course, I kept my fears hidden from Chamuka as there was no point in worrying her, but sometimes I wondered if I should say something, as then if anything did happen to me, at least she would be prepared.

My own dreams seemed to tie in with what Sai had told me about his dreams containing a mysterious assassin. The trouble was, because I knew it was coming but not exactly 'when' it was coming, I was constantly looking over my shoulder, and if there wasn't going to be anything that I could actively do to prevent it from happening, I would probably have been far better off not knowing about it. And as each new day began, I continued to be on my guard – always wondering if today was going to be the day.

Eventually three moons had passed by – and still there was no sign of my assassin, so slowly I began to relax a little. Maybe there had been some mistake, or perhaps something had happened to alter my fate somehow. I remember

Garenhir once telling me that although it does appear that some things are written in stone, many other things that we may experience, or encounter along the way are left unwritten, and our so called 'fate' may alter and change as we alter and change.

One morning after spending the night with Sai, I was woken to the sound of someone calling my name outside. I quickly got dressed and peered out through the kol doorway, and there standing outside was a young messenger who had been sent by my father to find me.

"Sha Pada wants to see you immediately," he said.

"OK – tell him I'll be along shortly," I replied with a yawn.

"It must be really important for your father to call for you so early – I hope everything's okay," said Sai, tying the golden sash around his waist which distinguished him as the Derkesthai of our village.

"So do I – I'll come back and let you know as soon as I can," I replied. And I promptly left and hastily made my way over to my father's kol.

Even though I got there as quickly as I could, I was still the last one to arrive. No one even bothered to ask me where I was, as there wasn't one man present who hadn't already guessed, as it wasn't as though my relationship with Sai was a secret any more…well, at least not in our village anyway.

"Ah, Manu Kai…well, that's everyone I think," said my father, clapping his hands loudly together in an attempt to bring everyone's attention back to the pending matter at hand, and away from me.

"Sorry to keep you all waiting," I said awkwardly as I walked over and took my rightful place at my father's side.

Merren and Aptien were both there looking at me with a knowing air of amusement at my obvious embarrassment. I was careful to avoid any eye contact with anyone; at least until the matter in hand was well under-way, and my some-what awkward moment was past tense.

My father asked us all to sit down, and we all seated ourselves on the cushions surrounding the low wooden table on the right hand side of the kol, a 'modus operandi' of the Huns, and one that my father had seen fit to incorporate into the way in which we conducted our own political meetings here in Scythia.

"Right!" he said rather loudly, "I've called you all here today to let you all know that I've received word that the Italians are back in the area, and by the sound of things they are very keen to resolve our differences and to re-kindle communication between us, with a mind to re-establishing our covenant of trade.

You will all recall Cornelius…and just in case you've forgotten…he's the Italian soldier who lived with us for a little over one cycle of the sun, in order to learn to speak our language. He's what they call a cavalry officer now – which basically means that he has risen to a higher status amongst his own people, and has earned himself some power and influence in the process. And he, along with an Italian envoy, and an accompaniment of Italian cavalry, will be visiting us in a couple of days for talks, and Cornelius will be acting as their appointed spokesman." There was a moment of stunned silence by all, and although I'd mellowed a lot over the years, I still found what my father had just said a very bitter pill to have to swallow. Cornelius had been the only Italian that had ever managed to earn my respect, but I still hadn't been able to forgive the Italians as a whole for the killing of my cousin, wife, and my son; or for all the mental pain and anguish that they'd managed to inflict upon me the last time that they were in this area. I looked across at Merren and Aptien, as I knew that both of them would have been watching my every reaction. I was doing my very best to remain calm, and they must have known that, so I just nodded to both of them to let them know that I was in control of my emotions, and I was not about to explode into an uncontrollable torrent of rage. I looked back towards my father who looked understandably apprehensive as he awaited my response.

"Is there anything else, Father, – as I'm sure you'll understand if I excuse myself right now," I said with such perfect manners, that no one would ever have guessed at the tsunami of anger that I was actually managing to hold back right now.

"That will be all for now, Manu Kai," he said with an obvious look of relief on his face.

"Thank you," I said respectfully bowing to him before making my exit.

Just before I left, I caught sight of my father subtly signal to Merren and Aptien to follow me outside, so with the speed and efficacy of an arrow at close range, they were both there at my side. My father knew me well enough to know that I may have taken the news very sedately on the outside, but what was going on under my apparent calm exterior may have been quite a different matter entirely, and my inclination towards impulsive autonomous behaviour, would have certainly given my father good cause for concern.

"How are you doing there, Chief?" asked Merren, doing his best to try and gauge my level of emotional distress.

"I'm not happy obviously! But I'm not planning an insurgence if that's what you were thinking."

"Well, that's a relief at least," said Merren, carefully studying my expression for any covert signs of impending wrath. "You seem to be taking this news very calmly, Chief, in fact a little too calmly…if you don't mind me saying."

"What do you mean by that? Are you implying that I have a hot temperament?" I said wryly. "Hmm…'Me' imply that 'you' have a bad temper. I wouldn't dare – you might hit me," he said with a stupid grin on his face.

"Yeah, very funny I'm sure," I said sarcastically.

"Look…all joking aside, Kai, we know how you must be feeling right now, so why don't we all head for mine and we can talk about it there, it'll give you a chance to get it off your chest…eh?"

"I'm okay…honest. I'm going to head straight back to Sai's, as I promised I'd let him know what's going on. Besides he gives a better shoulder massage than either of you two," I said, already beginning to walk off.

"Fair enough…just as long as you're not going to do anything we might all regret," said Merren, calling after me.

Merren waited until he thought I was well out of earshot before I heard him say to Aptien:

"He's not alright you know – he's taking this far too calmly for my liking." I never did get around to telling them about my exceptional hearing.

I didn't bother to respond to Merren's comment. Perhaps he was right to be worried…who knows, so I just kept right on walking until I reached Sai's kol where he had been patiently waiting for me to return. I told him what had been said during the meeting, and shaking his head in antipathy, he sighed and tutted to himself before asking me if I needed a tonic. Sai's tonics usually consisted of an herbal sedative which although fairly mild, was very useful in helping me to cope with very stressful situations.

A few days later, my father received word that the Italians would be arriving in a couple of days' time, so at least I had a little time to prepare myself, as I was going to have to somehow find the strength to be able to stomach their nauseating presence here once again. I'd always hoped that we had seen the last of their kind around these parts, but I guess that was just wishful thinking on my part. So when the time finally came for their arrival, I mentally shielded myself from their vile emanations, and standing at my father's side, I stood and faced them with such cool indifference and professionalism, that if you didn't already know, you would never have been able to guess that there had once been such a violent and tempestuous history between myself, and far too many of them to recall.

A few moons later, Chamuka gave birth to our third son, we named him 'Gerrin', and Nymadawa had also given birth to my first grandson. She named him Kai after me.

Meanwhile the Italians had continued to pay us regular visits, and Cornelius had once again become a familiar sight in our village, and I must admit that when I'd had a chance to get to know him a little better, surprisingly enough I'd actually found him to be a very reasonable and likeable character, and gradually he even began to grow on me a little, so much so in fact, that one day I even found myself inviting him to come and join me and my family for a meal at our kol. And it was all down to him that I eventually allowed the Italians to re-establish their connection to our inner and outer trading posts, and this in turn allowed them to further their own eastern interests, by giving them direct passageway through the more established east Scythian trading links. One morning as I was making my way over to the training area to meet up with my young students for some weapon training, I was suddenly taken by surprise by the sight of Gaidres who was just a little way ahead of me seated on a horse. And even though he wore his hair much shorter now, and was wearing the helmet and the full uniform of the Italian cavalry, I would still have recognised him anywhere. The last time he'd been to our village we'd parted on some-what unfriendly terms, and if I remember rightly – I'd actually humiliated him and bloodied his nose, and to be honest I'd never expected to ever see him here again…so what was he doing here now? As soon as he noticed me he rode over to where I was standing, and looking down at me from the saddle of his horse, he said:

"Long time no see, Manu Kai."

Just then two of my young students eager to begin today's lessons ran up to me, I smiled at them and told them to go on ahead of me, and that I'd be joining them very shortly. Little did I know that I was never going to be able to keep that appointment, as unbeknownst to me, an evil plan to have me assassinated had already been set into motion by my own brother, as he knew that my father was shortly planning to hand the position of leadership of our people over to me, and he obviously thought that if 'I' was out of the picture, my father would then be forced to hand the title over to him instead. What my brother didn't realise was that our father would never have willingly surrendered the title of Sha Pada over to him under any circumstances, and he'd already had the hindsight to have chosen someone else over him, who with the backing of my father's finest warriors, would step in and forcibly take the position if necessary, should anything unfortunate ever happen to me. My father had been very careful to make damn sure that all of the right people were made well aware of this, so that they'd be ready and prepared to take care of all the necessary arrangements, and make sure that his instructions were all diligently carried out if ever the time should necessitate that it should be so.

"Yes, it's been a while – but I see that you're still working for the Italians," I said with a slight but detectable air of contempt.

Wiping his nose with the back of his hand, Gaidres continued to leer down at me from the elevated height of the fine-looking steed that he was presently seated upon, but I had the distinct impression that he was looking down his nose at me in more ways than one.

"Yes, I'm still working for the Italians, and I must say that it's had its rewards over the years. I can see that you haven't progressed any further than teaching small children how to draw a bow. It's such a shame you didn't listen to me when you had the chance. You could have been somebody instead of rotting away here."

"Hmm…is that so? Well I'd rather rot away here and be true to myself, than to sell myself like some cheap whore to the highest bidder…like some people I know. So, tell me Gaidres – why have you come here? Surely a man of your great standing has far better things to do than to waste his time with such a lost cause as myself."

"Well, you've certainly got that right at least. I can see now that you're a complete waste of my time. I suppose I was hoping that punch your boyfriend gave you all those years ago might have knocked some sense into you by now, but I think that what your boyfriend said was right; it is about time he gave you another one, as it obviously wasn't hard enough the first time," said Gaidres, with a really annoying smirk on his face.

I felt a wave of anger begin to well up inside me: "What do you mean by that?" I demanded to know.

"Oh! Sorry – didn't he tell you? We had a little chat about you earlier. He told me all about your 'little secret' Manu Kai – and a few other things too. I haven't laughed so much for ages."

And giving his horse a little kick, he turned his back on me, and began to slowly ride away. "What? ...Don't you dare insult me and just ride off like that. Get down off that horse right now and face me like a man," I yelled after him.

"I would if there was a man to get off my horse and face, but from what your wife's being telling everyone, you're not really much of a man at all...are you, Manu Kai," he said, continuing to slowly ride away from me.

I was so angry that I felt as though I was going to explode. I knew that Sai or Chamuka would never have said those things, and Gaidres couldn't possibly have known about any secrets that I may have shared with Sai, but the rational and judicious side of me had been replaced by a red cloud of anger, which had succeeded in clouding my logical mind so effectively that I just couldn't think straight anymore, and I wanted to grab him by one those stupid sandals he wore, and yank him down off his high horse. Gaidres always did have the knack of knowing just the right buttons to press in order to make me angry, and it was clear that he hadn't lost any of his old talent. How was I to know that all of this was part of a well-designed and carefully orchestrated plan to try and get me to react in a very precise manner, and unfortunately – it was working!

"Don't you dare just ignore me and ride off. Get back here and face me you coward," I shouted after him.

"Why don't you come and get me?" he shouted back.

And like a fool I quickly looked around for the nearest harnessed horse, and without so much as a single thought about the possible consequences, I jumped on the horse, and with Gaidres galloping off ahead of me, I gave my borrowed horse a sharp kick, and sped off after him. I don't know why I allowed myself to be manipulated into following Gaidres that day, or what I intended to do if I'd actually managed to catch up with him. I know that I didn't intend to kill him. I was just so angry that I really had lost all sense of rational thinking. When I actually look back and think about it, my brother had been spending quite a lot of time with some of the Italians lately, and even though I had noticed this, I hadn't really taken all that much notice...if that makes any sense!!!I should have guessed that he was up to something, but not in a million years could I have guessed at the depth of depravity that he was willing to sink to in order to get what he wanted, which of course was the title of Sha Pada; which would have put him in the position of power that he so greatly desired above all else, and that he saw as rightly belonging to him.

My brother had cunningly managed to convince about a dozen or so of these Italians, that 'he' was the rightful heir to the position of Sha Pada, and that 'I' was an evil and corrupt sorcerer, and I'd only managed to gain my father's favour by using dark sorcery, and I must never be allowed to gain the position of leadership, or it would bring doom upon them all. He had very shrewdly promised these rather naive Italian cavalry men, that if they co-operated with him in a plan to get rid of me once and for all, he would see them all rewarded with riches beyond their wildest dreams, but of course they must never reveal this plan to their superiors (such as Cornelius) as they would never believe any of this, as 'I' had successfully managed to entrance them all.

My brother was obviously well aware of my volatile nature, and how Gaidres seemed to have a natural ability to press all of the right, or depending on how you see it the 'wrong' buttons, and had in the past managed to precipitate a very angry reaction from me. In such a close-knit community such as ours, it was almost impossible to keep these things private for very long.

I find it ironic that the very first time that my brother and Gaidres had set eyes upon one another; Gaidres had stood up against him, and had saved me from taking a real beating from him. Gaidres had befriended me that day, and I honestly believed that our friendship would last forever.

But due to the twisted turns our lives had taken along the way – we were now enemies, or at least Gaidres had become 'my' enemy, as I'd never really considered him my enemy…not in the true sense of the word, as deep down inside, I'd always remained hopeful that one day we'd be able to overcome our major differences, just as we'd been able to do several times before. But unfortunately, I'd overlooked the powerful grip that misplaced pride, and the illusion of glamour, can have on the misguided and easily influenced. So with Gaidres enticed on board as the bait to draw me away from the protection of our village – the plan was now set in motion.

I raced after him, but he'd got such a good head start, and the horse that I'd 'borrowed' wasn't exactly the finest specimen that I'd ever ridden, that I was having some difficulty in catching up with him. He seemed to be heading towards the forest, and as I continued to chase after him, I gradually began to calm down, and as I did, I suddenly became aware that there was something very wrong with this whole situation. I felt a strange ringing in my ears, and a sudden clarity of mind which seemed to catapult me into a realisation of the reality of my situation, so much so in fact, that it actually made me feel physically sick. I don't know what transpired between Gaidres and me at that precise moment in time, but he instantly turned around and looked at me, and then suddenly changing direction, he headed off in a north westerly direction instead.

I brought my horse to a sudden standstill, and all my senses were screaming at me to get the hell out of there as fast as I could, but rather than following my instinct to run, I just kept staring towards the forest instead. I didn't have very long to wait before the truth was finally revealed, as more than twenty Italian cavalry men on horseback, suddenly appeared from out of the cover of the forest from what was to have been my ambush, and were now heading straight towards me. They had obviously realised that I wasn't going to oblige them by riding straight into their ambush, and had decided to engage me in a head on attack instead. What made me decide to stand my ground and fight them and not to try and out-run them instead, I shall never know. I was greatly outnumbered, and I didn't stand a chance against so many – and I knew this. I think I must have just grown weary of all the killing, and I was finally ready to face my final nemesis. But I wasn't going down without giving them a fight. If this was going to my very last sardonic act of defiance against the Italian army, who had plagued me for the best part my life, I was certainly going to make it count. So drawing my bow I steadied my aim and loosed my arrow. I'd managed to bring down seven of them before they had even got anywhere near enough for one of them to have speared my horse, and as the poor animal crumpled to the ground beneath me, I grinned at them nefariously. I felt more compassion for this poor horse than I did for any of the soldiers that I'd just managed to wound or kill. Or even for myself for that matter. They were upon me before I knew it!

I managed to draw my bow twice more, before being knocked to the ground and trampled by one of their horses. However, I wasn't done yet, and I drew my swords ready to lash out at anything that came within slashing distance, but with so many of them surrounding me it was all over pretty quickly, as I suddenly felt a searing pain as one of the soldiers had managed to bring me down with a single spear, which had penetrated straight through my right shoulder. Slumping to the ground I allowed my swords to fall besides me, I knew that this was it…it was finally all over.

The premonitions had come to pass after all…and at last, I had finally come face to face with my nemesis. It had taken the co-operation of people from three separate nations to bring me down, but it was me, and me alone who had made it all possible for them to carry out my brother's heinous plan to have me assassinated. If I hadn't been so quick off the mark to react, no matter how well devised the plan may have been, it would have failed pitifully, as the whole plan rested entirely on my predictability. And true to form – I had reacted exactly as predicted.

One of the Italian cavalry jumped down off his horse, and grabbing me by my braided hair, he was about to finish me off by slitting my throat, when I heard Gaidres shout out in the language of the Italians, "Leave him be…he's done!"

It was odd – but even though I couldn't speak the language – I could somehow understand what Gaidres had just said.

The Italian soldier stopped what he was about to do…and sliced off my braid and threw it at me instead.

"There…job done! Now let's get our dead and wounded and get out of here," he said. "Go on ahead of me, I'll catch you up," said Gaidres, dismounting from his horse.

I was still conscious, but I knew that I probably didn't have very much time left here in this body. The Italian soldiers quickly gathered up their dead and wounded and rode away. I looked at Gaidres and just happened to make eye contact with him. I knew that he'd purposely intended to lead me to my death, but I couldn't even bring myself to ask him why. I didn't feel any anger towards him any more – just a deep and resounding sadness that once upon a time we had been such good friends, and now he had coldly been part of a plot to kill me by intentionally leading me into an ambush. I thought of Tihanna and Kern, and Chamuka and our young sons, and my daughter Nymadawa, and of my mother and father, and all my dear friends and family that I was going to have to leave without saying goodbye, and I thought of my life-long companion on this planet…Sai, and my heart was filled with such a deep and heartfelt longing to be with them all again, if even for one last single fleeting moment. And as I watched Gaidres pick up my severed braid from the ground and firmly tuck it into his tunic.

"That was done by request of your brother," he said, turning away from me.

I remembered the time that my brother had threatened to cut off my braid when I was around fifteen winters of age, and how I'd almost succeeded in strangling the very life out of him. It was something he'd never got over, and his final revenge fitted his lifelong obsession with cutting off my long hair, which he knew was so much a part of the Hunnic side of my tradition and personal beliefs.

Gaidres bent down, and grabbing my arm, he pulled it around his shoulder and hoisted me up off the ground.

"I'm not asking you to forgive me, but for what it's worth…I'm really sorry," he said, as he struggled to help me to get on his horse. "I honestly don't know what came over me. It was as if there was someone else in my head. I was supposed to lure you into the forest, but suddenly I began to come to my senses, and I remembered all the times that we had spent together as children, and the many years of friendship that followed, and I quickly changed course; hoping to draw you away from the forest and out of harm's way. But you didn't follow, and I didn't realise this until it was already too late. All I can do now is take you back to your village, and what happens to me after that rests in the hands of the gods; or if you can hold on long enough, you'll have the satisfaction of letting your people know what I did, and I'll probably be executed."

I still hadn't said a single word, but looking Gaidres squarely in the eyes I said: "Just get me back and I'll say nothing of your part in this. We'll sort this out in another life…"

I could feel myself drifting in and out of consciousness, and only my will alone was keeping me alive right now, as I wanted more than anything else on this earth to leave this world surrounded by the people who cared for me. But how I managed to hold on I truly don't know. But true to his word Gaidres brought me back to my village, and as we rode in, word soon spread like wildfire that I was wounded. Merren was one of the first on the scene, and with the help of Gaidres he got me down off the horse, and after single-handedly carrying me into my kol, he carefully lowered me down onto my bed. Aptien was the next by my side, quickly followed by my mother and father. And as soon as my mother saw me lying there bloody and close to death she immediately burst into tears. I guessed by her reaction that I obviously didn't look too good!

Gaidres walked straight up to my father and handed him my severed braid. Sai was the next to arrive, and immediately set to work determining the severity of my injuries, and what…if anything could be done for me, but for all his efforts we both knew that I was fading fast.

"It's my time, Sai, we knew it was coming, and not even you can save me this time great Magus," I said, trying to raise a smile. "A part of me will always be with you, Sai, and I don't know how I'm going to do it yet – but someday I'm going to return."

"I believe you," said Sai, taking my hand in his, "Because guess what? You already have, and I know that you don't remember it right now, but one day, in another life, you'll remember." I didn't quite know what he meant, and I didn't have enough time to question him on this, as I could feel my life force ebbing away, so I quickly beckoned Chamuka to come to me. Sai stood aside in order to allow Chamuka and my sons to get close to me.

"Chamuka," I said, "I don't have very long; so please listen to me and do what I say…you have to take our sons and move back with the Hun, it's not safe for you here anymore."

"Please, Kai – you can't leave us. What are we going to do?" said Chamuka, sobbing.

"I can't stay, Chamuka…but you'll all be well taken care of…of that I'm sure."

I told each of my sons that I loved them, and looking up at my mother and father who were stood close by the whole time I said: "I'm sorry…I really messed up this time."

"Tell me who was responsible for this, Kai," asked my father, kneeling down by my side.

"It was an Italian soldier that threw the spear, but you'll have to ask your first born why." Cornelius who had been staying with us for the last few days had been stood by my father's side the whole time listening to everything that had been said.

"What!" said Father, angrily looking all around to see if he was anywhere in sight, but, of course…he wasn't!

Father immediately ordered five warriors who were standing nearby to go and find him.

"Find him and bring him to me," he ordered angrily.

"I'll go and try and find out which of the cavalry were responsible, and I'll have them executed the moment I find out," said Cornelius.

I suddenly remembered what Garenhir had said to me about the premonitions that he and other members of the Agari had received concerning the welfare of our people, and how the terrible things that they'd seen would not take place during my life time, 'if' I decided to remain in Scythia, and it suddenly dawned on me what Garenhir must have meant by that. He was obviously trying to warn me that my life span here may not be as long as my life span if I had decided to move to Britain with him; so in a nutshell, those things that were predicted could actually take place any time after my death here. I knew my time here was drawing to a close, and that the sultry wings of death would soon come to carry me away...but I had to summon just enough strength to warn him...

"Father, you need to make arrangements to get our people out of here before it's too late. I don't have time to explain...so please...you'll just have to trust me."

"Don't worry," he said, "I'll do what needs to be done."

I looked up at the faces of my trusted and loyal friends Merren and Aptien, who had both remained by my side through thick and thin, and had always been as dependable as a well-trodden mountain pass...and I said my final goodbye.

"Farewell for now, my friends, we'll meet up again soon...in another life."

And as I felt my eye lids close for the very last time, I found it very frustrating that I had to relinquish all that I'd been in this life, and that I had to be parted from the ones that I loved. But very soon that frustration was replaced by a feeling of inner peace, which gently washed over me like a warm shaft of sunlight shining through an open window...and my troubled soul was finally at peace.

I had lived by the sword, and I had died by the sword. Well, by a spear to be exact, but it all amounts to the same thing. And although, I'd finally realised that I preferred to be a healer rather than a killer, my failings had finally managed to catch up with me.

Turning his attention to Gaidres who was still standing nearby, my father asked him what had happened.

Gaidres hesitated for a moment before he replied: "It's true...it was all planned by Buemod Sha Pada."

My father studied his face carefully before saying to him: "But how could you know of this, Gaidres, unless, of course, you were a part of it too? For some reason Kai has decided to absolve you of any blame, as he could have easily pointed the finger at you at any time if he'd had a mind to, and you must have been aware of this fact, but even so you still chose to remain. I know you had something to do with this Gaidres...but you did bring him back, and I can see that there is genuine sorrow in your eyes right now; so I'm going to give you a chance to leave this place and never come back here again...and if you do...I'll kill you myself. Do we understand each other? Now get out of here..."

When the men my father had sent to look for my brother returned the next day, they did so with his dead body. My father never found out who killed him, as his men had told him that my brother was already dead when they found him. The truth of the matter was that after Cornelius and my father's men had managed to track him down, Cornelius had killed him himself. And after finding out which of the Italian cavalry soldiers were involved in my ambush, and having them all executed, Cornelius quit the Italian Cavalry and was never seen by my people again.

My father lost two sons in the course of as many days, and he also lost the will to continue to withhold the position of Sha Pada of our village, so he handed the title over to his chosen next in line before taking my advice. And along with my mother, sisters, Chamuka and our sons, Merren, Aptien, and their families, Nymadawa, Tesyrian, and my little grandson, and well over a hundred others, he left Scythia for ever and joined forces with the Huns, who welcomed them all with open arms.

My oldest son Altan eventually became Khan, and was to continue the blood line which would eventually fulfil the original prophesy that my Derkesthai Garenhir had made to my father before I was even born, and that was: 'That the Huns and the Scythians would one day join together, and for a while at least, would become the most powerful nation on earth. And the curse that I'd put on the Italians the day that they'd killed my cousin Altan, echoed throughout the course of history, until at last it came full circle.

Sai had chosen to move to Don (South Wales in the UK) with the remaining members of the Agari, and many others who had chosen to go with them. Sai and his entourage had arrived with just enough time for him to say goodbye to Garenhir, as only a few hours after they had arrived, he was destined to die of old age. When Sai told him what had happened to me, he just gave a little nod of his head and said: "I know…I felt it." And with that he closed his eyes and peacefully left this world of sorrow for a well-earned rest.

Sai quickly gained respect as a wise and powerful Druid, and had a great deal of influence across the land. He told magical tales of mystical beasts, and great warriors and kings, and he taught his knowledge of medicine to all those who had a thirst to learn, both male and female, and just as Garenhir had done before him, he taught the ways of the Sacred Serpent. And often when he was alone in his hut at night, he'd reminisce about the life that he once lived in Scythia, and of his half Mongolian, half Scythian lover, friend, and companion, 'Manu Kai', who he remained ever faithful to – even until death.

And now…as I gaze out of my window silently reflecting upon my incredible journey of self-discovery, I watch as a little robin flies down and perches upon the head of the resin cobra that sits in amongst the rose bushes in my front garden, before flying onto the window sill for his favourite daily treat of grated cheddar cheese. I look at the clock on the wall…he's five minutes late this morning, that's so unusual that I double check the time, and I find that he's not really late at all…it's actually my clock that's running five minutes fast. I smile to myself and adjust my clock to the correct time, and I pause and reflect upon the wonder of it all for a moment or two, before suddenly grabbing my coat from its peg and heading straight towards the front door. And as I step out into the cold icy chill of a mid-winter's morning, I pass my favourite tellurian neighbour, who was just about to throw a large heavy suitcase into the boot of a black taxi cab that was parked in the driveway. "Going somewhere nice?" I quizzed.

"Bloody place is haunted…I wouldn't stay another night in that place if you paid me," he snivelled, as he stamped out the remains of a cigarette, before clambering into the back of the taxi cab.

I suppose there was no point in telling him that he was most probably responsible for whatever spooky goings on that were now plaguing him, or that it would only be a matter of time before they caught up with him again. So wishing him well, I climbed into my car and fastened my seat belt. And as I pulled out of the driveway and headed off towards the market, I wondered if my mysterious friend would be there today…I hoped so, as I'm pretty sure that I can remember where I'd met him before now.

The End